STORGY®
BOOKS

Cover Art by Crap Panther
Cover Design by Rob Pearce

First Published in Great Britain in 2019 by STORGY Books

1st Print

London

Published by STORGY BOOKS Ltd
London, United Kingdom, 2019

10 9 8 7 6 5 4 3 2 1

www.storgy.com

Printed and bound by Page Bros Group, Mile Cross Lane, Norwich NR6 6SA

Edited & Typeset by Tomek Dzido

A CIP catalogue record for this title is available from the British Library

Trade Paperback ISBN 978-1-9998907-2-8
Ebook ISBN 978-1-9998907-3-5

"A sick thought can devour the body's flesh more than fever or consumption."

- Guy de Maupassant -

MAP LEGEND

1 - Hospital

2 - Arkady Asylum

3 - Police Station

4 - Library

5 - Superstore

6 - Sea Port/Pier

7 - Church & Cemetery

8 - Cinema

9 - Hut Near Devil's Gorge

10 - Bubba's Bazaar

11 - Abandoned Mine

12 - Jack's Tavern

13 - Lighthouse

14 - Junkyard

15 - A House of Interest

16 - Shallow Creek School

17 - Lumbermill

18 - Silverpine Forest

19 - Neville Cliff

20 - Croskell XXX Shop

21 - Jeffery Motel

22 - Wasek Joke Shop

23 - Rob's Rifle Range

24 - Self's Swamp

25 - Ramsey Woods

CONTENTS

FOREWORD

FOREWORD

Ladies and Gentlemen,

Allow me to introduce myself, my little curious concubines.

My name is Mallum Colt—purveyor of all things occult and proprietor of a quaint curiosity shop located in the centre of a splendid town called Shallow Creek. I'm glad you found me, my little pineapple frittata, otherwise you could have blindly stumbled onwards, without realising the reason why you're here … holding this tome of the macabre in your quivering hands.

There is little to distinguish Shallow Creek from any other fading boomtown on the outskirts of civilization. I'm sure you wouldn't have given our little slice of heaven a second glance if I hadn't beckoned you here. The night air, though cool, is painfully dry and dusty, the unpainted wooden buildings peppered with dry rot, but if you look closer you'll see the subtlest of movements from the corner of your eye …

There's a lot to for us to do, but if you'll permit me a small indulgence, I'll inform and guide you through Shallow Creek. You can quench your thirst at Jack's Tavern, but make sure to tip the cantankerous bar owner, he's known for his temper. For amusement there's the dilapidated fairground, owned by Bubba Cody—and if you listen closely you might hear the distinct calliope music playing through the snaking tangle of streets … just be careful not to tread through Silverpine forest late at night, the Creek has countless reports of wild animals stalking the land or escapees from Arkady Asylum hiding out beside the Hanging Tree. There's a lighthouse manned by the mysterious Jud, its bright beam of light forever guiding lost souls back to land. And don't forget to check in with Gertrude Saggery, Shallow Creek's resident witch.

This town loves me in ways no person ever has. And I love her just as fiercely. She listens to my footsteps, the clicking of my polished heels against her dirty pavements early on a Monday morning. She sees me smile from ear to ear when I marvel at the library's windows as they reflect the orange glow of the afternoon sun. She hears my satisfied sigh in winter as the first sip of morning coffee warms my throat and thaws my freezing hands. The city sees and hears and feels every second of my life. This Town understands.

As you approach Shallow Creek, my little intrepid adventurer, you'll become aware that something in this town is wrong. Despite the lateness of the hour, no light shines through the windows of each house. Instead, the town lies beneath a blanket of silence, the only source of light the fire burning beyond the northern border of the junkyard. On the face of it, my job did not appear too onerous; to repopulate the empty streets by publishing an anthology of tales so dark, so delightfully twisted and heinous that tourists could not resist but flock back in their droves to the town that sleeps with one eye open. I'm told that Dark Tourism is a roaring trade these days …

My first task was to create a competition to lure writers into town.

And how they came.

I assigned each of the hopeful participants a **resident** to base their story on and a **location** to investigate (you can check the map in this very book to see the areas of special interest). Lastly they were equipped with a single unique **item** … a totem, so to speak, to be included in their story. Never in my wildest dreams did I expect to receive so many entries of such high quality, but what you now hold is a collection of ghoulish tales that summarise the quintessential ethereal aura of my town. You can find out more about the competition and Shallow Creek at STORGY.com— an online magazine dedicated to the short story form.

But what is a short story, I hear you ask. Eager pundits love to explain that a short narrative piece must consist of a single situation, a short space of time, a defined cast of characters, a specified number of words, and so on and so on. My little terrifying avocados, these restrictive demands have existed for aeons, but what makes a spooky tale so gripping, so terrifying, so enthralling that you simply *must* read on until the frightful end? Such stories are terribly difficult to write. The best ghost stories, for instance, often do not involve a ghost. Or at least, you should not *see* the ghost. You should feel its presence by skilled and subtle means.

As a small boy, I grew up reading anthologies of horror stories containing a delicious mix of spooky houses, abandoned theme parks, damp and darkened cellars, but they were far too often all un-themed. Presently, market forces dictate that anthologies should explore a specific theme, therefore we regularly read books and stories full of zombies, vampires, or ghosts. With Shallow Creek, there is an entire city to explore—from high schools and hospitals, to lighthouses and junkyards and forests and mines—Shallow Creek contains it all.

I see you have a predilection for the macabre, so let me whet your appetite with the following tales of terror. Does it feel heavy in your hands? Does it pulse with a faint ferocity? You can't quite seem to close it, can you? That's why I need you, dear reader … this book consumes all who risk to read it. This book of endless horror … is hungry …

To this day no rational mind or means can explain the horrors that took place in Shallow Creek—as you too, my little pina colada, will discover when you encounter the tales locked within these pages. So abandon any hope of escape. Abandon hope. Right. Now.

DAVE DANVERS' LAST FORAY INTO ALL THINGS WOO WOO

by J Stuart Croskell

Get a grip, Danvers. You can do this. You're holding the hand of the prettiest girl in the world, a switchblade in the other.

You never could keep it simple.

You're getting ahead of yourself.

To the beginning of this strange day. To the gathering storm clouds and cranky bus cresting the hill into Shallow Creek, me its only passenger. All on my lonesome, afflicted by the usual anticipatory disappointment when visiting towns traditionally associated with anomalous activity and high strangeness.

I allowed myself to daydream that Shallow Creek would be *the one*. The place that finally lived up to all the hype. If you saw yourself as a roughy-toughy bona fide dark tourist, a fearless legend tripper, Shallow Creek had to be near the top of your to-go list. As for me, well, Shallow Creek would be my last investigation. If nothing happened here—which it wouldn't—I'd hang up my monster hunting boots and take up beekeeping. If it was good enough for Sherlock, it was sure as shit good enough for me. It had been fun visiting the world's Fortean hotspots, exploring locations I'd researched and read up on so many times they felt like friends. But they never delivered, not really. A couple of echoes, a glimpse or two.

Maybe. Yeah, maybe.

We passed the "Welcome to Shallow Creek; population 8,013" sign. From my elevated vantage point, I could see a river bisecting the burg. The town itself, a blue-grey jewel set in a crown of lush forest, mountains rising majestically behind. At the river entrance, a lighthouse loomed like an exclamation mark. Really! Do you *really* wanna come here?

Up in the clouds, though, looking down, it looked alright. Nice view, nice prospect.

The bus hissed to a halt. A guy dressed in an immaculate pin-striped suit, crisp white shirt and paisley tie stepped on. I wouldn't have glanced a second time were it not for his clown make-up and fluorescent green wig. The driver didn't miss a beat, business as usual. Must be a regular pick-up for the clown. As the bus pulled away, the guy walked up the gangway. I looked away. I wasn't in the mood. It was too early in the morning. Maybe the clown was for my benefit. Wow, Shallow Creek, what a crazy place, man.

The clown didn't sit next to me, but did the next worst thing. He sat immediately behind. Tapped the back of my shoulder. Here we go. I sighed, turned to face him.

"You the guy?" he asked.

I shook my head. "I doubt it."

"I mean, the guy come to put us back on the map?"

He had me there. I was, indeed, that guy. "That'll be me, Dave Danvers."

"I loved your shows, Dave Danvers," the clown said. He seemed sincere. "I've read your books, too, but I preferred the shows."

"Thank you, Mr, er—"

"Clown, Mr Clown. First name Krinkles, middle name *the*, last name, well I already told you that."

"Thank you for your kind comments, Mr Clown," I said.

Like most paranormal TV show guys, I got my break in the noughties, my calling card ghosts and hauntings. Later I branched out into cryptids, UFOs, anything, really, within the ambit of Strange Doings. And then I got tired of the arguments and bickering that goes with the whole TV thing, and decided to focus on the books.

"You were the best," he said. "The others were more entertaining, sure, but they were phonies. Not much happened on your shows, but when it did, boy was it quality. Are you a believer, Dave Danvers?"

"Agnostic," I said. "Keeping an open mind."

"You know, Dave Danvers, I think you'll be alright here. I think you'll find what you're looking for."

"Okay, yeah. Thanks. I hope so too."

Anyway, people got fed up with the whole paranormal gig. I don't think they stopped believing in ghosts or experiencing weird stuff, they just got bored with the way the supernatural was disseminated via ghosthunting TV shows. It got old. I mean given the way things are in this world right now, if a UFO did land on the White House lawn, would anyone give a shit? It's just *tired*, man. It was hyperreality that did it for our ghost shows. TV became more real than life itself. It made the damn thing so common-place that Strange Doings became Regular Doings. And yes, most of it was fake. Most of it.

Krinkles leant towards me, entre nous. "Do you want to know why the clown get-up?"

Not really. "Yeah, sure."

"It's so I don't have to smile all the goddam time. The makeup does it for me." He laughed. "Genius, isn't it."

I nodded enthusiastically. "You got it, partner."

He nodded to himself, kind of self-congratulatory. "I sure do." He thought for a moment. "They taking you up the mountain?"

"Uh-huh."

"Devil's Gorge? Where those kids died back in '59."

"Uh-huh."

"You reckon you got it in you?"

"To get up the mountain?"

"Oh, you'll get up the mountain alright. I was thinking about the other business. What you have to do when you get there."

"I'm not sure I follow," I said, convinced there was nothing to follow, that the clown was full of crap.

He sat back. "Perhaps I've said too much." He added, sadly, "Maybe I should shut the fuck up."

I studied him for a few seconds, and while he didn't seem dangerous, you can never tell. "Sir, you've made my journey more enjoyable than I anticipated. Thank you for your input."

He seemed satisfied and stared out the window. I turned around to face the front. We were entering the town limits. "All change," the driver said. The clown and me stood up as we arrived in what looked like the town square, shops and bars lining its perimeter. We thanked the driver and strode out into the crisp air. Krinkles held his hand out. I shook it. "Good luck, Dave Danvers".

"You too, Mr C," I replied. "Take care."

"We're all rooting for you," he said and walked off, oddly dignified despite the clown thing.

It was cold out on the street and I zipped up my coat and searched for Mallum's shop.

What was I doing here?

When my wife died, after I'd resurfaced from that first deluge of grief, I became aware of a curious silence. Not really a silence, I suppose, more of an absence. *Duh.* Yeah, I know. That's what you would feel, dead wife and all. But it wasn't a localised silence resulting from the absence of one woman. It was more, much more. I realised that this silence had been present for a while. My wife's absence merely enabled me to tune into the larger, more profound, absence. It was like the world had gone … *quiet.* I could still hear birds and traffic and other random shit, but I knew that behind all the regular, everyday noise, something sloped off. Something exited the building, the world, the whole damn universe, for all I knew.

Ah, Shallow Creek. Back in the 20s—last century 20s—something happened in Shallow Creek that almost wiped it off the map. Even the FBI was involved. It's all on record, if you care to check. But just what they were involved in, well, that's up for debate. And then there were all the skiers that died at Devil's Gorge in '59. Synchronously, the exact same thing happened at Dyatlov in the then USSR.

Yep, it happened. Dyatlov *and* Shallow Creek. It's a matter of record, despite the lack of details.

So when Mal got in touch to ask if I'd do a dark tourism piece for my impressively popular blog, I thought I'd kill two birds with one stone. I'd been putting off visiting Shallow Creek for a long time, leaving the best till last. I could take the disappointment of all the other sites because I still had Shallow Creek. Shallow Creek wouldn't let me down. Shallow Creek *would* live up to its reputation. Of course, *now*, I didn't believe *that* one damn bit. None of it was real. It was all smoke and mirrors. No bigfoot, no spooks, no little green men. The bastards. Only us. *Us.* Jesus.

As I stood in the middle of the square, an old couple wearing tight little smiles and winter gear, shouted, "Good luck, Mr Danvers!" I waved back.

Yowza! I was a big deal in this town. It was sweet. The kind of sweet I used to feel when I was a big TV star. The kind of sweet my wife once gave my life. I scanned the buildings and searched for Colt's Curiosity Corner. Ah, there she was, squashed between two wonky colonials. I stamped my feet, and blew into my hands, thumbed my rucksack straps and hiked over the cobblestones.

A man with his dog waved, yelled, "Yo, Dave! Way to go!" His face carried a tight smile too. Even the dog seemed to smile. Just like the in-sync couple and the driver. What a smiley place this was.

The items in Mal's window were bathed in a warm glow, immediately seducing me. The display was artfully done: a dab of Dickensian curiosity here, a pinch of steam-punk chic there. Wilfully anachronistic, but somehow not too twee or whimsical. Hard to pull off. Way to go, Mr Mal.

Thematically, the items in the window promoted early twentieth century comedy. There were life-like busts of Chaplin and Keaton, Lloyd, too. Faded sepia photos of long extinct burlesque halls, a bowler hat, its provenance unclear, allegedly belonging to Mr Stan Laurel. Among the last century funny-guy stuff were items—artefacts, I suppose—that defied categorisation, beyond the grasp of even the most gifted taxonomer. Of these, one particular object caught my attention; a three-dimensional *thing* in a glass case, suspended by no visible aids, its shape and colour shifting, its composition alternating between organic and inorganic. I leant in for a closer look and immediately felt a sharp pain in my forehead. Shocked, I realised I was pushing my brow against the window. I tore myself away. Weird.

Warily, I entered the store, an actual bell ringing above my head. The sprung door shut behind me. First impression. The store was like an old-fashioned proscenium arch stage set, the back of the room fading into the distance, a perspective created by talented scene painters rather than any accepted version of reality. The smaller items sat at the front of the store with incrementally larger items staggered behind, gradually disappearing into the darkness, infinitely, for all I knew. From the gloom, a tall, thin fellow emerged and calmly approached me, smiling. His high forehead, angular cheekbones and sweptback greying widow's peak gave him the look of a genteel skull, the spit of Peter Cushing, the famous horror film actor. He was immaculately dressed in a fine tweed three-piece, trailed by someone still in the gloom. Chris Lee?

"Mallum Colt," he said, shaking my outstretched hand with a firm grip.

"David Danvers."

"Of course you are. Who else would you be?"

Good question.

"Tea?" he asked. Mal, too, sported the Shallow Creek Look, the tight little *smile*, though not as *tightly*, as if his version was bespoke and not off the peg.

"Thanks, but no. I want to get started," I gestured vaguely to the town square. "The weather's looking none too promising."

"Oh, the weather here is always promising," Mal said. "The question is; will it deliver on that promise?" He turned to the ratty guy now stood beside him, the Look on Ratty too and a damn sight tighter than Mal. I offered my hand. He didn't.

I got to the point. "Mr. Mal, I'm not sure I fully understand what you want. I mean, I know you want a *story*, a yarn to put the Creek back on the radar, but I could have written it back in New York."

He placed his hand on my shoulder, "It's not about what I—we— want, it's about what you want. The story *you* want, need, can only be written here. In the mountains, at Devil's Gorge."

I nodded. Mal was as crazy as the clown. He removed his hand and turned to Ratty. "Allow me to introduce your guide, Barney Slyvester. Mr Slyvester will take you into the mountains."

I gave Barney a little wave and he tipped his head, almost imperceptibly.

"In this town," Mal continued, "Mr Slyvester is the wellspring of all knowledge. His family have presided over the junkyard for generations beyond recall. Eventually, all things come their way. We have much in common, Mr S and I. We both deal in *used* things. We are on the same retail continuum, you might say."

"Uh-huh," I said sagely, looking around, checking out the shrunken heads, sundry two-headed beasts.

Barney said, "Best be off, Mr Danvers."

"Dave," I said.

Barney picked up a worn canvas haversack. "If'n you wanna be back 'fore dark, *Dave*."

"Sounds good, *Barn*."

"Oh, Mr Danvers," Mal said softly. "Before you go, I'd like to give you a gift." He pressed something wrapped loosely in brown paper into my hand. "A token of my gratitude."

Before I could utter a reply he'd ushered us firmly out into the street, the door already closing. I slipped the small package into one of my jacket pockets and followed my guide northwards across the square. More folks, more tight smiles.

Hey, Dave. Keep it real.

'Appreciate what you're doing, Mr Danvers.

You're the coolest, man.

I looked up at the mountains. What the hell was supposed to happen up there? What was my role in all this? Gotta be some kind of a show, laid on for little old me. Krinkles, Mal, Barney, all from central casting. Gotta be. I couldn't understand the smiling, though. Didn't fit the dark tourism profile. I caught up with Barney.

"What's the joke, Barn?"

"Suh?"

"What's everybody smiling about? Are you all laughing at *me*?"

Barney stopped and faced me, his face as grim as one could be while smiling. Said, "This smilin' business ain't no laughin' matter. No, suh. We got to smile. We got to 'ccommodate it. Though, we don't have to smile *all* the time. Gotta strict rota. I got a day off tomorrow. Thank the lord."

"Okay," I said. "Thanks."

"Pleasure," Barney muttered, striding off.

Less than a minute later we were climbing into a blue dinghy tied alongside a concrete jetty beneath a groaning bridge. The dinghy had seen better days, but its outboard motor looked fairly new. I plonked myself on the centre thwart while Barney sat by the tiller. He untied the mooring ropes and the dinghy slowly slipped out into the river. Barney let us drift for a few seconds before firing the engine. We manoeuvred into the centre and sped down stream.

"How's the junk business, Barn?" I shouted over the whine of the outboard.

Barney studied me. I had the feeling he was weighing me up, judging me to see if I passed muster. After all, according to Mal, he was the local fount of all knowledge. Before answering he pulled out a small tin and extracted a plug of chewing tobacco, shoved it in his mouth between his lower lip and muddy teeth, and let it soak.

"Junk's a funny thing," he started. "People is kinda junk, you know. If'n you stay alive long enough. We all fall apart. But some folks, they want to become junk before their time. Like they wanna fresh start. They wanna be broke, dismantled, taken apart. Some say, if'n it ain't broke don't fix it. I say, if it ain't broke, maybe you should break it … maybe that's where the *fixin'* starts … when the real healin' process begins … you know, searchin' for your *authentic* face, your real self … the *thing* itself." He spat rusty saliva into the river and steered us starboard, up a feeder tributary.

We were headed north again, into the mountains proper. I wondered what Barney meant about a need to be broken. It sounded like creepy martyr-type shit to me. Not my cup of coffee, no sir. Maybe Barney was intimidated by Mal, and out here on the river and far away from him, he felt safe and free to let it all out. Whatever the hell *it* was. Man, could he yabber.

"Take yourself, Dave," he resumed. "If'n you don't mind me sayin', *you* need fixin'. Yep, let yo'sel' fall apart, let yo'sel' become fractured, let your *psyche* shatter. Create a li'l space there for the real you to emerge. And Dave, trust me, a joke's a good place to start. Maybe have yo'sel' a little laugh. Maybe not stop laughin' until they take you away. It's why folks is fascinated with junk. We all on the way to being junk. All depen' how you wanna take yo'sel' apart. Personally, I like the idea of laughin' until I ain't fit to do nothin' else. That's the best way to get broke, screamin' and heavin' until you's fit to pop. Laugh yo'sel' into the junk yard. That's what I say."

"Uh-huh I said, taking a deep breath. "Barney?"

"Yep, Dave."

"Like, where the fuck are we going?"

"Gertrude."

"Gertrude?"

"Yeah. Didn't Mal tell you? Gertrude's gonna be your, um, *shaman*, I guess. Hold your han' while you ride the smile. Can't do it without Gertrude. Too dangerous."

Shaman? Boy, gotta give it them. They sure were pulling out all the stops.

The tributary narrowed. Thankfully, Barney knew what he was doing, like he'd done it a thousand times before. The dense forest on each river bank gave way to sparser terrain as we moved higher into the mountains. Eventually, low-slung wooden pilings appeared around one tight meander. Barney tied the boat up and we stepped out onto a shaky jetty.

"Gertrude's hut's up there," he said. "It's a climb, for sure. We better get goin', if we're goin' to make the Gorge."

I followed him up the narrow track. He was fitter than he looked and I found it hard to keep up. Every so often he stopped and sniffed the air. "What are you doing?" I asked.

"Checkin' for snow."

"You can *smell* snow?"

"Oh, yeah. Different weathers different smells. Like a calling card."

"And what does snow smell like?"

Barney looked at me like I was stupid. "It smells of white."

Was he yanking my chain, or did he actually have synaesthesia. If so, I hoped to hell it wouldn't affect his navigational skills. Anyway, I didn't pursue it. I was lost for breath.

Apropos of nothing, Barney said, "Yeah, you in good company up here, Dave. The best, really. Back in the day, they all used to come here. Just to see how funny they really was, just to see if they really did have them bones, you know, the funny ones. They all wanted to ride the smile, ride the laugh. Stan Laurel, he came here in '23. Rode the smile. Easy-peasy, a born natural, Stanley. Took the whole smile and some laughin' too. A few months later, he got his big break. I reckon Mr Hardy coulda rode the smile too. But Stan said he couldn't get him off the golf course. Didn't matter, Stan was riding the smile for the two of 'em. We had a coupla easy years after that, in Shallow Creek. We didn't have to grin so stupid all the time. Stan had bought us those years. Chaplin, he came too. And Keaton and Lloyd, all those guys. Last big star we had here was John Candy back in '82. He took to the smile like a duck to water. Had the whole world at his feet, did John. But he didn't look after himself and fate did the rest. I miss him. I miss the films he never made."

Barney sucked in a final sniff and pushed on. We emerged from the forest, beyond the snow line, boots crunching crisply. The mountain eventually levelled out and on a wide ledge, attached like a limpet, clung an oddly constructed wooden shack, as if it were organic, having grown from the ground. Its precarious tenure on the mountainside secured not through firm foundations, but biotic roots plunging deep into the earth. It reminded me of snail stuck to the side of a leaf, always there, defying all logic and gravity.

"Funny, ain't it?" Barney said.

"Who built it?"

"Accordin' to Gertrude, Gertrude."

As we closed on the snail-hut, I noticed a tiny garden. Flowers of all cast and colour sprouted from it like explosions. They should not be here, in this soil, on this mountain. Gotta be fake. Gotta be.

We reached the garden and I tugged on a petal, expecting it to remain fixed to the plant on account of it being a fake, but it pulled off like a regular petal. I sniffed it. A regular petal it was.

Barney caught my surprise. "I know. Beats the hell outa me too."

"Shouldn't be a thing," I said. "Not at this height."

"Yep," said Barney, spitting out a great gob of baccy, careful not to hit the plants. "She's a witch, you know. So maybe that 'splains it."

Again, I studied Barney for signs of mockery. Again, nothing. "A witch, you say."

"I do," he said, knocking on the oval-shaped hobbit door.

Yowza. If this *was* a show put on for the purpose of my edification, someone had gone to a lot of trouble. Mal, probably. But that urbane Englishman didn't seem the right fit to launch something *this* peculiar, especially at this altitude.

The door, if indeed that was the right word, opened inwards. Inside the hut smelled of marijuana and … something else I couldn't place. Sour, but pleasant, a counter to the scent of hash. Barney leading, we stepped inside. It was gloomy yet cosy, lit entirely by candles and old-school hurricane lamps. There was no fire, but it was warm, and the uneven floor was covered with expensive-looking rugs. A woman pushed through some hanging blankets, two skittish dogs following close behind. Sixties, medium height, long dark hair framing her oval face. Despite her age—or maybe because of it—she was beautiful. Objectively, that is. There was no need for subjective-eye-of-the-beholder malarkey. Not here. No, sir.

"Gentleman," she said softly, doe eyes checking me out.

Barney cleared his throat. "I, um, didn't let you know we was comin'. I figured you'd, ah, know, anyhows."

"You presumed correctly, Barnabas. And this is …"

I felt like I was in the presence of royalty, a crass incomer who knew nothing of the appropriate etiquette. "David Danvers," I said, resisting the urge to bow.

"How can I help?" she asked, knowing, I guessed, how she could, whether by spellbinding skills or a script written by Mal. I couldn't tell.

I looked at Barney. He nodded. "I want to ride the smile," I said, feeling ridiculous.

If she was laughing at me for being a shmuck, there was no trace of it. In fact, she looked deadly serious. She didn't, however, exhibit the Shallow Creek Look, the regulation *tight little smile*.

"I don't have to," she said, apparently reading my mind. Neat trick. "I'm part smile, part human. It doesn't affect me. It's why I can hold your hand while *you* ride the smile."

"Will you take me to the gorge?"

"You know about the kids who died there in '59?"

I nodded.

"And that their bodies," she continued, "were torn apart and mutilated like they'd been in a high-speed car accident."

"Yes, ma'm," I said with conviction. "I do not believe they were skiing accidents."

"Correct, Mr Danvers. Those kids, they weren't skiing. They'd gone up to ride the smile, but they were reckless, unprepared. They didn't have me. The smile ripped them apart, not one of them could … take it."

"Unlike Stan Laurel," I said.

"Unlike Stan Laurel," she replied. "Dear Stan."

She plucked a yellow peacoat from the back of a chair and slipped it on. "Come. We need to go. We can talk on the way."

Gertrude eased passed us and exited the hut. We followed her out into the darkening day, the louring sky.

"Snow," she said. "Soon."

"Yep," said Barney. In the presence of greatness, Barney was once again his one-syllable self.

We trekked in a line, moving higher up the mountain, towards the pass that would lead us to Devil's Gorge.

"Are you aware of the risks, David?" Gertrude asked.

"Sure," I said. "Barney told me all about it."

"Have you got the knife, just in case?"

"Knife?"

"Mallum gave you the switchblade?"

I removed the package from my pocket and tore the paper off. A pearl handle switchblade. Beautiful. Deadly. I pushed the button and it flicked open.

Gertrude stopped, faced me. "Do you think you'll be able to use it, if needs be?"

"Use it?"

She looked at Barnaby as he shifted on his feet like a naughty schoolboy. Clearly, Barn had neglected to tell me something.

Gertrude sighed. "If the smile becomes too much, if you can't take it, you have to open yourself up. It doesn't always work, but it's the only chance you've got. If you want to go back down the mountain, that is."

"I have to cut myself?" I asked.

"You might be alright," she said. "How's your sense of humour?"

"Not too good these days," I admitted.

She gave Barney another look, turned back to me. "Are sure you want to do this?"

"Sure I'm sure," I said. After all, this was all a set-up, a show. Barney wasn't really Barney. And Gertrude wasn't a witch. I mean, *come on.*

As we trudged through the pass, snow fell in earnest, and increasingly I felt wrapped in a dream. I tried to imagine John Candy in this very same pass. Stan Laurel. Chaplin. All the silent guys. It was impossible. I couldn't picture it. Of course they didn't come here. It was nuts. Nuts. *I* was nuts to even be here. How glad I was for my last foray into all things woo woo. It was crap. All of it. Utter crap.

Gertrude halted and turned to me, shouting above the rising wind. "We're here. Devil's Gorge."

I stood beside her. Was it my imagination, or was she younger? Stupid altitude thingy, gotta be.

It wasn't much of a gorge, and it was hardly devilish, either. But that was the nature of such things. The places, the locations, they never stood up. When you looked closer, it was like trying to unearth the end of a rainbow.

Through the flurrying snow I gazed down the muzzle of Devil's

Gorge. Shallow Creek sat silently within its sights. From here the seaside town looked charming and haunted in equal measure—but I knew if I went down there, I'd see it for what it was: a town that'd seen its best days. Just like me. The real thing was never as good as the movie, the photo, the *idea*—get too close and it'll fall apart.

"We gonna get back before nightfall," I asked Barney, but he was nowhere to be seen. Had I imagined him too?

I was scared, I realised. *Strange.*

"Can I hold your hand, Gertrude?"

"Sure honey," she replied. "But make sure you've got the switchblade ready."

"Just in case," I whispered.

"Just in case," she agreed.

Far away, across the mountains, there was a deep whirling dervish of a roar, drawing ever closer.

You can do this, Danvers, I told myself. You've got everything going for you. You're holding the hand of the prettiest girl in the world, a switchblade in the other.

Just in case.

BEHIND THESE EYES

by Alice Noel

"Dad, I'm home." I call through the hallway, dimly lit by a lone bulb hanging from the ceiling. Whether he's left it on for me, or just left it on, I don't know. "Got assigned a new house today," I continue as I move to the kitchen—the constant sound of my voice will stop me from surprising, from scaring him—"it's one of the big five, you know, up by the hospital?"

The kitchen is empty.

"Apparently it's not been lived in since something like nineteen-ten." I step into the living room to find his familiar outline in the armchair in the corner. I didn't really expect to find him anywhere else. His deep brown eyes gaze vacantly past the TV, still on the same channel I left it this morning, humming low in the background.

"Dad?"

"Hm?" He turns slowly and looks, first through, then at me, pupils steadily focusing like a lens. His eyes study me, mind working through the puzzle. These silences still hurt, but I'm used to them now. I can see the frustration building on his face, but then his mouth and brow relax, the lines on his forehead melting as he closes his eyes.

"Chelsea," he sighs. "Chelsea Brittany Sanders. Born October thirteenth, nineteen ninety-nine. Six pounds, twelve ounces … It was raining." His eyes open again.

"That's right, Dad," I reply, a sad smile spreading through my lips. "Born for real estate." He laughs, not remembering this is the same joke we share every day—a poor stab at the commerciality of my name. He rises from the chair and embraces me, his warm smell reminding me of evenings curled up on the sofa, reading. My eyes slide to the tray on the coffee table: the plate sits empty, so does the pill pot.

"Did you enjoy your sandwich, Dad?" I ask as I pull away.

"I ate a sandwich?" I remind him that Helen, our neighbor, came over to transfer the sandwich from fridge to table, and to make sure he took his pills at twelve thirty.

"Oh. I suppose so." He looks around, lost. Then his head snaps up, and he grins at me with a beaming smile from a better time. "Is it dinner time yet, Gull?"

"Sure, come on. Let's see what we've got." He picks up the tray, and follows me through to the kitchen, soft carpet turning to cold linoleum under my feet. I need to vacuum. He pulls out a chair and sits down, drumming his hands like an impatient child.

"So, chef, what's for dinner?" He cocks a thick black eyebrow. I yank open the fridge door weighted with magnets, and hum along with the freezer fan as I scan the shelves and inspect the vegetable drawer.

"Well—" I pull out a bag of kale and cross the kitchen.

"Naw, not more of the green stuff? It's bad enough you've got me eating coconut toast for breakfast, Gull."

While I cook the butterbean stew, we chat about old vacations and older jokes. In these he is fluent, and we talk and laugh without interruption. Once I've served dinner, we empty our plates slowly, enjoying the warm kitchen which cocoons us from the chilly late-summer evening outside.

When the food is gone, he stands.

"Right, Gull. I'd best be off to bed as I've got an early start for work tomorrow." My face falls.

"Dad, you don't work anymore, remember? You had to stop because you weren't—aren't—very well." He pauses, confused. His dark knuckles grip the chair in front of him, fingers twisting into the gaps in its spine.

"Yes." His voice is quiet, fragile. "Yes, I must have forgotten. How silly." Embarrassed, he turns and trudges slowly out of the kitchen, and I wait for the sound of his soft footsteps on the stairs before clearing away the dishes. I wash up and wipe the counter, leaving everything as immaculate as when we entered earlier.

I switch off the light as I leave the kitchen, and pick up the laundry basket on my way through. As always, I tour the photo gallery leading from the hallway up the stairs to Dad's room. I pause at my favorites— photos of us down at the beach when I was four, maybe five, me running around, imitating the gulls sweeping across the sand—the origin of Dad's pet name for me.

When I've removed my stuff from the basket, I leave it on the landing under the photo of my high school graduation—offer to study science in hand—next to my dad's door. It's important he keeps doing small chores. I stick my head around the doorframe: the light is off, but I can see his shadowy figure sitting motionless on the bed, pajama top on, but no bottoms.

"You not gonna put on some pajama bottoms, Dad?" I'm careful to keep my tone light, non-confrontational.

"Hm? No. No, not tonight."

"Okay." Sometimes—over the little things—it's not worth arguing. "You cleaned your teeth?"

"Yes, at least, I think so." With my eyes now accustomed to the darkness, I can see the mixture of confusion, sadness and pain on his face as his tongue searches his mouth.

"Don't worry, Dad. I'm sure you have." As he slips under the duvet, my eyes drift to the large print on the wall opposite the foot of the bed. The whole family managed to squeeze into one frame for my dad's fifty-third birthday, only a few years ago now. Each of them has gradually fallen away—uneasy, unsure or unwilling to help. Like everyone else, they didn't know how to react when Dad began to struggle with his memory—"it's just old age" the most common phrase. Even laughter wasn't safe, the awkward amusement frustrating him because they couldn't see it wasn't a joke. It was real, and it hurt.

"Night, Dad." As I pull the door to, I spot the overflowing wastebasket, crammed with crumpled pieces of paper—countless drawings of clock faces, his exercises set by the doctor. I enter my room, dump my clothes beside the bed, and I pull on a pair of worn pajamas. Stuffing today's wear into the closet, I glimpse my little wooden cross buried at the bottom. Raised Catholic, I lapsed after Dad's diagnosis. It's surprising how many people claim to be Christian and yet never seek to help other anguished souls. Besides, no God could do this to a person.

I shuffle through to the bathroom, eyes drooping, exhausted from the effort of maintaining my mask of positivity—both at work and at home. The tiles are cold under my feet, and I work through my usual routine: brush, floss, mouthwash. I splash my face with cold water to conclude the ritual, long dark hair falling around my face as I lean over the basin. I let the water wash away premature creases in my forehead—well-aware that those same lines will re-group by tomorrow evening—before smothering myself with a towel still not quite dry from my shower this morning. Chin no longer dripping, I open the cupboard above the sink to return my purging tools, though there's little space among all Dad's E.O.A.D medicine. Shoving them in, I slam the door shut and stare at my face in the mirror; something I've been avoiding with greater resolve. With the realtor make-up erased, my face is façade-free, natural.

Shattered.

Hollows bleed from under my eyelashes, more noticeable now the layer of foundation is gone. My eyes stare into their reflected twins, bloodshot irritation clearly visible where water has leaked from duct to socket. Eyes exhausted from the effort of living this dual life, seeking solace in a lifeless reflection which knows nothing of deception, hazel staring into hazel, searching for hope in the depths of each other's darkness.

***

His eyes are black, feral, bloodshot; the mirror's glass stained and dull, dark bands marking the exposed silver nitrate. He dowses his face in freezing water, then storms from the room, droplets painting a dark trail on the wooden floor, like blood on snow. He pauses at the top of the staircase, ears cocked. A slight scuffle prompts him to approach the room at the far end of the passage, his footfalls cautious, deliberately avoiding the boards known to creak. The flaking door is already ajar, and he spies on the sole inhabitant through the mirror he placed there months ago. This is made easier by the room's sparse furnishings—a carriage clock ticking softly, yellowed face peering through clouded glass, an armchair, splitting at the feet, upholstery picked and frayed, and a rocking horse. The horse stands motionless, its tail matted in a thick clump, the varnish chipped, lines running through the paintwork as though it has been sprayed with alcohol. Its dark eyes swallow the room, open mouth jeering while the body creaks loosely on its metal axis as the house shifts.

The resident occupies the armchair. Saliva dripping from his chin, watery blue eyes— once clear as ice—vacant, as he murmurs to himself and his invisible companions. He—the father—takes counsel, while the son listens, enraged. There isn't enough money to fund a room in an asylum, and he won't receive his inheritance until the madman is dead. He entertains the possibilities, playing each one through in his mind.

"What was that, Henry?" the old man asks, his conversation gaining clarity. "No, he shall have none of it. I will burn it all before he can touch it, ablaze in a raging bonfire—imagine the heat." He pauses, and then—stern tone replaced with curiosity— "I wonder, if the fuel is green, will the flames be green, too?" Oblivious to his son's presence, his mutterings dissolve into drivel once again, his son sweating behind the door. He places a hand against the wall to steady himself, palm sticking to the wallpaper. He looks first to his feet, then to the large, dark window at the end of the hall. The rain outside distorts his reflection, his jet black eyes remorseless as his echo weeps.

***

A Chevrolet honks loudly behind me.

"Shit." I step on the gas and dart past the green light, the heaters in my car pulling the smell of pancakes from my clothes, filling the car with the sweet scent.

It is Tuesday. Pancake Day. Mom used to insist the British version— her version—was better. The calendar on the kitchen pinboard marks the passage of time for my dad, and although he can—with help—tell the days of the week, he insists that every Tuesday is Shrove Tuesday. Perhaps it's because Mom died on Pancake Day.

I've gone onto autopilot again, and barely register that I've parked the car, crossed the sidewalk and entered the office, when I hear my name.

"Chelsea! Hey, Chelsea?" I turn and see Josh, Oak's Estate Agency admin, waving a piece of paper in my face. "Your list—" he thrusts it into my hands— "I was going to put it on your desk, but you're here now, and I'm here, so uh … Yeah."

"Thanks." I flash a quick smile before turning my attention to the names and addresses listed on the paper. "You'd think, given the size of this town, that people could just walk to a property." I shake my head. Some of these folk live only five minutes away from the properties they view.

"I guess, but it's company policy, so what can you do?" He shrugs. "Anyway, you know what the weather's like around here—you can't expect clients to wander around houses dripping wet, can you?"

"Well …" I snatch some inquiry slips from my desk, and back out the door.

In the car, I attach the papers to a clipboard and check my stash of pens, before turning the key and setting off to meet buyer number one. No need for Google Maps here—I've known every street in this town since I was twelve.

Clients greeted and ushered into the car, we drive from their large house to an even bigger one, exchanging fake smiles and appropriate small-talk. I hate this job, but Shallow Creek is short of options, and is where I have to stay.

We pull up at the house—a colossal brick structure, the antithesis of the wood-slatted buildings that dominate the town—and I step out of the car, wincing against the sun, to open the doors for my clients. I offered them the choice of driving up to the front door, or parking on the road and walking up the driveway. They opted for the latter—a redeeming feature. There's something about driving up to a house that disconnects you from it, car windows forming a filter, a barrier against clear vision.

Although the driveway was originally gravel, there's no crunch under our feet; soft green moss a dampening carpet. As the drive winds around an ash tree in the center of the front yard, we are teased by closer views of the imposing structure. The russet and terracotta bricks mottle the exterior, juxtaposing the dirty white frames of the windows. Leading the two clients up the steps to the front door, I hear them murmuring—they love it already. Gothic is so in this year.

The entrance hall is vast and empty aside from the staircase sweeping down from the first floor—the hollow heart of the house. Our shoes knock on the dulled wooden floor as I guide them through each room, reciting the notes I memorized over my morning pancakes. They nod as I talk, their eyes distracted, consuming the stone-floored kitchen and grand living room. When they query the age of the fireplace, I expertly deflect and avoid this small lacuna in my knowledge, assuring them it is indeed an original feature—no construction work has taken place since the house was built; even I'm not sure how it remains standing after decades of neglect.

Once the clients have seen the house, I leave them in the overgrown garden and wander back inside. Despite loathing the fake smiles required for real estate, I can't help but revel in exploring empty houses, the shadows of previous inhabitants lingering in their walls. I sweep my hand up the smooth oak banister as I ascend the stairs, which billow from the first floor down into the hallway like a ballgown. The carpet in the center of each step has faded; it'll definitely need replacing.

At the top is a wide passage, the far wall occupied by a large window and the center of the corridor absent of flooring, providing a bird's-eye view of the hall below. I amble along the landing and follow a trail of dark stains infused in the wood, stains I had prevented the clients from spotting when we toured the house. I pause at the door where the drops stop, squinting as I look up, the sun filtered by filthy glass and dust, yet blindingly bright. I poke at the door panel, intrigued by the unexplored room, and quickly pull a sweaty palm away, brushing off the flakes of paint which have stuck to my skin. The door inches open at a touch, and as I step inside, my nose is confronted by the familiar smell of disuse that once filled my grandmother's attic. Coughing, I stumble to the far wall, reaching out to open the window. I manage to wrench the frame upwards, though a broken runner leaves the glass askew. I gulp at the fresh air flooding into the room, finally able to register its contents: an ancient armchair, a small clock on the table beside it, and a rocking horse.

I move toward the rocking horse and run a hand over its smooth wooden muzzle—now dulled from neglect. As I tease my fingers through its knotted horsehair mane, a faint buzz hums behind me. Perhaps a fly snuck in through the open window? I swivel around to check, but see nothing, so I turn back to study the looking-glass behind the old child's toy. The glass is consumed by cracks and chips which have collected so much filth they are now black, mirror rot lining its edges, encroaching on the surface. Another, longer buzz. *Damned fly.* My eyes slide from right to left across the mirror, resting on the blur over the armchair's reflection—likely just a hand smear.

The buzzing becomes louder and more frequent, sounding more like groans, followed by cracks. I snap my head around.

The horse.

Creaking from the rocking horse.

But it's not moving. It hasn't moved in years.

Slowly, I step toward it. I should be downstairs with the clients, all fake smiles and champagne. But instead I approach the creature, its wide, blank eyes fixed on me, carved mouth screaming white noise, filling my ears, stoppering all other sound.

Then silence.

Wailing, creaking, the breeze outside—all stripped from the room.

I pause.

The horse lashes forwards, rockers thumping against the floorboards. A tidal wave of hissing hits me hard. Ticking surges from the broken clock. I put my hands up to guard my ears—to mute the noise—but it slips under my palms, leaking in and flooding the canals from the monsoon hammering my eardrums. The grating sounds swarm around my head—whispers burrowing deep into my brain.

Chelsea.

The first word forms like a hot poker searing into the center of my skull.

"What?" I croak, mouth dry from fear.

You know what I need from you.

With eyes clamped shut I see them—the clients. Here and then not; two, insignificant people, gone.

And what I will give in return.

My father, no longer vacant. Once again *my* father, not a stranger sat across a breakfast table.

Throat devoid of moisture, I'm unable to answer, but it—whatever it is—knows my response; that I would give anything to save my dad from himself.

Footsteps thud on the stairs as the horse ceases to move.

"Chelsea? Chelsea, are you up there?"

I spawn enough saliva to rasp, "Yes." But I don't turn towards them as the sound of their approach draws nearer, nor as they appear at the doorway in the crook of my eye. A hand touches my back.

"We'll take it—the house—we'll buy it."

"Chelsea, are you all right?"

I close my eyes, trying to shut off the guilt, the part of me that knows this is wrong. With one final thought, I slam that door shut.

Yes.

***

He drags his fingers over the old man's eyes, closing the lids—shutting away the vacant pupils. He rocks back, knees filthy from their grinding against floor beside the body, and shifts his focus to the metal stake skewering the corpse. The wooden panels creak as he stands, one arm extended to wrench the metal free. There is a wet, tearing sound as he pulls the rod from its victim, a few dark drops dripping onto the floorboards. He continues to stare at his father, makeshift spear in hand—a Grecian statue.

For how long he stands like this, he does not know. The carriage clock reads quarter to two, hands frozen. But the sun—high in the sky when it happened—has begun to sink, and he knows he must move now. He turns to the disassembled rocking horse, its body lying rigid beside the base. Carefully, he inserts the metal into the notch in the center panel, the wet tip pointing upwards, blood dripping down its length. He gathers the horse in his arms, lifting the carcass, before ramming it down on the spike. The hooves whack against the wooden slats across the front and back of the rockers as they meet, the horse gored deep into its stomach—the dried blood on the metal swallowed by its barrel.

With the weapon returned, he gravitates once again toward the corpse lying on the floor. He'll bury the cadaver, then leave. Claim his inheritance and desert the house, the town. He lifts the body, no more precious to him than the figure of the rocking horse, and heaves it to the door, pausing only at the sight of himself in the mirror, whites glinting in the dark room, charcoal pupils merging with the encroaching blackness.

***

"Chelsea?"

My eyelids flutter open at the sound of my name. It's Josh, leaning over my desk with a grin on his face. "How're things going? Not seen you since before the vacation." I notice his tan—dark skin clashing with blond hair, blended with lighter, pink patches.

"Oh yeah." I'd been sleepwalking through work, only coming to life at home.

"Florida, right?" I return the smile.

"Yup." He shifts his weight to the other leg. "Hey, I noticed you're still on that big property up by the hospital—not found a buyer yet?

"Not yet, no." I keep it short, not wanting to get dragged in.

"Weird, I thought you'd found a couple of folks who were interested?" He lowers his tone. "I always heard something creepy went on there, a guy killed his old man or something." My eyes fall to the computer screen in front of me, lips pursed.

"They're probably just stories." The tone of my voice tells him this topic is over, and he hurriedly searches for a new subject.

"Er, so is your dad any better?" I meet his face again, his grey eyes inquisitive, yet soft.

"Yeah, actually—" I lean back and run a hand through my hair— "they're not sure if it's the pills or the exercises, but the regression seems to have stopped." I pause. "To be honest with you, he seems to be recovering." Though it's medically impossible. Neurons don't resurrect their dead.

"Really?" The grin spreads across his face at the success of finding a safe topic. "That's great."

I don't mention how Dad's changed—sterner and less joking than his old self, that he's still drawing clocks, all stuck at 1:45. Nor do I say anything about how he's spending more time in our shed, promising me a 'surprise'. Or that his eyes are no longer a rich, deep hue. Josh's head turns to the window, then back to me, then to the watch on his wrist.

"Look, I'm at the end of my lunch break and I've got to go collect some clients—" he pauses— "but do you want—I mean, would you like – to go get dinner sometime?" He nervously scratches the short, fair hair at the base of his skull.

"Maybe, but I—"

He steps back, waving his hands nonchalantly. "Yeah, don't worry. Family—I get it." He keeps talking as he retreats backwards towards the door. "Just let me know, okay?" He's gone.

I spend the rest of the day finishing up some paperwork, eager to get home in a way I haven't been since middle school. As I pull up in the driveway, I spot him on the front lawn, raking up fallen leaves from the birches on our street.

"Hey, Gull." He hugs me once I've stepped out of the car, coarse gardening gloves grazing my back through my shirt.

"Hey, Dad." I inch back and grab my bag. "Been up to much?" We walk towards the house.

"Well, I've done a bit of gardening, and I finally started that book you gave me a few years ago." He holds his hands up in surrender. "I haven't put that new lampshade up yet. I know you asked me to, but I got a little side-tracked with something else. Come see."

I follow him through the house to the garden, shedding work gear as I go, still in disbelief that he's made so much progress in less than a month. We amble down the freshly cut lawn and stop at the shed.

"Go on," he urges.

I push the door gently, its panels damp and splitting from autumn rain—like the creases in an old woman's forehead—and freeze on seeing what lies behind it.

The rocking horse stands in the center of the shed; a hammer, nails, and various paints and varnishes strewn around it. My mouth dries up, as if someone has stuffed a towel down my throat.

"Where …?" I wheeze.

"It was up in the attic—I'd completely forgotten we had it." He sidesteps me and stands beside it, admiring his work as he strokes the varnished head. "It was pretty battered. You used to ride it when you were about three, maybe four. But I guess you don't remember."

But I do remember. I remember a rocking horse—vaguely at least—a basic model, only wood. No mane, no paint, not like the one before me now. I've only ever seen a rocking horse like this in one other place.

How did it get here?

"What's wrong? I thought you'd be pleased." His voice is distant, muffled by the invisible cotton jamming my ears. I back out of the shed, avoiding his eyes. Numbness dripping from stomach to feet.

Unless he moved it.

"Yeah, just … Look, Dad, I'm really tired, okay?" I try to keep my voice level and calm, but my vision begins to fog. "Think I just need to go grab some food."

His eyes harden as I turn away, and I can feel his stare boring into my back as I stride up the garden, letting up only once I'm out of sight, safe in my room with the door firmly shut.

I cautiously approach the window and peer out, his stationary figure still there on the grass, staring up at the house. I retreat into the shadows of my room and wait for him to return to the shed. As soon as the door shuts, I run down the stairs and out the front, grabbing my car keys from the dish, knocking it to the floor, the sound of it shattering fading as I flee.

I keep driving, my eyes fixed on the road until our house is merely a faint outline in the rear-view. Mindlessly circling the town, I wind past the school and into Silverpine, only stopping when I reach the cliff next to the asylum, its lit windows winking at me in the darkness. Staring across the bay, I can make out the bright colors of the funfair on the far shore, sand flashing white beneath the watchful eye of the lighthouse. I exit the car and stand as close to the edge as I dare, wind buffeting me, waves booming on the cliffs like a fusillade of canons.

What if it needed their lives to get its own back? Then all it would need is a host …

I scrunch my eyes, trying to wish this whole thing away. But it's my dad.

I have to go back.

I climb into the car and wrench it around, flicking the wipers on as rain starts to pelt down like intermittent gunfire, bullets peppering the sand as I take the coastal road home. By the time I get back it's pouring steadily, and as I stand hesitantly on the porch, I'm completely soaked, water running like veins across the surface of my skin.

I place a hand on the cold, wet handle, and push down.

The door swings open and I step inside, feet crunching on splinters of glass. Ahead, light glows in the open mouth of the kitchen doorway, bleeding out into the darkness of the hall. I pause. My breathing is slow, quiet, but in the stillness of the house I can hear him, together with a soft tapping and the ticking of the hallway clock. Hands, slick with sweat, hang limply at my sides as I command myself to move forward. Through the gap I see the horse, now indoors, freshly painted black eyes glinting in the light. He's at the table, coarse fingers drumming on the wood, waiting.

"Yes. She'll return soon. We'll explain."

My toe stubs the baseboard with a dull thud. A pair of ice-blue eyes fix on me.

ARROWHEAD

by Daniel Carpenter

Bubba Cody paid big for the old Krinkle toys. All the classic cereal toys really, but especially the Krinkle ones. It was just another thing you did when you lived around Shallow Creek, if you found some old kids toys in your attic, or in some dusty cardboard box in your cellar. They had to be from cereals, mind. None of them fast food things. Bubba didn't like those, and he sure as hell wouldn't pay for them. First thing I took him was a red plastic Plymouth that I picked up from a yard sale just a week after I'd heard about his collection. Walking through the town towards the fairground, it felt heavy in my pocket, like a lump of gold.

Barely a soul went to the fairground, but it would be wrong to say it had fallen on hard times. To everyone's best recollection, only a handful every week went into Bubba's Bazaar. He still kept it running though. Everyone used to speculate how Bubba Cody could afford to run that place. As I approached it, the tinny carnival music caught in my ears; somewhere in the distance, adding to the noise, announcers shouted through annoys, 'Try your luck at the high-striker!' 'Who dares enter the House of Terror?' to the tiny group of people walking around.

I skirted around the Bazaar following the path towards the port. Bubba lived just next to the fair, his house a rickety shack two stories high that his pop had built by hand fifty years ago. Bubba lived there alone now. Rumour was he'd tried marriage for a while, but it didn't stick. On the edge of the Bazaar, the air stunk of cotton candy and machinery. Multi-coloured light penetrated the tree line next to the house, and the sound of the Black Bullet, the ancient wooden rollercoaster, rushed past me somewhere close, carrying no-one but running anyway, the telltale announcer kicking it all off with a 3, 2, 1, away we go, followed by a starter's pistol.

He opened the door as soon as I set foot on the porch, I didn't even need to knock.

"Lenny?" he said, as though he'd been expecting someone else, "What do you want?"

"I got a Krinkle toy."

That was enough.

Bubba was a big guy. Practically filled the hallway as he led me down it to his back room. In the dim light, I could see a handful of tattoos, thick black symbols, now dulled and faded to match the colour of his skin. He'd recently shaved his head, or at least that's what I assumed the scratches on his scalp were from, and as he walked he left damp footprints on the wooden floor. On the side of his neck I noticed a thick strip of duct tape, and what appeared to be rust around the edges.

"How's business?" I asked, not caring about the answer.

He turned and smiled at me, "which one?"

That shut me right up.

The hallway opened up at the back into a small kitchen. Unwashed plates and crockery piled high in the sink, underneath a stack of paper was a dining table of some description. In the corner of the room was a cupboard door with a thick padlock hanging from it. Bubba took a heavy wad of keys from his pocket and turned to stare at me.

I got the message and shifted to face away from him. Behind me, I could hear the jangle of the keys as he sorted through them, then, finding the right one, I heard the click of the lock.

"Go on then," he said, "show me what you brought."

Inside the cupboard was a treasure trove of toys: a clown mask from a box of Frosted Flakes, an action figure from a bag of Lucky Charms, and on the shelf above them all, a long line of plastic Plymouths, all different colours, none of them red.

"Red's the only one missing. Rarest one too you know, one in a thousand boxes. The blues, they were one in ten. Used to have whole lot of them. But red. Man, I never had the red. You're not shitting me are you? You did get it?"

I took the brown envelope from my pocket and held it out to him. There was a silence in the room, a flood of anticipation, washing away all of the noise. Bubba took hold of the package and unwrapped it, letting the little red car fall into his palm.

There were tears in his eyes.

"Oh yes," he said, "You go right up here with the others."

He placed the red car alongside all the other colours, and stood back to admire the collection.

"Look at you all, just look at you."

The air stunk of spores, food gone mouldy, damp walls, but underneath it all there was the sweetness of a bowl of cereal that took me back to my childhood, transporting me in such a sudden and awful way that I felt things I hadn't felt in a long time.

"The Krinkle toys," Bubba said, and it took me a second to realise he was talking to me again. "They're the ones to look for. Rarest of the lot are the Krinkle toys."

He took a roll of notes from his back pocket and handed it to me without counting it. I sat on my bed when I got home and took my time placing them down in front of me. He paid me five hundred dollars for a plastic car.

"That's what a Krinkle toy gets you," he said.

I had never seen that much money before in my life.

"Now," he continued, as though giving me all of that was nothing, "you want to make some real money? Find me an arrowhead."

An arrowhead? Like the dented old stone ones that were on display in the museum? Little flint things we used thousands of years ago to hunt. I asked him about those and he laughed.

"Do I look like a curator to you?"

I stared deep into the cupboard with all of his little plastic toys and I didn't say anything.

Bubba's arrowhead wasn't the kind you'd find deep in the soil. It wasn't even all that old. Sometime in the fifties the folk at Krinkle did a limited edition toy, a plastic arrowhead. All the kids loved their Cowboys and Indians. Loved to run around on their mom's broom pretending to be on horseback. An arrowhead must have seemed so perfect for the time. Of course there were accidents and of course Krinkle pulled the boxes from shelves, issued a massive recall. Only a couple of hundred got through the net. Just two hundred arrowheads out there.

Any one of them would be worth a small fortune.

***

I became a garage sale junkie, sifting through endless boxes of crap. Some people spend hours every day doing what I did. Mostly they are collectors, looking for records, books, those rare objects you chance upon once in a while. The thing that makes it all worthwhile. I started noticing the type almost as quickly as I became one. Gaze down, angled for peering inside boxes, awkward posture, almost hunched, trying to shrink, as though if we all got small enough we could clamber inside these cardboard treasure chests and find the real gold, the atomic rarities that the human eye could never spot. The men, and we were always men, gave each other courteous nods, though we never spoke to one another. I wondered briefly if anyone else knew Bubba, if any of them were also searching for the fabled arrowhead, but one by one they would show their true colours. An overexcited gasp upon the discovery of a first edition Detective Comics, or a smug chuckle at the sight of an original Blind Blake record. Whenever I saw someone find something and caught their poker face as it fell away, I felt as though they had betrayed us. But the truth was, I was jealous. They'd found it and I kept on coming up short. Yeah, I'd find the odd toy to sell to Bubba, a spoon, an action figure, and once, a whole set of trolls, their hair still in good condition. But each time I'd sell something to him, he'd ask me the same thing,

"How's the search for the arrowhead?"

And I would deflate.

I felt as though I would never quite do right by him, just missing the mark every time. Sure, he wouldn't look upset, and he'd pay, but you could tell that it wasn't quite right. He had this thing that he did, scratching at that bit of duct tape stuck to his neck, whenever you disappointed him. Some days that tape would be black, some days red, he replaced it all the time. I guessed that he had a tattoo he wasn't so proud of, maybe something he'd gotten whilst in he was prison all those years ago.

People do stupid things when they're backed into a corner. No doubt about that.

With the cash Bubba had paid me I'd been able to stay afloat for a while, making rent payments, keeping the lights on. Scraping by. There's not much work in Shallow Creek. Not much work anywhere. Sometimes it feels like not only have the cards been stacked against you but that you ain't even a card that belongs in that deck. When I found one of those arrowheads I'd buy myself a plot of land on the outskirts of the town and build myself a home. Nothing fancy, just a couple of a rooms, that's all. But it would be mine. I've never been so good with tools but I'd learn. That dream got through the worst of it, the weeks where I found nothing. I'd sometimes buy boxes of cereal and sell Bubba the toys straight out of them, still stinking of fresh plastic and sugar, but they'd never net me more than a dollar.

"They're good toys," I'd tell Bubba, "brand new, could be worth a fortune in the future."

"Need to be old, need to feel old," was all he'd ever say and I'd stand there holding a limp dollar bill watching as he scratched his forever itch, smoothing down the duct tape.

I got that. The feeling you get when you love something, a nostalgia for it that means more than the object itself. It didn't stop me from trying it on every now and then.

Sometimes I got this feeling, like I was enabling him. It was the way his eyes would light up, just a little, colour catching in the corner of the iris and spreading. Like the touch and feel of the toys woke him up after days or weeks of sleeping. Even though he'd always have his cupboard open, I noticed that he always held on to the toy for a little longer, hesitating before placing it on the shelf.

Then, the itch.

Then, the money.

But that damned arrowhead just kept on alluding me.

So when I say that I found it, and that it was under my nose the whole time, well, it makes me a prize motherfucker, doesn't it? I got a call from Mom, boxes of my childhood shit had been in the garage ever since I moved out and could I get my ass over there and move them? Sure. I'd be happy to.

She didn't seem so pleased to see me.

"Lenny, Lenny, Lenny," she shook her head as she embraced me, "I heard all kinds of stories."

"They're not true Mom. Promise."

"They never are, are they?"

"Not unless I tell them." That made her smile at least. I'm a fucker, sure, but I'm sweet enough.

The garage was thick with the warmth of the summer; a man could pass out sifting through junk in this heat. I couldn't see any of the walls anymore, instead they were piled high with boxes and crates. A whole bunch of them soggy and green with mould, some of the wet cardboard eroded away to reveal the insides, and only one or two repaired with stripes of duct tape that recalled Bubba's neck in a way that made me wince. Strapped to the ceiling was our little old row boat which we used to take out on the Silverpine back when Pop was still alive and kicking. Now though, cobwebs wove their way around it. Looking closely, I could see a batch of spider-eggs, laid and waiting.

Mom came out with a six-pack of beers and left them on top of one of the boxes.

"Your stuff is in the corner."

She pointed over at the front of the garage, next to the door. Four or five boxes scrawled with the words 'Lenny's Stuff' were stacked high in a single tower.

I grabbed the first one, tore off the tape, and there it was, in amongst ratty schoolbooks and broken toys. A plastic arrowhead, no bigger than my thumb. I turned it over in my hand and in tiny raised letters on the back, KRINKLE. This was it. The real deal.

No one ran quicker than me that day as I made my way to Bubba Cody's.

It was the middle of the afternoon and the Bazaar was closed, though the sound of fun lingered in the air, like the silence after a bomb goes off. I took the turning off towards Bubba's place and practically ran straight into the man in the middle of the path.

Bubba grabbed hold of me and I stopped in my tracks.

"Lenny, where you off to?"

"You got your money ready Bubba Cody? Because I've got something for you."

I saw a man cry that day. The arrowhead had felt so small to me, so light, but when Bubba took hold of it he gave it a weight I hadn't noticed it had.

"I had it, it was mine," I told him. "I don't remember when I got it, or how old I was or anything like that, but it was mine."

But Bubba didn't hear me, he was entranced by the object, tears flooding his face. I felt awkward stood in that room with him. I couldn't leave. Not without my money. So I stayed and I waited, and for a little while I felt alone, as though Bubba was not really there. His eyes had widened, and I saw colours within them I had never seen in a human eye. In between the tears, a smile crept up his face, gleeful and ecstatic. His face was that of a child at Christmas, eagerly opening presents, determining each one to be the most important object he'd ever have.

Then I caught the duct tape on his neck, in the corner of my eye, moving. It was a small movement at first, just a flicker of it across the surface. Then, a small cone, tiny, really, emerged from underneath it, like a finger testing the temperature of a bath. The tape stretched and then retreated. I looked up, and Bubba wasn't looking at the arrowhead any longer, he was staring straight at me.

"Is everything alright Bubba?"

"What? Oh, Lenny. I'm fine. You, ah, need something from me, don't you? Money. Money. Payment. That's it. Bubba remembers. I remember."

He shoved his hand in his pocket and brought out a wad of cash. Without counting it, he pressed it all into my hands, stared me straight in the eyes and said, "Thank you Lenny, sincerely, thank you."

And I knew then that I had to leave.

I went back to my mom's place the next day with a headache splitting my head, feeling hungover though I hadn't had a drop the night before. Sifting back through those boxes of old things of mine, I couldn't get the thought of that tape on Bubba's neck out of my head. The way something had pressed up against it. For a while I'd kidded myself that it was an injury or a tumour. The kind of horrible thing that he couldn't afford to have looked at by doctors. Hiding it away from himself was the only way to pretend it wasn't really there. But then that tiny little thing reaching out through his neck. What had it been? I tried to unpack the boxes, throwing old crap away that I didn't need, but I found I was grabbing objects from them and just staring at them. An old football trophy, the tarnished brass barely reflecting my face, glinted in my eyes as though it was newly polished. When I put it down, I could have sworn I'd only been sat there for a few minutes but nearly an hour had passed.

That's the power they hold, isn't it? These things from our past.

***

The money helped. For a while at least. Then the engine in my truck got fucked, then the storm hit, taking a part of mom's roof with it, then, then then. Always something new. Always something that cost. That wad of cash Bubba had paid me whittled down to nothing quicker than you could say Shallow Creek. I was never going to find another toy like that. He said it himself. The Krinkle toys were as rare as they came. Problem was I was never any good at anything. Useless son of a bitch. Finding that toy amongst my old stuff, well, that was the first time I'd felt like I'd be a decent guy my entire life. The look on Bubba's face. The money too. Of course the money. The first night after it all ran out and I couldn't afford food, I sat hungry in my bed, crying, holding my rumbling belly like a child.

When was it that I decided to rob Bubba? Was it that night, staring at my walls, understanding what it was like to dream of food? Was it the next morning? That week? I don't remember, but the idea came to me and when it did it cemented itself and became the only option I had.

I practised target shooting in the backyard with my pop's rifle. I was pretty good, though I was hoping to get through this without firing a single bullet. I just wanted the toys.

Bubba said they were valuable. Not just to him but to collectors.

I wasn't the only one who knew about Bubba's collection, and no doubt others had seen inside the cupboard, knew where everything was hidden. He'd suspect me, sure, but I'd just be one of a lot of people in Shallow Creek who were desperate for money. I'd be in and out of his cabin without him knowing I'd be there, so long as I made sure to go on one of the nights the bazaar was open. All that really mattered was shifting the toys and spending the money quietly. I could do that; I wasn't an idiot.

That evening it felt as though the sun set slower than it had before. In the distance, beyond the trees, I saw the lights of the bazaar flicker on, casting dusty pinks and greens across the sky. The music carried through the trees like birdsong. I wrapped my pop's rifle in a blanket and set off to Bubba's cabin.

There was no eerie silence around the cabin, not when the happy cries from the two people on the coaster and the screams of the scant few folks trying to make their way through the House of Terror echoed all around me. Still, easier to smash a window when no one can hear it. I shattered the kitchen window with the butt of the rifle and climbed in.

In the dark, the kitchen felt smaller and I felt clumsy. The table and chairs seemed to be in a different position to where they'd been when I'd last been there, and as I crossed the floor to the cupboard I found myself stepping into the path of some object or another.

The lock on the cupboard was sturdy, of course it was, if Bubba Cody wanted something locked away he'd for sure keep it locked away good. No chance of picking the thing. No chance of knocking it open with the end of the rifle.

I raised the barrel, holding it close to the body of the lock, and I waited

for the telltale noise from the Black Bullet,
 3
 2
 1
 away
 we
 go
 and I fired.

Beyond the cabin, a woman screamed as the coaster whipped its way around the corner. I knew that damn ride like the back of my hand.

The lock lay on the floor, a smoking hole in the centre.

The cupboard doors, one now hanging off its hinges, were open revealing Bubba's collection. There they were, my paycheck, and in the centre of the middle shelf, sitting on top of a small red velvet pillow was the Krinkle arrowhead. I grabbed it and pocketed it. That one was special. No way I'd treat it like the rest.

I opened up the blanket and lay it on the floor.

The Black Bullet would be nearly done and I wanted to be out quick. No telling when Bubba would take a break.

No need to be quiet, and no need to be careful, these things were mostly plastic anyway so they weren't going to break or anything. I swept my arm across each shelf, knocking the toys down onto the blanket. I took the corners up together and knotted them around the rifle butt. Must have looked a real sight.

A real sight.

Of course, I never got to see that. I probably blacked out long before I felt Bubba Cody whack me over the head.

***

There was dirt in my mouth. I coughed awake. Above me, the canopy of trees told me I was somewhere in the middle of the Silverpine forest. Long distance from the bazaar, in Shallow Creek terms at least. I was dazed but I didn't feel any pain, and when I checked my body I couldn't find any wounds except for a horrible lump on my head.

"Shouldn't have gone to the house, Lenny."

I blinked and saw Bubba sitting on a gnarled old tree stump rubbing his duct tape.

"Dammit Lenny, you shouldn't have. I like you, goddamn it, but you shouldn't have gone back."

"Sorry Bubba," I slurred, the knock to the head had gotten to me more than I thought.

"Yeah, I guess you are," he seemed exhausted, resigned. "And if it were up to me I'd … I don't know, let you off, but it ain't."

He tugged at the duct tape; I could hear it tearing at his skin.

"They say to do it in one quick rip, ain't that a lie."

Bubba stood up and grabbed hold of the corner of the tape with two hands and he yanked it, pulling the whole thing off. It would be wrong to call what was underneath it a scar; it was a gaping open wound, pink flesh. I felt sick.

"You like them Krinkle toys Lenny? They like them too you know. I tried them on all sorts, insects, animals, hell I even tried pet food," he put his hand into his pocket and pulled out the car I'd brought him all those months ago. I thought about the money he'd paid me for it. "But it's these things, I don't know why, it's what keeps them going."

He held the toy car up to the wound on his neck and I watched the skin bulge, like a tumour working its way up through his throat.

Something stuck of his neck.

A hand.

It was human, or human looking, and it was small, like a child's. Porcelain skin, clean, sharp nails.

"Here you go, here it is."

The hand whipped the little car from Bubba's fingertips and retreated back inside the opening. From within his throat I heard a chewing sound. Bubba gagged, struggling with the thing sat where it was.

It clambered back down within him.

"Please," I said, "Please don't kill me."

"Say, you kept that arrowhead from the Krinkle box for years didn't you? Like, decades, right?"

I nodded.

"Crazy thing. I bet when you were a kiddy you loved that damn thing. I used to try and make Momma pick up this thing called Raisin's n Flakes. Cried like a real shit when she didn't. They used to come with these little Cowboy and Indian toys. I loved them. Fucking lived for the next one. I'd grab that box and empty the whole damn thing out to try and find the toy in there."

The headache was going and my voice was coming back, I could feel it, and if I had just a few more minutes, I could run.

"I think they latch on to something like that, you know? Maybe it'll be different for you. Maybe it'll be money Lenny, fuck knows you got a love for that stuff. Whatever it is, you'll know soon enough," he pulled a new roll of duct tape from his pocket, tore a stretch of it off and smoothed it over the hole in his neck, "it usually kicks in an hour after they've nested."

There it was, the feeling coming back.

I picked myself up, and I didn't think twice. I ran.

There aren't so many paths in the Silverpine forest, though, if you've lived in Shallow Creek long enough you get to know some of the landmarks, at least on the outskirts. Where Bubba had taken me, I didn't know. The red maples grew tall, obscuring the sky but for the odd gap in the canopy where I caught the stars and the moon. I could barely see, it was that dark, but I ran anyway, kept on running and I only stopped when my lungs heaved and a sickness inside of me rose.

I looked around to see where I was but nothing made sense and inside, I could feel something.

An hour after they've nested, how long had I been out?

I took in a deep breath before realising I couldn't breathe properly, that something had wrapped around my throat, squeezing it with what felt like tiny fingers. Across the inside of my neck a tiny nail scratched, exploring its new home, teasing its way up towards my mouth. Instinctively I clamped my lips shut. This thing could not leave. I felt a tiny hand dragging its way up and across my tongue, reaching out between my lips to test the air. Another tiny finger played against my windpipe, and I opened my mouth just a little because what was in there could not stay in there. Whatever it was, it had to go. It had to come out.

But the thing inside me wouldn't budge.

I had no way of knowing how to get out. I could look for the edge of the asylum grounds, but who knew where they began. It's just the Silverpine, I tried telling myself. That's all, Lenny. Just the forest making you believe all that shit Bubba said.

But then I stopped breathing entirely and something closed its grip on me. I could see that porcelain skin inside me and I knew, I knew it was there, and it had to come out and there was no other way, and I thought about shoving my hand the hell inside my mouth and dragging the thing out. When I raised my hand above my mouth I couldn't and I knew that I'd die trying, until I remembered it, still there in my pocket.

The arrowhead.

Bubba must have thought he got everything from the blanket. Never thought to check me.

The little plastic point wasn't too sharp, but maybe, maybe with enough force it would do. This thing had to come out.

I held the arrowhead at arm's length, shut my eyes, and somewhere distant I thought I could hear the Black Bullet, and I heard that tinny recorded voice say 3, 2, 1

away

we

go

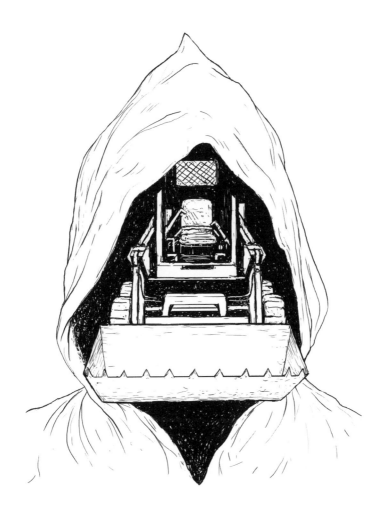

THE SOIL OF STONIER HEARTS

by Erik Bergstrom

When death arrived in Shallow Creek, it surfaced in the soil. The snow had peeled back in Spring like a coquettish debutante showing off her bruises, revealing ghastly yellow rectangles where the ground soured over plots of the buried dead. April rains came and went. Soon after were the familiar mists of May, sliding over town like a beaded curtain but failing to wash it clean, leaving behind the same fuming face of Devil's Gorge and filthy gutters outside Jack's. The dead rectangles of grass at St. Mary's were only the latest in a long series of blights upon the town, and, like all others, they refused to leave, even when the sun grew warm and the soil softened from fresh rain.

It was the time of year that Jed Sherman, groundskeeper of St. Mary's Catholic Cemetery, anticipated the longer he lived in Shallow Creek. With Spring came a revival; a chance to empty the dustbin of evil thoughts that lingered in the lonesome winter and resume the sort of honest work he'd been chasing for years. His tenure at St. Mary's began as a community assignment following the latest of his drunk and disorderly charges, though slowly it turned into his singular dedication. He'd given himself over to the cemetery's grounds, and, as in any healthy relationship, it paid him back with grass soft enough to stimulate his toes and leaves thick enough to shade him from the heat.

But then there'd been the arrival of the dead rectangles, carrying with them something strange and old and unwilling to be forgotten, shook out, or hidden.

Jed's troubles began when, during a hasty discussion in Sister Augustine's office, he was given orders to prepare the cemetery for an impending remembrance ceremony. He walked down the long, dark corridor afterwards, beyond the reach of light filtering through the red and yellow stained glass, suddenly heavy with a need to drink after the nun's dressing-down. He shamefully considered rooting for the communion wine like a pig in want of truffles even as he knew Father Frank was shuttered up in one of the hidden rooms, making himself more difficult to reach once the melted snow revealed the cemetery's new physiognomy.

Jed entered the room at the back of the church where he stored his gardening tools and stood motionless, as if an answer to the dead grass problem might simply jump out and cry, "Here I am! Use me!" But among the rakes and shovels and coiled-up hoses, only the telephone called to him, accompanied by a name he suddenly remembered—the name he'd telephoned only once before when his community officer asked for confirmation of his skills. He'd blurted out "groundskeeping" for the sole reason of once knowing a man who'd emigrated from Shallow Creek to become a professional landscaper in a town far away.

"Something's wrong with our soil, Gordy." Jed heard the short echo of his voice in Gordon Anderson's answering machine. He began to articulate the thoughts he'd never previously said out loud: "I think it's the dead stirring.."

He ended his message shortly after, then immediately began worrying over what he'd said and whether he'd come on too strong. There was a reason Gordon moved away from Shallow Creek, and Jed knew bringing up the living dead likely wouldn't sway him to return; for though the two had been inseparable in their youth, they were unlike in many ways. Gordon had grown up ramrod straight, while Jed slithered around town like a snake searching for his tail, always carrying a wild imagination for the secrets that were stowed away in buttoned-down houses and old curiosity shops. Soon Gordon was gone, and Jed's imagination dried up once he took to the bottle. But then that grotesque grass reared its lifeless face, hiding strange new secrets for him to unveil in the shapes it left behind.

The phone clanged loudly, nearly casting Jed into the coat rack. He hurriedly picked up the receiver. It was Gordon. A surprising relief washed over him, realising his friend still chose to reach out irrespective of their past or the present miles that lay between them.

"You test the soil at all?"

Jed wanted to answer Gordon directly, but his nerves, wild imagination, and phantom drunkenness consumed him once again, knowing all that separated him from the cursed ground outside were the thin walls of the church. "We never should've buried them here, Gordy. I knew it all along! We never should've buried them here!"

"What are you on about?"

"We put their sickness in the dirt!"

"It's likely the acidity. I've got a test. Won't charge you for it. I can come by next Wednesday?"

It suddenly seemed to Jed that not much had changed with his old friend. Whether this was simply a courtesy call or an absolution of his guilt for leaving, he'd always had an explanation for everything in Shallow Creek, until the day he didn't—which was the day he up and left.

"I'm happy to get you back here, Gordy." Jed stumbled excitedly over his words. "You might even see how much we've changed. Maybe this time you'll stay awhile."

***

June 1st - Took a nightcap to Father Frank. Looked for him for half an hour before I found him up near the altar, blessing the Eucharist. Something seemed to fill his thoughts as he set the toddy aside and busied himself with replacing the jug of wine beneath the altar. I'm sure it's got something to do with the anniversary of that forsaken event out at the gorge. And now, just to make matters worse, there's something off about the grass.

I don't understand how he figures to hold a remembrance service for all those wretched souls. I told him they broke a commandment by following that false prophet. But it's on his mind all the same, and there's no changing it. I know him too well to believe he'll never break his stubborn nature. So I kept quiet as he straightened the lineaments and ignored his drink. I can only hope his mind was in a godly place.

I'll confess mine isn't. Not always.

Those dead patches in the cemetery got to reminding me about the sick times, and of the man I kept seeing through it all. Made me wonder if more trouble lies ahead.

It always does, here.

***

They were corralled around Gordon's truck to eyeball the results of a pH test on the cemetery's grounds. Gordon looked up, the wrinkles around his eyes creasing as he surveyed the patches of dead grass. On the phone, he'd assured Jed that, over the course of twenty years, he'd discovered all there was to know about dirt and that there was likely an earthly explanation for their problem. It wasn't until he found himself back in St. Mary's Cemetery, shifting his eyes between the test results and the soil, that he suddenly remembered how the town's mysteries could coil themselves around a person rather than loudly announce their presence.

"How'd acid even get in the soil?" asked Jed, breaking the disquiet.

"Oh, any number of ways. Misplacement of nitrogen. Bad fertilizer. Could be there's too much sulfur." Though he tried to remain rational, Gordon knew something inexplicable had surely happened—as much as he tried to keep it at arm's length—what with how those rectangles appeared so neatly rotted whilst permitting the grass to remain so lush and green around them.

All at once, it came to him; they'd been in a fix like this before, working their minds over something that made so little sense even into their later years.

The two had often spent excessive hours at Jed's house during the summer, picking through his icebox or digging holes for their toy soldiers in the backyard. On days when it rained, they'd go up to the attic—and that's where they found the odd photograph hiding amongst the other relics. Gordon, dressed in a dusty frock coat, was rolling across the uneven wooden floor in a squeaky wheelchair while Jed sat nearby, peeling apart the laminate pages of a photo album. At one point he paused and cautiously placed a finger on the photo to rub it, stating, "This person's got no legs."

Gordon spilled out from the wheelchair and crouched next to Jed, anxious to see this real-life amputee. The figures in the photo were standing next to a church and celebrating a wedding, each of them sporting feathered hair and dressed in brash checkered suits and lacy dresses. The boys quickly recognized them as younger versions of their respective families—friends through the ages, it seemed—with Shallow Creek nurturing generations in its nucleus. A sudden shock seized Gordon when he focused on the man Jed was pointing at—it was his uncle, though with nothing but an eerie emptiness below his knees.

"Looks like he's floating," said Jed, rubbing at the page, trying to erase a blemish. But there was no blemish; his uncle, a diabetic, lost his legs when Gordon was a child—yet in the photograph, taken a decade or so before he was born, Gordon could clearly see the slats of the church where his uncle's legs should be. A trick of the camera, perhaps, though it felt to Gordon more like one of Shallow Creek's familiar oddities revealing its diabolical secret. "Odd, ain't it?"

Gordon snapped out of his reverie and turned to Jed, who, aside from his thinning gray hair and spider veins along his nose, looked every bit the same as he had in the attic all those years ago. "Come again?"

"Odd that it could be sulfur."

"How's that so odd?"

"Seems to me sulfur would kill off the whole grounds."

"Well, yeah. Though there's things that can be done." Gordon tossed his gloves into the back of his truck and lit a smoke. A gust of wind shook the leaves over their heads, and for a fleeting moment life existed again within the cemetery.

"Like what?" said Jed, his voice deadened.

"Well—" Gordon pointed with his cigarette, waving the smoke around like a smudging wand. "We can till in some limestone to fix the acidity. Would need to tear up the whole lot, more than likely."

"Oh, we can't do that! Father Frank would throw a fit!"

"Okay then, Jed. If you want it look like ghosts left their beach blankets behind, by all means …"

He noticed how Jed's eyes were wet and bloodshot from staring; first at the poisoned grass, and then beyond to where the setting sun flared up alongside the western face of Devil's Gorge. It seemed to Gordon that a familiar countenance consumed his friend, as if he were succumbing to the old, jealous nature of the town. At last Jed turned back to Gordon, eyeballs dancing and shadows spilling over his gaunt face. "I ever tell you about the sick times?"

"You've told me more tales about this town than I care to recall."

"But you must remember hearing about the hospital. How it got so full it had to turn people away?"

"I might remember something about that."

"Did you know Father Frank took 'em all in, even when we didn't know what it was making everybody sick? That he buried them all here?" Jed stopped to give the grounds another respectful moment of silence. "Had to bury them two by two," he said at last, his voice veering with the wind. "He put the bodies one on top of the other. But they just kept coming!"

The sun had quietly slipped away, leaving two old friends covered in deep blue shadows. Gordon grabbed his truck's door handle with a trembling hand, greasing it with his sweat. "All right then, Jed," he said. "You just let me know what your reverend says about the limestone treatment."

Jed looked back at Gordon with a frightening dullness. "Father Frank told me once, when there's no more room in hell, the devil's gonna send 'em back. Back to Shallow Creek."

**

June 6 - Well it seems Jed got mixed up in all kinds of trouble. Brought a man here yesterday from out of town who looked over the grounds and decided the whole thing needs tilling. How can he mean to till up the ground where the dead lie resting?

Didn't even bother delivering Father Frank his drink after Jed spoke to him. Knew he'd be especially out of sorts after hearing how the ground's got too much of something bad in it. Of course there's something bad in it! All those poor, sick souls buried there, faster than Father could ever bless them. Not to mention those bodies from the gorge. It's all so terrible.

I suppose it's why our visitor's returned. Saw him again the other day, come back to heed the dead like they belong to him alone. He's back with that demonic tool, too, ready to mow down another swath of Shallow Creek's godliest after leading them astray of the Lord, like he did with those lost lambs at the gorge. It took many blessings to be rid of him the first time, though it wasn't until the gorge incident that he finally disappeared, like some Grim Reaper come to cleanse the town.

Poor Father Frank. I didn't mean to withhold our communion tonight. But it seems to me there gets to be a point where a man's troubles can't be fixed with drink. He must instead turn to something stronger. A deeper kind of solitary prayer. That Jed's brought a lot of trouble down on Father Frank again, fooling with outsiders. Doesn't he know the only thing he's tilling up is the stonier soil of our preacher's wounded heart?

***

The day was not ideal for digging. A soupy, fetid air was wafting in off a nearby marshland and the sky was thickening with dark clouds—signs of an impending storm. Though after weeks of Jed's nervous stalling and visiting numerous towns to source equipment and supplies, Gordon was now short on time.

Jed, meanwhile, was nowhere to be found.

Gordon stood next to a featureless woman on the back steps of the church. He'd been expecting the priest too, but he was as mysteriously absent as his groundskeeper.

"How long is this process?" the woman asked. Gordon twitched at the sound of her voice, fully aware of how unwanted he was at the church. Even so, he pitied them, for he knew the nun and her priest would never fight the town's superstitious grip hard enough to escape it. They'd continue to live in their own ignorance, he felt, until it wholly consumed them both.

"It'll be a full day's work," he said. "Morning to till it up, afternoon to lay sod." He turned to observe Willy, his youthful, blotchy-cheeked apprentice, struggling to fix the tiller to their rented skid-loader.

The nun looked up to the sky. "And if the rain comes?"

"Then we'll work as long as we can in the rain."

She scowled at Gordon with a vile twist of her lips. "Seems awfully messy."

"If Zeus himself starts throwing lightning, we'll stop. Otherwise …"

Gordon paused upon noticing a swarm of townsfolk snaking around the corner of the church, their voices inextricable in the boggy air.

"Looks like you've caught their attention," said the nun, with a hint of a smile.

"No, no, no," Gordon said. "This won't do." He approached the swell of people, waving his hands in the air to attract their attention. He shouted over the racket to inform them of all the hard work there was left to do, he and his apprentice were already running behind, and the intrusion would only slow them further.

"You're disturbing their rest," said a man nearest the front, his accent thick and Scottish.

"Ain't you got any decency?" said another man who Gordon recognized as Jack O'Keeffe, whose tavern could be directly implicated in many of the harsher memories he had of the town.

"Why can't you leave them be?" added a younger woman with beautiful, ebony skin; professional-looking in a way, which left Gordon wondering how she got tangled up with such types.

"You're turning this into a whole lot of nothing," said Gordon. "We're just skimming her off the top. Giving her a little makeover."

The crowd erupted and Gordon pleaded with the nun for assistance, who, in an instant, quietened them all by repeating Gordon's words. "It's only a quick renovation to make the grounds look fit and proper for our remembrance in a week." She spoke with a calm determination that indicated she'd dealt with this lot before. "Now let these men finish their work. Longer you stand around, longer the job will take. We'll then be forced to find other ways to entertain our visitors."

Most of them splintered off, the core weakened, though a few remained—one of whom was the sheriff, asking to see Gordon and Willy's permits. The nun informed him that both had been vouched for by Jed.

"Monthly patron of the Shallow Creek jail, Jed Sherman?" the sheriff cried. "You trust any acquaintance of that drunk, you might as well trust the devil himself!"

"That's fine, sheriff," said the nun. "We completed the proper checks. They have their permits and all that other paperwork you and your deputies like to shuffle."

The sheriff smiled and eased up, yet there remained an ember of distrust burning in his eyes, rooted long ago. He hooked his thumbs in his khaki trousers and lumbered off, surveying the grounds as he passed. The way he looked out—the way all the citizens of Shallow Creek looked out at that cemetery—made it appear as if any and all warnings were less for outsiders like Gordon and Willy and more for themselves. Like the dead were a bad memory on the return.

It's what Shallow Creek was to Gordon, after all; a bad memory awakened when Jed came calling, disrupting the life he'd tried to build after freeing himself like a dandelion seed to be sown in richer soil.

Gordon watched Willy work the ground awhile, keeping his eyes on the townsfolk who remained at the perimeter of the cemetery. The sun had risen from behind Devil's Gorge, burning away the morning haze and waking the cicadas to their lazy drone. He shaded his eyes with his hand as he looked out at the Gorge, putting together the bits and pieces of all he'd heard about the incident. Jed had called those people "possessed", though what Gordon now thought, shivering even in the sunlight, was how the whole bloody town was possessed, and how, as a young man, he'd come close to joining them, escaping only when he'd learned what it was that held such power over them …

He was just about to take over from the boy, when suddenly, like an omen from his wandering mind, Jed stumbled into the cemetery, his clothes dishevelled and eyes ringed with fright.

"You got to stop the digging!" he shouted over the skid-loader's engine.

"What for?"

"You got to stop!"

Gordon stepped forward and waved Willy down. The engine sputtered and died, and the deceptive quiet of St. Mary's consumed them once more.

"What'd you need us to stop for, Jed?" asked Gordon. "We were coming along nice enough."

"I was leaving Jack's … through the alley," he spoke with labored breaths, "and I saw—I saw—"

"Christ, Jed! The hell were you doing at Jack's? You knew we had the dig scheduled—"

"I saw your uncle—" Jed halted, seizing up at Gordon's scowl that grew ten leagues long. "Hear me out," he continued, "I'm sober as a fox, I promise, and I know he's been dead awhile. But I swear to—" He stopped once more and looked up at the long steeple of the church, which cut into the clouds above. "To God, I guess, that it was him, Gordy. And it was just like that photo we saw—he was hovering there with no legs, out of his wheelchair, dressed in black. He was holdin' on to something too, something long and sharp, curved almost—"

"A scythe, Jed?"

"Yeah—"

"You calling my uncle the Grim Reaper?"

"I don't know what he was, but I could hear him clear as St. Mary's bells. I recognized the voice—it was your uncle, telling me—telling me—"

"Telling you what, Jed?"

"He told me that even in Shallow Creek, the graves run deep. Said it just like that—*the graves run deep*. Told me the dead had visited hell, and now they're comin' back!"

All at once Gordon was forced to acknowledge something he'd always known—that there were things in Heaven and on Earth that couldn't be explained by observable facts; that there were men and women who knew how to tap into higher planes of existence. Some of them had come to Shallow Creek—fallen into its orbit, it seemed—because it was one of the few weak spots in the universe's tether. There were those who actively sought more, like the man who'd led those poor people down to Devil's Gorge. Then there were people like his uncle, a simple farmer who'd stumbled upon his own secrets. He hadn't needed an imagination to uncover them, like Jed. He only needed a tool for cutting away the dense chaff …

Suddenly there was a loud, grating sound behind them. Gordon turned to find Willy battling with the controls of the skid-loader as it took on a life of its own, jerking and listing from side to side. The boy barked a short cry, calling for help, but as soon as Gordon stepped forward the machine jerked and threw Willy out. The engine roared and coughed thick black clouds of exhaust. Children screamed while others shouted at Willy to move, get up, do *something*! But the boy just lay helplessly in a shallow pit of his own making, reaching out for help as the skid-loader trampled slowly over him, cutting his cries short before continuing unimpeded towards the marsh.

Gordon broke away and screamed for the boy, hoping for any response. Yet when he found him—what remained of him—he knew there was no breath left in Willy's lungs.

He knelt over the body and sobbed until a clap of thunder rang overhead and a warm rain washed over him. Soon it was steaming off the hot granite headstones and transforming the soil to muck. To Gordon, it seemed as if the ground itself was moving—like there was a machine buried deep within the earth, churning mud like cake batter.

He removed his hands from the boy and yelled his throat raw, then stood to sprint from the cemetery in a direction he wasn't sure of; knowing only to keep to a straight line until he was far enough away from the boundaries of Shallow Creek and all its insoluble secrets.

***

July 2 - The big dig ended in tragedy. Another mark on the town, I suppose. There was a storm that came and went in a matter of minutes, though the mess those boys left behind will take weeks to clear up.

Father Frank held the Requiem Mass at the Town Square, much to the dismay of the victims' families. They wanted the service to be on the holy ground of St. Mary's where the devil couldn't reach their poor babies again. Father Frank told them there's nothing holy about St. Mary's anymore.

I pray I might find the words to tell him he's wrong, and how I believe, now, that our returning visitor is actually a guardian angel, arriving ahead of those godless outsiders like Dave Danvers and the possessed devils at the gorge. Makes me feel better, anyhow, since it seems he's taken to spending time with my Maura. He even left his cutting tool among the graves to show us he was here, keeping our holy ground safe from meddlers. I've got it stowed away now, in a place Jed can't misuse it; along with my other delicious little secrets, it brings me comfort to know it'll never be found.

Of course, telling Father Frank any of this right now might be the death of him after all he's endured. At the very least he may threaten to shut the church down again. He knows how I feel on the matter, even as he keeps telling me God left us long ago. That even the best shepherds lose their flock from time to time.

Now can you believe that? From an ordained minister?

There's no way I could let St. Mary's be shut down. Our town needs the church now more than ever before, what with all the strangeness that's been happening. And so, with Father Frank's blessing, or without it, I'll be sure to keep our church doors open, and I'll wait here as long as it takes for the grass to grow green again.

JANET'S VISION OF LOVE

by Tom Heaton

Janet Lopez was picking up coffee and donuts when Chief Hamilton called to say they had a suspect homicide up at the hanging tree.

'A what?'

'You heard it right, Janet. You seen that contortionist act down at Bubba's?'

'Uh yeah.'

'Fella folds himself into a packing box, writes an address and sticks the stamp on with his foot.'

'Kinda creepy actually.'

'Well you won't be seeing it again anyhow. He's the victim. You get me the Blueberry Frosted?'

'Still warm.'

Didn't seem like there was a need for the siren. Instead Janet punched the CD player a couple times. When it began playing 'Heartbreaker', she remembered the date. 'Oh Mariah, if only you knew!'

The chief was standing to attention outside the station, his hat on so straight he might've used a spirit level, the new crease in his pants at risk of making a slice in the upholstery.

'Looking fly, boss.'

'Got an upstate detective coming in by boat, maybe ballistics as well.'

'Discharged firearm?'

'According to the ranger found the body.'

Janet pulled out of the station and on to Main. 'Donut's in the bag. Don't get frosting on your jacket.'

The chief leant forward as he bit so the blueberry shavings fell into the footwell, his spare hand restraining his tie. He chewed awhile. 'What you looking so miserable about anyway?'

'One-year anniversary,' Janet said.

'Of what? Of Bobby leaving? That's a dumb reason to have an anniversary.'

'All I got.'

'Man was a known commitment-phobe.'

'The preferred term is relationship anxiety.'

'You're better out of it, Janet.'

'So everyone tells me.'

The road wormed its way up through the first of the pines, the sun twisting between the trunks and sitting pretty in the new growth. 'Doesn't look so bad on a bright morning,' the chief said. 'Almost friendly.' But when they reached the plateau, the canopy closed in sudden as an eyelid, as thick and dense as only silver pine can, and they entered the shadowy world of the forest, tall straight trunks crowding the road. The chief brushed sugar off his trousers. 'You know sometimes, I think maybe they should've built that highway. No offence.'

'Bullshit.'

'Natural response, Janet. You were committed, put your life on the line, but that was some years ago and no one's too fond of these woods. Truth is, they're unpleasant in character, and inhospitable.'

'They got their own agenda.'

'You talk like they're human, Janet, which they ain't. They're just lumber waiting to be cut. A six-lane highway might've brought something cosmopolitan to Shallow Creek, just saying. Turn here.'

Janet swung into a parking lot carpeted with pine needles. 'I know the way, boss. These woods are my babies remember. I saved 'em, which is why I'm so touchy on the subject. And you got frosting on your chin.' The chief let her dab at it with a tissue. 'Got it. You're dandy.'

***

The hanging tree was an ancient spreading oak that was somehow mixed up in a forest that otherwise preferred to grow straight. Maybe no one had ever been hanged off it, but its sturdy branches would sure be useful if that was your purpose. The pines maintained a respectful distance, as if anticipating malice.

Most summer evenings, kids from Shallow Creek drove up there and did what kids like to do. Alongside the path were crushed cans, empty packets of rolling paper, the occasional prophylactic wrapped around a fern like some species of woodland jellyfish. Janet speculated that all this human junk was why the pines hung back, and she wouldn't blame them.

Officer Jimmy Turner ran down the path towards them. 'Hey Boss, hey Janet. I secured the scene. Didn't have no tape, so I used pine cones. Here's the way in and out through that line of cones there. We got a witness—ranger who found the body. It's pretty grisly.'

Didn't matter how many training videos Janet had seen, with their surplus of bullet wounds in gory close up, it still delivered a wallop to see the back of someone's skull missing and a twenty bore sprouting from a gaping mouth. He was slumped against the hanging tree, wearing nothing but a T-shirt and boxer shorts, his hands chained around the trunk and secured with a padlock. 'Found the key,' Jimmy said. 'Over there, throwable distance from the deceased, marked by that large pine cone.'

'Looks like suicide, boss,' Janet said.

'How's a suicide supposed to chain himself to a tree and discharge a gun into his mouth exactly?'

'You seen his act?'

'What if I haven't?'

'He does this stunt called the reverse escape, trusses himself up like a thanksgiving turkey and tosses the key into a jam jar held by a member of the audience.'

'Right, and he placed the gun in his mouth using his feet, you suppose?'

'Nope. He put the gun in first, *then* chained himself, pulled the trigger with his big toe maybe. Look where his leg's fallen.'

The chief drew himself up and looked pointedly around the clearing. 'Listen, we got upstate homicide detectives descending to our little community, so as far as anyone's concerned this is a homicide. Or let me put it another way, Janet. Why would a man contemplating suicide, go to the effort of chaining himself up beforehand?'

'That I don't know, chief.'

'Precisely. Let's get an ID on that firearm. What is it? Some sort of ladies' hunting rifle? Filigree pattern on the stock there. Someone in Shallow Creek knows the provenance of that rifle. You've gone uncharacteristically quiet, Janet.'

'Making mental notes of the scene, boss.'

'Good. Jimmy, head back to the station, get some tape and secure this scene properly. I don't want any upstate guys seeing our pine-cone shit and taking us for hayseeds. Janet, take a statement from the witness.'

'Where'd you put him, Jimmy?'

'Her, some crazy name.' Jimmy checked his notes. 'Zsofia Horvat.

Waiting in the ranger's hut, two-hundred yards yonder.'

Zsofia!

Oh.

***

'Janet! Last time I saw you, you were throwing on a shirt and running out the door.'

In the shadows of the hut, a pressed green ranger's uniform, creamy blonde hair drawn back into a ponytail, mirrored aviator sunglasses.

'Hi, Zsofia.'

'You left your bra. I've still got it. Funny way to end a date.'

'Zsofia, I'm conducting a homicide investigation, this isn't the time.'

'Oh, when is the time? You don't call for one month, two months. I guess, you're not so bi-curious now, huh?'

Janet perched on the edge of a chair and took out her notebook. 'Let's address this before we get going. It's nothing personal. It's not about you. I mean, you're great. I was really into you. *Am*. I just felt guilty about Bobby—my ex.'

'Oh, I know Bobby. You talked about him the whole date.'

'I did?'

'Yeah, how much you loved Bobby, Bobby this, Bobby that. Bobby just disappeared in the middle of the night and left a stupid note.'

'I said all that?'

'And more. Anyway, I'm kidding. I'm not really angry. Happens a lot with the straight ladies. What do you want to know about the dead body?'

'You don't seem very upset, Zsofia.'

'Upset about what?'

'Discovering a corpse?'

'I see a lot of nasty things. Blood. Guts. Animals ripped open and hung from trees. Normal for Silverpine Forest. You done a search?'

'Not yet.'

'Piece of advice—don't go more than fifty yards from the trail.'

***

The trees were so close it was like they were covering some secret shame, blocking the light until Janet had to reach for her flashlight and play it on the ground to see where she was going.

A rectangle of white caught her eye, stark and angular against the forest floor. When she knelt to get a closer look, something bit her hand. Dark forest ants swarmed her fingers. She brushed them off. In the flashlight beam was a cereal carton, not a real carton, but more like something a child might make: taped together at the edges, crudely penned lettering spelling the word 'Krinkles', and beneath that, a drawing of a clown's face with a stupid mocking grin.

From the open flap, a string of ants carried clusters of cereal—Janet drew the flashlight closer—blackened shrivelled clumps of nuts that didn't look too appetising. They dropped each cluster into a hole in the forest floor and clambered in.

She pulled an evidence bag from her pocket. 'Sorry fellas, this is an item of interest in an ongoing investigation.' The ants didn't look too pleased.

Back at the parking lot, the chief was distracted by the upstate guys. 'Where you been, Janet?'

'Conducting a wider search, just a hunch.' She dropped the bag into the trunk of the car as casually as she could.

'Find anything?'

'Few trees. Guess it's not hunch day.'

'Get down to Leadbetter's, see if he's sold any fancy rifles of late.'

'Sure thing, boss.'

But she didn't go to Leadbetter's.

She already knew the provenance of the rifle.

It was her rifle.

The rifle Bobby took the night he disappeared.

***

Bubba's fat, cloddish fingers feverishly rubbed his neck, as if to relieve some relentless irritation.

'I already heard,' he said. 'Awful pity. People think us carnival folks are freaks and weirdos, but he was an enthusiastic older gentleman who enjoyed fresh air and the countryside—loved hiking in those woods - same as you might encounter in any walk of life 'cept he was unusually flexible in his joints.'

'Any enemies? Disputes you're aware of?'

When Bubba shook his head, Janet noticed a strip of duct tape peeling away from the side of his neck.

She pulled out the cereal packet, still in the clear evidence bag.

'What the Jiminy is that thing?' Bubba said.

'I'm asking you.'

'Looks like the cereal Krinkles was mixed up with.'

'You know about it?'

'Heard it from my pa. All those shrivelled-up kids, something wrong with the nuts. They had a jingle: 'Love those Krunchy Nuts,' something like that.'

'When'd you last see Krinkles?'

Bubba shook his head angrily. 'Leave Krinkles out of this. He in't nothing to do with it.'

'Why're you so sure?'

'Well, first off he's dead, most likely. That is, no one's seen him the best part of a decade. And second, most everyone's got him misunderstood.'

'That right?' Janet said. 'His police record is misunderstood?'

Bubba spat on the floor. 'Once was a clown myself. People think a clown is creepy and, worse, can't be trusted. Popular media got a lot to do with it. We're an easy target. Krinkles got a heart of gold, I tell ya. All he ever wanted was to be a child entertainer, and people got a problem with that? Even though they can't be assed to entertain their children themselves? How could you have a nobler calling than to make a child laugh, but some people got to drag it down. I don't know who made that thing.' He jabbed a giant finger at the cereal packet. 'But it in't got nothing to do with Krinkles. Hey, look at that.'

Inside the evidence bag, a group of ants removed a mouldy cluster of cereal and transported it to one corner. A nut in this particular cluster had sprouted, and the ants treated it with a strange reverence. They were chewing up a corner of the cereal packet and carrying the scraps over to the sprouting cluster. Others curled up on the shredded material and bit through the thin stalk that connected the lower segments of their own body. A thick layer of shredded paper and dead ants was slowly building up around the sprouting nut.

Bubba scratched at the duct tape on his neck. 'Well, in't never seen anything like that before.'

***

The first voicemail message was from Zsofia. 'Hey Janet, I didn't mean to be hard on you. I was just embarrassed, you know? If you wanna talk I'm up at the ranger's office. They put me on night shift in case anyone else wants to commit suicide, like I'm gonna stop them. Was nice to see you. Guess I've always been a sucker for a uniform.'

The second was from the chief, a dollop of barely-disguised disappointment in his voice. 'Hey Janet, they're calling it suicide. Only one set of prints on the rifle and they was his. Same prints on the chains and key. No sign of a struggle. So that's that. Case closed. See you in the morning. Pick up another one of those Blueberry Frosted, will ya?'

Janet sat on the sofa with a bar of the stupidly dark chocolate her father sent up from Fresnillo: thinking chocolate. She stared at the bright, florid letters attached to the opposite wall—LOVE—and let the bitter chocolate fill her mouth. As a piece of home decoration, the LOVE sign wasn't her style, but she hadn't bought it. Bobby had. And what sort of commitment-phobe purchases a LOVE sign of his own accord and spends a Saturday afternoon hanging it on a wall when he could be watching a ball game?

She took a fold of paper from the kitchen drawer, noticed how the ink was fading in the creases. 'Dear Janet, I got to go do something. I'm sorry. Love Bobby.' It was dumb, no doubt, typical Bobby, but there was no relationship anxiety there.

And that word again: love.

A stolen rifle. A dead man. Crazy cereal cartons. What had he got himself mixed up in?

***

She followed the line of pine cones until she arrived at the hanging tree. The body had been cleared away along with the police tape. All that remained was the circle of cones and some scuff marks in the dirt. She shone the flashlight across the ground, along the thick roots of the old oak, past drifts of acorn husks. A man perished here, she thought, and there's no trace of it. But what did she expect? That death would leave a stain, some residue in the air? There was nothing to discover here, even supposing she had an idea of what she was looking for.

At the fork in the path, her feet led her towards the music coming from the ranger's hut, some sort of hard dance she didn't recognise. A body—green and blonde—crossed the window. The door opened. A flashlight skimmed the undergrowth. Janet shrank back against a tree trunk. The harsh light sliced past her.

Zsofia's voice. 'Hey, anyone there?'

The beam flicked across the brush and then cut out. The door slammed shut and the music started again.

Janet didn't move, her nails dug deep in the bark of a pine behind her. She wasn't thinking about Zsofia anymore. In that final sweep of the beam, she glimpsed something strange. A body, pale and upright. A tangle of lean limbs, a wiry torso bent back to pass beneath a fallen pine.

The doop dums of 'Always Be My Baby' ripped through the forest air and Janet scrambled to her feet. 'Chief, what is it?'

'Hey Janet, I can hardly hear you.'

'I'm up at Silverpine.'

'What in hell you doing there?'

Deep breath. 'I got a theory about the case, should've told you about it earlier—'

'No time for that, Janet, listen up. I need you down at the morgue. Some sort of break in. Damndest thing. They stole a body and somehow dragged it out a window that was eight foot off the ground.'

'What body?'

'The contortionist, the suicide. They didn't touch a thing else. You there, Janet? You hear me? Janet?'

'I hear you, boss.'

'Can you hear me?'

'Boss, I just saw him. I saw the contortionist.'

'Hello, Janet? Hello.'

'I'm going after him.'

'Hello. Helloooo. Godamn. Janet. You there?'

***

A distant ghoulish glimpse of white in the flashlight beam, a loping gait, a whiff of camphor riding the night air. Whatever it was that looked exactly like the contortionist's corpse was making no effort to be discreet.

At Lover's Look, with its twinkling vista of Shallow Creek, the path petered out. The contortionist had cut through the brush. Janet followed through trees that pressed uncomfortably close, reminding her of certain Christmas parties she'd rather forget. She clutched her side to ease a developing stitch, thinking maybe the whole bar of chocolate hadn't been a good idea.

Tiny glowing eyes observed her. Forest noises hung in the branches: claws scrambling on wood, sudden peeps and hoots, the elongated creak of trunks flexing in the breeze. She followed the trail of crushed grass and broken ferns and after an hour found herself heading downhill, the ground soft and dry beneath her feet. Every twenty or thirty yards she collected a bunch of pine cones and built a low cairn to help her find the way out.

She reached low, flatter land where the trees were sparse and sloped gently along the course of a dry stream bed. A thin, high howl shuddered through the branches. Another answered. A blink in the flashlight beam. The contortionist? She stepped closer. It was another cereal carton.

Crouched low over the leering face and crude lettering, she became aware of something in the forest with her. She sensed it first: dark and otherworldly and vast, an atmospheric shift, a subtle gathering coolness. Now she saw it, or part of it. Nature had creased and crumbled the forest floor, but here the land was eerily flat and empty of life, smooth as the surface of a lake. Water might reflect a flashlight even on the stillest night, but this was an all-consuming void. She scrambled closer through branches that tore at her hair and face. A horizontal plane stretched away into the distance, blackness carving its way through the trees. Her fingers found the surface, smooth and rough at the same time: asphalt.

A highway. *The* highway—against the building of which a young and irrepressible Janet Lopez had protested, had found herself improbably adopting the role of civic leader. Here, where the asphalt abruptly ended, Janet had chained herself to the hydraulics of a giant yellow excavator that was ripping up roots from the earth. She'd held out for six hours before they finally cut her free.

As she stepped on to the blistered mossy surface, a lightness quivered within her. With every step, elation grew. She allowed herself to imagine the highway clogged with traffic and choking fumes. She grinned to see it empty and deserted. Vanquished.

In a broad clearing beside the road, abandoned equipment remained secured by rusted chains: dumpsters and diggers, sagging as they crumbled into the brush. Here the young Janet Lopez, serious and high-minded, but also cute in her cut-off army surplus, had given a rousing speech to her fellow residents of Shallow Creek. They had cheered, waved banners, sat in the road. Here, Janet Lopez had been arrested and taken off to the county jail. She'd so impressed Chief Hamilton that after he'd booked her, he handed over an application form to join the force.

A noise hung in the rafters of the pines, a lingering moan like the shriek of an owl. The flashlight caught movement: a shape, pale and imprecise against the misty blackness of the pines. It squirmed and vanished. Janet raked the beam across the surface of the highway, thankful now for the asphalt's evenness, its regularity and simplicity. Then a figure loomed out of the darkness, shuffling and stuttering towards her, head lolling and nodding haphazardly, white eyes rolled high into their sockets. His sockets. His beautiful eyes.

***

What happened to the young Janet Lopez anyway?

She could barely recognise herself as the firebrand speaker atop an oil barrel, loudhailer in hand, summoning mighty words and inspiring a sleepy and complacent community. That felt like a different Janet Lopez, someone on a higher and faster trajectory.

She knew the answer.

Bobby happened. Instead of rescuing trees, she'd rescued Bobby. Domestication happened. Getting a job on the force, officer training, buying a flat, settling down. A lower, steadier path. She felt a pinch of disappointment but knew she shouldn't because she had loved those things too.

Love grew in subtle ways. Love changed a person from the inside in a manner that was imperceptible and yet profound. The old Janet Lopez became this Janet Lopez, and love had made the change.

***

She drew her gun.

'Nice timing, Bobby.'

He lurched closer. Black mould covered one side of his body, ran up his legs and torso, all along the hand that grabbed towards her, deep in the skin like ingrained dirt but with a delicate peachy fuzz. Black mould ran up one side of his neck and over half his face. It seemed to extend into the cavities of him, into his eye sockets and nostrils and mouth. It was obvious that he was dead, or as close to dead as a man still walking can be. He stepped towards her and in the flashlight he became malevolent, his torn lip twisting into a sneer, his eyes rolling down with purpose, and something like a snarl sprang from that pretty mouth that many nights she had watched as he slept, for Bobby had been strangely winsome for such a large man.

She thumbed the hammer back. 'Bobby, I'm warning you. If I got to do this, I'll do it. You take a step back though and cooperate, we can get you up to the hospital.' He staggered so close he almost touched her. When he spoke, his voice was as it always had been. One word: 'Love.'

Janet was about to reply, though she didn't know exactly what she intended to say, when he spoke again. 'Love.' As if that explained everything. As if that was all there was to say.

He held out his good hand with simple insistence, the hand free of mould, and even in the harsh flashlight she could see colour in it.

'You got something to show me?'

Did he nod?

The hand was warm. A dark shudder ran through her.

'Bobby, what happened to you?'

Her body buzzed to be beside him again, to walk hand in hand. He led her along a worn path littered with plastic gas cans like carcasses from some bloody ambush. A fuel tank in a steel cage leaked honeyed beads into the earth. A generator hummed with life.

'What the hell, Bobby?'

Then they were in a larger clearing lit by floodlights, and at once she understood, but Bobby took her gun and tightened his grip on her hand. He dragged her past the dead contortionist, whose head was still half blown off but was now sealed with the same mould that covered most of Bobby. He was tying a young branch to a wire, a watering can at his feet. Beyond him was Mrs Lucinda Kemp who was registered as a missing person some four weeks before Bobby, and whom popular opinion held he had run away with. She had appeared more than once in Janet's fevered, angry dreams, but now held a plastic bucket as she gathered handfuls of mouldy nuts from trees that grew in tidy lines along a stretch of wire fences. There was Krinkles the Clown, hammering a new fence post, his clown suit strangely clean, his face contorted into a broad fixed smile. Beside him a mouldy hiker took mouldy nuts from his mouldy rucksack and planted them in straight drills. Another mouldy hiker sat at a makeshift table, making cereal packets from sheets of cardboard, drawing Krinkles on each box and finishing the letters in gaudy colours.

The air was heavy with the smell of nuts and the strange spicy scent of the mould and of freshly-dug soil and dry vegetation. Everyone worked in silence, with a slow, unquestioning purpose. They showed no interest in her.

'Love,' Bobby said as he pulled Janet towards a wooden shack that stood at one end of the clearing. 'Love.' He threw her inside. Here the mould grew thickest, blanketed the walls and smothered objects long since made indistinct. Spores drifted in the air thick as soup. Bobby smiled and his teeth were black with mould. 'Love those Krunchy nuts!'

***

There was a gap where the wood had warped and it must be how the contortionist escaped, but Janet could fit no more than her arm through.

She felt the mould inside her, stiffening her limbs. Her arms spasmed. Her mouth numbed, and saliva dribbled from her lip. Her eyes rolled helplessly upwards.

She would not give in. She would be the Janet Maria Lopez who saved the forest. Her same fierce determination would rescue Shallow Creek from the black mould.

But Janet was being erased. She could feel the mould in her head, disconnecting memories, infecting her mind so that every thought came clustered in nuts.

She would not let the mould rob her of herself. She resisted. She clung to those things Janet loved most: 90% dark chocolate, Mexican revolutionary politics, police training videos. The mould would not take these things from her. The provision of local recycling points, Mariah Carey albums, the LOVE sign. The smell of Bobby waking in the morning beside her.

Janet. Be Janet.

***

The door opened and Bobby stood there, just as handsome as ever. She barely saw him. Janet's movements were as jagged and lifeless as his. The tap was stiff but it squeaked open. She filled a watering can and shuffled along the neat rows, bathing the roots of the trees. The others were so slow-witted that it was only when she reached the last row that they realised. They came at her all at once as if by a signal, arms scissoring the air, howling like wild animals. Janet reached a rusted floodlight moments before they caught her. With all remaining strength and will she pulled it to the ground. A shower of sparks. Fire streaked along the ground in lines where Janet had tenderly doused the rows in gasoline from the leaking tank. Flames engulfed the hikers as they struggled to save the mouldy nuts. Mrs Kemp and Bobby flailed and thrashed in the haze of fuel. And Krinkles? Krinkles had vanished. But she heard manic laughter on the wind. Then the low branches of the silver pines caught alight, and the fire leapt from tree to tree until the whole forest blazed.

***

It was Zsofia and Chief Hamilton who found Janet and pulled her from the smoke.

'She's alive.'

'What's that shit all over her?'

'It's nothing. She's going to be OK.'

Janet didn't listen. Something pure and wild rose within her. She clenched her fist around the handful of nuts she rescued from the flames, their husks beautifully shrivelled and black with mould. She found her voice and sung

Craved through the ni-ights
Soooo crunchily (So crunchily-y-y-y-y-y)
Knowing the nut that I needed
Wo-ould get me eventually

ANCHOR

by Marion Coleman

My tears were not for my father, a drunk and a bully. I escaped him seven years ago when I was sixteen and only returned to the cabin to make sure he was dead. It had always been a prison to me, representing everything I hated about my life.

I unlocked the door and crossed the threshold. Cold shivers rippled across my skin and dread settled in my belly, irrational and unexpected. I should have trusted my instincts and stepped back outside into the sunshine. Instead I berated myself for being stupid and forced myself to look around the house.

Everything was much the same as it had been on the day I left, the same mess and chaos, but now that he was dead, it seemed to have shrunk, not smaller—just less, somehow. Maybe that's why I was ready to cry, because he'd seemed such a powerful monster when all this time he was just a pathetic loser—and now I had a truck-load of hang-ups over nothing.

I found the letter taped to the door of my old room. My name, Georgia, was scrawled across the envelope, inside—just a terse, *Your mother is at Arkady Asylum, Shallow Creek*. Now, the tears flowed freely. I had always hated my father, but until that moment I hadn't realised how angry I was with my mother for leaving.

He always said she was a crazy witch. When she left I believed she'd realise her mistake and rush back, but he moved us immediately to prevent her from finding me. Whenever he caught me crying he'd rant at me to stop blubbering over her, that she could never love me or anyone else. His tirades conflicted with my own memories of a smiling woman with an intense gaze who spoon-fed me soft food. After she left I learned to survive the hard way. I proved I didn't need anyone, but inside, in my most secret dreams, I longed to be taken care of, to feel the warmth of my mother's love.

Less than a week after reading my father's note I arrived in Shallow Creek. I had no ties to anywhere else, and when I smelled the sea I considered settling down there if I could find work. My mother could be my anchor.

But a sense of foreboding hit me again when I stood outside the asylum. It looked too old and imposing to be the friendly and caring place I expected. When I went inside my spirits plummeted further. Dark wooden doors loomed menacingly within grey walls. The black lino floor only added to the gloom and the reception desk was so big that I was forced to step around it to see no one was there. I didn't even dare call out hello. There was no sign ordering silence but I sensed the command from the oppressive atmosphere around me. Everything encouraged me to run, but I'd come this far and my mother was here, somewhere.

I crept along the corridor in search of life. Waves of laughter and applause filtered through a partly open door and I made my way towards it, faintly reassured by the cheerful noise. I pushed the door open wider and peered inside. The sounds were coming from a TV. The room was large and decorated much the same as the dreary hall. Around the perimeter, seated in a hodge-podge of armchairs of dubious comfort, were about twenty residents, all slumped like abandoned puppets, silent, eyes dull. A few rheumy gazes strayed in my direction. One man stared at me intently. He seemed terrified, and young too—not much older than me. Embarrassed, I looked away. What a horrible place, and how awful to lose your mind. At least the staff appeared friendly, judging by the nurse with her back to me, who was too engrossed in her work to notice my entry. She was gently coaxing an elderly woman to eat a spoonful of food.

I didn't hear anyone approaching me until I was grabbed by my wrist and hauled out of the room. My assailant, a woman in her thirties, closed the door behind me. If I was going to visit the Asylum regularly I didn't want to get off to a bad start, so I followed her meekly to the reception desk.

"Why are you snooping?" She spoke with an unfamiliar accent.

"I'm looking for my mother, a resident here."

"Name?"

"My name is Georgia F—"

"—Don't be stupid. Your mother's."

"Gina Fry."

"No."

"No?"

"No one of that name has ever been here."

I stared at her, bewildered. She was not old enough to have worked here when my mother was admitted. I hadn't expected to be so blatantly thwarted, though I was used to disrespect. My short stature and skinny frame made me look as if I was still sixteen. I attempted to be more assertive. "Don't you need to search your records or something?'"

"I make it my business to know everyone who passes through these doors. There is no resident here of that name."

I had to be careful. This woman was clearly not going to provide me with the information I needed. Thanks to my father, I had a good understanding of difficult people. I didn't want to get her back up. I believed her to have the capacity and temperament to make my mother's life unpleasant. I thanked her and left. I would return when someone else was on duty.

On crossing the bridge back into town I spotted a sign for the library and my beleaguered spirits lifted. A good omen. Libraries held records. Ten minutes later a grey-haired man helped me log into the library's database and I was soon scrolling through Shallow Creek's history. I found a 2010 article about the asylum that involved a day trip to the local fairground, an experiment that was never repeated, but there were countless photos of that singular event.

I carefully studied each photo, despite not having a clear memory of what my mother looked like. In 2010 she would have been in her mid-forties and I searched for anyone in that approximate age group. Her name wasn't listed under any of the pictures. One woman was photographed next to a man of similar age. His arm clung tightly to hers and her hand covered his in a protective manner. The caption read, *Krinkles the Clown without his makeup*. He seemed haunted and self-conscious and appeared to be avoiding the camera, but she was smiling confidently. It was the unusual locket around her neck—a silver acorn—that made me hold my breath. The certainty that my mother possessed a similar locket grew. I even remembered that in order to open it, the acorn cap had to be lifted.

I found plenty in the records on Edward Carnby, aka Krinkles the Clown. Turns out he had never been an inmate at the asylum. He avoided people and hid out in Silverpine Forest. The picture I'd found was proof that he'd once been close to my mother and and now I had a photo of it on my phone to jog his memory; he'd talk to me—I was certain of it.

The town map, displayed near the library desk, helped me figure out a route to the forest. I asked the librarian about Mr Carnby and Silverpine Forest but he warned me that the place was a hotbed of vile characters, full of dangerous junkies and delinquent teenagers, as well as the crazy clown, who, if rumours were true, harboured an unhealthy fondness for children.

And here was another warning, this time from a flesh-and-blood person, but I was certain I had nothing to fear from Krinkles. As for the delinquent teenagers, I used to be one myself and had dabbled enough with drugs to know the kind of junkies who hung out in forests. The only thing that bothered me was the size of Silverpine Forest. I could wander around for days and never find the man that could lead me to my mother.

Outside, luck smiled down on me again, because across the street stood Bob's Bits N' Bobs, and lounging against a bicycle bay a bunch of teenagers were trying to outdo each other in demonstrating how much they didn't care. Judging by the glares hurled their way from passers-by, I was confident these were some of the delinquents who frequented the forest.

For once my appearance might work in my favour. First, I bought some cigarettes from the store. It had always been the way to join any group—just wait for the right moment before producing them. If they take one and then ignore you, you're in; too much attention and you need to scarper fast before they turn on you for sport. The spotty kid on the edge of the group, a boy of about seventeen, seemed the most likely to fall for some female attention. I slouched against the nearest wall and waited.

My chance came when one of the group handed cigarettes to a chosen few and my target watched hungrily. As unobtrusively as I could, I moved towards him and offered one of mine. Five minutes later we were on our way to Silverpine Forest. Mike was eager to show me their hangout and I was willing to be impressed. Only one of the group, a girl with a spider nose-ring, watched us as we left.

Mike boasted of his exploits in the forest and it was easy to steer him onto the topic of Krinkles the Clown. I soon learned how Krinkles spied on the teenagers. They liked to chase him away by throwing sticks or beer cans. Occasionally they tried to hunt him down, but they had so far failed to catch him because he knew Silverpine better than anyone else. No matter where they went, he was always there, hiding in the trees, watching, as if the forest itself told him where to find them. It seemed meeting Krinkles would be easier than I thought.

The route to their hide-out at the Hanging Tree followed a wide path until Mike veered off onto a narrow track. We were only a few metres along when I felt the forest close in on me. Perhaps it was the densely packed trees blocking the sunlight, but I could sense eyes watching me from all sides. At this point I was close to turning around and giving up, but if I wanted to find out about my mother I had no option but to carry on. I linked my arm in Mike's. He seemed to relish my nervousness and took pleasure in elaborating on Silverpine horror stories, many of which I'd read about in the library.

The trail included occasional negotiations where brambles grew either side of the path and I had to relinquish Mike's arm. I was spooked by thorned tendrils that clung to my coat as if they wanted me to stay and never leave. There were enough unfamiliar sounds to keep me worked up, and I was furious with myself for being such a wimp. We had just cleared another thicket when I felt a tug at my shirt. Before I could free myself from the bramble a voice, low and eerie, begged me to stay. I burst forward towards Mike, screeching.

Wails and guffaws of laughter filled the claustrophobic air around me and three teenagers erupted from the darkness. While I struggled to regain my composure, the girl with the spider nose-ring grabbed Mike's arm and pulled him along. "If she likes that dirty old Krinkles so much we should let him have her." She laughed and broke into a run. Mike loped along behind them as they vanished into the gloom.

Despite the fright, I scrounged some dignity from the fact that my instincts were right. Someone *had* been watching. The dread refused to go away, but I drew comfort from knowing I wasn't alone—surely nothing could happen with so many people around.

I followed their trail and after several metres the path split in two. I took the wider one and soon heard rustling noises again. I hurled abuse, expecting the kids to jump out of the shadows, but they remained hidden. I waited, listening closely. A hand touched me on the shoulder and I spun round to see a man dressed in a scorched clown costume. I'd found Krinkles, and with that realisation, all sense of doom lifted.

He put a finger to his lips and beckoned me to follow as he moved away from the path. Several minutes later he stopped at a small clearing and we sat on a fallen tree. Up close I could see the childlike innocence in his eyes. The poor old man was harmless. I showed him the photo on my phone. His eyes lit up as he touched the screen. "Gina," he said.

My heart flipped in my chest. "Is she still here? Did you meet her at the asylum?"

"She takes care of me, feeds me."

I pointed at the locket and explained she was my mother. He held his fist to his mouth and began to sway back and forth. His excitement delighted me. After a few moments pause he stood. "Come," he said.

I jumped up so fast I was dizzy. He moved swiftly and silently, following no discernible path that I could see. At one point he stopped and signalled for me to be still. I could hear laughing and taunting in the distance. No doubt we were near the Hanging Tree. Krinkles led me away from the sounds and soon we were hurrying along again. I had lost all sense of direction by now so I made sure to stick close to him. We seemed to be going deeper into the forest so it was a surprise when we crossed a well-trodden track, and thanks to the break in tree-cover I could see the fading evening light. We plunged into the gloom on the other side and twenty minutes later we arrived at a lumber mill, where Rottweiler's growled behind locked gates. Out in the open the moonlight played on all the trees that lined the road, silver glimmerings that befitted the forest's name. We hadn't gone far when I recognised the distinctive silhouette of Arkady Asylum against the skyline.

On nearing the building, we detoured to one side, following a line of shrubbery towards the rear of the Asylum. We stopped in the shadowy blanket of a bush. The rear of the building was in complete darkness. Krinkles warned me to remain hidden and then he disappeared across the lawn. Several seconds later a momentary sliver of light broke the monotonous blackness and I fixed my gaze on that precise spot for signs of his return. Was he going to meet my mother? Perhaps I should have followed him, but there was no point now when I had no way of knowing where to go once inside. Minutes passed before the sliver re-appeared and the moonlight highlighted a hurrying form. No … two. I couldn't believe it. Was my mother with him?

When they finally reached me I immediately recognised her from the photo. She embraced me warmly and I clung to her, afraid to let go. Something inside me shattered and I began to sob. She gently shushed me and murmured in my ear about my father and how he hated the fact she did everything for me, that his jealousy spirited her baby away. Eventually, she held me away and her coat fell open, revealing a nurse's uniform. My mother wasn't an inmate;

she was a member of staff. She appraised me with the intense gaze I remembered. I blinked away tears as I reached out and touched the locket that helped me find her. She squeezed my hand gently and let go, then she reached up to the locket and pulled up the cap. She opened it carefully then tipped the powdered contents onto her palm. I leaned in closer to get a better look, surprised when she blew the powder into my face. My legs folded and I crumpled onto the grass. As consciousness slipped away from me, Krinkle's grinning face hovered above me. All trace of childlike simplicity vanished.

I wake up in a sitting position, unable to move. While I wait for my body to adjust I open my eyes. I'm in a large and dreary room Muted sounds filter out from a TV in the corner. Recognition comes slowly. This is the room with the immobile inmates, the one with the kindly and patient nurse. I try again to move but can't feel my limbs. The only part of me I *can* control is my eyes. I desperately search for help and lock gazes with the young man from yesterday. His eyes have the same intensity as before but he looks at me differently today—with pity. Too late I realise that yesterday he was pleading for help. Now there is no one to help. My mother is kneeling in front of me. A dish rests on a tray beside her. She is smiling at me, encouraging me to open my mouth, a spoonful of soft food in her patient hand.

BACKWARDS

by Adrian J Walker

C

I met myself in Silverpine Forest. And I'll never forget his grin.

There are certain places on this planet from which we flinch. That old house that sits alone on the street as if the others want no part of it. The shortcut home that's forever dark and cold, regardless of the hour or season. The cupboard, basement or hut in which you do whatever you must at twice the speed before getting the hell out.

Even Chicago, that boisterous city where I spent the greater part of my adult life, has such places. Working homicide in a big city tends to take a man to some mighty dark places, but no murder scene ever gave me the chills like Ivy's, the derelict printing shop on Denver Street with the shattered windows and invoices strewn across the floor, a crushed trilby and a young boy's duffel coat hanging on a hook, as if whoever abandoned it did so at speed. I'd always quicken my pace whenever I drew near, focusing my stare on the wet stone through which I splashed.

Some places have a depth to them. A *memory.*

And Silverpine Forest is one of them.

In the fall of '09 I spent a lot of time in Silverpine. It was not pleasant work. For most of September and all of October I scoured the forest with every cop in Shallow Creek and a hundred other volunteers, trying to shake something from those dense trees and bracken—a shred of clothing, a dropped pin, a clump of hair snared on a branch. Some sign of hope.

But there is no such thing in Silverpine.

The search party dwindled and grew less frequent until eventually it was just Lopez and me stumbling over the same old ground. By November we were done.

'Go home, Hamilton,' said Lopez. 'You look like shit.'

'I want to check the lumber yard again.' My flashlight flickered. 'Damn it, I need new batteries.'

Lopez grabbed my wrist, tears in her heavy eyes. 'Hamilton. We're finished. You know we are. Go home and get some rest.'

'I can't. Not while she's still out there.'

She struggled to smile. 'You want to help her? Then freshen up. Get sharp. Sleep. OK?'

I looked down at my flashlight's meagre beam. Finally, I nodded.

'I'll drive you home,' said Lopez.

'I'll walk.'

'Sheriff ...'

I set off down the track.

'Walking helps me think, Lopez. It's not far.'

'I'll see you Monday,' she called after me. 'We'll pick up some new leads, OK?'

'Sure,' I said.

But we both knew there were none.

I stopped at Jack's Tavern, a habit that resurfaced on the lip of every winter. This time of year always reminded me of my last few weeks in Chicago, which of course reminded me of her. I guess I just didn't want to be on my own.

Not that Jack's provided much in the way of company—a missing child tends to make a town less than hospitable, especially if you're the man who failed to find her.

Taking over as sheriff in Shallow Creek was never going to be easy, given the somewhat *backward* opinions belonging to a number of its inhabitants. It wasn't just that I was black—the town was well-represented in those terms—but more that I was from out of town, and from a big city to boot. Those tired and jagged prejudices were as hard to break through as that damnable forest. But break through them I did, and little by little folk became friendlier.

Now, though, I wasn't so sure. Eyes watched me from every corner of Jack's with the same suspicion I witnessed during my first week as sheriff. The roots of the forest grow deep, it seems.

'Good evening, Sheriff,' said a baritone voice from the end of the bar. There sat a hawkish man in a double-breasted suit with slick black hair and sunken eyes. It was Mallum Colt, owner of the old curiosity shop. He smiled as he twirled the cocktail stick in his martini. 'Looks like you could use a friend.'

'Colt,' I replied in low greeting, swiftly returning to my beer.

'Any luck with the search?' he asked, as if enquiring about a set of lost keys.

I shook my head, took a swig. .

'Well, well,' he said with a cluck. 'A strange one indeed. Virtually the whole town sees that little girl walk into the forest, but not a soul sees her leave. That's a real—'

I slammed down my glass and glared at him. 'I know what it is, Colt.'

The bar hushed. Colt blinked, his front vanquished by my outburst.

'My apologies, John,' he said at last. 'My intentions are good, I assure you. All I am pointing out is that if nobody saw her leave, then logic dictates she must still be in the forest.'

I scanned the bar, waiting for all those unfriendly eyes to fall back to their drinks.

'We've searched every square inch of that place,' I said, keeping my voice low. 'You were out there yourself, Colt. There's no sign of her.'

He raised an expansive eyebrow. 'Perhaps the forest still has some secrets, John. Perhaps—'

He stopped short as the door swung open, a frigid wind flooding the Tavern. I turned to see Chelsea Sanders stood in the doorway. Her hair was straggled, eyes gaunt and weary. Same as mine, I guessed. Her husband, Josh, appeared behind her. He closed the door.

She hovered for a second, then hesitantly stepped towards me. 'You find my little girl yet?'. Her voice trembled like a tree's last leaf.

'Chelsea,' said Josh, laying a solemn hand on her shoulder. She shook it off.

'Well, Sheriff? Have you found Cody?'

I looked back at her dumbly. She was furious with grief, but what made my chest heave was that somewhere in all that rage was the will to retain hope. This miserable man who had let her down, who had failed to find her daughter, and who I'm sure she longed to throttle and choke, might still have good news.

But I had nothing of the kind.

I turned away and looked down at the floor. She walked across the bar and found a booth. Her husband followed.

Colt continued to stare at me.

'Don't give up, John,' he said. 'There's always a new way of looking at things.'

At that precise moment my phone buzzed. I picked it up; three missed calls and a message. I dialled my voicemail, turning from Colt's curious stare.

An aged voice in my ear. Dogs in the background.

'Is that the Sheriff? *Heston get off me.* This is Gert. Gert Saggery. *Heston! Blade! Get back, you damn hounds!*' There was a wallop and a yelp. 'Sheriff Hamilton? You said to call if I found something. Well, I found something.'

'A box of Krinkles.'

'That's what I said.'

Somewhere between Jack's Tavern and Gert Saggery's shack on the outskirts of Silverpine it had started to rain. I stood on her porch, avoiding the fat drops that fell from its rotten roof. Her hounds yowled behind the half-open door. I had often considered getting a dog for company's sake, but if I ever did it wouldn't be one like Gert's.

Gert was a hermit, I guess, somewhere north of 50. As the door opened I studied her in the dim light of the shack; long yellow dress with a mud-soaked hem, wax jacket and heavy work boots—I don't think I'd ever seen her in anything else. A shotgun cocked over her arm. She looked nervous.

'Krinkles as in that old breakfast cereal?' I asked. 'The one with the clown?'

'Mr Krinkles, that's right.' She pulled a face and crooned. *'Makes me aaaall Krinkly'*. Her expression straightened instantly. 'Only they don't make 'em no more. You know, on account of the poison.'

'You brought me out here for an old box of Krinkles, Gert?'

'Ain't just any box of Krinkles.'

I was tired now. I wanted to go home.

'Right. And what's so special about this particular box?'

She pushed her head through the gap in the door, checking for eavesdroppers.

'It ain't right. There's something off with it. Writing's all back to front, words don't make no sense. Even that old clown looks different. His face, it's … it's like it's not supposed to be here. Do you understand me, Sheriff?'

I sighed and dropped my head.

'Thank you, Gert. I'll get someone to look into it. Where did you say you found it, the Hanging Tree?'

'Yes, but you don't understand.'

I turned to leave.

'Good night, Gert.'

She reached out and grabbed my arm. Her grip was like an iron wrench.

'What the hell, Gert?'

Her wild eyes trembled in the moonlight.

'It ain't the box,' she whispered. 'It's what's holding it.'

Gert led me through the sodden forest. With my flashlight next to useless I followed her swinging beam, my boots squelching the wet bracken. Her dogs darted in and out of thickets, whining constantly.

'They've been like this all evening,' said Gert. '*On the scent*. There's something out there, Sheriff, and they don't like it. Whatever it is.'

She came to an abrupt halt.

'Here. The Hanging Tree.'

She pointed her beam at the vast oak tree that had no place beneath the slender, gloomy pines. It sat there like a gnarled and ancient claw.

'I left it there, didn't want to touch it. Go on, take a look.'

I approached the tree. Gert waited behind.

'And don't even think about suggesting one of my dogs did that. There ain't no possible way. Cut's too clean. Heston? Blade?'

Her beam suddenly swung away.

'Gert?'

But she had already stomped off in search of her dogs.

'*Heston! Come back here, you mutt!*'

Her voice faded away until I was standing in the dark with nothing but the rain. I pulled out my dying flashlight and flicked the switch. Nothing.

'Come on.'

I shook it until a faint beam spluttered out. I trained it on the trunk. There at the foot of the tree was a box of Krinkles, just as Gert had described. It was clearly unopened, and even from distance I could see what she meant; it wasn't right. It wasn't just the backward writing or its strange hue that hung between red and orange, it was the thing itself. Like she had said; it didn't belong there.

But what also definitely didn't belong was the hand that held the box, severed beneath the elbow in a perfect diagonal line.

Bracken crunched behind me.

'Gert?'

'You appear to have found my arm.'

I spun round and my beam struck a face. I staggered back in fright. It was a face I knew well.

'And the rest of me too, it would appear,' said the man who was, without question, me.

I fell on my ass. Well, what would you do if you saw yourself? Not just a reflection, but another human being, an actual flesh-and-blood *you*. I guess twins see themselves all the time, but I was an only child as far as I knew, and anyway, this was different. This wasn't a reflection, this wasn't my twin, this was *me*. It's hard to explain but I could feel it, and I knew he could too. We were the same.

Apart from that smile of his.

'Well isn't this a to do?' he said, sweeping a pine stump and sitting down. His face shone with sweat as he held his right arm, blood pumping from the same clean cut as the thing on the ground between us.

He nodded at my belt. 'Spare me that, John? I'm bleeding awful bad here.'

'How do you know my name?' I asked.

We both knew how.

He looked down at the bloody stump. 'Awful bad, John.'

I removed my belt and threw it at him. He tied a deft tourniquet above his elbow, tightening it with his teeth. When he was satisfied he patted his arm.

'Much obliged.'

I was still on the ground, my throat arid and raw. 'This is a trick.'

He cocked his head. 'Sitting here with half an arm, in a place I don't know, bleeding all over the ground and looking just like you. Hell of a strange trick to play, don't you think, John?'

I wished he wouldn't say my name like that. It made my blood run cold.

I fumbled for my flashlight, hoping it wouldn't give out, and directed it to the glistening stump.

'What happened to you?' I asked.

'Well, you got me there. One minute I'm carrying groceries to the car, trying to find my keys, the next I'm staring at a space that wasn't there a moment ago.'

'Groceries?'

'Yeah, milk and eggs and all the other shit she forgets to buy during the day. Every fucking evening. *Oh, John, I forgot apples for the pie,* or *John, Sarah needs Krinkles for the morning.* Krinkles.' He scowled at the box in his severed hand. 'Sarah needs her fucking Krinkles.'

'Who's Sarah?'

He turned to me.

'My kid, of course.' He narrowed his eyes. 'You ain't got one?'

I shook my head and he looked at me with a dead-eyed stare. 'Lucky for you, John. Lucky for you.'

The rain continued to pour around us. I wiped it from my face and got to my feet, trying to shake the shock from my bones.

'They haven't made Krinkles for decades,' I said. 'And anyway, what do you mean, *groceries?* This is Silverpine Forest, the nearest store's over three miles from here.'

'So this *is* Silverpine,' he said, scanning the scene in wonder. 'Well what do you know?'

'What the hell do you mean?'

'Where I come from, John, there ain't no forest. Silverpine was cut down thirty years ago by Hank Lanegan to make way for the Northcreek Mall.'

'Lanegan? Never heard of him.'

'No. I suppose you wouldn't. Well, Hank built Northcreek back in '94. Made him rich, and boy—' he heaved a dry laugh '—does he have some stories about Silverpine. "Best thing I ever did for Shallow Creek, John," he says, usually three beers in, "was tearing that fucking forest down. There was something in there, something bad. And not just *in* it, but under it too. Wait till I tell you what we found beneath those roots." Has a touch of the theatrics about him, know what I'm saying? What are you doing out here so late anyway?'

'A child went missing two months ago. Cody Sanders.'

He blinked, indifferent, then drew a deep breath and admired the canopies.

'Nope,' he went on. 'It's just concrete and steel back there now. No trees, no trees at all. Save for that one.' He nodded at the Hanging Tree's ugly knot. 'That one's still there, slap bang in the middle of the Swift-e-Mart parking lot.'

'What do you mean, *back there?*'

He was shaking and clutching the open wound. Nevertheless, that relentless smile endured.

'I was almost at the car when I saw it.'

'Saw what?'

'This space, like a door that shouldn't be there, full of trees. I checked if anyone else could see it too, but it was late and nobody was around but me. Then the thing just blinked out, so I shook it off and made for the car. But then it opened up again. Same place, same trees. I swear, it was bone dry in that parking lot but rain streamed in from that door. Same rain we're sitting in now. I walked up to it this time and you know what I did? I pulled that box of Krinkles from the bag and stuck it in, that's what I did. Guess I wanted to see what would happen. Well'—he grimaced and raised his stump—'turns out this is what happens. That bastard thing snapped shut like a crocodile and took half my arm with it. I didn't even scream, barely realised what happened when it opened up again and I saw my arm just lying there holding the box. I jumped in after it, instinct, you know? Then the thing snapped shut and hasn't opened since.'

He shivered on the tree stump.

'Bullshit,' I said.

He glared at me. 'It ain't. Wish it was, but it ain't.'

'You're talking about, what, some kind of portal? A gateway?'

'I guess. I don't know.'

My mind began to churn with possibilities, which must have played out on my face.

His lip curled.

'And no, John, nobody found a strange child wandering around the Swift-e-Mart parking lot two months ago asking for her mommy.' He kicked the dirt at his feet. 'All I know is I'm stuck here. And that fucking bitch will be waiting on me.'

'Who are you talking about?'

'Jodie, of course.'

I straightened like a tree trunk. He noticed my new stance and the smile returned.

'You ain't with Jodie here, are you?'

I shook my head, dumb with shock.

He sneered. 'No kids, no wife. Ain't you the lucky one, John.'

My head spun. 'You and Jodie...you're married?'

He spat in the dirt. His face glazed with a sickly sheen. 'Yeah, we're married.'

'And Sarah, she's ...'

'Our fuckin' kid, yeah. Nice work, Sherlock.'

I glowered at him, this wretch slouching in the rain. It was at that precise moment that our likeness—no, our *sameness*—fell away entirely. Apart from our appearance I no longer recognised anything in him that was me. I felt hatred.

And—there is no question of it—envy. He had everything I wanted.

I moved towards him, my flashlight beam making sharp shadows of his face.

'You don't seem particularly happy with your life,' I said.

His eyes narrowed. 'Nor you with yours. The question is, why are they so different? I'm married and you're not. What happened?'

'Jodie left me in Chicago.'

He clucked his tongue. 'Now why would she do that, I wonder. Must have been something big...you have an affair or something?'

'No.'

'No.' He looked me up and down. 'Don't seem your style. You're too
…'

He stopped abruptly, eyes flashing.

'Wait,' he said, 'you went through with it, didn't you? Yeah, you did.
You killed him.'

If there are places from which we flinch, there are people too. Vincent
Dutt was such a person. During my life I have encountered all manner
of denigrates, villains and lowlifes, but none of them ever came close
to Dutt. He shouldn't have been here, that was my opinion. He just
shouldn't have been here.

In the spring of 1996 Dutt kidnapped, tortured, maimed, raped and
performed all manner of acts I wish I didn't know on seventeen girls
between the ages of six and fourteen. I know because I was the man who
caught him. Three of the girls died, including the youngest, but of all the
godforsaken evidence, what stays with me the most are the words of one
victim's mother. Her daughter couldn't sleep, she said, not because of
memories or nightmares, but because she couldn't expel the taste from
her mouth.

I was plagued by that as Vincent Dutt smiled at me on the courthouse
steps, a free man.

All of Chicago knew he was guilty. Even the judge hung his head as
the case was dismissed. But Dutt wasn't just a monster, you see, he was
also a successful businessman with powerful friends who didn't want a
petty hindrance like justice to affect their financial interests. Strings were
pulled, evidence disappeared, dirt on witnesses was fabricated. They did
whatever they had to do.

And Dutt walked.

I couldn't take it. Three girls were dead and fourteen more were
fighting their way back their nightmares, while he walked and grinned
his way through steaks and wine that cost more than their therapy. It ate
me up inside.

'You have to move on, John,' Jodie said. 'You have to find a way
through it and move on.'

But I couldn't. And that's why on a miserable night in the fall of '97 I
stood in the rain outside one of his grand buildings with a gun concealed
in my coat, and when he skipped down the steps I shot him dead, right

between the eyes.

There were four witnesses. None of them uttered a word.

'Yeah, I killed him,' I said. 'You mean you didn't?'

He shook his head, face twitching with tremors that racked his entire body. 'Almost did, but I chickened out at the last minute...I couldn't do it... just couldn't. What happened? You … you didn't get caught?'

'Everyone knew what I did.'

He grimaced. 'But you got away with it all the same. Well ain't that nice.'

'If that's what you call purgatory. The commissioner found a way to bury the case on the condition that I left Chicago for somewhere … quieter.'

'Like Shallow Creek.'

'Like Shallow Creek.'

'So why did she leave you?'

I looked at the damp bracken. 'Because killing Dutt didn't make any difference, and she couldn't cope with what that made me.'

'Easy enough to call her, ain't it? Sort things out, if that's what you want.'

'I can't.

'Why not?'

'Because she's dead, that's why. She died in a car crash just before I left.'

He was silent for a moment.

'Huh,' he said, and spat.

My envy flared. 'And yet she's alive where you are. And she stayed with you.'

He flashed me a vile look. 'Yeah. I guess she did.'

'How come you moved to Shallow Creek?'

Pale and shaking, he still managed that dreadful smile. 'Change of scenery. Jodie said it would be a good place to raise a family. How about that, John? Looks like we were destined to be here.'

There was a sudden flash and we both turned. In front of us flickered a rectangle of yellow light through which we could see a red Ford Focus and an empty parking lot.

'I'll be damned,' I said.

'Told ya.'

I stared at the strange line which traced the border between this world and the one on the other side. Could it be true that beyond that door was an alternate version of my life? One in which the woman I loved was still alive and married to me? One in which we had a daughter?

'Well go on,' he said. 'Do it.'

'Do what?'

'Shoot me dead with that gun of yours and take my place. I know that's what you want. It's burning you up inside you want it so much.' He let out a maniacal hoot. 'Hell, I don't mind, I hate my goddamn life. You'd be doing me a favour.'

'Why?' I said. My hand hovered over my gun. 'Why do you hate your life?'

His face twisted into a seething knot of rage. 'Because I didn't fucking do it, that's why. I didn't kill Dutt. So go on, shoot me. That thing won't stay open for long.'

I looked between him and the door. It would only take a shot and a few steps. My body tensed, ready to act.

But my hand fell, and I exhaled wearily.

'No.'

He stamped a foot. 'Why the hell not?'

'Because that ain't my life, it's yours. And besides, somebody here's counting on me.'

A memory struck me.

'Wait.' I shone my beam on his face. 'What did you say earlier about this forest?'

'What?'

'That drinking buddy of yours, Lanegan. You said he found something underneath it.'

'Lanegan's full of shit.'

He glanced at the door. It was beginning to flicker and fade.

'What did he say he found?'

'Underground tunnels, caves and shit. A collapsed mine shaft from way back full of dead bodies.'

I thrust the beam in his face. 'Where?'

'North of the lumber yard. Why the fuck are you so interested?'

The door blinked out and dimly reappeared.

'Get up,' I said, hauling him to his feet.

'Hey, get your fucking hands off me.'

I pulled out my gun and pointed it squarely at his face.

'Get up and go through that door. You get back to that family of yours and you treat them right, you hear? You spend time with your daughter and you tell Jodie that you love her.'

'Fuck you.'

I pushed the barrel against his forehead.

'You listen to me, you son of a bitch. I got some business to take care of here, but something tells me this ain't the last time that door's going to open, and the next time it does, I might just pay you a visit, *John*. See how you're doing. What do you say?'

He said nothing. I withdrew the barrel and motioned for the door.

'Go on. Go home.'

He spat in the dirt one last time.

'Suit yourself.' He scooped up his arm and that box of Krinkles and leapt through the door.

A moment later the light was gone, and I was alone again with only the rain and forest for company. I holstered my pistol and ran north.

I found Cody Sanders in a tunnel twenty feet beneath Silverpine Forest. She had fallen down what you would have sworn was a rabbit hole, but was in fact an access shaft from the first gold rush to hit Shallow Creek, two hundred years before.

She was skinny and afraid, and as I coaxed her towards me I wondered how she'd managed to survive, given that she'd been alone for over two months. Then I saw the empty packets littering the ground, each daubed with the familiar image of that creepy clown.

To this day I have no idea how a shipment of Krinkles breakfast cereal found its way down in that mine, and of all the mysteries with which my life has been afflicted, it is the one I care least about. I'm just glad I found Cody alive.

As is her mother, of course.

It's spring now and I am the owner of a dog—a mongrel named Bob with whom I take long walks through Silverpine Forest. Squirrels, hares, finches, buzzards and a hundred other types of animal scurry through those trees at this time of year, and the bracken is carpeted with bluebells and daffodils through which Bob darts like a rocket. I never appreciated how different a place can seem—as that queer old fish Mallum Colt once said to me, there's always a new way of looking at something.

We've become friends, I guess, Mallum and I. Sometimes we'll share a drink in Jack's, where eyes have regained their friendliness, but mostly he'll join Bob and I on our walks through Silverpine. He saunters beside me in that suit of his, tossing a coin or chewing a cocktail stick. Occasionally we'll visit the Hanging Tree.

'What happened here, John?' he'll ask.

The door has never re-appeared. I have no inkling of why it opened on that particular night, but it hasn't since, and perhaps it never will.

Or perhaps it's waiting for a reason.

'Well?' says Mallum.

My answer's always the same: 'Nothing out of the ordinary, Mallum. I just gave myself a good talking to, that's all.'

And he'll smile, and we'll walk on, and Bob will skitter off after something he'll never catch, and the pines above us will swish with life, whispering down their hopes.

SECRET INGREDIENT

by Heather Cuthbertson

Sister Augustine's low-heeled shoes snap the asphalt as she approaches the police station. She makes this visit twice a month, always in the same week, but never the same day. In her arms she cradles her famous banana bread, made with an ingredient not found on any recipe list, and red dahlias wrapped in brown paper.

She pushes open the glass door. Officer Lopez's desk is right behind the receptionist station, although there hasn't been a receptionist in over five years.

Lopez stops typing when she sees Sister Augustine.

"Sister," she says, getting up. "You have to tell me your secret. You have better skin than I do."

"Goodness." Sister Augustine waves her off. "Maybe thirty years ago, but not now." She sets the banana bread on the counter and offers Lopez the flowers. "Here, Janet, these are for you. It's just a little something to brighten things up in here."

The designer who renovated Arkady Asylum in the fifties also reworked the police station. Both buildings share identical chartreuse wall-paint, the speckled avocado countertops, and the lime-stained linoleum floors. Green, as it happens, provides an excellent contrast to blood.

Officer Lopez accepts the dahlias. *"Gracias,"* she says. "They're beautiful."

"Maura helped me cut and arrange them and bake the banana bread too."

"You'll have to tell her thank you for me. How is Maura?"

Sister Augustine takes a breath and exhales. "The same, I suppose. Sometimes I think she is getting better, but then other days, worse. Of course, the doctors are of no help."

"I know how much she means to you," Lopez says with a sad twinge in her voice. "I've been lighting a candle for her."

"You think some people will be with you forever." Sister Augustine's eyes water. "Seems like yesterday Maura and I were taking our final vows together, but like they say, time is a thief." She removes a scarf with embroidered flowers from inside her habit. She dabs her eyes with the antique silk. "It's all in the Lord's merciful hands, but enough about me. How are you? Things staying quiet?"

Lopez groans. "Too quiet. The boss likes it, but I don't. This town is so dead that I just got a report of a ghost outside Jack's Tavern."

"Count your blessings, my dear," Sister Augustine says. "I'd take a roomful of harmless ghosts over some of these criminals I hear about on the news. Every time I turn around someone is either going missing or a body is found. It's the devil at work, I tell you."

"I suppose you're right, Sister."

"Don't worry too much about it, Janet. Besides, the carnival is in town. I have no doubt that should keep you busy."

"A bunch of drunk and disorderlies. Can't wait. You going?"

Sister Augustine grins. "I never miss it."

***

Tucked away on the grounds of St. Mary's Church is the small cottage Sister Augustine shares with Maura, a stone's throw away from the small Catholic school she heads. The home nurse waits outside. She is there to spend the evening with Maura, assisting her with whatever she needs. It's typically a job handled by Sister Augustine, except for the occasions when she's required at the school or when the carnival beckons.

Sister Augustine opens the door and the nurse steps inside. "How is she?" the nurse asks, glancing toward the living room where the only noise comes from the television.

"She seems to be enjoying her program," Sister Augustine replies, "but she hasn't done much else all day."

Maura sits in a wheelchair before the TV. Her hair dangles like wispy cobwebs around her shoulders and her veined hands clutch the armrests. The TV channel is fixed on the same station, playing the same show, night after night, year after year. She's watching a rerun of a game show. The screen splits from the host to the happy-faced contestants.

Sister Augustine says, "I can normally get her up and moving, even a little, but today she's refused to budge. Maybe you can try while I'm gone."

The nurse stares at Maura. "Age has really crept up on her it seems."

"It does us all."

"Not for you," the nurse says. "You haven't aged a day."

"I feel it even if I don't look it."

Maura mumbles, "Momma. Momma. Momma."

Sister Augustine sighs. "She's been doing that a lot lately. I'm worried that her dementia's getting worse. Note anything out of the ordinary. Her doctor was very adamant that any unusual behaviors must be documented."

"Certainly," the nurse says.

Sister Augustine shoves her scarf with the embroidered flowers into the pocket of her habit before fussing with Maura's blanket. She presses the remote in Maura's palm and kisses her on the forehead. As Sister Augustine turns away, Maura clutches her sleeves, murmuring words too soft for most to hear.

"Let go, dear." Sister Augustine pulls away; the sound of tearing fabric follows her. She picks up a black bag, turns to the nurse, and laughs; there's a nervous edge to it. "Are you sure you will be alright?"

"Yes, Sister Augustine. Everything will be fine. Don't worry. Enjoy your evening."

***

Powdered sugar and diesel fumes coagulate in a plume above the carnival.

Sister Augustine trudges through, dodging carnies with fistfuls of stuffed animals and kids sprinting to join the Zipper line. She arrives at the entrance of a tent where Bubba Cody waits inside.

She approaches two of his thugs standing guard. They have a drowned way about them as if they've been dredged from the muck out of the bay. One combs his bangs and watches her closely. The other spits chew into a Gatorade bottle. She steps past them and pushes through the flap of the tent. She can smell Bubba Cody's cigar the moment she enters.

Bubba Cody turns his head toward her. He's wearing an expensive suit that looks cheap on him. "Sister Augustine. It's always a pleasure."

"Good evening, Mr. Cody," she says.

"After all these years, you still don't call me by my given name."

"I'm not altogether convinced it *is* your given name." She fixes her gaze on him. "You have it?"

"I always deliver, don't I?" He takes another drag on his cigar and motions behind him. "This one I picked up a few states back. Fits your criteria."

Sister Augustine opens her bag and gives Bubba Cody four stacks of $100 bills. She then removes a pair of latex gloves and slides them on.

Bubba Cody tips his head to her and says, "See you again next year."

After he is gone, the only noise is the steady swoosh of the nearby rollercoaster and the fading screams of its riders.

Sister Augustine moves in the direction of the other room in the tent—the belly. She pushes the flap aside. Strapped to a chair in the middle is a naked girl in her late teens or early twenties. Her wrists and ankles are bound in duct tape. Two strips of tape cover her mouth. Off to the side is a surgical table adorned with instruments for cutting, clipping, and sawing. Blue tarp stretches across the floor.

The girl's wild eyes settle on Sister Augustine with a look of relief.

***

The TV is still on when Sister Augustine returns. The racket blaring from the set muffles the clank of metal as she drops her purse next to a ceramic cat with jewelled eyes.

The nurse puts down her phone and gets off the couch.

Sister Augustine asks, "Any issues while I was gone?"

The nurse shrugs. "No, not really. All she did was go through the photo album." She gestures toward a leather book with a beveled cover. "She kept talking in another language. Sounded so pretty, but I couldn't place it. Finnish, maybe."

Sister Augustine laughs. "It must have been something from one of her shows."

"That's funny," the nurse says. "It seemed like she was fluent."

"Oh, you can pick up a little of anything from the television these days." Sister Augustine gives the nurse a check for more than the agreed amount. "Thank you so much for coming. Bless you, child."

The check disappears into the nurse's wallet and Sister Augustine leads her to the door. With pre-recorded laughter rumbling in the background, she watches from the venetian blinds until the nurse vanishes around the bend in the walkway. Sister Augustine sets the alarm and returns to the living room where the light from the TV dances across the bookshelves. She watches Maura's muted expression before, without warning, Sister Augustine slaps her hard across the face. The papery skin on Maura's cheek blooms red. A photograph flutters to the ground.

Maura whimpers and turns away, shoulders heaving.

Sister Augustine seethes. "Do you want to ruin everything?"

A trickle of blood seeps from Maura's nose and she smears it across her cheek like cheap blush.

"It was a curse the day I was burdened with you." Sister Augustine snatches the photograph from the floor. She looks at it and brings her hand to her mouth. Her eyes glisten. Sister Augustine drops to her knees before Maura. "Forgive me. Oh, darling. I didn't mean it. You see what you're doing to me? My heart is breaking. There might still be time. If only you'd—"

Maura turns and shakes her head.

"Very well." Sister Augustine grits her teeth. "You've made your decision," she says, wiping her eyes and standing. "I don't know why I keep putting up with you in the first place. Why don't you do us both a favor and be quick about it, hmmm?"

Sister Augustine grabs her bag and disappears down the hallway towards her bedroom. The only decorations are a cross above her bed and a gold-inlayed mirror, a family heirloom, on the opposite wall. She opens her closet and reaches for a suitcase on the top shelf. As it tumbles toward her, she can hear its contents shifting. She sets it on the bed and unfastens the leather clasps.

Inside are countless human fingers in various states of decay. Most are in plastic bags where the flesh has turned black and withered. The others are in tiny jewellery sacks containing nothing but bones within their gossamer nets.

Sister Augustine removes a sandwich bag from her coat pocket and studies it. Ask any art student which part of the body is the most difficult to draw and they will say the hands, but the true difficulty lies in the fingers. To Sister Augustine, they are like individual flowers, full of expression and beautiful in their own way despite their various calluses, torn nails, arthritic joints.

Blood has smudged the plastic but that will eventually dry and flake away. Sister Augustine holds it up and admires her newest addition nestled at the bottom. On this one is a tattoo with the words *Bella Vita* written in looping greenish-blue ink, stretching from stump to tip. When she's done, she adds the finger to the rest and shuts the suitcase.

***

As leftover tickets and flyers from the carnival marinate in coffee grounds and cracked eggshells, Sister Augustine sets the alarm and locks the cottage. She'll return every hour to check on Maura. She runs her fingers along her veil before setting off down the walkway toward St. Mary's Catholic School. To the trained eye, the somber black cloth cannot hide that her skin is glowing with a preternatural aura. But to the majority of folk with kids to dress, lunches to fix, and jobs to rush to, Sister Augustine appears as if she had spent a refreshing weekend by the beach.

She steps over the groundskeeper, Jed Sherman. Next to him is an empty bottle of moonshine. It was full when Sister Augustine left it by one of the graves last night. Since the incident with the soil last spring, Jed's ramblings of the dead rising from hell have echoed all over Shallow Creek, but all the devils Sister Augustine has ever known were aboveground—not beneath. But still, she'd rather Jed press his nose up against his favorite vice than discover any more of St. Mary's secrets.

Still asleep, Jed scratches his stomach and grunts as he rolls over. Sister Augustine's lips curl in disgust. Before her students' doting-parents arrive, she'll have to ensure he is safely hidden away. She grabs Jed's feet and drags him behind a bush and drops the bottle beside him. She wipes her hands and turns to continue her short trek to school, but just as she steps on the path, she spots something and stops. Lying before her is a finger.

It is only polished bone and could have easily been mistaken as part of a toy, but Sister Augustine has no doubt it is one of hers. An artist always recognizes their art, and this one had been plucked from her early days.

Other than Jed, there's no one in the courtyard. Sister Augustine removes her scarf and picks up the finger. After wrapping it with care, she slips it into her pocket and hurries toward the school.

Inside, clusters of students already hang around the commons; their voices carrying along the metal lockers like the ebb and flow of ocean waves. They say, "Good morning," to her. Sometimes she returns the sentiment.

Sister Augustine unlocks the main office and veers toward a door with *Mother Superior* engraved on a golden plaque. She fastens the latch behind her and closes the blinds, shutting out her view of the creek. She turns to her desk. On a stack of invoices for new class equipment is another finger, this one merely a few years old, taken from a drug addict Bubba Cody picked up in Minnesota. Chunks of flesh have shriveled from the bone beneath. If left too long outside of its plastic bag, then more of the flesh will disintegrate. She peeks out the blinds as if expecting the person responsible for leaving her tokens to be standing there, ready to reveal their identity, but there is only the oak tree and an empty bench beside it.

The main office door swings open and there is a shuffling of feet followed by the strong scent of coffee. It's her assistant. She moves away from the window, pulls out her scarf, and places the finger in with the other.

Sister Augustine leaves her office. Her assistant is distracted by his computer, the skin under his eyes is red and swollen. He's spent the weekend shoveling tickets into his kids' outstretched palms, guzzling "guaranteed natural," lemonade, and throwing up after riding the Gravitron.

He jumps in his chair when he notices Sister Augustine standing quietly over him. "Everything okay?" he asks. "Was the AG room broken into again?"

"No." Sister Augustine replies. "Nothing like that. Can you take care of things here for a bit?"

"Y … yeah," he says, his voice hemorrhaging with anxiety. "Sure thing."

"Very good." Sister Augustine smiles. "I'll return momentarily."

The folds of her habit flap behind her like the blackened wings of a raven as she quickens her step on the sidewalk. She's never arrived at the police station empty-handed before, but today is not a normal visit. She leans forward as if pushing against an invisible force.

Officer Lopez is on the phone when Sister Augustine enters. It's the tail-end of a conversation. When Lopez ends the call, her eyes widen in surprise. "Sister Augustine?"

"Good morning, Janet." She grips the counter. "I'm sorry for the sudden intrusion. Are you having a busy morning?"

Lopez examines her. "Same as always, for the most part. What's going on? You look like something's bothering you."

"Oh, me? Heavens no." Sister Augustine shrugs. "Well, maybe there *is* something. We've been having some vandalism up at the school. Seems to happen every time the carnival is in town. I thought I'd file a report this time. Unless you're busy. I can come back later."

Sister Augustine turns to leave, but Lopez gets up. "No worries, Sister, I can take the report. It's not like there's a whole lot going on at the moment. I did get a missing persons case over the weekend, if you can believe it. Some detectives are looking for a girl that they're convinced hooked up with some carnie."

"Goodness. Like she ran away with the circus?"

"Something like that. Maybe you can help me for a second before I take your report. You went to the carnival last weekend, didn't you? Here—" Lopez hands her a sheet of paper "—do you think you might have seen her?"

Sister Augustine glances down at a photocopied photo of the girl Bubba Cody provided. In it, she is smiling and peering over her shoulder: a pose Sister Augustine has seen a hundred times from graduating seniors. There's a list of biographical information included at the bottom, along with the date and time she was last seen. Under identification marks, only one item is listed: a tattoo on right index finger, "Bella Vita."

"Her family is really torn up," Officer Lopez says. "Wealthy too. They're offering a $300,000 reward for information on her whereabouts. I suppose you can't really put a price on your little girl." Lopez looks up at Sister Augustine "Well? Did you see her?"

Sister Augustine returns the paper. "I'm sorry, dear. I can't say that I did."

"It was worth a shot," Lopez says. "I got ahold of Bubba Cody. That's who I was talking to when you came in. When I told him how much the family is offering, he perked up and said he might know something, but you can't trust a guy like that. Know what I mean?"

"I believe I do," Sister Augustine says. "For her family's sake, I hope the girl is found. In the meantime, I'll be praying for her safe return." She spins around and disappears through the rigid doors.

Officer Lopez calls after her. "Wait. What about your report?"

***

Sister Augustine rushes up the walkway to her cottage, crushing a pink chrysanthemum in the process. She unlocks the door. Once inside, the only noise is the clattering of applause from one of

Maura's gameshows. What she doesn't hear is the shrilling of the alarm. Someone has switched it off.

She shuts the door behind her.

"You got your wish," Sister Augustine yells. "We're leaving, and it isn't because of your little stunt either."

The volume on the TV increases.

Sister Augustine heads to her bedroom. "Next time you try and pretend that you can't get out of that wheelchair, I'm going to throw you out of it. You hear me?"

She retrieves the suitcase from the closet, but this time there is no shifting of weight within as she pulls the case down. It's as light as a bird's wing. She rips the clasps open and lifts the lid. Other than yellowed fingernails scattered like cracker-crumbs, the suitcase is empty.

"Where are they?" she shrieks and rages into the living room. "Where are they, you little—"

Sister Augustine gazes around, her chest rising and falling with each rapid breath. On every available surface lie her precious fingers, pointing in her direction, as if staged for the precise moment she'd enter the room.

"How …" she begins, staring at Maura who is in her usual spot with the blanket draped over her in the exact manner it was less than an hour ago.

Maura motions for Sister Augustine to turn around, and as she does, she notices the dark figure of a woman standing in the hallway. She is wearing a carnival uniform and her hair is pulled tight from her face.

"Who are you?" Sister Augustine demands. "How'd you get in here? Did Bubba Cody send you?"

In the woman's hand is a large wrench. She is missing an index finger.

Sister Augustine pales and slowly backs away. "Get out of my house," she says, barely above a whisper.

Another figure joins the carnival worker. This time a younger girl dressed like a peasant. Then another appears. And another and another. Some are children. Some are not. Seemingly, they have nothing in common, save for the one thing Sister Augustine stole. She runs toward Maura. "Come," she says, attempting to grab her.

Maura pulls away.

"This isn't the time to fight with me." Sister Augustine stands behind the wheelchair, preparing to give it a shove, but Maura engages the brake.

Sister Augustine snaps, "What in Christ's name are you doing? We have to leave. Can't you see? Can't you see *them*?"

Maura's eyes flutter toward the visitors and she nods.

Sister Augustine leans against the chair. The murky figures close in. Soon, they'll be trapped like spiders in a glass jar. "Don't make me choose, Maura."

"Momma." Maura reaches her gnarled fingers toward her. "Momma, please."

A sob escapes Sister Augustine as she takes Maura's hand in her own and kisses it.

The figures spill into the living room. Maura opens her arms as if greeting old friends. Sister Augustine trembles behind her, barely able to peer upon the familiar shadows she'd once trimmed like rosebushes when they were flesh and bone and full of blood.

The carnival worker stands before them, clenching the wrench.

"Don't," Sister Augustine's voice quakes. "I beg you, don't do this."

Maura closes her eyes.

The last sound in the cottage at St. Mary's Catholic Church is the high-pitched scream of a game show contestant winning a brand-new car.

***

Abandoned on the front step of the police station is a faded leather suitcase with a single red dahlia on top. Beneath the flower is a recipe for banana bread and a black and white photograph of a woman cradling a newborn in her arms. The woman's face is turned away from the camera, but she is wearing a silk scarf with embroidered flowers. Written on the back in faded script is 'Baby Maura and me, Čachtice, Slovakia, 1867.'

DISTRACTION

by Brian Wilson

One two three four five six seven. Count them. One two three four five six seven. Seven cigarette butts. Seven crimson eyes. They hang out at the pier after dark, slumped against the fractured balustrade, untouched by moonlight. Without cigarettes they'd be an amorphous black blob. I'd have no clue how many lurk in the shadows. Smoking is a dirty habit. One two three four five six seven.

Angus is late. Usually his tugboat pulls up a couple minutes after midnight. What can I do? The man has me by the balls. I'd do anything for Marjorie after what happened to our daughter. She was only three years old.

One two three four five six seven. C'mon, Angus. C'mon, you son of a bitch. Don't make me wait all night. I can feel them staring at me. Why don't they say anything? Why don't I ever hear them speak?

"You want some advice, kids? Quit smoking. I gave up six months ago. Best decision of my life."

No response. Probably smacked out of their minds. Probably don't even know I'm here. Takes a certain kind of person to hang around a place like this. The stench of ruined wood is unbearable. It's so foul you can actually taste it. Shallow Creek pier burned down years ago. No-one knows who or what started the fire. My guess? Some nutso's idea of a joke. Town's full of them. The man I'm waiting for is no different. I'd heard rumours about Angus Runt's criminal past. Turns out they're all true.

One two three four five six seven. I only count the cigarette butts so I don't have to look at the sea. If you ever find yourself in Shallow Creek, try not to look at the sea. It's got this way of talking to you. Inviting you. Makes you feel like you can run across the surface. Get away from here.

You've got to find a distraction.

One two three four five six seven. I dug out the pond myself. It was the first thing I ever made for the garden. The project was Sarah's idea. She's one of my employees down at Bob's Bits N' Bobs. We were having lunch one afternoon when I mentioned I was getting cravings again. "Nothing like a bit of DIY to take your mind off it," she said. "Works a charm for me. I've been off the death sticks for two and a half years. And I've got a beautiful garden to boot."

Sarah was right. It felt so good, dashing the shovel into the ground and tearing up the earth; moulding it to fit my vision. The smell was delicious. Fresh grass and wet mud. When the hole was big enough I filled it with sand. Then I went down to Bob's for a plastic tarpaulin to use as underlay. Marie was excited. "Daddy," she said. "Can I help you?" "Of course you can," I told her. "Grab a bucket and get mommy to fill it up at the kitchen sink."

She did just that. She waddled in and out of the kitchen for an hour straight, bucket suspended between tiny clenched fists. When she reached the edge she dumped the contents into the freshly-lined pond, laughing with delight as her meagre contribution merged with the whole.

One two three four five six seven. How much of the pond did Marie help fill? Not much, probably. Her bucket was one of those small lime green numbers used for making sandcastles on the beach. In the following days Marj decorated the perimeter with stones and bright flowers. We were so proud, Marj and I; so proud of what we had made. We couldn't stop admiring it. So then how did we miss her falling in?

One two three four five six seven. Angus arrived four days after Marie's funeral. He knocked on the door three times. He was carrying a leather briefcase. "I know what you're going through," he said. "I can help you." I didn't know what he meant but I let him in anyway. Our house was a wreck. Marjorie wasn't sleeping. She lay in bed all day gazing at the ceiling, as though the real Marjorie had oozed out of her ear and left behind a Marjorie-shaped husk.

"Where is Marj?" Angus asked. I didn't like that. It was overly familiar for a man I'd only seen at the store a few times. "Upstairs," I said. That's when he opened the briefcase. "Look," he said. I looked.

A dozen syringes embedded in foam, each filled with liquid clear as water.

"What are you doing here?" I asked. "What is this stuff?"

"Do you want your wife to feel better, Maurice? Do *you* want to feel better?"

I asked again: "What is this stuff?"

"She'll sleep, Maurice."

That got my attention. I saw Marj's face; those slumped, pallid features; the way her skin sagged as though her skull had caved in.

"Don't worry," Angus said. "I'm here to help you. That's what I do, Maurice. I help people."

Angus removed one of the syringes and offered it to me.

"Take it. Try it and see what you think. Inject it somewhere no-one will notice. If you want more, meet me tomorrow. I'll be at the pier at midnight."

"Wait," I said. I had so many questions. But he left in spite of my protests.

One two three four five six seven. That was the first night Marjorie slept in over two weeks. I shouldn't have done it. Shouldn't have bunched up her nightdress and pressed the needle into her thigh. I was desperate. You understand that, don't you? Marj didn't even look at me. Her eyes remained fixed on the ceiling. But when I saw the expression on her face I knew I'd done the right thing. Her head lolled back and her lips curled upwards.

A smile. She was smiling.

Of course I wanted more.

One two three four five six seven. One two three four five six. Fuck.

I recount the burning blots. One. Two. Three. Four. Five. Six. Again.

One. Two. Three. Four. Five.

Oh *fuck.*

What happens when they finish smoking, Maurice?

I wheel around and face the sea, overwhelmed by a surface so smooth you could glide a curling stone a hundred miles with a single throw.

Don't listen. Don't listen. Don't listen.

What happens when it's just you and me?

That's it. I'm done. Angus, buddy, our business is concluded. If you wanted my custom, you shouldn't have kept me waiting. We don't need your help. Not anymore.

But Marjorie can't sleep without it.

It's true. That first time she slept the whole night through. The next day she even got out of bed to use the bathroom. She washed her face with lilac soap. The scent filled the house. It was a miracle. Then she changed the sheets and climbed back into bed. That's when I knew I had no choice.

One two three four. I arrived at the pier an hour early. By then Marj was back in her trance. A couple more nights sleep would do her a world of good.

One two three four. I didn't see the kids show up. As soon as the sun goes down it's impossible to see anything beyond the shadowy contours of shattered wood. There's no sense illuminating a desolated pier, not when there are so many lights sucking up juice at the fairground next door. One moment I was alone, the next that seven-eyed beast was slumped against the balustrade, staring right at me.

One two three four. Angus's tugboat appeared at five minutes past midnight. He docked by the pier and invited me on board. His grin revealed a set of straight white teeth. And there was that leather briefcase.

"This time," he said. "It doesn't come free."

I tried it myself that night. Brought home two syringes. After I'd done Marjorie I removed my jeans and administered it. Within seconds the dull, heavy thing I'd been carrying inside me began to dissolve. In the morning I was able to admit it: I hadn't been sleeping right either.

I've been meeting Angus twice a week ever since.

One two three four. I risk another glimpse at the sea, scanning for any sign of Angus's tugboat. The water is empty. To the right of the pier and across the bay, the lighthouse winks in steady mockery. Jud, the lighthouse keeper, is doubtless inside. He's nutso too. The month before the accident, Marj and I brought Marie to the lighthouse for a tour. We had to cut through a copse of trees next to Arkady Asylum, and Marie wailed the entire time. I don't know why. There was nothing out of the ordinary about the trail. When we reached the lighthouse, Jud was pleased to see us. I don't think the man gets many visitors. He was especially happy to see Marie. He noticed her red, puffy face and asked if she was okay. When I told him what had happened his expression changed. He took my arm and led me away from my wife and daughter. The smell of cigarette smoke was heavy on his coat. "I think, perhaps, maybe, I can't be sure; Molly—I mean Marie—hears them too. The voices of the folk in Arkady. They rise at night when sleep will seldom come. They rise at night when William's far away."

I was about to cut his inane babbling short when a burst of static erupted from inside his coat pocket. He mumbled something and pulled out a battered-looking walkie-talkie. Then we got on with the tour. I remember standing at the top of the lighthouse looking out at the ruin of the pier. Somehow it seemed even more hollow during the daytime, as though a seagull might land on the wrong blackened slat and cause the whole thing to collapse into the water. When we were finished, Jud offered to take us back into town in his rowboat. I refused. I had no intention of putting my family's life in the hands of a man who professed to hear voices.

Tell the truth, Maurice.

Is that …? Could it be …? Yes. A faint light on the horizon. Angus returning from wherever he's been; from wherever the hell a man like him has business.

Five minutes pass. Ten. The light remains a blip. What is it they say? A watched kettle never boils. We learned that when Marie was a baby. You wouldn't believe the screams. Sometimes it took hours for her to settle. Sleep, my baby. Sleep, my precious thing. Lights out.

I turn back towards the silhouette. Three eyes now. One two three. I can feel them on my skin, itching like insect bites. My fingers claw at my jeans, trying to reach my inner thigh.

"Please," I say. "Please. Just a bit more time."

The eyes continue to blaze.

"Please."

Facing the water again. The light on the horizon is bigger, isn't it? Yes. It must be.

Come on, Maurice. Tell the truth now, Maurice.

"The truth?" I say aloud. "You want to know the truth? There's a reason the church is a stone's throw from the cinema. It's because they sell the same damn thing. All those people stuffed inside that pathetic grey building on a Sunday morning—they're delusional. How can they believe in a God that would take away my little girl? A God that would turn her skin so cold and blue? It's some kind of sick joke."

Silence. Who am I talking to? Get a grip, Maurice. Get it together. It's the sea. Didn't I tell you? It's got a way of burrowing into your brain. That's why distractions are important. That's why you've got to keep counting.

One two three. One two three. One two three.

I'm being punished. Angus is punishing me. He's sitting out there in his tugboat and he's laughing his fucking head off. Last time we met we got into an argument. I told him I don't like meeting at the pier. I told him the sea makes me nervous.

That isn't the real reason.

One two three. One two three. One two three.

The real reason is you were thirty dollars short.

That was part of it, sure. I'll admit it: Money has become a struggle. It's only been a month since Angus came knocking but already we've nearly run out. Marj isn't working and I've just started back. It's hard to sit in a cramped office in the store where you bought most of the tools that facilitated your daughter's—

No. Angus's help doesn't come cheap. But it *does* help. Marj and I have talked about it. We just need to stay on for another month. Two at the very most. Angus was furious when I didn't have all the money. Threatened to cut us off completely. In the end he relented half a dose, enough for one person. I gave it to Marj. The rest of the weekend was spent trying to scrape together the funds for next time. Tonight I'm only seven dollars short.

One two. The kids are finishing up. One two. They are kids, right? One two. Don't leave me here alone. One two. The stink of charred wood. One two. And Angus's boat having drawn no closer.

Relax, Maurice. Why not bum a cigarette?

"Quit tempting at me!" I cry, stomping in the direction of the kids. For an instant I hope the pier gives way and we all fall down.

Ashes! Ashes! We all fall down.

Ashes! Ashes! We all fall down.

Ashes! Ashes! We all fall down.

Shut up shut up SHUT UP!

I lodge my fingers in my ears and close my eyes. Yet the voice remains crystal clear.

Smoking is a dirty habit, Maurice.

How do you know about that? How can anyone know?

When I open my eyes again a feeble groan escapes my lips. Those eyes, that pair of blood-red embers pulsating like living things …

They're gone. Replaced by a dim outline. A short figure with skinny arms and skinny legs and sticky-up hair. I'd recognise those pigtails anywhere.

"Marie?"

It's not darkness that obscures my vision now but tears, and I fumble for the thing in my pocket; the thing I shouldn't have—the thing I promised my family I had thrown away for good. Hands trembling, I remove the lighter and thumb the wheel on top, producing a tiny, wavering flame.

Tell her you're sorry, Maurice.

I take a step towards her, keeping my arm as steady as I can. Somehow I know that if the flame goes out the entire world will plunge into darkness.

"I'm sorry," I say. "I'm so sorry, baby."

Another step. The itch in my thigh makes me want to scream.

Tell her the truth, Maurice.

I stop so suddenly the flame almost extinguishes. Something inside me cracks and gives way.

"It was an accident. Marie, sweetie, you've got to believe me."

The lighter starts to slide through my sweaty palm. I grip it tighter and step forward.

"If your mom found out I'd started smoking again she would have been so disappointed. I promised her, Marie. It was the one thing she asked me to do and I couldn't do it."

The wood groans beneath my feet.

"But it was you I let down most. You hated it when I smoked. Hated it. When you were a baby the smell made you cry. Do you remember what you said to me on my birthday? The day I vowed to quit? *Daddy*, you said. *Smoking is a dirty habit.* You must have heard it on TV."

Close now. So close I can almost make out her face.

"I was only gone for five minutes. Nipped into the shed to get out of sight. You were sitting on a blanket playing with your toys, singing that damned nursery rhyme for the thousandth time. Ashes, ashes, we all fall down; ashes, ashes, we all fall down. What happened? What made you wander over to the pond?"

At last the flame's glow reaches the balustrade, and then I see her—my little girl.

"You forgive me, don't you? You forgive daddy?"

"Fucking creep!" A voice says, and then Marie is gone, replaced by the beast, and the beast breaks apart and disperses with the sound of frantic footsteps. "Junkie fuck!" calls another. Then it's just me and the pier and the tugboat's distant light.

Attaboy, Maurice. Doesn't that feel good?

I'm still staring at the place where I swear I saw my daughter.

"Marie," I whisper. "I haven't smoked a single cigarette since. I promise."

Get a hold of yourself, Maurice. Marj is waiting for you. You don't want to keep her waiting, do you?

Too weak. Too weak to fight it anymore. Slowly, I turn towards the sea. Angus's tugboat still hasn't moved. Yet somehow the light is brighter.

"Angus," I try to shout, but the word is suffocated.

She's waiting for you, Maurice.

"I can't get to him," I say. "He's too far."

You'll make it.

I lower myself into a sitting position, legs dangling in mid air. The sea stretches for eternity; its surface a flat, solid plain.

I promise you will make it.

I push off. For a horrible moment I think my feet will pass straight through the water, but they don't, and then I'm running, and it's cold—*so cold*—but I am moving towards the light. Don't worry, Marj. I'll be home soon. I've taken so much from you. The least I can do is bring something back.

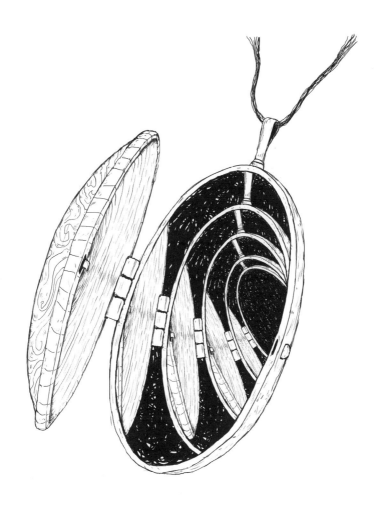

AND THE WORLD FADES TO BLACK

by Adam Lock

Ruth Usiskin sits on the chair next to the bed, leans back and crosses her legs, a gold chain and locket held loosely over her thigh. The bell in the tower clangs. Her patient, Donny Dakin, is sedated, fastened to the bed by leather restraints. Ruth holds the locket out in front of her, letting it swing freely before placing it in her palm. She turns it over, reads the inscription on the reverse: Forever. Ruth pushes her fingernail into the fissure and the locket springs open. Inside, is a lock of hair. There are flames and there is pain, and the world fades to black.

Ruth holds the locket out in front of her, letting it swing freely before laying it in her hand. She turns it over, reads the inscription on the back: Forever. She waits, her fingernail pressed against the opening. A crow squawks outside the window and her fingers cease to stir.

'Mr Dakin?' she asks, the patient rousing. 'Mr Dakin. It's Ruth Usiskin. Do you know where you are?'

The patient's head rocks from left to right, tipping towards her before resting on the pillow. His eyes slide down her body and fall on the locket cradled in her hand. His lips curl, not entirely a smile, more a snarl.

'Daisy?' he asks.

'It's Ruth Usiskin. You're in Arkady Asylum.'

His chest sinks beneath the sheets and his dry, crusted lips part. 'Open it.' The pink-creaminess of his eyes flash in the darkness of the room.

She looks again at the locket, and pushing her fingernail into the opening, it springs open. Inside, is a lock of hair. There are flames and there is pain, and the world fades to black.

'Open it,' he says. The pink-creaminess of his eyes flash in the darkness of the room.

She looks again at the locket, and rests her fingernail against the opening.

'What's inside?' she asks.

The patient smirks, and his head falls back so he's staring at the ceiling. 'How much longer?' he asks.

'For what?'

'How much longer do we have to go over this, time and again?'

'I don't understand.'

Again, his head swivels to the side so he can look at her.

'Do you know how many times I've died? How many times I've watched you die?'

Ruth uncrosses her legs and sits forwards in her chair, the locket resting on her skirt, between her legs.

'How many?'

One eye is bloodshot, the other lazy, an eyelid drooping across a silver eye.

He lifts his head, the muscles in his neck twitching. 'Open it. And this time, try and remember what it feels like. Really try and remember.'

Ruth's eyes narrow as her fingers work the clasp of the locket.

He nods slowly. 'Concentrate.'

The locket springs open. Inside, is a lock of hair. There are flames and there is pain, and the world fades to black.

***

Daisy Fontaine locks the front door of Jack's Tavern and parts the curtain to peer outside. There is only her reflection and the beads of rain sliding down the glass.

She runs through the bar, removes her apron and enters the room at the rear of the tavern.

Donny Dakin is stood in the centre of the room waiting for her.

'We don't have long,' she says, throwing her arms around his shoulders.

'I don't understand,' Donny says. 'What's going on?'

'I know, I know. I can't explain *how* I know, but I know.'

'But he's not been in the Creek for weeks. What makes you think he'll be here tonight?'

She lets go of his neck, straightens her hair, and stares at the ground.

'Told you. I dreamt it.'

'Your old man? Here—tonight?'

She nods, moving threads of hair behind each ear.

'So why don't we just run away? Leave the Creek.'

She shakes her head. 'It's no use. Wouldn't help.'

'We wouldn't be here. And he wouldn't find you. How can that not help?'

She approaches the window that overlooks the yard behind the tavern. She pours a bourbon and downs it, then stretches her back, inhaling deeply.

Donny watches her, twisted away from him.

'There's something we can do,' she says.

He waits, then edges towards her.

'But I don't know the price,' she says. She turns so he can see the profile of her head against the darkness of the glass.

'I'll do anything,' he says.

'You shouldn't say that.'

'Tell me what we have to do.'

She reaches to the back of her neck and unfastens the chain and locket.

The wind blows the trees outside the tavern and they rattle against the roof. Over her shoulder, the curtain billows into the room and slowly settles again.

'I think I can give us one more night,' she says.

'Daisy, I don't understand any of this. Your dad. It was just a dream.'

She lifts the blanket from the chair and lays it on the timber floor. She places a knife and candles in the centre and sits crossed-legged before them. She indicates for Donny to do the same.

He sits on the blanket and watches her light each candle, the flames trembling in the draft.

There's banging on the tavern door.

Donny turns, rising to his knees. 'What's that?'

'Don't. We still have time. I don't know the price. But if we do this, we'll have one more night together.'

He goes to speak, but sees a calmness in her eyes, a reassurance, and sits back down.

Louder banging at the entrance of the tavern.

Daisy places the chain and locket on the blanket beside the candles.

'It was my mother's,' she says.

Donny looks behind. More banging.

Removing a small envelope from within her shirt, Daisy pulls out a lock of hair.

'Father's,' she says. 'I took it knowing this day would come.'

She takes the knife, and holding a clump of her own hair, cuts. She shifts on her knees and reaches across for Donny's hair. He closes his eyes, feels the tug as she slices a lock of hair. She arranges all three locks of hair on the blanket and proceeds to plait them.

Daisy whispers something, her eyes closed.

The wind rises again, blowing the curtains into the room.

Then there's banging at the window over Daisy's shoulder, above the table. There is a dark figure and a fist pounding on the glass.

'Daisy? You in there?'

'Ignore him,' she says, and continues muttering under her breath.

More banging at the window.

'I know you're in there, Daisy!'

She folds the lock of hair, pushes it inside the locket, and seals it closed.

'Daisy! Open up, Daisy!'

She grabs the knife, leans over the locket, and etches something onto the back.

'Will you?' she asks, handing Donny the locket and turning around.

His hands shake.

The window rattles.

Finally, he fastens the chain around her neck.

Daisy turns and kisses him on the lips.

And the banging, the wind, the rain, stops.

'One more night,' Daisy says.

She's so pretty, he can think of nothing else.

***

'How many?' Ruth Usiskin asks.

One eye is bloodshot, the other lazy, an eyelid drooping across a silver eye.

'Well? Do you remember?'

'Remember?'

Donny coughs, his upper body convulsing, the straps binding him to the bed pulled tight, the veins along his arms pulsing.

Ruth stands and searches for the syringe in her pocket.

'Wait,' he says. 'Wait.' His eyes fix on her pocket. 'Don't do that.'

She can't remember him ever having that expression—of fear. She removes her hand from her pocket.

'We're not done for today,' he says. 'We need to try something different. I'm growing tired of this. Over and over.'

She walks around the bed and stands beside him.

'Something different? I don't understand.'

He coughs again, his chest gurgling, throat rasping.

'Open it. But don't look inside.'

Ruth holds the locket in the palm of her hand.

'You talk as though we've done this before.'

He closes his eyes and sighs.

'You could say that. Open it. But don't look.'

Her fingers work the clasp of the locket. It springs open. She waits and then looks. Inside, is a lock of hair. There are flames and there is pain, and the world fades to black.

He closes his eyes and sighs.

'Open it. But don't look.'

She feels the clasp and waits.

'Why can't I look?'

His head rocks back and forth until he's looking up at the ceiling. 'You always look.'

Ruth clenches her fists, feels her forehead creasing.

'Mr Dakin, you've been here two days. We really need to talk about what happened.'

The patient laughs, his chest aflame, crackling and guttural.

'Two days,' he says. 'That's a beauty.' He laughs again and coughs.

Ruth reaches for the syringe.

'It's OK. It's OK—wait.' He stares at her pocket. 'We don't need that. Not yet.'

Ruth sits down on the chair at the foot of the bed. Outside the bell in the tower clangs.

'This time,' he says, 'open it, and then drop it. And don't look.'

'I don't understand. This time?'

'Do it. Please.'

Her fingers work the clasp. It springs open. She drops the locket. It lies on the ground, open, revealing a lock of hair. There are flames and there is pain, and the world fades to black.

'Do it.'

Her fingers work the clasp of the locket but something stops her.

'You looked,' he says.

'Mr Dakin, we need to talk.'

'I know. You said that already.'

Ruth goes to speak but stops, a strange sense of déjà vu consuming her. She wavers, her mind clouded, hands reaching for the railing of the bed.

He clasps her wrist, the leather straps permitting such minuscule movement.

She reaches for the syringe with her free hand.

'She didn't know the price,' he says, eyes heavy and sad. 'If I'd known…'

She pulls out the syringe.

'Might as well,' he says, and releases her wrist. 'We'll have to do it again soon.'

His smile changes, shifting between bitterness and spite.

Through the open window arrives a smell of damp earth and rain. A crow squawks. Something in the way the patient jerks his head, she knows she'll not gain anything worthwhile today. She'll try again tomorrow. He doesn't flinch as she threads the the needle into his wrist. She pushes the locket into her pocket and backs away from the bed, watching him the entire time. His chest rises and falls beneath white sheets. The bell in the tower clangs.

'Daisy?' he says, drowsy.

She turns and opens the door.

Ruth Usiskin sits on the chair next to the bed, leans back and crosses her legs, a gold chain and locket held loosely over her thigh. The bell in the tower clangs. Her patient, Donny Dakin, is sedated, fastened to the bed by leather restraints. Ruth holds the locket out in front of her, letting it swing freely before placing it in her palm. She turns it over, reads the inscription on the reverse: Forever. Ruth pushes her fingernail into the fissure and the locket springs open. Inside, is a lock of hair. There are flames and there is pain, and the world fades to black.

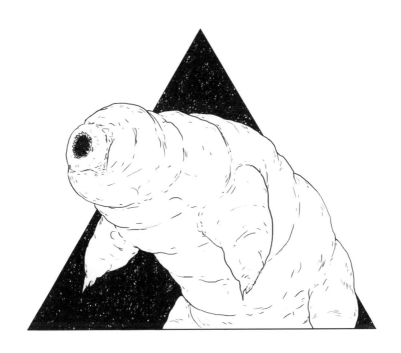

THE LURID TRANCE

by Gregg Williard

I received a large envelope in the mail, well-travelled in time and space. The original return address from the Brooklyn Board of Education had been stamped over and replaced by other address labels from other departments and divisions of teacher certification. It had been forwarded several times, and somehow made it to my current address, in a different city and state, years later.

The envelope was tightly sealed in multiple layers of postal tape, and, beneath that, yellowed masking tape old enough to crack and crumble. I thought of a mummy's wrapping. When I finally opened the envelope with an inelegant attack of pinking shears the smell inside was of play dough, crayons, mimeograph ink and mildew. Not quite the tomb of Imhotep. Between sheets of cardboard was an 11" x 14" diagonal of white drawing paper. On the horizontal was an unfaded drawing in black ink. It was an intricately detailed but boldly rendered landscape of a junkyard at night. There were rows of wrecked cars, trucks, motorcycles, construction equipment and other, harder to identify vehicles and machines, possibly airplane parts, pieces of carnival rides or funhouse props, even spaceships and science fiction weapons. In the distance stood a lighthouse. The detail was amazing, lit from above by the moon, and below by trash can fires and cigarette lighters. Clustered around the fires were gatherings of children, teenagers and adults in the style of 1930's or '40's Reginald Marsh urban dwellers, or 1950's-'60's teenage and juvenile delinquent movie posters and paperback novels. Some of the girls and women looked more contemporary, with black hoodies and bleached white hair. Their faces over the lighters were luminous, and their eyes had a night vision sheen. The darks and lights, the complications and inventions of faces and machinery were somehow held together by a firm, prodigious mastery of line and form I studied with keen envy.

It was my drawing, completed in a room full of art teacher candidates, forty years ago. It was a timed exercise to evaluate our drawing ability and imagination. I never heard anything from the board and assumed I'd been turned down, again. I forgot about the drawing, and any hope of being a teacher, or an artist. I moved many times, and changed. The drawing found me, but I never found myself. Maybe I was lost overseas, or wandering in another homeless envelope. I saw another paper in the bottom, a faded, official form. It was a typed evaluation: shows great promise. Accepted. Only the applicant name wasn't mine. Someone named Bridey Hatfield had been accepted on the basis of my drawing. Now Hatfield was sending me the evidence. To be forgiven? Or to gloat?

It was too easy to track down Hatfield. A simple google image search of my scanned drawing linked me to a town called Shallow Creek. Hatfield lived across from the Shallow Creek hospital and the old School for Wayward Girls in a place identified as "A House of Interest." When I arrived, a note on the screen door directed me to Jack's Tavern where I would be "teaching a drawing class." Great. The tavern was a few blocks past the town square, and I drove by to take a look. There wasn't much: a little roundabout surrounded by mostly empty store windows and a shuttered municipal building, and in the center a 19th Century-style bronze figure on a granite pedestal. I pulled over and got out. My distant impression was confirmed: the statue had no face. The clothes and body were realistically modeled in bronze (or perhaps faux bronze, like the cheap, coated-tin confederate statues that were being torn down all over the states), but the figure's head was a cyborg-like shell, highly polished and smooth. The features had not been disfigured; they were never there, or were yet to appear. It stood sentinel over the listless foot and motor traffic in a stiff pose, wearing a frock coat and holding a sextant before him with both hands. Not a sea-faring man, more an accountant or scrivener out of Melville, taking full measure of his preference for naught. Appropriately there was no identifying plaque.

Jack's Tavern had a back room that resembled a grudging idea of a coffee shop. Three tables were pulled together and covered with sketchpads, pens and pencils. At the table were four young women, two dark and two light. All had slate gray eyes and bleached blond hair, wearing black hoodies, long skirts and heavy boots. The women in my drawing. I sat in the empty chair but couldn't meet their eyes. I sighed at a twist of pencil shavings and watched it rollaway.

I finally asked, "Where's Bridey Hatfield?"

They looked at each other. One of them groaned and rolled her eyes. Another drawled, "Like, sitting right in front of us?"

"Bridey is a woman's name."

The one who spoke shrugged and said, "Shallow Creek's fluid." She nudged the pad closer to me. "Teach us how to draw ourselves twenty years before we were born."

"I can't." I got up and lurched past the bar to the bathroom. I closed the stall door and sat on the toilet seat, trying to count four beats in … four held … four out. Combat breaths. What I'd learned.

When I came out I'd got the shaking down to a tremor. The table was cleared. The women were standing with their hoodies zipped, and khaki back and side packs slung. "We'll take you to Liz Warren at the Shallow Creek Cinema." The talker said, "We can do our lesson there."

I followed them with more resignation than curiosity. I had no plans to stay, but no plans to go. Outside I walked into a short, barrel-chested man with long white hair pulled back in a pony-tail. His Buddy Holly glasses were steamed over. "Oh, sorry man! So sorry!" He took my hand in his. It was hot and wet. "I had to cover for the dishwasher. Drunk again."

"You work at Jack's?"

"Actually, I'm the town librarian. We're closed today for mold removal. I help Jack from time to time for some extra scratch. James Cooper, Esquire. You're Bridey Hatfield. You're the dude that drew Buba Cody's junkyard, and the girls' portraits twenty years before they were even born."

"Fuck you James, we're not girls," the women said in unison. James ignored them and pulled me aside with a wink and (eerie) smile. "Hey, you don't remember me, do you, Bridey?"

"I'm not Bridey.

He leaned in closer, steering me around a crew of homeless crusties on the sidewalk sharing a sparking joint. "I know you're not, brother. I'm not James Cooper, either. It's Tim. Tim Ferris? 1972. V.A. psych hospital. Bangor, Maine. Ward 7. You were the C.O. Psych Orderly. You ran the Thursday night group therapy. Remember me?"

I didn't. "Tim. Sure."

"A whole platoon of psychos, only some of us were fake. I always wondered if you were there to weed out the phonies, shake out the 4-F's into nice juicy 1-A's, ready for the grinder.

I stared at James/Tim, but couldn't remember him. There'd been so many patients, and so many years.

"And you know what, Denys? I *was* faking! Oh, I know it wasn't you who ratted me out. You actually helped me. Remember that therapy technique you used with us? 'Repressed Cheap Horror

Movie Trauma Syndrome?' We all thought you were tripping us out, man, but I actually had it! Remember?"

I gave him rueful shake of the head and weary laugh. I didn't have the heart to tell him I couldn't remember, but as he went on about Repressed Cheap Horror Movie Memory Syndrome, something clicked, fell into place like a long-frozen lock finally tumbling open. It was as if my own repressed memories were being released, not about horror movie trauma, but horror reality trauma.

We arrived at a cross street with an old masonic lodge on the corner. "Hey girls!" he called out. "Let's take Argyle to show Bridey some of the town."

The women walked ahead, giving us the finger and trilling out, "Fuck you James, we're not girls."

James continued in an excited rush: "Remember my trauma? It was the memory of a living black umbrella that enfold my head and suck out my brains", and with an icy jolt, I did: it wasn't a living umbrella. It was a flying bat creature, a little rubber bat on strings, released from a tube to earthlings, under the control of Paul Birch, the space vampire in Roger Corman's *Not of This Earth* from 1957. In a trance I heard myself tell James, "You saw it when you were five, or six. You were sneaked into the theater by your older brother, who was stuck babysitting you and he put you in the back row so he could make out with his girlfriend in the balcony. You forgot all about the movie, but the repressed memory messed with your head, and had you screaming at night and wetting the bed for years."

James gripped my arm. I could feel the heat of his hand through my sweatshirt. His eyes were clouded with tears. "I was still wetting the bed in the damn hospital, which helped my psycho case, but not enough. Once you identified the movie, and showed me some pictures in that "Famous Monsters" magazine, I remembered! We waited for *Not of This Earth* on the late show, and once I saw it—saw it was nothing but that little rubber bat thing, I stopped the wetting, the screaming. You changed my life. You cured me, man, and I'm grateful. Of course, they reinstated my 1-A in nothing flat. That's how I ended up here and became James Cooper. Back in the day we had a whole little community of draft dodgers in Shallow Creek. Hard to say how many of the town are descendants of the pseudo psychos. I'm the last original. But hey, I heard something happened. That they sent you to 'Nam as a medic ...?"

"I chose to go."

"You chose to go? That must have been ..."

"It's amazing how many people our age were traumatized by cheap horror movies. Not just horror movies, too. Exploitation. Girlie. Elvis. Sci-Fi porno. Noir zombie snuff. Even commercials. I remember one of my patients had a thing about Howdy Doodie, and Captain Midnight Ovaltine Commercials ..."

"That's why we called you, Denys. You did that drawing forty years ago of Buba Cody's junkyard, with pieces of the fairground, all the condemned rides, the Tilt-a-Swoop and Chute of the Lost Cookies and the Dimension Creeper, and his Time Travel Bulldozer and Inner-Vision Arcade. You even show Jud's lighthouse in the distance, right where it ought to be. But you've never been here before, have you?"

No."

"I knew it. Some of the others say this is all more chamber of commerce BS spearheaded by O'Keefe and his crew back at the Tavern, just crying for some local ghosty stories or urban legend jizz, clairvoyant-cannibal back country mutant moose-men kinda thang, 'cause that's the problem: Shallow Creek's got no stories at all, no local mythology, no history, no memory, no nothing."

"I wouldn't say that, James. Every place has its ..."

"Look around, Denys. Look at the stores. Look at the locals. Do you notice anything odd?"

We'd circled back along a street of closed or might as well be stores, and wood frame houses.

"It's a little ... depressed, but then, most small towns ..."

He tugged on my arm again, and we stopped. He swept his arm to indicate all that was before us, or rather, wasn't: shells of former video rental, pet store, radio repair or book store Quonset huts, stunted trees, a handful of cars with duct-taped windows and dragging tailpipes. There were homeless crusties, a couple of lounge lizard outside Jacks, and some lumpy shoppers pushing wobbly carts across the Super Store parking lot, which was crisscrossed with fissures sprouting gray weeds. I thought of the statue in the town square. Surely there was a story there.

James said, "Ah, that would be The Man with No Face."

I waited, but James only shrugged. "Ask any of the residents of Shallow Creek. That's what you'll get: 'Ah, The Man with No Face.'

Sometimes, "Ah, The Faceless Man.' Shit, Denys, I'm the town librarian, keeper of the histories, and that's all *I* can think to say! Ask the girls there …"

They were a block ahead of us chanting, "Fuck you James, we're not girls."

James smiled. "They're the only ones with any life left. But it'll hit them, too. It starts with the eyes."

"What does?"

"Do you see any bright colors here, Denys? Do you see anyone with dark eyes?"

"I just thought, you know, maybe …"

"C'mon. Look at my eyes, Denys. What color are they?"

"Blue. Blueish. Gray, I guess …"

"When I came to Shallow Creek they were brown. I swear to god."

"What does that have to do with stories. Or no stories?"

"Listen, Elizabeth—Liz—she's the owner of the Shallow Creek Cinema. She can explain this better than I can, but before we get there, let me just ask you, have you ever heard of a movie called *The Tingler*?"

My memory clicked awake again: *The Tingler.* 1959. Vincent Price. Directed by William Castle. Price plays a doctor who discovers a heretofore unknown physical mechanism in the human body: when experiencing intense terror, an insectoid slug detaches from the spinal cord and snaps the spine in two. The only way to stop it is by screaming. And it seemed the only way I could access my past was through horror movies, science fiction, noir, exploitation, teen and rockabilly… and 'it' would come back again, the 'it' of the war, the 'it' of the peace, the 'it' of every nothing that followed. Did I really want that? Did anyone?

"Yeah," I said. "*The Tingler* was famous for its 'revolutionary new film technique': 'Percepto'; little electric buzzers installed in random seats in the theatre where the movie was being shown. They'd activate when the tingler in the movie was removed from the body, and began crawling free around the floor. It's also famous for the first dramatization of an LSD trip, I think that part filmed in color."

"Right. Right. That's it. Boy, Liz is going to be happy to have you. It's supposed to be a surprise, but you're the guest of honor at the film festival. Your movie posters are in the lobby, and we're showing a whole bunch of Lurid Trance movies."

"My what? What movies?"

At the end of a long hedgerow of pale, metallic-colored leaves was the Shallow Creek Cinema, a small brick building with twin silver doors and a glass box office situated in the middle. Above it was a large marquee with bright bulbs illuminating the surface. In the graying afternoon light, the radiant promise of the cinema was a reprieve. I could finally see what was missing from the rest of Shallow Creek. I could almost imagine that all life contracted down to this place. How much longer could the cinema hold out against the blight?

Across the marquee in red plastic letteri were the words:

SHALLOW STARE, LURID TRANCE FILM FESTIVAL

James held the door for me. "Guess the girls—the women—are already here."

The lobby had a dim glow of red velvet and gold. The air was warm and smelt of popcorn, and I could hear the muffled words and music of a film in progress. The theater was much larger than it appeared from outside, with long walls of movie posters, and a velvet rope divider running down the middle of the carpeted floor lead to the theater doors ahead. James said, "I'm going to go find Liz and the girl women. Enjoy your posters. We couldn't put all of them up, but Liz is curating a complete record. The exhibition notes are here, together with the schedule of films."

Stacks of schedules and program notes for "Re-Imagined Movie Posters by Bridey Hatfield" covered the surface of a low table. Bridey and Elizabeth had curated the show and film series together. The films were all too familiar: part and parcel of Repressed Cheap Horror (and Teen, J. D., Beach Party, Blackploitation, Gore, Surreal) Trauma Syndrome canon, the films of my now intermittently reappearing childhood, and, presumably, the stuff of Bridey Hatfield's enigmatic world as well:

Santo: Vengeance of the Mummy
Roustabout
The Robot vs. The Aztec Mummy
Not of this Earth

Hillbillies in a Haunted House
Panic in the Year Zero
The Man from Planet X
The Brain Eaters

Night of the Blood Beast
Horror of Party Beach
Archangel
Hot Rods to Hell
Tales of the Gimli Hospital
Gidget Goes Hawaiian
Goliath and the Vampires
How to Stuff a Wild Bikini
They Saved Hitler's Brain
Hootenanny Hoot
House on the Haunted Hill
Hot Rod Hullaballoo
House
Jesse James Meets Frankenstein's Daughter
Kissin' Cousins
Viva Los Vegas
Mesa of Lost Women

Muscle Beach Party
The Mysterians
I Was a Teenage Frankenstein
I Was a Teenage Werewolf
Atom Age Vampire
The Human Vapor
The Horror Chamber of Doctor Faustus
Twenty Million Miles to Earth
The Angry Red Planet
The Brainiac

Terror from The Year Zero
Night of the Blood Beast
Curse of the Crying Woman
Detour
The Frozen Dead
Planet of the Vampires
The Tingler
I Walked with a Zombie
Santo vs. The Evil Brain
Fantomas
The Gamma People
Attack of the Crab Monsters
The Invisible Boy
Twenty Million Miles to Earth

The Angry Red Planet
The Incredible Shrinking Man
The Horror Chamber of
Doctor Faustus
The H-Man
The Human Vapor
Riot in Cell Block 11
Shock Corridor
The H-Man
Queen of Outer Space
The Invisible Boy

Jailhouse Rock
The Heart of the World
The Creeping Unknown

I lost myself in the titles. Finally, I came around and picked up the exhibition notes with the same flutter of recognition. A long time ago I had steroid shots in my spine to treat a back injury and felt a similar chill spread through me, followed by a warm, numb spell that seemed to mean a homecoming, a dread and a wonder of release all at once.

Who is Bridey Hatfield?
Who Was I?

The Lurid Trance: Movie Poster Dreams and Abstractions

Part movie homage, part graphic experiment, the fifty prints in *The Lurid Trance* use the form of the movie poster as a metaphoric projective screen, and refractive lens. On it and through it, drawing influenced by mid-century noir, science fiction, horror and atomic modernism reimagines movies as biomorphic dream machines. Like films processed through an alien consciousness (that more and more may be our own), the posters establish and inhabit a liminal zone between the movie as artifact, and as dream, (like the refugee in-between state known in Spanish as *nepantla*). Rather than promotional or advertising images, these "movie posters" become documents and generators of dissonance, longing and mystery: the movies they herald are on show for one night only, and only in the theater of your (own) heart. The prints also map the wilderness of a childhood spent in movie theaters or lost in movie poster gaze, constructing counter-narratives to make sense of an often-inexplicable movie of a life. In the manner of early surrealist manifestos the titles bear a special poetry of hysteria and trance, often translated into Spanish, Italian or French as a kind of "making strange" strategy for the English language viewer/reader (like myself), and as a small tribute to the many Mexican, Italian, French and Canadian films that exemplify the spirit of the *The Lurid Trance*.

The Lurid Trance bracketed the movie-going experience. Before the credits rolled you would stare down at the ads all week in newspapers, or while standing in front of the movie theater, the posters for films currently showing facing the street, the coming attractions on the inner walls. You fell into the posters, the visual cacophony of screeching, shivering, flaming, exploding, dripping title letters, jostling for space in the distressed three foot by five-foot zone of panicked, screaming, fighting or erotically transfixed faces and bodies, writhing before flaming cities, rampaging monsters, looming, grasping, embracing.

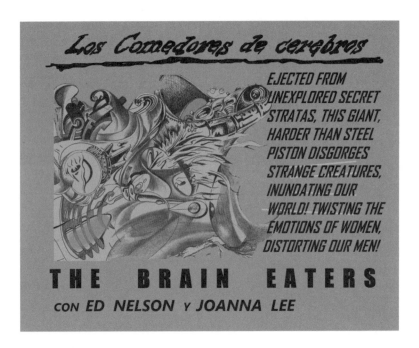

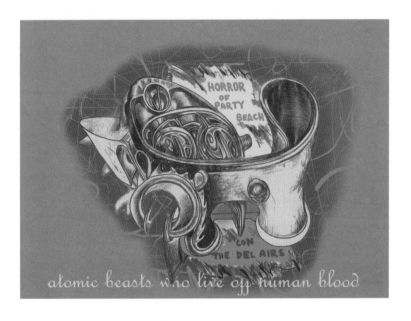

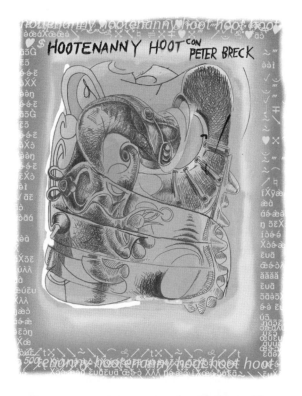

Where was James? I looked away from the posters, trembling. Where was James? I looked away from the posters, trembling. My body was a shining key that suddenly slid into the right lock. It turned. I backed away and wandered into a dark hall to the side, feeling my way along the velvet walls. I reached a door with light leaking from the gap beneath, and voices hidden beyond. I entered and found myself on the stage of a small black box theater. The house lights were bright and waiting and watching was an audience of perhaps forty people. On stage was James, the four fuck you women, three other men I didn't recognize, and a black woman with close cropped hair and a red dress, all seated around a table. The woman turned at the creak of the door and smiled when I came into view, waving me forward with a smile and urging me to take a seat. She said to the audience, "The last member of our panel has joined us. Please welcome our guest of honor, Bridey Hatfield." There was modest applause, and I took a seat beside the woman. James resumed speaking as she leaned in close and whispered, "Happy to meet you, Bridey."

"Same to you, Elizabeth."

"… and personally, I used to read Kafka with great interest and pleasure, until human-sized cockroaches started waking up next to me in bed. That's …"

The man at the end of table, a cadaverous man with deep set eyes and a white beard, said, "They're not cockroaches, James, they're gigantic Tardigrades."

There was a stir in the audience. Someone called out, "Mallum, could you explain what Tardigrades are again? Some of us arrived late."

The man named Mallum leaned forward and answered, "Tardigrades are microscopic bugs that live in skin and dust motes and just about anything. They are marvelously adaptable and virtually indestructible. They are popularly known as 'water bears' and are only about half a millimeter long, though they more closely resemble diminutive crabs or beetles with pointy feet. We've got them all over us, and around us, and in us, but they're too small to matter."

The man beside him, a large man with a glistening face and booming voice chortled, "Man, what you showed me looked more like some ugly ass centipede with high heels." He let off a rasping laugh but no one joined in. Elizabeth scowled. "A lot of people in town have encountered these creatures, Bubba. It's no joke."

"What we want to know," an audience member said, "is where they came from …"

Another person cut in: "… and how they got so freaking big, and how do we kill the suckers?!"

Many people were talking at once. There was fear and fury in the air. Elizabeth called for order and Mallum addressed the audience, his voice exuding a calm authority that settled the space.

"We have a theory." He motioned to the projection booth. "Could we show the first visual?"

The lights dimmed and the screen ignited with a power point image of the same Shallow Creek map that had been linked to my drawing, but with the addition of two red lines intersecting at one precise spot: the lighthouse.

"As you all know, one of the first reported sightings of the giant Tardigrades was at the top of my lighthouse, which is the intersection point of two signals emanating from two stations of the LIGO—that's Laser Interferometer Gravitational-Wave Observatory—in the U.S., the bottom two points of the triangle being the lab in Washington State, and in Louisiana. LIGO has leased out our lighthouse as the apex of the signal triangulation for the past six years, to stabilize calibration signals. I have just learned that LIGO has been conducting experiments trying to identify and reproduce where the laws of quantum physics pass into the classical, macro world, the world that we live in. The experiment wants to explore the possibility that macroscopic objects—the stuff of our world—can behave in quantum ways …"

"We talking about teleportation from entanglement of distant particles and time travel?" James asked.

Mallum held up his hands. "I don't know. Theoretically, yes. But this was far more modest. The experiment uses a millimeter-size membrane of silicon. It looks like a tiny trampoline. Can we see the next image?"

The screen filled with a drawing of a square of 'silicon substrate' supporting an inner area of "silicon nitride membrane." A red laser beam was striking the center membrane. In a graphic insert, a drawing of a Tardigrade—which did resemble a centipede in high heels—was vibrating atop an "oscillating membrane." Mallum explained that the laser could set the membrane vibrating at two different amplitudes simultaneously, creating the condition for quantum decoherence and collapse into a single amplitude: the fabled state of transition from the quantum to the macro world, with the microscopic Tardigrade along for the ride.

Elizabeth added, "And the quantum to macro decoherence middle ground strangely echoed in Bridey Hatfield's *Lurid Trance* "Nepantla" zone …"

"Never mind that!" Bubba protested, suddenly skittish as he toiled with his scarf, eyes scanning the theater. "It sounds like Mallum just said that the States are beaming us materialized interdimensional monsters, with the receiver in Jud's goddamn lighthouse!"

The audience roused again, so Elizabeth stood up and shouted "All right, everyone! Please! Calm down!"

Mallum sipped his water, entirely composed. I wanted to leave, but Elizabeth looked at me imploringly and touched my hand.

Mallum said, "This goes beyond 'interdimensional monsters,' I'm afraid. All of us know something is happening to Shallow Creek. We stir from dreamless sleep into waking trances. Our eyes are blank and light has forgotten all color. Barney's junkyard is crammed with machines no one can recognize, and the fairground boasts rides befitting torture, or transformation into things far worse than Tardigrades …"

"I just can't think straight anymore!" Someone called out.

"It's like I was saying," James cut in, "how do we find our way when nothing seems real?"

"It's from the States! The fucking President!" someone screamed

"No. It's bigger than that." James said. 'It's multiverses colliding, time travel and movies blurring into reality. Look at the intrusion of alien machines and the re-imagining of movies in the posters outside. Who hasn't turned a corner in town and not run into something from those posters and been incapable of explaining it, and then, later in the day, unable to even remember happened? I mean, who the hell is THE MAN WITH NO FACE?!"

The audience rooted in tribute and rage.

Elizabeth nodded and waited for silence. "That's what has brought us all here today, the Shallow Stare, Lurid Trance exhibit, and the visionary message of our special guest, Bridey Hatfield. Forty years ago, Bridey saw what would become of Shallow Creek. He recognized the warnings, portents and images that would haunt our town and challenge our way of life, our sanity and our very lives. Bridey saw the quantum Tardigrades, the alien machines in the junkyard, and the echoes of the future in the films of the past. I bring you, Bridey Hatfield."

I stood up, dazed. Mixed between the applause were fragmented shouts and screams. One after another yelled, "There's Tardigrades here! I felt one crawling on my leg!" "Here! They're over here!"

I remembered the movie, *The Tingler*, or maybe Bridey Hatfield did. Guided by something bottomless and far bigger than me I called out to the room, "I want everyone to stop. Take a deep breath. And

SCREAM

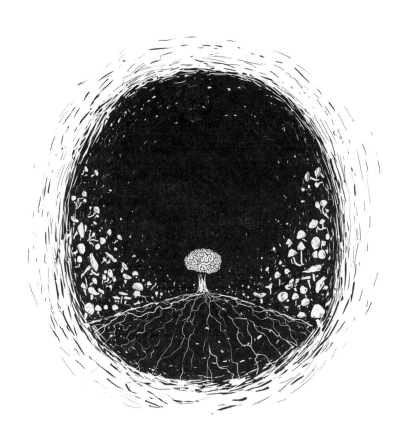

WE LIVE IN DIRT
by Ian Steadman

Miles was emptying the food scraps into the compost bin when he saw Natalie pull up in her Mini. *It looks like a child's car*, he told himself, whacking the plastic bucket with the heel of his hand to dislodge a particularly tacky piece of banana skin. *She's a young woman now, she should be driving an appropriate vehicle, not this … toy.* Her visits always raised his blood pressure, even when she was trying to be nice. The banana still wouldn't budge, so with a tut he dipped his fingers into the bucket and scooped it out, flicking it into the compost with a wet *plop*. The slugs and red wrigglers could fight over that one.

Wiping his fingers on his dressing gown, then wiping the dressing gown with his palm as he realised he'd left a slimy trail down its faux-velvet front, Miles ambled back indoors. He knew she would give him a hard time for emptying the food scraps in his pyjamas again. Last time he'd pointed out that he wasn't always in pyjamas, sometimes it was just his dressing gown and Y-fronts—but that hadn't helped. Neither had his protestations when she'd shown him the dirty brown holes worn in his slippers by the daily trudge up the path. Looking down, he could see a yellow, horn-like nail protruding from the tip of the right one. Well, maybe she had a point there.

Pushing open the back door, he dropped the bucket into the sink and ran some water over his hands. Realising that he'd forgotten to remove the towels from the dryer, he dried them on his dressing gown.

She was taking an age coming in, and for a moment he wondered if he'd got it all wrong. Maybe it wasn't Natalie's car—these mix-ups were happening more often, he'd noticed, as if his brain was slipping loose from its moorings. It worried him that he might be losing his mind, that his understanding of the world was fractured by a series of cracks, and those cracks were widening. Lord knows his job was hard enough already, but if they discovered the mayor was drooling into his soft-boiled eggs …

There was a click as the front door unlatched, and he heard footsteps on the parquet floor in the hall.

'Hi Dad! I would have called but I'm running late. I've brought you something for your tea tonight, or maybe lunch, I don't know, so I thought I'd just—'

Natalie's monologue stopped mid-breath as she surveyed the

dressing gown, the stained, threadbare slippers, and finally the food bucket upended in the sink. In her hand she held a wicker basket, which she ceased swinging abruptly.

'Oh, for God's sake. I've told you before, Dad—you can't be wandering outside in your pyjamas for all and sundry to see. What would the press say if they got wind of it? Or half the city council? For heaven's sake. You have to think of your standing in town—Is that your toenail?'

Her gaze had wandered down to his feet, and on cue Miles wiggled his big toe.

'Yes. Yes, I believe it is.'

'Oh Dad. I'll get you a new pair for your birthday. But today, I've brought you these.'

She lifted the basket onto the worktop and pulled aside the checked tea towel. For a brief moment Miles thought it was a severed head, and his fears for his sanity—and his daughter's—resurfaced. But it was too pale, and too … well, *round*. A big, spongy football, then. Only there were some mushrooms scattered around it, ceps by the look of them, and a couple of waxy yellow chanterelles, their caps like half-digested miniature sponge cakes.

'Ah, you've been foraging! A puffball, how delightful.'

Natalie squinted as if he'd said something ridiculous or unfathomable. It was a look he'd grown used to over the last twenty years.

'Yes, of course I've been foraging—that's what we've been talking about, isn't it? Keep up, Dad. Now, you know what to do with these, I'm sure. The chanterelles need soaking in milk for ten minutes or so, and the ceps will need a good clean, but otherwise you're—'

'Yes, yes, I was picking mushrooms in those woods before you were born. I know what to do with a cep or a … a …'

'Chanterelle, Dad.'

'Exactly, so don't you worry about me. I must say, though, that's the biggest puffball I've ever seen. I remember finding them when I was a kid, but they were never larger than a fist, or maybe a cantaloupe; but my word, this one's a beauty.'

'It was Simone at work who told me where to go. I told her I'd been shrooming around the lower edge of the woods and she said no, not there, you need to go to the mouth of the old mine. It's the dark, or the damp, or something. Anyway, she was right. There they were, right next to the entrance: clusters of ceps, field mushrooms and morels too. Then I saw this bad boy sitting there, almost glowing in the dark. I figured it would do you for a couple of meals at least.'

Miles frowned. He didn't like the thought of his daughter poking around that old mine, not with what Freddy told him about all the noises out there at night, and that Cody Sanders, who'd fallen through an access shaft and almost died. Even more than that, it brought back memories of the Bell girl and the police investigation back in the eighties—an investigation that had very nearly put an end to his political ambitions. He'd handed over a great deal of money to make that particular ghost disappear, and the last thing he needed was Natalie stumbling over it. Nor did he need her—or anyone else—to discover the other disused mines full of Krinkles Crunch, or the deal he'd struck to bury the deadly cereal in exchange for illicit campaign donations.

'Listen, sweetheart, do you really think you should—'

'I don't have time to stay and chat today, sorry. Shouldn't have taken this long really, but I thought you should have them fresh, maybe a late breakfast or something. Up to you what you do with them.' She was walking back up the hallway, her fading words punctuated by her heels on the floor. 'Enjoy them, though, won't you? And call me sometime about next weekend, I think Saturday would be best. Oh, and Dad? Change out of that tatty old gown, will you? Before someone sees you …'

The door slammed.

Miles teetered for a moment, his head spinning. It was often like this when Natalie visited, his daughter whipping through the house like a tornado, leaving him stunned and disorientated in her wake. He took a deep breath and checked his pulse. Not too bad—a little high. Maybe a chamomile tea before showering and donning his robes, then. There was a function at the church today, and he was expected to attend in all his mayoral finery.

When he lifted the puffball it was heavier than he expected and he was at a loss for what to do with it. Usually he'd fry up a thick wedge, like a steak, but one this size wouldn't fit in his pan. In fact, looking at it up close, it wouldn't even fit in the fridge.

Picking out his longest carving knife, he steadied it on the wooden worktop and began to saw through it, making the cut as close to the middle as he could. Once it was halved he could squeeze it into the fridge between the eggs and butter. Halfway through, the knife hit something hard. He tried again, but was faced with the same result—there was definitely something solid in the middle of the puffball. Puzzled, he pulled the knife out and slid his fingers into the incision. The flesh of the puffball was cool and moist, like a giant chilled marshmallow, and the sensation triggered an involuntary shudder in his shoulders. His fingertips struck a solid object that felt like plastic. Pulling his hands apart, he ripped the ball in two, the flesh splitting with a slight sucking noise.

In the middle of the mangled puffball was a VHS tape. Between the two spindles, peeling away from the surface and spotted with mould, was a white sticker. The last thing Miles remembered before passing out was the crude message, scrawled in thick black marker: I'VE BEEN WATCHING.

***

Two days later, after another meeting about proposed zoning changes opposite the library, Miles changed into his rambling gear, laced his thick-soled hiking boots, and headed out the door, the VHS tape buried deep inside his rucksack. He was almost at the edge of the forest when it occurred to him that he should have brought some food or water, but it was too late to turn back. The light was already blushing orange and only one or two hours of daylight remained. He could always use the light on his mobile, if he remembered how to turn it on.

He didn't need a map to find the mine. Everyone in town knew about it, of course, but he knew better than most. Back when Julia Bell disappeared they'd all participated in the search, night after night, thrashing the bracken for the slightest sign of her. A couple of kids had seen her walking around the fringes of the forest on the day she disappeared—and then she'd vanished from the earth. They never found so much as a footprint, never mind a shoe, or a foot. She was gone.

He knew of her, though. For the final weeks before her disappearance, Miles had enjoyed the briefest of flings with the girl. He'd been in his mid-twenties and she was only eighteen, so they were wary of scandal—they kept it all hush-hush, behind closed doors. She'd had a high school boyfriend too, but Miles had been her 'fancy man'. He'd liked that phrase, and it had stuck with him all these years. He couldn't recall another instance in his life when anyone referred to him as 'fancy'.

Snapping a dry branch from an oak, he swished it through the ferns as he soldiered on, watching with childish glee as the delicate tips severed and fell to the dirt. He certainly didn't feel fancy now, but he imagined that was often the case. Life had a way of fraying your edges.

It hadn't taken long for the police to arrive. Clearly their clandestine liaisons hadn't been as secret as they'd thought. Not only had his neighbour pointed a finger at him, but they'd reported hearing raised voices the day before her disappearance, an argument spilling from his one-bedroom flat into the street. He couldn't remember the details, but it had involved the boyfriend, her refusal to let him go. He'd wondered in that moment if the boy was being cuckolded, or if he himself was being played for a fool. He'd called her 'whore' and pushed and pulled, but she had finally escaped, running and crying, into the street. The revelation had been enough. He'd been cuffed and driven to the station.

Shaking his head, Miles whipped the foliage so hard that the branch snapped, the broken end dangling loose. Frustrated, he hurled it into the brush with a grunt. He knew that venturing out here would bring it all back, but he'd thought he could handle it. Apparently, he was deluding himself. Again. The light was beginning to dim, the trees bleeding colour as the day drained away. He should arrive at the mine soon, but he couldn't dally. Night was closing in fast.

He'd explained about the argument to the detectives who'd questioned him. No law had been broken, had it? But still, he'd felt sickened by the way they regarded him, their eyes probing, judging. So many memories had fallen away, but not that one. It was etched far deeper than the others. He was in that sad, boxy room for only three hours before his release—but it had felt like years.

And during those three hours, not once did he confess the truth of his last encounter with Julia Bell, several hours after the kids spied her entering the woods.

The rucksack shifted on his back and the corner of the VHS tape dug into his spine, snapping him out of it. When he'd come around two days ago, sprawled on the kitchen floor in his shabby dressing gown, it had taken him a moment to remember what had happened. He'd been lucky not to land on the knife, or smash his head open. All in all, he was remarkably unscathed. Then he had seen the two halves of the puffball, ripped apart like a Halloween mask, and the black cassette nested inside. It had all come rushing back and he'd vomited into the sink.

He'd still made it to the church, naturally—such official functions paid the bills—but he'd excused himself shortly afterwards and had spent the afternoon searching through drawers and cupboards for his old VHS player. He hadn't seen it for several years, but knew he wouldn't have thrown it away. He held on to everything, just in case— it was another quirk that Natalie harangued him about whenever the opportunity arose. But it also meant that he'd buried the SCART cable and crackly headphones deep in the cluttered drawers in the garage, or, better yet, in the cobwebbed recesses of the attic. She'd never find them there, he thought, and the knowledge that they remained safe under his roof afforded a sense of security. One less piece of the past gone forever.

Only, the VHS player had vanished. After hours of scrabbling through boxes of mildewed school photos and other damp ephemera—a blond wig he once wore to a party, a portable radio tuned to a station that no longer existed, a Rubik's cube—he had to admit defeat. Without the machine, he'd never know what was on the tape, not unless he found a store in town that still sold ancient video recorders. He'd heard of folk that converted tape to DVD, but how would he stop them from watching the tape while they did it … no, it was impossible. Until he knew what was on the tape, it simply couldn't leave his possession.

He'd slumped in a chair, clutching the cassette, staring at the label and the words 'I'VE BEEN WATCHING' while he finished a bottle of disgusting cinnamon-flavoured vodka that someone had left behind last Christmas. He'd woken in the dark, his head pounding and his lips tingling as if he'd been chewing on bark.

Pushing through a stand of saplings abutting the entrance of the mine, the taste of that vodka came back to him, sweet and cloying like the scent of pine. Although he hadn't watched the tape, the handwritten label was enough. Somebody knew something. It riled him that he'd never seen this day coming, never put contingencies in place. And here he was, soon to be exposed, and the only link he had was that damned puffball. Someone had planted the tape for his daughter to find—maybe her friend, Simone. Maybe they were sending him a message. There was no choice but to follow the call.

As the trees thinned out he could finally see the mouth of the mine, gaping wide and empty. There were theories that Julia Bell had plummeted down an old shaft, or fallen victim to one of Shallow Creek's landslips, when the ground reclaimed its hollow bays. Miles knew otherwise, but they were feasible explanations. In time, he'd almost come to believe them himself.

At the entrance to the mine the rotting leaves were trodden flat, and as he strained to see inside he wondered just how many people visited this place to pick mushrooms. From a nearby thicket the old narrow-gauge tracks emerged, barely visible amid the fallen leaves and decomposing slivers of bark. The wooden sleepers had long since rotted away, their dark stains entrenched in the dirt. In the centre he could see a footprint. Stepping over a stump, black and splintered, he stuck his head into the open mouth.

'Hello? Anyone here?'

He'd expected an echo but his voice was muffled by pillows of moist earth. He doubted his words had travelled further than a few metres.

'Hello!' he shouted, projecting as best he could. 'I'm coming in.'

Pushing aside the foliage above the entrance, he ducked and stepped inside. Immediately the temperature dropped, and he was reminded of the meat locker in the store he'd stacked shelves at back in the seventies. He was a young man then, before any of this happened: the Bell girl, the cover-up, Candace leaving him, and now the VHS tape. He wondered how his younger self would have coped, if he might have done better with the cards fate dealt. Probably not.

Miles crept forward with hunched shoulders, feet barely shuffling more than an inch at a time. The roughly hewn ceiling was a few feet above his head yet he had an innate sense of it close to his scalp, biding its time before cracking his skull open. Rummaging in his pocket, he removed his mobile phone and fumbled for the flashlight app.

When it finally sparked into life he almost dropped the damn thing. The light was stark but pale, stretching no more than a few metres into the blackness. Surrounding him, however, were hundreds— no, thousands—of fungi, branching from the walls in brackets the size of dinner plates, sprouting from gaps between clusters of pale brown caps no bigger than a thumbnail. He recognised ceps like the ones Natalie brought him, and field mushrooms spread like brown umbrellas, and morelles dark and pitted like rotted honeycomb. Puffballs too, although none as big as the one he'd found the video tape in. At the edge of the beam of light, disappearing into the darkness, he thought he saw a cauliflower fungus the size and shape of a human brain.

Shining the light closer, he could see the fungi were all connected by fine white threads which stretched across the soil like hair, or a spider's web. It was everywhere—above his head, across the walls, tangled around the rails beneath his feet. Most of it seemed firmly rooted in the dirt, but here and there he could see loose ends, twitching in the breeze blowing in from outside.

'Oh my …'

Miles shrugged his rucksack from his back and dropped to his knees. With his fingertips he traced the network of threads as they branched and expanded, always splitting and spreading, splitting and spreading, blanketing the entire surface like a mat. It felt cold and firm and slightly springy, suggesting layers upon layers of tendrils like an organic carpet.

He tried to stand, but couldn't. His fingers were glued to the ground.

No matter how hard he tugged and pulled they would not budge or break free. White lines snaked up his hands, encircling his wrists, pulling him towards to the soil. His knees were wreathed in webs now too, stretching and winding, cocooning him in a mass of pale threads. He tried to scream and felt them worm between his lips, tickling his throat as they wriggled their way inside him, a sudden squirm in his stomach, alien and unwelcome; and then nothing at all.

***

Officer Janet Lopez grabbed herself a cup of coffee from the machine and swiped a donut from the meeting room on the way to her desk. The VHS tape—or 'Exhibit A', or whatever the hell she was supposed to call it—was wedged under her armpit. She didn't think it could be considered tampering with evidence, but once back at her seat she dropped it into a clear plastic bag, just in case. It never hurt to play things safe.

Not that there'd been a crime, as far as she could tell. When Mayor Woodrow had failed to turn up for work three days in a row they'd been called to investigate, but there was none of what Sheriff John liked to call 'foul play'. His house was a pigsty, but he *was* a bachelor, so Janet hadn't been all 'Shock! Horror!' about any of that. She thought he could have used a maid, but that wasn't a criminal offense.

When the daughter's hysterics had finally died down, she'd mentioned how the Mayor had mumbled about the mine, on and on ever since she'd picked some mushrooms there a couple of days previous. Janet thought it was likely the old man dropped dead from a poisoned shroom, knocked off by his daughter's stupidity, but she didn't say anything.

They'd found the old man's backpack down in the mine, but nothing else. No body, no foul. But there was a strange mass of mushrooms inside the entrance—all gnarled and yellow looking— and the backpack, with nothing but a big black video cassette hidden inside.

It was Sheriff John who'd suggested she watch the tape. He'd brought in a clunky old machine from home and spent twenty minutes cursing and punching the wall as he tried to wire it to the flat screen TV. But finally he managed it, and she'd blocked out her diary and sat for an hour, watching and waiting, hoping to uncover the truth.

Turns out it was an episode of some old TV show called *Krinkles in Town*, but she wasn't paying much attention—had people actually watched this shit? Krinkles the Clown. Really? She knew the shows on her planner weren't highbrow, but they were better than this.

As for how it related to the mayor's disappearance, she hadn't a clue. Maybe he was a fan of the Clown. He was certainly odd enough—both Mayor *and* Clown.

It was only when she started to seal the bag that Janet noticed something stuck in one of the spindles. Digging the object out with the tip of her nail, she held it up to the light. Damn. Looked like a mushroom, of all things. She dropped it into the waste bin. Cramming the rest of the donut into her mouth, she sealed the bag.

The daughter wasn't the only one who had mentioned the mine recently—it seemed more and more people were foraging there.

Maybe, once her shift was over, she'd make a stop there too, grab herself a funky-looking mushroom. If they weren't trippy, she'd eat her badge.

KNOCK, KNOCK, KNUCKLE BONE

by Allyson Kersel

I know as well as anyone that when the tide goes out, the estuary pukes up the town's secrets. Each cautious step, laced with the dreary squelch of gritty foam, releases the briny stink of decay and putrid weed; tiny bones and scraps of shell crunch underfoot and, coy beneath an inch of water, the algae-covered skulls of mooring buoys peep up through the mud as I scour the estuary for flotsam.

My eyes are sharp enough to catch the gleam of objects caught up in rippled sand or webbed beneath a curly head of bladderwrack. Here, the desiccated corpse of a herring gull, tangled and splintered at the tide line; there, the ice pick glimmer of a fisherman's lure. Beer cans, bottle caps, a pair of sunglasses, a set of keys—all of these can be found lodged in the gullet of Shallow Creek where they will either be retched immediately out to sea, or remain for years to rust and rot and become the homes of mud crabs and worms.

Further down the river mouth, towards the humped backs of the sandy deltas and silver crested rocks at the foot of the lighthouse, stoops the bowed figure of Angus Runt, dredging the early morning mud for clams. I wave to be polite but receive nothing in response save a reticent nod, so I lower my eyes to the ground and resume my search. Already, the sun is high and damp heat reeks from the riverbed. I wipe my forehead, relieved that I got up early to catch low tide, rather than waiting for the suffocating afternoon haze when the estuary sinks into an oasis for mosquitoes.

It's rich pickings today. I've been searching for half an hour and have already found several items of interest, a mermaid's purse and the fragile, lace-like skeleton of a dogfish among the best. I place the objects carefully into my bucket, and continue my search.

I'm making up for lost time over the summer vacation. This is my last chance, and what I want to do is capture the town—its history, blood, bones, and secrets.

I've called my project "Dissection of Shallow Creek", and every time I think about it, I shiver with morbid pride, knowing that I'm stripping back the town's skin, laying its organs bare. It's a good concept. The problem is tying it all together in some meaningful way. I've got all year to work on that though, so I'm not too worried. I can sense the narrative behind it—a gorgeous, weird fable of nightmare, memory, and maritime curses. For the first time in months, I am pleased with myself.

I take off my boots and toss them up to the dry sand beyond the tide line, the sickly squidge of mud emerging between my toes. A frail crab skitters sideways out of my shadow and, as I wade further out, a flurry of silt marks the frantic departure of a flounder. The tides have been unusually extreme this summer, sucked and pummelled by a large, lingering moon that haunts the sky. Though the deepest part scarcely reaches my knees, I can feel the urgent pull of its currents, begging me out to sea. Even beneath the mildest of moons, the river can be treacherous, with drownings in the estuary almost every year. In fact, there have been three this summer alone that happened, quiet and unnoticed, in full view of the school as I smoked and sulked behind the bleachers. Bathory caught me, confiscated the dope and hauled me to her office, where only the faint portent of wailing sirens and the approaching lick of blue police light saved me from further punishment.

I move slowly, keeping my balance against the demands of the current and a careful eye out for unexpected holes and ankle-snapping roots. Trailing weeds and discarded shreds of plastic brush my skin and rolling clusters of pebbles shift underfoot when I feel a sudden stab and sting of salt. I yank up my foot and topple into the water, barely managing to keep the bucket upright as I thrust out a hand behind me. Blood blooms and I grope around, searching for whatever it was that cut me, expecting to discover a shard of shell or broken glass, when my fingers touch upon rough metal. I fling it in my bucket and limp back to shore.

The cuts are bleeding profusely but I ignore them, more interested by far in examining my find to assess if it is of use to me. A corroded chain, the sharp edge of which sliced my skin, protrudes from the slimed neck of a bloated leather bag. The knotted cords at its lip are so swollen with salt and sea water that it takes almost ten minutes to pries it open.

The object within is repulsive, a faded figure in deep-set clay, two thumbprint eye sockets howling out from a featureless face; round-bellied and scarred with tide-worn whorls, sutured into something whole and unholy with rusted iron and knuckle-bone limbs. It rattles when I shake it and my teeth rear up in response.

"Anything good, Michael?" Runt's shadow falls across the back of my neck as I crouch in the sand, tracing bone with my finger.

"This," I reply, gesturing to the object. "Any idea what it is?" Runt will have an opinion and, whether informed or fabricated, it's bound to be interesting.

He leans upon the peeling handle of his dredger and scrutinises the clay figure.

"Corp-criadhach," he says decisively.

"A what now?"

"Gaelic, boy. Clay corpse. Witch's dolly. An unco wee poppet for mischief and revenge. Mould someone's image in clay and leave it somewhere secret where it can slowly wear thin and take them with it." Runt leans closer and squints. I feel the sour scratch of smoke-and-whiskey on my cheek. "Old. Dangerous. I'd leave it well alone if I were you."

"Yeah? Why's that?"

"You'll find out if you don't." He sighs, face folding like a leather pocket over a tooth-sparse mouth. "Course, what you should really be asking is, was it something the tide brought in, or something uncovered when the tide went out? That's the important question. What happened to your hand, son?"

"It's fine."

"Wash it. The water's clarty and thick with germs." He pronounces it "gerrums".

"Sure thing, Mr Runt." Seated in the mud, I flash him a grin, and he slouches away, dragging his dredger behind him. Caught in its steel teeth, small pebbles click and whirr, tumbling over each other, bones clacking on bone. People say that Runt is almost as mad as I am. Maybe he is.

I have found something very special today. I can feel it.

***

At school, in an empty classroom in the Art Department, I caress my find with cold water until it is free from grime. Using my thumbnail, I scrape away the furry beard of weed from its face and pick a rash of baby barnacles from its belly, flicking the scabs into the sink.

I examine the bones, wondering if they are human. How do you tell if bones are real?

Scratching my nail along a knuckle bone, I tip my finger with a crescent of dark brown muck which sloughs from the creature like skin. The sound makes me shiver, conjuring the acrid stench of brine, decay, and cold, dead iron.

The knuckle-leg pulses with something that feels alive but shouldn't be.

I wrap the poppet in a plastic bag and place it in my backpack.

On my way out of the school, at the end of the corridor along the side of the assembly hall, I run into Bathory.

"Hello, Mike," she says, surprised. "What are you doing here?"

"Hi, Miss. Um. I've just been up in the art department, working on my project."

Bathory nods, thin-lipped. At the end of term, she reluctantly gave me permission to use the school facilities. I think she was feeling sorry for me at the time—understandable, given the circumstances. Bathory never could decide whether I was a lout or a genius. My grades dictate misunderstood misfit, but common sense and my appalling attendance record suggests otherwise. I smirk. She looks like she regrets it now. No doubt she was looking forward to a summer of peaceful, light admin—a chance to burrow her snout deep into bureaucracy and root around without anyone to disturb her. But now, well, here I am. I grin.

"Oh, yes," she says with a sigh. "Very well. Did you turn the lights off after you finished up?"

"No, Miss. I left them on. And the tap too. With the plug in."

"Hm. Very funny, Mr Pollock. Just make sure you leave everything as you found it, OK?"

"Yes, Miss." I wince as the clay corpse seems to snarl and twist inside my backpack. Bathory stares at me.

"What was that?"

"Sorry, Miss. I skipped lunch."

Bathory sweeps off, a bashful wedge of paperwork stuffed under her arm. Teachers like me more than they should. They don't know why, but they do.

I let myself out of the school, and step out into a hot guff of concrete air from the parking lot. Shifting my backpack on my shoulders, I feel the bony jab of the corp-criadhach against my spine, and the sky dulls. Did it really move? It was probably me, and the strange snarling noise was caused by the bones rubbing together. Imagination, nothing more. A sea breeze threads up from the estuary, tepid and damp, thick as an eel. It winds around me, coiling in my lungs and, shifting the backpack again, I follow the thick breeze home.

***

I spend a long time that evening wondering about the clay corpse—who put it in the river and why? Realistically, it can't be that old. If it was, the leather pouch would be rotted through, and the clay itself would be even more degraded than it already is.

What was it Runt said? A poppet for mischief and revenge? He would know. Everyone says he's a vengeful man

A quick search online confirms that this is exactly what a corp-criadhach is. According to the stories, they were used by Scottish witches to defeat those who wronged them, often left under streams or dripping water. In theory, the wrongdoer's body would waste away as the clay dissolved.

So, who had gone to the trouble of dredging up old folklore from halfway across the world and why? Having spent considerable time making the dolly, why had they just tossed it in the estuary?

Perhaps it's time to make a social call on Mr Runt. For all I know, he could have dropped the damn thing in the estuary himself as a talking point for his boat tours. My mother has already started her night shift at the hospital. I'll go tomorrow morning before she gets home from work and I'll make sure she's asleep by the time I get back. I don't need her questions or concern.

***

Runt sleeps in a nest on the peeling floor of his tugboat; a rumpled sleeping bag like the shed skin of a snake; discarded packets of chips and chocolate, boxes of smokes, and, within pillow's reach, a bottle of Jack with only the dregs remaining, a cigarette bobbing in the murky liquid. A message in a bottle right there—a man forsaken; cigarettes and whiskey; the grimy ash-and-booze breath of morning despair. Until recently, he rented a nice house on the riverbank, but I guess business has been slow since those kids drowned.

He's drinking scalding, tin-tainted liquid out of a thermos, hunched on a stool next to the engine. A mosquito lands on his neck and bites, sucking for several seconds before he notices it. I picture its tiny shoulders heaving as it attempts to slake a desperate thirst. It will get nothing from him. Eventually, Runt slaps it, and the mosquito transforms into a gory smear beneath his jaw.

He offers me tea from the thermos, and I decline, knowing it will taste of nothing but ancient metal and the riverbed.

"You're here to pick my brains about the wee poppet you found, aye?" he mutters into a lit cigarette before I can speak.

"I—yeah. How did you know?"

He shrugs, purses his lips upon the cigarette and exhales through his nostrils. Runt smokes like he used to breathe—in out, in out, without pause.

"I gave you a nice wee titbit yesterday. Course, I knew you'd be back to hear the rest. You like to chew on things, Mike. The stories and that. You chew them over, then spit them out."

"Um. OK. I guess. So, are you going to tell me anything else?"

"What d'you want to hear?"

"Why would someone in Shallow Creek have made one of these things? And why would they leave it in the estuary?"

Runt will make something up if he doesn't know. He sucks on his cigarette, but it's gone out. He fumbles for a sodden box of matches and fails to relight it. He sighs, flicks the half-smoked cigarette overboard, and picks a wet frond of weed from his hair. Water puddles around his feet.

"It could've come from anywhere," he muses. "Washed down from the forest, choked up from the gorge, brought in on the tide. Now, I ken the estuary fairly well, aye, and I can tell you the now, it's been hiding down there for years, quiet as a wee mouse with the dogfish and eels."

"Very … evocative," I say. Runt never disappoints. "But if it's been down there for years, wouldn't it be more damaged?"

"Would it?" Runt pulls another cigarette out of a crumpled packet but again, as he tries to light it, it turns damp under his touch. "I don't know about that, lad. It's been down there since the town spread over the river, I can tell you that much."

"How do you know that?"

"After a certain point, your bones begin to know things. I know all the secrets now." The match suddenly flares, and Runt sucks the cigarette triumphantly. "Even your secrets, Mike."

"What can I say, I'm an open book." I glance up at the sky. The sun is climbing, bright and hot, draining the last misty coolness of the morning. "I'd better go now, Mr Runt. Thanks for answering my questions."

"Nay bother, Michael. It was grand chatting with you. Don't get many visitors these days, ken." He pokes his tongue into a gummy crevasse between his teeth. "Here, if you ever find my wallies - my false teeth—on your searches, gie them to me, aye?"

I halt, one foot on the pontoon, the other on the boat.

"I will," I tell him, my chest suddenly tight. "I'll see you later, Mr Runt."

"Take care, lad. Watch yourself." The old man turns away before I can reply, and as the sun illuminates the pallor of his face, I see the web of every vein in his neck, turgid and useless, and the congealing, black mess of the dead mosquito.

***

The clay corpse takes particularly well to charcoal and, holed up in the deserted Art Department, I sketch the corpse over and over again in smudged fragments of dead willow. The school is empty and quiet apart from the faint buzz of the ceiling lights. Every second yawns, dismaying the steady tick of the plastic clock on the wall, grasping at single moments for just a fraction too long. I love the silence and the halting lapse of time; it means that I am here, solid, real, and the world can eddy on without me.

It means that I am a rock or the stanchion of a bridge. I watch, implacable, as the river does its work.

The corp-criadhach leers at me and, for an instant, it looks almost cute, wide-eyed with a goofy grin. The ceiling lights flicker and crackle, and the corpse's mouth turns sharp, those deep, damp eyes betraying the gaping horror of the ocean floor. Thumbprint eyes; footprint eyes; sight, memory, truth—gouged out, gone. If it could, the thing would weep blood. I mix ink to the right shade and drizzle red onto the cheeks of my latest drawing. The eyes of the dolly in my hand glisten scarlet and I blink, momentarily horrified, until I realise that my stained fingers have smeared ink across the corpse's blurry face. Something thrashes in the corner of the room like the flicker of a troubled fish. My heart hammers; I need a break.

I go to the sink and wash the ink off my hands, shivering as the water turns rusty and my nostrils fill with the imagined iron tang of blood. As I scrub my hands, my nails catch dry frills of eczema. I dig harder, relishing the painful itch. After several minutes, I stop gouging and allow the stream of cool water to soothe my skin. The dolly watches, slumped, cadaverous, from the workbench.

***

That afternoon, bruised clouds roll in and humidity smothers the town. Something rumbles, guttural above the mountains, and finally, it starts to rain.

It rains as though the sky has been eviscerated. The creek bulges with the tide, flaring at the edges, silken with mud and thorny with debris. The river, pitching down from the mountains and crashing through the bony trees of the forest, is furious. It surges, round-backed, through the town, slicing rock and lore and ancient timber from the reclaimed floodplain with a single, feral bite.

The river is hungry. It needs to be fed.

We have stories of river Gods in Shallow Creek. River Gods, demons, ghosts, and cryptids, some passed down for millennia by the town's first inhabitants, others brought as baggage by those who came later. I stand beneath First Bridge, just outside the plaster and plywood cubes of the High School, watching the weaving humps of the river sweep by. In my backpack, the clay corpse claws and spits against my spine, and I wonder which one this storm creature is.

I hate that I can still see them, small heads bowed, playing in the mud on the far side of the bridge. I close my eyes, blind to everything but the death rattle of rain and the insidious hiss of the river washing them away forever.

***

As I work long into the night, the plaster walls grow sodden. Bathory thought I left hours ago and locked up as I hid in a closet, sealing myself inside this drowning ribcage of a building. The rain clatters on the roof like falling teeth, the poppet gleaming slyly under the fluorescent light. I sit at a dingy table in the art department, my project spread in front of me, sketching frantically as mildew seeps in bats and blood across the walls.

The dogfish skeleton shifts and shimmers and, tricking my eyes, something small—an ocean tadpole—writhes inside the mermaid's purse.

The clay corpse watches, a smile playing upon its lipless face. Every now and then, I swear it growls, a guttural hiss rumbling from its belly, but I know it's just the buzz of the strip lighting.

The eczema on my hands is getting worse and itches unbearably. I try not to dig at it, smearing my skin liberally with medicated cream, but as the hours scrape by, I find my nails buried in my flesh. My fingers bleed rusty streaks on my page as I draw but it doesn't matter. That's art. Flesh and blood; eaten up by my own charcoal. My work is good - we're onto something. The poppet smirks, and I smirk back.

The light dips and the poppet winks. I wink in return. I hear something knock, an air bubble inside the pipes.

I get up to use the bathroom and, standing at the sink, I'm horrified to see the state of my hands, scaly and raw; swollen and painful as threaded skin sloughs away. Something oozes down the walls behind me, a creeping stain of briny liquid. The floors are soaked and the place reeks of seaweed. I rub my eyes. What's happening here?

I hear something shuffle in the corridor outside.

"The janitor," I mutter to myself. "Just the janitor."

But the school has been empty and locked for hours.

It's a damp and dragging sound, like that of a limping figure trailing a web of heavy weeds.

I'm imagining things. I must be. I clench my fists and my scabbed hands crack, blood beading like tears on my knuckles.

"You're being stupid," I tell my reflection. "There's nothing there." But in the corner of my eye, beneath one of the half-closed cubicle doors, I see the ragged flash of a skeletal dogfish disappear behind a trash can. I lurch backwards, tripping over my sneakers.

"OK, OK," I say shakily. "You just need a break. It's late. You need to sleep."

The dogfish hisses across the linoleum, spraying across a mist of brackish water. Inch by inch, the pool on the floor deepens, water gushing from the sinks and cisterns as the drains choke up the ocean.

I run, blindly slamming the bathroom door behind me. I hear bone splinter and don't look back to see the shards of the dogfish broken on the tiles. There's a hammer on the floor next to a fire extinguisher, and a plaster-dusted pile of nails abandoned by maintenance. I seize the hammer and sprint towards the exit. A strange, slouching shape appears up ahead, and I swerve into a closet, shutting myself in, clutching the hammer, my breath rasping from my lungs.

A cold drip trickles down my neck.

Something damp soaks through my sneakers.

A child's voice whispers in my ear, a sound that stops the blood in my veins, followed by a tiny tap, knuckle bones rapping on sodden wood.

I sink to the floor.

Small heads, bowed, playing castles in the mud; I'm behind the bleachers, smoking weed and watching the rapid swell of waves along the river. I knew what was coming; I knew what the river could do. It had been raining all afternoon, and the water was rising. The river was crashing down from the mountains, through the rock and bone and petrified wood, and I knew it would burst its banks before long. They were too close to the edge, especially the little one. He was sailing mussel boats in the shallows.

I should have shouted. I should have told them to go home.

Instead, I watched, horrified, fascinated, as the tide rose and trapped them.

Runt, securing mooring lines in the bay behind the deltas, heard them screaming and rowed towards their voices.

But all I did was watch and roll another joint. It didn't feel real. There was nothing I could do.

Was there?

The tide is rising as I crouch inside the cupboard, lapping at my feet. Knock-knock. Knock-knock. I can hear them. The ocean sloshes against battered paint tins and empty bottles of disinfectant. A cardboard box of toilet roll dissolves and the sodden clumps of paper float in ghostly islands.

Knock-knock … Knock-knock …

I'm sitting in deep mud and sand now, clutching my head as fronds of weed and fishing line knot around my legs.

He almost made it back. The kids almost made it home. Almost.

But almost was not enough; the boat capsized, caught by one edge of a twisting wave. It came to rest against a jutting rock, undercut and perilous, where the panicked knocking from beneath the wooden boards took an eternity to slow and cease. By this time the bridge was drenched in blue light and sirens howled, announcing the shipwreck. Bathory led me away from the scene, appalled by what I had just witnessed.

Knock-knock, the water rises. I stand up and pin myself against the wall. I can feel it watching me, the clay corpse. It's been there the whole time, waiting. I knew Angus Runt was a vengeful man.

The water is at my knees now, surging through the cracks in the door. I realise now what the poppet is, a sentinel, placating the battle between river and sea. And sometimes a sentinel requires sacrifice. Something hard and spiny tugs at my leg, dragging me down, deeper and deeper. The linoleum floor is shifting silt and the walls dissolve to waterlogged clay. I clutch futile fistfuls of it, nails, teeth, anything that might prevent me becoming the boy who drowned in a closet, but it drags me further, down and down.

Down and down until I realise I'm floating.

The moon wavers above me, as innocuous as looking up through a glass coffee table, but it's all I can do not to scream.

If I scream, I'm dead.

My lungs burn; my chest is caving inwards and outwards at the same time. I feel the pressure of the last vestiges of oxygen inside me as my ribs creak and buckle, ready to snap. Knock-knock. I try one final, desperate kick and force my way to the surface, clawing my way up the shelves. Somehow, I retrieve the hammer.

The corp-criadhach slumps on a dripping, plywood shelf, eyeing me with its eerie grin, and my head spins as I haul oxygen back into my lungs. I lurch forwards, hammer in hand, and smash the leering thing to pieces.

Shards of clay and bone fly past my face, glimmering in the moonlight, peppering the muddy walls as I catch sight of a pearly strew of tiny teeth.

I pick one up. It rests in my hand, innocent, harmless, a childhood memory so fierce that I poke my tongue around my own mouth, searching for a gap. Horrified, I fling the tooth away, freezing as I hear the shick-shick slip and slide of the clay creature behind me.

The knocking starts again, and I know it will be the last thing I ever hear.

I clutch the hammer to my chest as something cold and wet grips me by the ankle and starts to pull. A shadow falls, blocking the insipid gleam of the moon across the paint tins, and everything is smudged to darkness, but not before I see, illuminated in the fading light, the fleshy plastic plate and bright, sharp incisors of Angus Runt's false teeth.

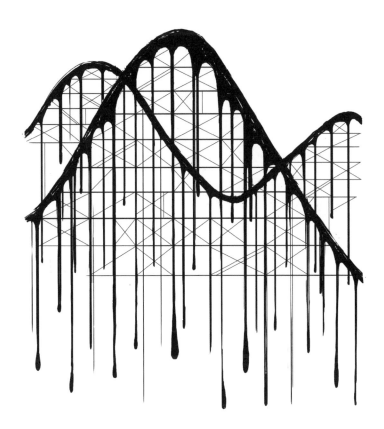

PENTAMETER

by David Hartley

I think, perhaps, maybe, I'm not too sure;
the sea has more waves on it than normal.
Crests of white, too many to count. And gulls,
riding thermals, the likes they've never felt.
Not sure, Molly, if this says change is here,
or trouble. I hold the walkie-talkie
and think of William. Should I tell him this?
No. He will see it soon enough I'm sure,
and if I am needed, he will tell me.
Ships that avoid us seem further off too;
specks on an agitated horizon.
Our lighthouse must be no more than a star.
  A winking warning of consternation,
  a pinprick lost from its constellation.

Today, Runt told me I was dead to him
because restless waves don't yield too much fish.
I came to you, Molly, and cried it out,
but your eyes told me; take it on the chin.
Without you my love, I am far too weak,
It's at times like this I'm so glad you stayed.
The walkie-talkie crackles into life:
"William to Jud. Forest tonight, full works.
Flush out them new kids, send them home weeping."
I count the pentameter on fingers,
it's perfect and I flick my hands in glee.
I press the button twice, confirm the job.
  That night I stalk Silverpine, ghoul of trees.
  Entrails and wicker, teens screaming on knees.

I know that I am Jud, lighthouse keeper
and once I was a husband, a lover.
But that's a zapped-out time, removed, no more.
I know it happened, you are proof, Molly,
and so is William. But those times are gone.
New times come each day and night, but I cope.
I play the bogeyman of Shallow Creek,

and blink-blink away ships that don't belong.
That's it. My life. In between I whittle
and read the collected works of Shakespeare.
I like the sonnets and soliloquies,
They make my voice feel right; a sense of good.
>   There's comfort in these rhythms, there is peace,
>   for a man with a once-life, now deceased.

A knock at the lighthouse door. It wakes me.
The girl lets herself in. Sian Runt. Fifteen.
"Hey, Jud? It is Jud, isn't it? Can I come in? It's ok, it's just me; Dad's out on his boat.
Wow, I like your place, it's so cute. Sorry, were you asleep?"
She doesn't speak the rhythm, I am lost;
too many words, questions, body language.
I shrink back, turn away. Why won't she leave?
"I've always wanted to see in here, lighthouses are so cool. Can I go up to the top?"
I leap up, block her way, manage a "No!"
Sian Runt is not afraid, she shrugs and smiles.
She sits down. I do not know why she's here.
She keeps talking but I tune out her voice,
wait for our home to become mine again.
>   I sprawl back on our steps and think of you.
>   My Molly, who always knew what to do.

Sian picks up a model, a highland cow.
I whittled it from driftwood just last week.
"Too cute," she says, and then she starts to cry.
I knew the restless sea meant something bad,
and here it is. Should I touch her? Soothe her?
I don't know how it works. I am useless.
Is she scared, or—"I'm sorry, sorry. Bursting in here, crying all over your beautiful
lighthouse. It's just—fuck him! You know? Fuck him to hell! Sorry. It's my Dad, being
a total prick. You know what he's like."
Among her words I hear mention of Runt,
her father, the boatman, with spittle eyes.
He thinks I am a pervert, a sex pest;
he will kill me if he knows she is here.
I want her to leave. Why won't she just leave?
>   She is beauty inside my ugly home
>   She is kelp, silver scales, puffs of sea-foam.

She stops her tears and laughs. I can't keep up.
Her smile is sudden, a leaping dolphin.
"You don't say much, do you? That's ok, though. I'm sick of voices. Dad shouting, mum whining, me screaming. I expect you hear it all, even up here. Dad doesn't like you much. Says you should still be in Arkady. Were you in Arkady?"
"Arkady," I say, "yes." The asylum,
where old Jud was zapped into this shadow.
"Fuck's sake. Creepy. Was it fucking awful?"
I thrill at her pentameter and smile.
She must think I liked Arkady. Not true.
"Ooh, tell me everything. I love shit like this. I mean, if that's OK?"
It's not. Don't want to. I hated that place,
but I can't find words, her stare is intense,
then pop: the walkie-talkie comes to life,

       it's behind where she sits, can't get to it,

       I panic, freak out, she should not hear this.

"William to Jud. The fairground, after hours.
That ride, the new one. It's not been approved.
I want those contractors gone. Scare them good."
Sian's face changes and I cannot read it,
but she stands up and steps towards the door.
"Who was that?" she asks. Her mouth is smiling,
but her words crack, shells under heavy feet.
"William Shakespeare. It's time you went home now."
"Shakespeare? Okay … It's fine, I'm going and going. I'm sorry to disturb … whatever it is you've got going on here. Enjoy the fairground. See you."
She dances out like water escaping
and dust motes whirl, lamenting loss of her.
The room feels lighter somehow, more joyous.

       The bard breaks the spell; "Did you get that, Jud?"

       I press the button twice, confirm the job.

I take a bag of bones to the fairground.
High-vis workmen clank away at the ride.
The Screamer. Too shiny for Shallow Creek,
so says William. An eye sore for sore eyes.
I make skulls appear, then vanish them away.
I make the sounds of orphan kids laughing,

and playing Ring-o-Roses in the dark.
I smear bloodied words on safety signage,
I loom atop looped track, axes aloft.
With a boom, the lights go out, torches fail,
my pentameter voice says *dismantle*,
be gone, go home. This place is not for you.

> There is not a man left by three am,
> the clowns of the fairground will smile again.

I take the long way back to the lighthouse;
shoreline, sand dunes and cliffs. The moon is weak,
but our sweeping light catches worsened waves,
which crash at the rocks in angry vengeance.
They will look to me, Molly, for reasons,
like I'm some Poseidon, salt in my blood,
or King Lear with a storm to rage against.
But I'm just Jud; I'm nothing and no-one,
a shadow for hire and—"Hello." It's her.
"Sian." She grins. "You do know my name. That's sweet."
Our light sweeps past and gives her brief halo
or is it your jealous and searching stare?

> I'm sorry Molly, I'm trying to be good,
> but the Creek gets to me, it wants my blood.

"I've been watching you. Down at the fairground. Scaring the shit out of those workmen.
Is that what you do? Does that voice tell you to do things? Hey, Jud, talk to me. Are you
in some sort of trouble? I can help. I don't mind helping. Hello-o?"
"I can only speak in pentameter.
I can only hear in pentameter."
"Sorry, I really don't know what that means."
"You just did one." I hold out both my hands,
count each beat off on my fingers and say;
"*But soft, what light from yonder window breaks?*"
She laughs, I blush while she tries it herself;
"Shakespeare. I get it. Weird, but I like it."
She grins, she claps, she's thrilled by the rhythm.
"I promise to talk in pentameter."
"I have to go." I turn and head for home.

> She follows like she is my Juliet.
> Oh Molly, by moonlight, we are ill met.

"You cannot be here. You have to go home."

"Just … tell … me … ab-out … these things that you do."

She's proud of herself for catching on quick,

her head bobs, her hair jumps as she counts it.

My heart is hot; I *like* talking to her,

she doesn't back off or frown or tense up,

she talks in my language, lets me be me,

and she's nothing like her father at all.

But I'm covered in blood, I need a wash,

and these bones should return to the graveyard.

"Tomorrow. Morning. Come back if you want,

And I'll tell you all about me. OK?"

      "Aye, aye, Macbeth, I'll be back with the sun."

      She twirls, takes a bow, sweeps out and is gone.

She doesn't come back with the sun, or at

           all.

I pace, I moan, I spit and I swear and

           my

pentameter fucks up and I'm *sorry,*

           Molly,

Shush-shush, you say, *calm those hands down a while.*

Make her something, Jud. She may come by yet.

I whittle her a dolphin, like her smile,

but the sun goes down and no Sian, no Sian,

I snap the dolphin in half and burn it.

In the night the sea attacks the lighthouse,

great crashes, like shocks, they say *Ar-ka-dy*.

The asylum itself looms on the hill,

where old Jud's forgotten, still locked away.

      I hide from it all, my head in your lap.

      I'm a twirling corpse in the hangman's trap.

By morning, its calm, but made itself known.

The Creek is unnerved; what might waves wash up?

And down at the fairground the work resumes,

and still no sign of Sian. I am numb, mute.

I hear, on the wind, the shouts of old Runt,

at me, or Sian, or the waves, I'm not sure.

I keep out of sight, keep myself busy,
and the promise of Sian starts to fade off.
Then a pop, a crackle, the bard is back;
"William to Jud. Your old games did not work.
These fuckers are stubborn, they won't scare off.
The Creek will not be the next Disneyland.
      Their boss has moved in, up by Banker's Mile.
      Be best if his kid went missing a while."

A chloroform pad for the mouth of Jack,
and a sealed-up shaft in the old tin mine.
My ghoul mask gives him nightmares forever,
but there's enough food and drink for three days.
I feel bad for the kid, I say to him;
"Stiffen the sinews, summon up the blood."
I don't think he's read much Shakespeare, Molly.
My easy clues make a harrowing trail,
he'll be found safe and well by the weekend.
On my way back, I spit threats at the sea
as it crashes and bites at the shoreline.
Its laughing because it knows what awaits:
      Sian's at my door, her smile has been stolen.
      She's black, she's blue, her eyes are both swollen.

"Hey Jud, you should have seen the other guy."
But it's a joke so it's also a lie.
"Can I stay here with you? There's nowhere else.
It won't be for long. I'll figure it out."
I unlock the door and let her go in,
and then do what I can for her bruises.
She lies down on my bed, curls up her legs.
"Sleep here. You must not go up to the top.
I'll be upstairs. Call me if you need me."
"Thank you, Jud. You are a total sweetheart."
Another night with you Molly. It's nice.
I lay you down so we are side by side.
      You and me and Jack and Sian and William
      Grains of salt tossed in sea. One in billions.

The angry fists of Angus hit the door,
Sian slips beneath the bed and out of sight.
"Oi! Are you in there? Get out here now, Jud."
He seems to always be pentameter;
it hypnotises me. I go to him.
Food-flecked beard, cracked eyes, cuts on his knuckles,
he reeks of mackerel. "Where is she?" he spits.
"My Sian. Do you have her here, you pervert?"
He shoves me aside and stomps his way in,
he holds me back as he looks round the room,
then he heads for the stairs. I grab his sleeve.
He spins, eyes flaming, harpoons in his teeth.
    "I saw her. She passed here, headed for town,
    Early this morning, as the moon went down."

"You're sure it was her? Did she look at you?"
"There was blood on her lip. Her face was bruised."
He thrusts up close, he looks set to explode.
"And you didn't think to help her, dickhead?
Or come to tell me what you saw? Fuck. You."
He shoves me again and stalks out the door,
leaves behind a greasy air, a foul stench,
and now this room feels claimed, stolen from me.
Sian crawls out, her cheeks wet but her face hard.
"If he comes back, we'll face him together."
She takes hold of the plays and finds *Macbeth*
and flicks her way to act one, scene seven.
    "But screw your courage to the sticking place."
    I am thrilled by the look upon her face.

That same day young Jack is found safe and well.
The new police chief vows to track me down.
There's no cease of clanging on The Screamer,
and the sea puts a storm into the sky.
"That kid was well lucky. He would have drowned."
If she knows it was me, she does not say,
but asks all about the walkie-talkie.
She wants me to tell her who William is,
but I don't have answers to satisfy,

and she soon backs off. Instead we read plays.
She swishes her dress as Lady Macbeth
and pulls funny faces for Iago.
>Runt does not come back. We're trapped by weather.
>Perhaps we can be like this forever.

"William to Jud. Fucking fuck those fuckers.
The old methods are not working no more.
We need to up our game old friend. Be strong.
Tonight at midnight. Sticks of dynamite."
Sian's eyes glow in the waning evening sun.
"What does he mean, Jud? Blow up The Screamer?"
I nod but I'm scared of what she'll do next.
She grabs the walkie-talkie, presses twice.
"Let me help. I'll scare away the workmen,
you blow it all to hell. Ka-boom, ka-boom!"
"No. It's too dangerous for you, Sian Runt."
But I don't mean it. She smiles. She can tell.
>"We are a team now. Sian Runt and old Jud:
>the Scourge of the Creek, the Witch of the wood."

We go to School Bridge where supplies are left,
find the explosives wrapped in cheese paper.
Sian fidgets, she's wild, she won't settle down
and the flow of the river looms too large.
There's almost no moon tonight, heavy dark.
One false step and we'll fall. Molly, I'm scared.
There's no talking Sian down, she's fired up
and she hurries us both to the fairground.
The contractors are a new firm, fresh men,
I wonder if there's an endless supply.
The Screamer is uglier than ever,
it thinks it takes our town and makes it fun.
>These city boys don't know fear, don't know pain,
>and Shallow Creek is not their swamp to drain.

Sian strips down to a ripped and stained night gown,
and lets her dark hair fall onto her face.
She has opened up the wound on her lip

and smears streaks of blood all over herself.
She cackles and creeps towards the workmen;
I don't know if I feel pride or worry.
But her passion is infectious Molly,
you would have liked her as well, I'm quite sure.
She climbs onto the track and starts to groan,
when the men find her with torches she screams.
But they do not run, they're ready for this.
Someone throws a switch and floodlights come on.
  Night becomes day, the men just scoff and laugh.
  One whistles, one shouts: "Tits out for the lads."

Phones up, they film it; I'm going to be found.
Sian's trying her best, head twitches and groans,
but she just gets mocked, zombie moans all round.
One man steps forward and spits at her feet,
then digs out his cock, limp slither of meat.
Rage fills me, I charge, a wrench in my hand,
with one hefty swing, I smash in his skull,
then grab Sian and run, ignoring her cries,
past the pier, round the school, into forest,
not stopping until I'm back at the beach.
I put Sian down, but she's dizzy and sick.
"What the fuck have you done? Is he dead? That guy, did you kill him? Oh fucking fuck,
Jud. Shitting fucking fuck, this is bad."
  I sit on the sand, hands over my ears,
  try to ignore all of Sian's deepest fears.

When I look back up, she's halfway to home.
I run to catch up, but the sand is sludge,
and waves have washed up impossible stuff.
Vast splinters of shipwrecks and carcasses,
old trollies and bike frames and licence plates.
Weeds grab me, catch me, I fall many times,
the flotsam slices new wounds into me.
From town I can hear wails of the sirens,
and the fairground flashes, blue-red, blue-red.
When I get home, Sian has bust her way in,
and she's shouting at the walkie-talkie.

"Answer me you utter dickwad. We need you! Jud needs you! Come on *William* this is all your fault, you penis."

> She hands it to me, thinks through the rhythm
> "Tell him to help, I can't go to prison!"

"He won't talk to us, that's not how it works."
I put the walkie-talkie back in place.
"You do know that's not William Shakespeare, yeah?
It's some guy gets you doing this shit and—oh fuck it. Whoever he is, he's controlling you Jud, don't you see? You're doing the stuff he can't do or won't do. Kidnapping? Blowing shit up?"
I fall to the floor and cover my ears,
I rock back and forth and squeeze my eyes shut.
Sian grabs my shoulder, I shrug her straight off.
"They're coming! Police! They'll lock us away!
We have to clean up Jud and hide. Come on!"
I push her away and run out of the door.
They can have me, I'm done, I'll take the blame,
but the sirens aren't here, they've gone straight past.

> Down at the docks is the scene of the fuss;
> they're at Sian's house, they've arrested Angus.

I grin, I flap, this is William, I know.
He looks after me, makes sure that I'm free.
I go back inside to tell Sian the news.
She's hidden away, she's under the bed.
"We're fine, they've arrested your Dad for it,
you can stay here with me, we're safe again."
She doesn't come out, I lift up the sheet.
Darkness. She's not there. Above me, a creak.
I am drained of all feeling. My head spins.
I sprint up the stairs, around and around,
they seem to go forever and ever.
At the top Sian is waiting, white as death.

> She stares at you, Molly, with bulging eyes.
> She reels from the stench of formaldehyde.

I've tried my best to keep you fresh, my love,
but the heat from the light makes it tricky.

William keeps me supplied with the fluids;
I've grown fond of the upkeep massages.
I know this is weird and some think it's wrong,
but I won't have you burned up or buried.
Worm-food and ashes, what's wrong with people?
Preserving makes so much more sense to me;
we're together, you'll not be forgotten.
For Sian its too much, she won't look at me.
"No, no, no, no," she says. "Keep back, stay back."
I don't want to hurt her, I move away.
      Between us the light pulses on and on.
      Outside the sirens have faded and gone.

"Just let me go. I won't tell, I promise."
Pentameter still, I can't help but smile,
she sees it and whimpers, tears in her eyes.
I cross the room, take hold of you Molly,
try to think of what I can say to Sian.
"I'm sorry, Sian." It's all I can manage,
but it sounds all wrong. She bolts for the stairs.
A wave hits the lighthouse, I shout out; "No!"
It's too late; she trips on the first step down.
She tumbles, she falls, her bones against stone,
a guttural cry, breath stolen from lungs,
a sickening crack then silence; no more.
      You whisper to me; *It will be OK.*
      I hold you close so the world drifts away.

I'm brought back to life by her soft, small voice.
"Help me," she calls, the words broken and cold.
You slide from my arms and say; *go on, Jud.*
I descend the steps, just one at a time
to the twisted shipwreck of her body.
All that can move are the fish of her eyes;
they swivel to me, as if caught in nets.
She moans as I take her into my arms,
as light as driftwood and just as shattered.
I take her downstairs, go straight out the door,
to be met by the worst storm I have seen.

I have to take her to the hospital.
I have to take her to the hospital.

The town of Shallow Creek is waking up
                              with
bankers and shop clerks and vagrants and jog
                              gers
and me, with Sian Runt, half dead in my arms,
and I don't know the way. Which way is it?
                              Which way is it? Which one of-
Which one of your buildings is the hospi-
tal. How can she get better with no hos-
pital? They all look the same, like Arka
                              dy.
Arkady, Arkady, Jud and Molly,
Arkady, Arkady, William and Jud.
"Are you OK, mate? What's happened? Hello?"
"I have to take her to the hospital."
"It's the other side of town, mate. Why don't you put her down in here, out of the rain?
We'll phone for an ambulance, yeah? Take it easy. Take it easy, come on."
"I have to take her-"
"I'll phone for an ambulance. It'll be much quicker, much better. What's your name?"
"Arkady. Arkady. Arkady. Ark."
"Arkady? Have you come from the asylum? Is there someone with you, or ...?"
"Or?"
"Look, you just put her down, I'll get that ambulance, OK?"
        With a grumble and groan, thunder rolls on.
        When his back is turned I grab Sian and run.

Once knew this town like the back of my hand.
Arkady, Arkady, Arkady, Ark.
But I was different, I did not belong.
Arkady, Arkady, Arkady, Ark.
Lost jobs, lost women, lost friends, family.
Arkady, Arkady, Arkady, Ark.
Spent time on these streets, saw the backs of things.
Arkady, Arkady, Arkady, Ark.
But I couldn't explain, couldn't make sense.
Arkady, Arkady, Arkady, Ark.

They sent me away and there I remained.
Arkady, Arkady, Arkady, Ark.
      The one shining light, the woman inside;
      Molly, enchantress, my mental health bride.

The hospital.
I find it.
I can't go in.
They'll take me.
I can't go in.
I lay Sian down. An obvious place.
I don't look closely at her.
I don't know if she's still breathing
or not.
I can't lose another.
I can't do it.
I can't lose another.
They won't let me keep her.
I couldn't even be with you, Molly.
It wasn't allowed. We married,
but it wasn't allowed.
                    *

A day goes past, two nights. The storm won't leave.
I don't see Sian. I don't even see you.
I'm hidden downstairs, I whittle and read.
William is silent. So are you. Me too.
Angus is not. I hear his shouts, his rage.
They released him, last night. No evidence.
He's not come up here. He will. I'm not scared.
I'm numb, mute but calm. That workman? He died.
I've spent the hours rehearsing the rhythm.
Pentameter, my unfailing ally.
It holds me, it folds me, inside its loop;
all words can fit in its infinite grasp.
      I know who I am, I know I am Jud.
      I'm skin above bones glued fast by my blood.

"William to Jud. It's all over my friend.
Done my best to keep things straight at my end.

But its all gone to shit, I'm sorry Jud.
They're coming for you, it's not looking good.
I've bought you the night to pack up your stuff,
they'll come at first light, I hope that's enough.
That girl you were with. Sian Runt. She alive.
Was touch and go, but you got there in time.
This walkie-talkie, throw it in the sea,
I can't have these things coming back to me.
I'm so proud of you, my brother-in-arms,
but the Creek's had enough of our alarms.
            If you'll take my advice, end it tonight
            I believe you've still got that dynamite."

Dawn comes, the forces are gathered outside,
behind them a mob, with Angus in charge.
I watch him a while through binoculars.
Revenge, for Sian, is still high on my list.
Propped up at the top, you're still there, Molly,
but the time has come for goodbyes, my love.
At least you will go in a spectacle;
Angel of Arkady, love of my life,
when the wire is tripped, you'll light up the sky.
The walkie-talkie. Still got it. It's here.
"Jud to William, I am coming for you.
I've recalled your face and know what you do.
            I'm Jud, I'm human, a person, a freak:
            the bogeyman and the Scourge of the Creek."

BLOOD MOON BOB

by Simon Billinton

'**T**he dreams have started again.'

'And what happened in this one?'

Eileen Bathory thought back to this morning, waking up covered in sweat.

'It seemed like Hell. I was in a massive cavern of fire and lava. Something was coming for me. Something black and smoky. Its eyes were on fire and it kept on saying the same thing to me. *Burn. Burn with me.*'

'And what were you feeling?'

'Terror. Complete terror. I was screaming.'

'Do you know what may have triggered it? Have you seen John recently?'

'No. I think it was something a student said.'

'And what was that?'

Eileen looked out of the open window. The sound of clunking metal and heavy machinery drifted in from the nearby junkyard.

'I taught Barney, you know.'

'Is Barney the student?'

'No. Barney owns the junkyard over there. He was a good kid.'

'Do you want to talk about Barney?'

'No. Just thought of him is all.'

'And why's that?'

Eileen continued to gaze out the window.

'I guess it's just some kids are inherently good, and some kids … well, some kids are nasty little shits.'

Eileen said nothing more.

Ruth Usiskin glanced at the clock. 'We have to finish now. We can talk about this next time.'

Eileen gathered her bag and shawl. 'Sure. No problem. Oh, can I get another prescription? I'll run out soon. Thanks.'

Eileen waited for Ruth to write up the form and said her goodbyes. She headed down the back exit as usual. She didn't want to give the town gossips more to talk about. She'd had enough of that since John. She got in her station wagon and drove back into town. Fall in Shallow Creek was in full swing. The air cool and crisp, the mattress of fallen leaves growing by the day. She drove past John's library, checked her watch, and slowed to see if he was leaving early.

A shiver ran through her body and her cheeks burnt. Stop it, she thought, this is embarrassing. She pressed the gas pedal and drove on to the pharmacy. She parked up and held her rosary beads.

'I'm sorry,' she whispered to God.

She waited for a response and sighed when none came. After collecting her prescription, she drove to the diner to grab some food before tonight's town party at Devil's Gorge. It was set to be the first blood moon Shallow Creek had seen in years.

***

'I need to pee'

'How long does it last?'

'Bob's gonna get ya, Bob's gonna get ya.'

'Stop scaring your sister, Joey, and tie your shoelaces.'

Chattering voices drifted through the car park as children ran around with glow sticks, teenagers snogged behind pick-up trucks, and guys unloaded coolers laden with six-packs. From the license plates, Eileen could see that a lot of people had travelled from far-off counties or even out-of-state. Shallow Creek was a big draw on nights like this, particularly as everyone knew the story of Blood Moon Bob, the old-time preacher who rises from the dead every lunar eclipse to seek out sinners. Eileen was far more scared of real priests than imaginary ones.

She walked into the darkening woods that led to the lookout. Children raced past her, calling back and waving, 'Hello Mrs Bathory.' She waved back with a smile. At the top of the path, a tall police officer held a lantern to help guide everyone along.

'Evening, Eileen,' said Sheriff Hamilton.

'Hi Sheriff.'

'How you been? School keeping you honest?'

'If I told you what I'd like to do to those kids some days, you'd lock me up.'

The Sheriff winked. 'Best keep it to yourself then.'

Eileen chuckled. 'I didn't see you at Gert's last night for poker?'

'Yeah, had to go see Father Frank at the church. There was a break-in. Someone had stolen a big old silver crucifix. Probably just kids,' he leaned in closer and glanced around, 'or some of these out-of-towners.'

'Really? Well, I hope you find it.'

'I ain't even gonna pretend we'll recover it.'

She laughed. 'I'll let the local criminals know.'

He tipped his hat and smirked. 'I'd be much obliged.'

She said her goodbyes and upon reaching the lookout she saw hundreds of people huddled together in couples, families, and friends. The ragged valley of Devil's Gorge stretched far into the horizon, but the main attraction tonight was the lunar eclipse. Eileen mingled and caught up with friends and the parents of her students, until finally she found a spot to watch the Earth's shadow inch its way across the face of the moon.

The hush was broken from behind her by a soft voice. 'Hello, Eileen.'

Eileen tensed. A cold wave washed over her body and her heart fluttered.

'Hey, John.' She turned to face her ex-husband.

He smiled at her like always: warm, gentle, comforting. The moonlight erased his wrinkles and he looked young again, like the early years of their marriage.

'You look well,' she said.

'Thanks. Been doing a lot of hiking recently. It's keeping me fit. You look good too.'

She averted her eyes from his and thanked him.

'How's Jackson?' asked John. 'I miss him.'

'He's fine,' she smiled. 'Getting old.'

'Aren't we all,' he said chuckling to himself.

A moment of silence fell, and John looked up at the moon. 'Quite something isn't it?'

The moment of totality was fast approaching. The Earth's shadow would soon extinguish the moon and it would be reborn as fire in the sky.

'It is. I don't think I've actually seen one before. We always seemed to miss it. Sorry … I didn't mean to …'

'It's ok.' John touched her hand. 'You don't need to apologize.'

Eileen looked down at her feet. 'I always feel that I do.'

A group of high school seniors standing behind them, sharing cigarettes and beers, whispered and giggled. Eileen glanced at them and her stomach twinged when she caught sight of Kevin Horgan in the center of the group. John followed her eyes. 'Some of yours?'

'Unfortunately.'

'I always thought the kids liked you?'

'Most do. He used to. But nowadays …'

'Well, ignore him. You're ten times the person he is.'

She nodded faintly. He always knew what to say. They stood together gazing at the moon as it was finally engulfed by the darkness before a red luminescent light bathed over its surface, igniting the infinite night sky. The blood moon was born.

From the woods behind, a wild, howling cry pierced the silence; part animal, part man, both dying. Everyone exchanged glances and tittered. One of the kids behind Eileen and John howled like a wolf; his friends laughing and joining in like a pack of wolves. Eileen rolled her eyes and groaned. Just one day without school-kids' nonsense, she thought. She turned and hissed, 'Shhhh! Be quiet.'

They exchanged glances and looked at Kevin. Under the red light of the moon his face blackened. He glared into Eileen's back and flicked his lit cigarette in her direction.

'Anyone got any air freshener?' Kevin asked his friends, loud enough for Eileen to hear. 'There's a bad smell round here.'

A chill surged down Eileen's back as the group stifled their laughter.

'No one? Damn. It really stinks. I might throw up.' He mimed retching.

'Someone mustn't have washed. Urggh. Must be hard to scrub off shame I guess.'

The gang giggled hysterically and Eileen shuddered inside.

Kevin continued, 'My dad says he doesn't know how women can go outside stinking like that.'

Eileen's cheeks flushed and her stomach burnt. She turned to look at Kevin and saw a smirk on his face. John tried to hold her back but she pushed his hand away and stormed up to Kevin. He was a high school footballer, tall and wide, but despite his size she got right up in his face.

'You and me are going to have a serious talk tomorrow.'

He stepped back but continued to smirk.

'Can't wait, Ms.' He turned back to his friends and laughed.

A fire blazed deep inside and tears welled in her eyes. She hurried away from Kevin, from John, from everyone, hiding her face as she fled into the woods. The laughter drifted away as the towering trees cocooned her from sounds. Moonbeams bled through soaring branches and fell in pools of crimson light on the ground. She slowed to a stop, closed her eyes, and drew in long, deep breaths. The air smelt rich and earthy; pine, fir, and moss lacing the crisp, cool, night air. She stood motionless in the dark, letting her muscles and breathing relax as the trees embraced her.

A twig cracked somewhere to her right. Her ears pricked and she peered into the darkness, straining her eyes but unable to see anything. Probably an animal, she thought. A rustle rose from the undergrowth and her feet inched backwards.

'Hello?' Her voice trembled.

Silence fell and she felt the hairs rise on the back of her neck. In the corner of her eye something flashed through a pool of light, making her gasp. She spun round to check but there was nothing there.

'Hello?!' She called out again. Twigs and branches began to snap, moving ever closer.

'Kevin?! Is that you?!' She tried to run but in the total darkness she stumbled and almost fell over. Her heart pounded in her chest. 'Please, this isn't funny!'

In a pool of moon light up ahead, something appeared making Eileen stop dead. A figure of shadow and smoke, fire and ash, stood bathed in the light of the blood moon. Eyes of molten fire locked on to Eileen's, piercing into her soul. Her legs crumbled and she collapsed to her knees.

'Nooo!' she cried, clutching her rosary beads.

The figure glided toward her, wisps of fire and smoke streaming from its shadowy form. She burrowed her head to the ground and prayed, scrabbling through her mind to remember the prayers she once cried out as a child, alone in the dark.

The figure stopped in front of her, radiating a heat that scorched the air, and spoke with the hiss and crackle of fire, turning her words of God to ash. 'Burn ... burn with me! ... siiiinnneer.'

She felt as though her skin would melt, her blood ignite, her soul turn to flame. Her entire being screamed as fire consumed from her within.

And then it was gone. Cool, crisp air rushed into the void it left behind. Silence returned. The blood moon shone again and the trees of Devil's Gorge exhaled as Eileen collapsed in a heap and wept.

Eileen drove home in a daze. What she'd seen was seared into her mind. She tried to rationalize it, repeatedly telling herself it wasn't real, that she was just tired and emotional from the encounter with Kevin and from seeing John which even now, almost a year later, still affected her. But it was surely impossible. Blood Moon Bob couldn't be real, could he?

She entered the house and threw her prescription on the side table, pausing in the hall to soak up the heavy silence. The only sound was the soft ticking of the clock above the fireplace, and she felt her heart suddenly ache at the memories of nights spent with John by the fireside, reading, talking, drinking. The house was too quiet for her until a throaty bark sprang from the kitchen and a golden labrador burst through the swing doors and jumped on her, barking and wagging his furry tail. She rubbed his head and hugged him tight.

'My baby. I'm so glad you're here.' Jackson writhed and wriggled in her embrace, licking her face. 'Come on you. Time for bed.'

At the mention of bed he broke free and raced up the stairs. She found him on the bed, circling on his usual spot. She undressed, got into bed, and stroked him to sleep whilst thinking about what she'd seen earlier. A passage from the Bible her mom used to read to her popped into her head, *Therefore, just as through one man sin entered into the world, and death through sin, and so death spread to all men, because all sinned.*

***

'Come in, Kevin. Close the door behind you please,' Eileen called from behind her desk, her hands resting on a thick folder. Her head ached, her stomach grumbled, and her mouth was dry. She'd overslept, missed breakfast, and forgotten to take her meds.

Kevin dropped his bag on the floor and slumped into the chair.

'So, we seem to have a problem,' said Eileen.

He stared at her. 'I got no problem, Ms.'

'Well I do. I expect students of my school to treat staff with respect. But you don't seem to understand that.'

'I do. But not everyone deserves respect.'

Her brow furrowed as she leaned backwards. 'Do you mean me?'

He looked straight at her and shrugged.

'I see. And why's that?'

He didn't reply.

'Ok Kevin, look. We can either talk about this or I'm going to be handing out detentions all semester. Your choice.'

He chuckled to himself.

'You don't think I will?'

'I don't care if you do, Ms. You have no power over me.'

His words triggered something in Eileen's memory. She remembered a former student, sat in the same spot, saying the same thing, *You have no power over me.* She opened Kevin's file and ran her finger down the page until she reached his grades. Just like the other student, Kevin's grades were once consistently high, but earlier in the year they began to tail off. She studied his face and wondered if the cause was the same.

'How's things at home?' asked Eileen softly.

His eyes flared. 'Why?'

'How's your mom and dad? I haven't seen them at parent-teacher meetings in a while.'

'My dad's great.'

She held his stare. 'And your mom?'

'I don't know where she is,' he leaned forward, 'and I don't care either.'

Kevin sat back and looked down at his scuffed boots. Eileen thought for a moment. She didn't want to make the same mistake as last time.

'Kevin. I'm sorry to hear things aren't great at home. It must be hard.'

He didn't respond.

'It can be helpful to talk sometimes. We have a counsellor in the school you could talk to. She's very experienced and can really help. Would you like that?'

Kevin's jaw tensed and he clenched his fist. 'What I would like, is for all you stupid bitches to leave me the hell alone, ok?!'

She recoiled at his words. 'Kevin! You can't say—'

'Save it.' He grabbed his bag and stood. 'I don't give a shit what you think!'

He stormed to the door, yanked it open, and slammed it behind him.

Eileen shook her head. 'That little shit.'

For the rest of the day Eileen's stomach churned. Thoughts of Kevin, John, and what she'd witnessed the night before consumed her mind. Was it real? Or had she dreamt it all? She needed to talk to someone and Ruth was out of town until next week. There was someone else, but her throat tightened at the idea. It was time, she thought. Leaving school early she drove to church and sat in the car for fifteen minutes, staring at the vast oak doors. She took a deep breath, exhaled, and stepped out of the car.

Day turned to dusk and a deep hush enveloped her as she entered the church. Candles flickered in the half light and the aromatic scent of incense pricked her memories. It was empty except for one person deep in prayer and the priest, stood in the doorway of a side room speaking to someone within. He beamed when he saw her and she returned his smile whilst motioning towards the confessional booth. Nodding, he raised a finger, and mouthed 'one minute.' She entered the booth and settled herself in. The smell of the musky wood triggered memories good and bad, followed by the image of fire and smoke, ash and embers, and the smoldering figure in the woods.

She shut her eyes, crossed herself, and whispered, 'Help me, God. Please.'

The adjoining booth's door opened and closed and she cleared her dry throat.

'Hello, Father.'

'Hello, my child'

She paused and drew in a deep breath. 'Forgive me, Father, it's been a while since my last confession.'

'How long has it been?'

'A year or two. I … I've been too scared to come.'

'Why?'

'I don't think people like me are welcome.'

'All of God's children are welcome.'

She lowered her head and swallowed down a lump in her throat. 'Even divorced people? It's a sin, isn't it?' I failed John, and I failed God.'

'Sin is what defines us. Sin is there at the beginning and so it will be at the end.'

Tears welled in her eyes. 'I know, I know.'

'Sin is forever and cannot be undone.'

The tears rolled down her cheeks. 'Please help me. I don't want this.'

'You must repent your sins.'

'How? What do I need to do?!'

'Sin must have its reckoning.

'What does that mean?'

'Sin needs the flesh. The flesh must burn. Burn...burn with me...burn!!'

Eileen recoiled with a scream as two blazing eyes of liquid fire peered through the small grate between the booths. Smoke seeped in under the door and the paneling began to smolder. She scrabbled for the door, burst out of the confessional, and ran for the exit. She tumbled out and crashed into someone on the steps outside. She fell to the floor and scrabbled to break free from the stranger helping her up.

Sheriff Hamilton looked down at her. 'Jesus, Eileen! It's me. Are you ok?'

'Let me go! He's going to get me!'

'What are you talking about?'

'Please! He's in there! Help me!'

'Who is?'

She stared up at him, wild eyes bulging. 'The priest! He's … he's Blood Moon Bob! He's come for me!'

The Sheriff held her steady by the side of her arms. 'Eileen, I was just with Father Frank in his office. He's definitely not Bob.'

'You don't understand!'

'Then explain it to me.'

The Sheriff helped her up and led her trembling body to his patrol car and listened as she told him about the confession booth, the woods last night, and her dreams. He waited for her to finish and then considered her for a moment.

'Ok, first I have to ask, have you been drinking or taking any drugs?'

'Sheriff! You know I don't.'

'Sorry, I have to ask.'

'I know it sounds crazy.'

'Look. I've seen all kinds of things in the twenty-five years I've been doing this job, so crazy doesn't surprise me. But facts are facts, and Bob is long dead. I know. I was there. I pulled his burnt body from the fire.'

Eileen's eyes widened. 'So he was real?'

'Sure. Bob was a preacher. A real fire and brimstone kinda guy. The town grew tired of his sermons about how they were all sinners. They wanted him gone. And what happened was … just an accident. I guess some folks took the opportunity to make up a ghost story. Good for business, as they say.'

'So I'm just seeing things then?'

'I'd say maybe you need a break from those kids. And isn't it around a year since you and John split up? I know I go weird around the anniversary of Maggie's death. Guilt can really screw with us.'

She nodded. Maybe he was right. Maybe she'd been wrong to try and run away from what happened with John, and maybe it was all catching up with her now. Ruth was always telling her to face it.

'This is the first time I've been in Church since John and I divorced. I couldn't come. How's Father Frank been? I've missed him.'

'Not too good actually. He seems lost, like he's struggling with his faith. And the robbery hasn't helped. He was just telling me - and I probably shouldn't say this—It's just a coincidence ok, but that missing crucifix? … it belonged to Bob.'

The Sheriff chuckled. Eileen's stomach turned to ice.

On her drive home, Eileen stopped at the 7-Eleven for cigarettes and matches. She sat in her car, lit up, and drew in a long drag. Her lungs rebelled and spluttered out smoke. She sucked in one puff after the other, forcing her lungs to accept the cigarette until the nicotine finally kicked in and her trembling hands relaxed. She closed her eyes, leant back, and inhaled the cloud of smoke.

An old Chevrolet banged and lurched into the parking lot, screeching to a halt by the row of bushes at the rear. Steam billowed from beneath the hood and the driver's door flew open. Kevin emerged from within, kicking and screaming at the car, 'Jesus fricking pile of crap!'

He pulled out his cell phone and dialed. 'Hi. Is that Barney? … I need to get rid of this hunk of junk … Ok I'll drop it off tomorrow morning. Bye.'

He popped the hood to let the steam escape and retrieved some water from the trunk to fill the radiator. As he closed the hood, a small stray cat emerged from the bushes and walked toward Kevin. The cat meowed at Kevin, but he ignored it and walked on. It followed him and rubbed itself against his legs.

'Get lost, you stupid thing!' he said, stepping back and kicking the cat square in the stomach. The cat screeched and fled into the bushes as Kevin laughed and hooted.

Eileen's cigarette fell from her open mouth. An image of Jackson yelping in pain flashed before her eyes. Fire seared through her veins and every muscle ignited. She flung her door open and yelled, 'You. Goddam. Piece. Of. Shit!'

She stormed up to Kevin and slapped him so hard the impact knocked him to the ground. She leant down and shouted into his dazed face, 'If you hurt any animal ever again, I will kill you!'

Kevin crawled to his car, fired up the engine, and spat at Eileen through the window as he wheelspinned away. 'No bitch does that to me!'

She stood motionless in the car park watching him roar off, adrenaline coursing through her veins. As the fire inside her faded, a cold sweat spread across her skin and a sinking feeling swelled in her stomach. Oh shit, she thought, what have I done?

***

The students swarm around her. Their eyes on fire, faces melting. Her office crumbles to ash and she's falling into a cavernous void. Alone. Fire burns the darkness. Screams echo to infinity. Molten lava scorches naked feet. Skin roasts, bone turns to ash. He walks through the flames. Black as the void. Black as death. Burn with me he says, burn with me. The flesh must burn. Burn your sins … Burn!

Eileen woke up screaming like a dying animal, the sound retching from her body rising from somewhere deeper than hell. Her chest heaved, clawing for breath, sweat bathing her shaking body. She staggered to the window and gulped at the cold, morning air.

It's just a dream, she told herself. Just a dream.

Her breathing settled and the sweat chilled on her forehead. She felt Jackson's furry head nuzzle against her leg and glanced down to stroke him, but he wasn't there. She scanned the room and couldn't see him. Rubbing her eyes, she went out on to the landing and a smell of smoke made her nostrils twitch. At the bottom of the stairs she saw shadows flickering on the floor and heard the fire crackling. Her head was heavy and dazed, but she didn't remember lighting a fire. All she remembered was coming home and crying herself to sleep over what she'd done to Kevin. She plodded downstairs and found a fire roaring in the fireplace. The air was hot, smoky, and tinged with something else, something charred.

As she went to put the fire out something between the logs caught her eye. She took the poker and parted the wood. Nestled amongst the smoldering logs glistened a large silver crucifix. She gasped and recoiled, treading on Jackson's furry tail.

'Oh Jesus!' she cried, spinning around to check if he was ok.

Her heart instantly shattered. She fell to her knees and screamed out every last part of her soul. Jackson lay unconscious on his side, his golden fur burnt and singed, and seared onto his hind leg was the blood red branding of a crucifix. Tears poured down her face as she clutched his lifeless body, the dog she and John had raised, the dog that held them together, and held her alone ever since. The one last remnant of that life was gone.

A car banged and spluttered outside and Eileen's ears pricked. It can't be, she thought. She peered out of the window and glimpsed a car turn the corner. It looked like Kevin's car. She stared out the window into nothing, tears streaming down her cheeks, her mind numb. Jackson was no more and there was nothing left for her in this world. Visions of the blood moon, the flaming figure, of Kevin, flashed before her eyes, and she roared until her throat burned. She scrambled for her keys, ran to her car, and gave chase, racing round the neighborhood in search of Kevin, but there was no sign of him. She thumped the wheel and screamed. *Think, Eileen, think!* She glimpsed the clock on the dash which read 9:35am and knew where to go.

She floored the gas.

Barney Sylvester came out of his ramshackle workshop and his eyes beamed. 'Mrs Bathory! What ya doing here?'

'Hey Barney. I got some car trouble. I was coming back into town and it just stopped out by the mill. Can you take a look?'

'Sure thing. Let me get my tools and we can get going.'

Eileen hesitated. 'Umm … I have an appointment in town … so

would you mind going ahead and fixing it? I'd be real grateful.'

'No problem. I'll get that old thing up and running in no time.'

Eileen smiled. 'Thanks. You always were a good kid.'

He blushed, waved goodbye, and drove off in his pickup to fix her car. Eileen was now alone in the junkyard. She hurried into Barney's workshop and rummaged through his tools, testing the weight of hammers and wrenches, examining the blades of knives, when she spotted a jerrycan in the far corner. She lifted the can and shook it; half full. She found a filthy rag and an empty beer bottle and her ears pricked when she heard the sound of a banging and spluttering engine approach the junkyard.

The battered Chevrolet pulled up outside the workshop and Kevin honked his horn, 'Hey! Anyone there?'

Eileen appeared in the doorway with one arm behind her back. Kevin gaped. She strolled up to his door and propped herself against the roof, leaning into his window.

'What are you doing here?' he sneered.

She stared down at him. 'Come to get rid of some junk.'

He returned her stare. 'Whatever. Is he here? That retard?'

Her eyes flared. 'Barney is ten times the person you'll ever be, you nasty little shit.'

Kevin laughed. 'You are *so* over. Like all the other whores, you'll be hawking your saggy old body for booze and drugs by the time I've told the school and press what you did.'

Eileen chuckled. 'I don't care anymore, Kevin.'

She took out the cigarettes and box of matches from her pocket. 'Fancy one?'

Kevin ignored her.

'Quite right.' She threw the cigarettes away. 'It's a filthy habit.' Kevin looked at her puzzled.

She struck a match and watched the flame flutter. 'This is for Jackson.'

She lit the rag from the gasoline-filled beer bottle she'd placed on top of his car, took a few steps back, and hurled it through his window. The bottle shattered and the interior of the car ignited in a flash. He screamed as a fireball engulfed him, searing his skin. He clawed at the door, but the flames were consuming him whole, becoming him, feasting on his flesh. The raging fire devoured the old seat fabrics turning the car into an inferno. Kevin was burning alive and nobody could hear him scream.

And then Eileen saw him, flickering in the flames. The figure from the woods, from the church, from her dreams. The figure with fire in his eyes. Now she knew. It was clear. Sin must have its reckoning. Sin must have its flesh. Blood Moon Bob called to her, 'Burn. Burn with me … burn with me!'

Eileen walked around the blazing car, opened the passenger door, and slid into the flames.

***

Sheriff Hamilton broke down Eileen's front door and entered the house. Smoke and ash drifted in the rays of sunlight peeking through the curtains. His heart ached when he saw the photo of John and her she'd kept on the sideboard, knowing he'd be the one to inform John. He began searching for any evidence when a whimper came from beside the fire. He looked behind the armchair and saw Jackson, burnt but his eyes half open.

'Oh Jesus.'

He radioed the station for a vet and hurried to the kitchen. As he filled Jackson's bowl with water, he noticed a row of unopened medicine bottles on top of the fridge, their seals intact. He picked up the nearest bottle and examined the label; antipsychotic pills, prescribed three months ago, untouched.

He exhaled and shook his head. 'Oh Eileen. What happened?'

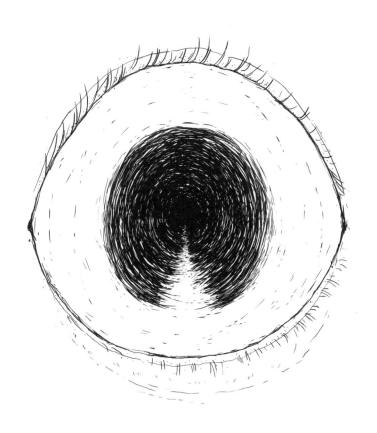

THE EYES HAVE IT

by Sarah Lotz

An hour before he received the call that would eventually send him spiralling into malfeasance and murder, Father Frank had been pacing around St Mary's, boozing and brooding about his lot in life. Self-medicating with the moonshine that he bought on the sly from Jed, St Mary's monosyllabic grounds-man, had become a nightly ritual. Frank was past caring if Jed judged him for it. He was past caring if anyone judged him for it.

He couldn't decide if it was the town itself or its people that sucked the energy out of him, dulling his mind and weakening his limbs as if he were being slowly poisoned. Not that it mattered. He wasn't in Shallow Creek to spread evangelical zeal or save souls. In fact, he suspected the souls of his congregation were long past saving. Among them were Chelsea Sanders, who had a habit of nipping at his fingers when he placed the communion wafer on her tongue, and Mayor Woodrow, who dispassionately confessed his lustful, incestuous inclinations each week after mass. No one showed any curiosity as to why the diocese had seen fit to send Frank to this town in the arse end of nowhere. Shallow Creek was the kind of place where the church banished those who'd transgressed. The kind of place where folks wouldn't ask questions. Because he *had* transgressed at his last placement, hadn't he? Transgressed grievously.

The phone shrilled, breaking his reverie. He almost let it ring out, but some vestige of duty sparked into life and he picked up the receiver. Daisy Fontaine's whiney, little girl voice whispered back at him. Ever since Donny was incarcerated in Arkady Asylum, Daisy tended to smirk her way through mass, as if she knew a secret he didn't. Perhaps she did. Malicious gossip was her stock in trade, and it was she who'd let slip that Frank's predecessor, Father John Mackinnon, had hanged himself in Silverpine Forest. Suicide may be the mortal sin to end all sins, but Father Frank almost sympathised with the late priest. But gone was her usual, self-satisfied tone: 'Father, I need you. It's my father. He's dying.'

Frank wasn't aware the woman even had a father. 'Have I seen him at mass?' *Had* he? Possibly. He was quite often drunk and the faces had a tendency to blur into one.

'No, Father. He lapsed many years ago. But he needs you now. Please hurry, he doesn't have long.'

It wasn't unusual for people to magically rediscover their faith when the grim reaper came knocking, but a call to give the Viaticum was rare—the last rites were more the realm of war zones and unexpected deaths; most people had time to put their affairs in order. Mind muddied by booze, it was the last thing he needed, but he could hardly refuse. He collected his vestments, and stumbled out to his car. He wasn't worried about a D.U.I. The cops were as corrupt as the rest of the townsfolk, and he knew their secrets.

Daisy lived at the edge of Silverpine Forest, the site of Father John's last hurrah, and as he wove up to the front door, the pines whispered around him, their brushing branches sounding almost like laughter. Daisy ushered him in, idly scratching at a patch of psoriasis on her chin. 'He's in the bedroom, Father.' Gone was her distraught tone.

He followed her up a dusty staircase, along a corridor lined with a fool's gallery of papal portraits, and to a room at the end. As she opened the door, he was hit with the dual odours of excrement and pain. Someone had tried to mask them with air freshener and Clorex, but that always made the stench of death worse. Breathing through his mouth, he approached the shape on the bed, sidestepping a stinking commode. A large moon-faced man with yellowish skin stared back at him through pain-wracked eyes. It was obvious from his laboured breathing that he didn't have long.

'Daddy, this is Father Frank,' Daisy said. And then, shooting a trademark smirk at Frank, she scuttled away.

Frank dragged a chair up to the man's bedside. The second he sat down the man snaked out a hand and gripped his wrist with surprising strength. Frank fought the urge to shake him off and wipe away the clammy feel of his palm. 'I'm scared father. I'm scared of what comes next.'

'There's nothing to fear, child.' *Child*. Ridiculous. This man was twice his age.

'What if I'm destined for hell?'

'Hell? You're a good man by all accounts.' Was he? Who knew? Frank certainly didn't. All he cared about was escaping this stench of shit and death as fast as humanely possible.

'Forgive me Father, for I have sinned.'

'When did you last confess?'

Mr Fontaine whispered something Frank couldn't make out,

then dredged up a second wind from somewhere. His eyes cleared, and Frank steeled himself for a tiresome catalogue of venial sins: Gossip, bad thoughts, envy, perhaps. This doughy man couldn't have anything too repugnant in his past—could he? But it seemed that he could. It was a struggle for Father Frank to keep his features serene as Daisy's father huffed his way through it, for he had a past blacker than Bundy's. At the age of fifteen, and tasked with caring for his younger siblings, he'd murdered three of them with rat poison. Their deaths were put down to a virulent strain of gastroenteritis, which was typical of Shallow Creek. The town was the kind of place where you could get away with murder. He'd done it to free himself up to see his girlfriend at the time.

When he paused, Father Frank asked: 'Are you penitent?'

A tear leaked from the corner of an eye. 'I am, Father. Only … there's more.'

There *was* more. A *lot* more. It became almost unintentionally hilarious: just when Frank thought it was finished out wheezed another crime. Among Fontaine's victims were two ex lovers, a dry-cleaner who'd ruined his favourite coat, and a neighbour who'd had the temerity to question their shared boundary lines. He'd even attempted to murder Daisy, his daughter. 'Only the bitch wouldn't die, Father.' That didn't surprise Frank.

He asked again: 'Do you repent?'

'I do, Father.'

His temples throbbed with the spectre of the hangover to follow. 'I absolve you from your sins in the name of the Father, and of the Son, and of the Holy Spirit.'

The man's breath hitched. His jaw muscles slackened, face caving in on itself. He was really crying now. 'God will forgive?'

'Christ will take you to his bosom, my child. He is merciful.'

Fontaine gripped Frank's wrist even tighter. 'Thank you, Father. I am so sorry for what I have done … I am …' He looked past Frank, and let out a low, guttural moan—a sound of such anguish that it appeared to emanate from a place deeper than his throat. Father Frank jumped, snatched his hand free, and turned to look behind him, unsure what he'd find, but certain it had to be something truly horrific. There was nothing there. Then: 'You lied, father, you *lied*. Oh … it hurts, it burns, it hurts … You *lied*.' His eyes widened, eloquent with a terror so potent and primeval that Frank was only aware he'd backed away when he felt the door handle spiking into his spine. The large body bucked, and from his throat came a hiss, followed by the death rattle. There was an emptiness to him now. Fontaine's soul had fled; the body on the bed nothing more than a meaty shell.

It took all the resolve Frank possessed to make his way back to him and do the necessary. He closed Mr Fontaine's eyelids, pressing down firmly for several seconds in case they sprang up again. He did this more for himself than out of respect. He couldn't bear to look into those glassy orbs again. Although empty of life, the stain of that terror was still evident.

Before he left the room to give Daisy the news that her father had passed on, he took a moment to compose himself. His pulse roared. His mind reeled. His stomach churned. Mr Fontaine had confessed. He was penitent. Of that Frank was sure. But to hell he still went. Of that he was *doubly* sure.

So where did that leave Frank?

***

In the days following the man's trip into hell, Father Frank could think of little else. Was *he* responsible? Had his own wrongdoings negated the sacramental absolution? No: he'd confessed his sins. He too was repentant—*wasn't he*? His overriding emotion was fear for himself of course. That look in Fontaine's eyes, the man's final words, contradicted every tenet of the Sacrament of Penitence. Because they meant that the doctrines on which he based his faith were false: there was no forgiveness for mortal sins. If you'd transgressed then you were destined for hell, and *there was nothing you could do about it*. The dread of this consumed him. Convincing himself that he was mistaken was impossible: he'd seen similar horror-filled expressions in the eyes of other sinners who were seconds away from death. Up till now, he'd put these down to a natural fear of letting go. But now he knew the truth: they were looking through the doorway that led to their eternal damnation.

Destined for hell. Unless … unless the soul could be grounded on earth and trapped here somehow. Clinging to this strand of hope, Father Frank scoured the bibles and theological texts that filled his predecessor's eclectic library, and then downloaded more. He read all he could about the nature of duality, devouring the writings of Thomas Aquinas, drifting into philosophy and then, on to neuroscience and string theory. The murkier corners of the internet were rife with tales of practitioners who'd brought dark energies *back* from the dead, but there was nothing about how to prevent the soul from slipping into purgatory. In desperation he turned to writings on other religions: Hinduism, Judaism, the Kabbalah, Islam, Buddhism. There was no one in whom he could confide, so he filled notebooks with feverish notes:

The soul (spiritus, pneuma) = Ghosts??? Are ghosts a manifestation of the soul finding corporeal form on earth?? Proof that it is possible to avoid eternal damnation??? Is it better to be trapped on earth or in a rotting shell of a body than burn in lakes of fire for eternity? (yes)

Ancient cultures believed the soul manifested through the breath. Is this the answer? Does it leak out, waft through the orifices when the final breath rattles out? Possible to stop it from escaping? Could it be as simple as that???

Burying bodies at a crossroads to confuse the soul??? No. The soul left at the moment of death. Too late.

Soul/ghosts: the spirits of vengeful people??? Those with unfinished business?? Those who'd died in great pain. i.e the rumours of the witch who haunts Silverpine. She burned to death. Possible method???

That Sunday, he stumbled his way through mass; barely listened as the usual suspects babbled their way through their weekly sins in the confessional. When the last of them tricked out, he breathed a sigh of relief, then made his way to the ineptly rendered Plaster of Paris Jesus who hung above the altar. He hadn't found solace in prayer for years, but what else could he do? A cough sounded from behind him. He started, and turned to see Ivor Perrin, one of the orderlies at Arkady Asylum, seated in the front pew. As always, Frank felt intimidated by the man's presence. Ivor was a brute of a man, morbidly obese, and well over six feet tall. Ivor had never slid into the confessional, but Frank suspected the man must need to salve his conscience. Arkady Asylum— (*Asylum*—it was typical of Shallow Creek that it still used this outdated terminology) —was a depository for the criminally insane, and according to Daisy Fontaine, *things* went on in there.

The last thing he felt like dealing with was a needy congregant, but he asked all the same: 'Do you need to talk, Ivor?'

'No, but you do.'

Taken aback, Frank automatically blurted out a denial. But then he looked into the man's eyes, and something passed between them: A glance of understanding. *You know your own.*

'I've been watching you, Father. Something's burning at you.'

Perhaps it was Ivor's apt choice of phrase, perhaps it was the exhaustion—he'd barely slept all week—perhaps it was the loneliness of keeping such a game-changing discovery to himself, but Father Frank found himself spilling the beans. He had enough sense to skirt over the details about his own transgressions (although 'transgressions' was a massive understatement), but the rest vomited out. The man's demise and plummet into hell, his own fears for his immortal soul, and the conclusion he'd come to, that the only way to avoid Mr Fontaine's fate was to find a way to tether the *animus* to this realm. Ivor merely listened, his slab of a face expressionless.

'I've been studying various methods, Ivor. But how could I possibly hope to be sure?'

Ivor leaned forward and whispered. 'I know how.'

***

The call came at three a.m, disturbing Father Frank from a booze-addled slumber.

'I have one.' Ivor said in lieu of a greeting. 'Name of Murray Abrams.'

Father Frank was instantly awake. 'He's dying?'

'He's dying. Pancreatic cancer. Terminal.'

'And you're sure that his mind isn't broken?'

'He's a fake. Conned his way here to avoid the chair.'

Choosing a *One Flew Over the Cuckoo's Nest* subject had been one of Frank's main criteria. His faith may be shaken, but he refused to believe that God would send the mentally tortured to hell, however foul their sins.

Pulse thudding, Frank gathered his things and ran for his car.

Once again the pines mocked him with their whispering sniggers as he rocketed along the twisting road that led to the Asylum's gates. In the distance came the sound of crashing waves; ironically, the asylum had the best views in town, set as it was on a cliff at the fringes of the forest. Ivor was waiting for him on the front steps, his usual implacable expression in place. The immediate entrance of the building, like the exterior, bizarrely resembled a kitsch 1920s hotel, but any illusion of comfort and grandeur was shattered as Frank made his way through the reinforced glass doors that led into the heart of the asylum. The place reeked of nervous sweat and disinfectant, the lights were too bright, and the walls were painted in shades of despair and fuck you. The building seemed to be holding its breath; if anything, it had the atmosphere of a place long-abandoned. The floor squeaked beneath his feet as Ivor wordlessly ushered him in to an elevator with damp, carpeted walls. Up, up they crawled.

Frank's mouth tasted of old pennies. He swallowed, made himself speak. 'He's catholic?'

'Yes.'

'And his sins? Mortal not venial?'

In answer, Ivor handed over a manila folder. Inside it were notes written in spidery handwriting: 'Murray Abrams: Sexual deviant, malignant narcissist, admits to sexually assaulting the corpses of his victims after death.' The notes were signed 'Dr Ruth Usiskin', the facility's psychologist, who clearly wasn't averse to doodling on her reports. In the margin, next to 'sexual deviant', she'd drawn a smiley face.

Faintly nauseated from the elevator's jerky movement and the thought of what he was about to do, Frank followed Ivor along a series of corridors that had a utilitarian, 1960s vibe to them. Through a barred door labelled 'maximum security', past an empty nurses' station, and along another corridor that stretched indefinitely like an optical illusion. The walls were lined with white metal doors punctured with suicide watch spy holes. Frank hadn't expected the silence—he'd been imagining screams of anguish and hopelessness— but again, all he could hear was the squeak of his shoes and his pulse thumping in his ears.

Ivor paused outside a door and took out a fistful of keys. 'How will we know it's worked, Father?'

Frank would know. He'd see it in Murray Abrams's eyes. He'd know if the man was destined for hell or not.

Ivor slid the key in the lock and stood back to let Frank enter the room (or cell) before him. Frank had been steeling himself for a Victorian horror, but it was a portrait of clinical blandness. White, empty but for a stainless steel pan, a hospital bed and a halogen lamp bright enough to illuminate the blocked pores on Ivor's nose.

The man on the bed was borderline skeletal, his skin the same dull yellow as Mr Fontaine's. His eyes, watery brown stones that dripped with pain and contempt, followed Frank as he approached. 'Fuck off, priest.'

'I am here to help you.' Frank jumped as the door clanged behind him.

'Don't want ...' —a wheeze, a grimace of pain— '... help.'

Frank reached into his bag to retrieve the mirror. After much thought, he'd decided to experiment with the tenets of the Kabbalah. According to his readings, during Shiva, mirrors were covered so that an evil spirit wouldn't fill the void left by the soul of the dying. But what if the dying subject was forced to stare deep into his reflection as he expired? Would the soul become confused? Remain locked inside? More than likely it was nothing but hokum, but it was worth a shot.

'Will you repent?' Father Frank didn't care if the man repented or not, but he supposed he should put on a show of saving the man's soul—even if it was futile.

'Fuck off.' This time, Murray's voice wavered.

Frank turned the mirror to face Murray, angling it so that the man was forced to gaze into his reflection. 'Look at yourself. Look into it. I am trying to save you.' *And myself.*

'Wha the fuck?' The man batted at the mirror, almost dislodging it from Frank's grip.

Moving surprisingly speedily, Ivor strapped Murray's left wrist to the bed. Murray twisted his weakened body and lashed out with his free hand. Ivor ignored the blows, then casually elbowed Murray in the stomach. Murray let out a whoof of pain, then stilled. Frank didn't get the sense that Ivor was enjoying himself, but this display of violence certainly didn't seem to bother the man's conscience.

'Look into the mirror, Murray. See yourself. *Do it*. It's your only chance.'

Perhaps Murray could pick up on the desperation in Frank's voice, for something seemed to soften inside him. His bottom lip wobbled. Once more, Frank held the mirror directly above Murray's eyes. 'Do you repent? Do you repent?'

Murray let out a sob. 'I repent. Save me, Father.'

Was Murray's penitence genuine? Frank didn't care. The man's chest was barely rising now. Time was running out. 'Then tell me what you see. *Tell me what you see.'*

He didn't need to be told. Frank could see a cruel echo of that terror in Murray's eyes as the man succumbed. It hadn't worked. Frank turned away.

'He's gone. We failed, Ivor.'

Ivor shrugged. 'Too bad.'

'What of his body?'

'I'll take it to the morgue in the basement. Cremate it.'

'Won't there be questions?'

'No one questions anything here.'

'We failed, Ivor,' Frank said again, despair staining his voice this time.

'There will be others.'

***

There *were* others. Many others.

Their second subject, a woman who'd helped her fiancée kidnap young boys for depraved purposes, was on her last legs after a botched overdose. This time, Frank decided to investigate the notion that the soul exited via the final breath. It was Ivor who took care of the practicalities, of course. He'd straddled her, then slipped a plastic bag over her head. See-through, so that Frank could verify the look in her eyes as she died. Another failure—if anything, her expression as she looked into the next realm was more horror-stricken than even Murray's or Mr Fontaine's.

Before long, as his desperation to find a solution grew, Frank's criteria that their victims had to be terminal, catholic and of sound mind went out of the window. All that mattered was that the subject had a backlog of mortal sins. Frank salved his conscience by distancing himself, going about their experiments in a clinical fashion, and collating notes that echoed Dr Ruth's Usiskin's:

Subject #6
Name: Peggy Anne Morris
Age: 32
Sins: Infanticide.
Proposed method: to seal all orifices and wrap the skin in plastic to prevent the soul escaping not only via the last breath but through the pores of the skin.

Subject succumbed easily. No last rites given. There was a moment of hope when she seemed to find peace, then …

FAILURE

Subject #9
Name: Damien Peter Gray
Age: 65
Sins: sexual deviance, paedophilia, matricide.
Proposed method: Embalming alive and trapping the soul within the body's shell (the Egyptian method). Subject was restrained by Ivor, and the fluid was inserted intravenously.
Result: FAILURE. Subject's last words were 'it burns, it burns.' Impossible to be sure if subject was referring to embalming liquid scouring his veins or had begun to feel the fiery pits of hell.

Subject #12
Name: Petrus Humar
Age: Indeterminate
Sins: Found living at the edge of Silverpine Forest in 1987 with the mummified bodies of what were assumed to be his parents. He had 'done things' to their skin.
Proposed method: Calling on the preliterate theory of animism & belief that the souls who walk the earth are vengeful spirits that have suffered greatly at time of death. Great pain and suffering can confuse the soul keep it trapped here on earth. Ivor suggested burning alive the subject in the asylum's crematorium.

FAILURE (although difficult to be sure because of the screaming)

***

Weeks slipped into months, but Father Frank wasn't aware of the changing seasons. A fear of death had begun to metastasize inside him, so much so that he no longer dabbled with moonshine, and became almost pathological about looking after his health. He was young; he could have another fifty years before death came knocking. But what if it took him unawares before he found the answer? A car accident, a funny-shaped mole on his skin, a bad gene ticking inside him like a time-bomb. The experiments had become more frenzied.

More *desperate*. He re-read the literature he'd obsessively collected, even considered dabbling in the darker arts. Then Ivor reported that Dr Usiskin had begun asking questions about the whereabouts of her patients. According to Ivor, it wasn't out of concern for their well-being, more that she wanted them for her own purposes. 'We'll have to slow down, Father.'

He couldn't slow down. He found himself considering other possibilities, perhaps harvesting those who slid into the confessional: Daisy, with her weekly litany of debauchery and deviance; Mayor Woodrow with his lust for his daughter that was barely kept in check. If he *did* use them, it would be for their own good. They, like him, were destined for hell. But no: They'd be missed. He had no choice but to depend on Ivor and his catalogue of lost souls. (In any case, if he did find a way to trap his essence on earth, he reckoned he'd enjoy haunting his appalling congregation).

Fuelling this desperation were his dreams. The children had begun visiting him at night, the children from his first placement, the St Martin de Porres School for the Deaf and Disabled, a charitable institution situated in a backwoods town in South Africa. The nuns, all Polish, were diligent. So was he—at first. But they'd needed love, those boys and girls. They were so desperate. So *very* desperate. Most were survivors of shack fires and violence, casualties of struggling families who had no means to care for them. He hadn't meant to do it. It had grown in increments. They'd come into his room, and he'd spend quality, *special* time with them. Only he'd become brazen about it; pushed it too far. So far that the rumour mill had cranked into life, and the nuns had started asking questions. He'd confessed in the end, to Father Luke Masego. Frank had chosen his confessor carefully. Father Luke was loyal to the church and wouldn't want to sully its reputation further with yet another scandal, but Frank had still been punished, sent away to Shallow Creek, and his own kind of purgatory.

***

Frank cornered Ivor outside the church directly after mass, rudely pushing past Mrs O'Donnell who'd snagged at his vestments, no doubt eager to pour out more of her vitriolic gossip.

'We have to talk, Ivor. I need you. I need them. What if we took the subject to the forest? Did it there? I've heard things about—'

'Not here.' Ivor cocked his head in Jed's direction. The grounds-man was weeding around the gravestones and shooting curious glances in their direction. 'I'll come to you tonight.'

The hours passed slowly as Frank waited in his study for Ivor's arrival. As the clock reached midnight, he gave into the temptation to dip into his last bottle of moonshine. He lost count of the number of times he filled his glass, the liquid burning a trail into his soul, gazing at the books he'd scoured for clues, and at the statue of St Martin de Porres, the same one he'd kept on his desk back at the school, which stared back at him with its infuriating piety. It was the only personal possession he'd brought with him from his last placement. He wasn't sure why he'd even done that.

Finally the bell trilled, making him jump and sending the bottle smashing to the floor. Adrenaline vanquishing the moonshine's mugginess, he ran for the door, and ushered Ivor into his sanctum.

'There are no more, Father.'

'There must be.'

'There aren't. I can't help you. It's over.'

'But you came to me in the beginning. We have to see this through to the end.'

'It's over.'

'We can't give up. Why would you even suggest we do this if you weren't going to see it through?'

Ivor shrugged. 'Everyone's got to have a hobby.'

Frank brushed this insouciance away. 'You have to help me. We're in this together. You've done things too. Bad things. It's as much in your interest as mine to find a solution.'

Something sparked in Ivor's eyes, and then he smirked. 'There is no solution, Father. It's over. You're on your own.'

'Please, Ivor.

Ivor came closer, leaning forward until their noses were almost touching. 'It's over, priest.'

Frank looked deep into the man's eyes, desperate to find a trace of pity, hope, or *anything* in there. And then, it came upon him in an instant. The answer to his prayers was so obvious, how could he have not seen it before? Frank knew exactly what he had to do now. When Ivor turned away, Frank reached for the statue, weighed it in his hand and struck the back of the man's head with a strength fuelled by zeal. Ivor staggered, roared, and whirled around, ready to defend himself. Frank struck again. And again. Down Ivor went, crumpling over the desk, and then sliding to the floor. Frank sank to his knees and checked for a pulse. The back of Ivor's head was a spongy mass, but the man was still alive—*good*. Frank heaved Ivor over onto his back, then reached for a shard of the splintered moonshine bottle.

***

With Ivor's body cooling in his study, Father Frank hurried into the bathroom and stared at his reflection in the cracked mirror above the sink.

As Ivor lay dying, bulbous body twitching as if attached to electrodes, he'd gouged out the man's eyes, hacking through the optical nerves. Frank had saved him from a fate worse than death. His only regret was that it had taken him so long to find the answer. He should have figured it out when he gazed into Mr Fontaine's eyes, and those of the other unfortunates. It was there in the writings he'd pored over endlessly: Matthew 6: *The eye is the lamp to the body.*

The eyes are the windows to the soul.

The eyes are the windows to the soul, and his needed to be sealed. It would be agonising, but it was better than what was coming. If death did take him unawares at least now he'd be ready. Hands steady, albeit sticky and stained with Ivor's blood, he opened the rectory's First Aid cabinet, and removed the curved suturing needle. And, as he dug the point into the tender flesh of his lower eyelid to make the first of many stitches, he was completely unaware that he was smiling. For the first time in months he had hope.

THE ALTERATION

by Aliya Whitely

"I was a projectionist," says Madeleine. "In the cinema, on the south side of town. Did you know that about me? It's a skilled job. People don't appreciate that. I was good at it too. We're meant to be modest, aren't we? About our skills. But surely enough time has passed so I can say it, if only to you. You've been such a constant friend to me, haven't you, uh …"

"Ruth."

This is their regular route. Around the walls of Arkady, every day at three o'clock in the afternoon, pushing Madeleine's wheelchair along the gravel path in a clockwise direction. They've reached the turning that leads through the orchard to the pond. It's early autumn and the apples have not yet fallen from the trees; that is still to come. For now, there is the scent of fruit to enjoy, heavy and on the verge of the commencement of rot.

"That's right," says Madeleine. "Ruth Mortimer."

"My surname is Usiskin," Ruth tells her. "Mortimer is your surname."

"No it isn't!" she says, all astonishment. "Do you think I don't know my own name?"

It is not wise to contradict the confused, but Ruth finds it difficult not to attempt to steer the mind as she steers the wheelchair. She wants to stop progress down this particular path; she knows too well where it leads.

"Of course," she says. "Of course you know."

"I should think I know my own name." She sniffs at the crisp air. "It's one of those days. I can smell the change coming."

Ruth knows what she means. She's always enjoyed those days herself, when the blending of one season to another is palpable. They are like a secret seam found by fingers that tiptoe over a smooth, long length of material. They remind her of the perfect craftsmanship of the world. God makes such days to help humanity appreciate his skill and dedication.

"It's on you, too. The smell. The cinema used to stink of it, at the final showing," says Madeleine. "They'd roll in from a night at Jack's Tavern, across the street, and they'd shout and cheer through the midnight performance, whatever it was. All the better if some poor actress was taking off her clothes. The Portlin brothers were the worst. The three of them, drunk as skunks, yelling the worst things at the screen. And when the show was over, they'd talk about all going back to the eldest brother's house and sharing his wife out, like she was a bag of sweets. I'd see her in the superstore sometimes, putting things tenderly in her trolley, worn delicate with it all. I don't know how they could bear to do it to her."

"There are no Portlin brothers," says Ruth. It is for her own benefit, not for Madeleine's. It is to stop reality from sliding away. These stories sound true, but she has checked, and nothing is correct about them. Nothing but the details about Shallow Creek itself. The businesses and the homes.

"Not any more there isn't," Madeleine replies equably. They follow the low brick wall around the back of the orchard. The pond comes into view. It's not big, but it has a pleasing symmetry and a calmness that appeals to Ruth. "One night there was just the three of them at the late screening, and I started the film for them and put up with their noises for as long as I could. Then I set a fire going in the booth. Film stock burns very well, goes up quick, doesn't need any help. By the time I left and locked up tight behind me there was already smoke in the lobby. I don't know how long it took for the Portlins to smell it. I went home and put myself to bed. I do miss that old cinema, though."

"It's still there," says Ruth. "It never burned down."

"Just ruins," Madeleine says. "Just ruins now."

They reach the pond. At least, upon this spot, there will be silence for a while. Madeleine finds her own sort of quiet contemplation in the view, of the trees overhanging the water, and the leaves changing their shades.

Ruth tells herself—the words are loud in her head, and in her native tongue—*I can help. I will help.* She will find a way to reach them all. She looks out over the green algae that spreads on the pond, and thinks on it.

***

There are five inmates within the walls and three of them never receive regular visitors. The doctor and contracted nurses, even relatives, might come and go, but Ruth Usiskin is the only fixed point in the asylum, present day and night. She considers herself to be the best contact these people have with sanity.

It's on her mind as she works on her dress, which she has been sewing for three months, in the hours afforded to her between her duties. She has a narrow room on the ground floor, with a single bed next to the window. Behind the door she keeps a tailor's dummy that holds what she has completed of the dress so far: pink, floral panelled skirt, gathered bodice. The sleeves, collar and buttons are needed for it to be complete.

A utilitarian dressing table holds her scissors, pins and reels along with the travelling bible her father gave her on the day she left Sweden. She felt a calling, when she was younger, but there were few places left that wanted a person to become the light in the dark, the caretaker of souls. So she travelled, and talked, and followed the whispers of the worst things around the world, and finally arrived at Shallow Creek. *There is no other place like this left*, she thinks, as she sews. *And I will wipe it until it is clean.*

She has studied hard to reach this point in time. While travelling, she worked as a care nurse in special wards wherever she found them, hidden in the mazes of clean white hospital walls. She oversaw pills and therapies. She took courses and allowed the experts to tell her of certain paths out of misery that only needed to be walked. She still believes this. Walking the path, allowing the bad words and thoughts to flow out and away, will heal the mind. What would her father have quoted? Proverbs 16:24:

Gracious words are a honeycomb, sweet to the soul and healing to the bones.

She will keep her words gracious, and Madeleine will start to do the same. One day they will have a real conversation.

***

"I was a schoolteacher," says Madeleine. "I taught Class Two. Not the littlest ones, but the ones who were just beginning to find their feet, to know themselves. I loved watching them discovering who they were, a bit more every day. I like to think I prepared them to become members of our town. Moral leadership is very important, isn't it, er ..."

"Ruth."

"Who's that?"

"I'm Ruth."

"Who's Ruth?"

Ruth pushes the wheelchair onwards, trying to measure out her steps. She could rush but that would only eat into Madeleine's only meaningful contact for today. But it is so difficult not to rush, sometimes. She didn't sleep well. The state of the body affects the mood. Walking will help.

"I could smell them changing. Just like you. There'd be times when a certain child would bear the odour of change for a few days. It wasn't unpleasant but it's strong, isn't it? Tyler Stone was one of the worst. I saw him rising up taller and looking outwards, over the girls and boys in that room with him, and then at the world beyond the window, and I realised that he was becoming capable of terrible things. So I told him to stay after school to help me clear the paints away after an art lesson."

"There was no Tyler Stone," Ruth tells her. She pushes through the orchard, and notices the first of the apples have fallen.

"I told him to come with me to the supply cupboard, and then to stand still while I put the plastic bag from the paint supplies over his head, and there was enough good left in him to do as he was told. I wrapped tape around his neck to hold the bag in place and he stood still for a minute, at least, then reached out with his arms and I left him to it. I came back later and took his body to the basement and burnt it in the furnace, and that was that."

Ruth can't help herself any longer. She says, "You never did that thing, Madeleine, I promise you. You were never a schoolteacher, I swear it, and I don't believe you have it in you to do such a thing."

She doesn't reply.

Of course she doesn't reply; they have reached the pond, and the time for talking has passed for another day.

***

The first time.

She thinks and she sews.

The first time she walked into Arkady. The retiring full-time nurse showed her around, and how calm the place was! So few inmates for such an imposing building, with a grand central staircase, fitted with a stair-lift on either side—grandeur punctuated with practicality. The white statues of posed figures in front of each long window that looked down over the driveway, and then the thick locks on the doors. The bell tower, clanging out the hour, competing with the digital clock on the wall of the old kitchen, used as a dispensary. Pills for Bridges and Dakin and Fallowes and Tan. And Mortimer, of course. A privately-owned house held still between the past and the future. *There's no government interference here*—said the nurse. *You do things as you see fit. Nobody much cares.*

That was why she took the job. Not to do as she saw fit, but because nobody cared. The nurse hadn't cared. Not any longer. She knew she could do better than that.

For the first time it occurs to Ruth that possibly that old nurse had cared, once upon a time. But that time had ended.

The collar is nearly complete. It is a frothy, careful work of cotton embroidered with small green leaves, dotted in a loose pattern of her own devising. She stands up from the bed and approaches the tailor's dummy so she can put the collar against the dress. It looks just as she imagined it would.

She tacks it in place with pins.

The first time.

The first time she met Madeleine. Only a few months ago. An older woman, delivered to the doorstep, escorted by a policeman and the doctor. She was small and folded up in herself, arms and legs pulled in tight, like a newborn. They helped her into the wheelchair and pushed her inside.

"Ruth," said the doctor. "How are things?"

"Everything is fine, thank you, Doctor."

"This is Miss Mortimer. Here's her file." He handed her the paperwork, and Ruth read it later that afternoon, once the rooms were quiet once more:

The patient was found in an unresponsive state by authorities after a neighbour reported not seeing Mrs Mortimer for several days. Mrs Mortimer, in her late eighties, was found deceased at the property, having suffered a stroke.

Miss Mortimer was also found at the property in an uncommunicative state. She was taken to hospital and found to be suffering from dehydration and malnutrition, as well an underdeveloped musculature from prolonged inactivity. A birth certificate was later tracked down for Miss Mortimer. There are no records of school attendance or employment.

She still does not communicate, and shows no ability to care for herself.

Recommendation: private referral to Arkady.

And who was it who funded these private patients, this enormous house, the drugs and the daily care and her own small salary?

She had asked the doctor once. He said, "The town."

The first time Ruth heard Madeleine speak she had thought it was a miracle. Then she had started listening to what Madeleine was saying.

She sews on the collar, one tiny stitch at a time. The dress is nearly done.

***

"I was a lumbermill worker," says Madeleine. "Did you know that about me? That's why I'm still so physically fit. Look at my arms." She holds up her arms and makes fists, in a strongman pose. "I can lift twice my own weight. That's what happens when you shift heavy logs all day, every day, for thirty years. I wasn't a lumberjack, just to be clear. That's different. I wanted to be a lumberjack, but working at the mill was as close as I could get. I liked it, though. Good work. Good honest work, er—"

"Ruth."

"Really?" Madeleine's arms drop back down. She folds them over her body. "You're kidding me."

"I promise you, it's Ruth."

"But that was her name. I met her at the tavern one night, and walked her home, and then she started coming by the mill with things for me. A coffee, or a muffin she'd baked. She was much prettier to look at than you. You can't be a Ruth. Ruths are all good nature and sunshine. She would smile at me, and I'd smile back, and then I started to smell it."

There are more apples on the ground than there are on the trees. Somebody should be collecting them up, maybe putting them outside the gates so passers by could take them home. *It's a waste, but it's the same every year*, thinks Ruth. They'll lie on the ground, softening until the frost comes. Then they'll freeze. She tries to keep her mind on the apples.

"It wasn't her. It was me. In me. I was changing, and it got worse the more she came around. She brought it out in me, and I found I liked that smell, that deep, wet, red smell from inside. But I thought nobody else would like that smell. Definitely not her. I tried to keep my distance, but one day she brought me a coffee on my lunch break and sat beside me on one of the logs. She sniffed, and said—*You smell nice, Johnny.*"

"Johnny?"

"That's my name. And I think it's the way she said it, said my name out loud, that made me believe her. So I knew I had to let the alteration have its way."

Ruth walks faster as Madeleine's voice drops lower, and grows husky. They are leaving the orchard, and the pond is close.

"So I whispered in Ruth's ear and told her about the smell coming out of me, and how I wanted to put it in her. She shook her head and shook her head, but it was too late to take it back. She wanted the smell in her and I put it in her and I said her name over and over while I rubbed that smell in her hair, in her face, up under her dress. I said *Ruth, Ruth*, while I did it, I said, *Ruth, Ruth Usiskin—*"

"What?" says Ruth. "You said what?"

But they've reached the pond.

"What happened then?" says Ruth. "What happened?"

Madeleine looks out over the water, serene. She'll say nothing more.

***

To the sound of the wind blowing hard against the window, the last button is stitched in place. The hands that pull away the loose thread don't feel like they belong to Ruth. She has been watching herself all evening, as if she is a stranger in her own room. She does not feel like the woman who owns the travelling bible on the dresser, or like the daughter of the man who gave it to her. Her skin does not feel familiar to her. She does not smell right.

She takes off her white jacket and trousers, folds them, and places them on the bed. Then she removes the dress from the tailor's dummy and slips it over her head. It falls over her body easily. Surely she knows her own measurements, but the fit is looser than she would have liked, baggy over the chest and under the arms. She has lost weight.

Still, she likes the swing of the skirt as she turns. She decides to wear it tomorrow, forgoing the usual uniform. It might cheer the patients. For now, she undresses and puts it back on the dummy. It can be new for one more night.

In her plain white underwear, feeling the chill of autumn that the old heating system cannot defeat, she opens her bible and finds one of her father's favourite passages. Ephesians 5:25-27:

Husbands, love your wives, as Christ loved the church and gave himself up for her, that he might sanctify her, having cleansed her by the washing of water with the word, so that he might present the church to himself in splendour, without spot or wrinkle or any such thing, that she might be holy and without blemish.

How he had loved Ruth's mother in her clean, white dress for Sundays, but white is now the colour of work for Ruth. She thinks he would have liked to see his daughter in this soft pink. It might not suit her now, but at some point in the future, when she has aged and carries more weight, it will be right for her. This dress will be a reminder of this place. These patients and the good she did for them, to them.

It gives her the strength to go on.

***

"Don't wait for retirement," says Madeleine. "Don't wait for some time in the future because it won't come. I found that out when my husband died, two months into his retirement. All that time he had been talking about what he was going to do, and then there was no time to do it. No money, either, after that, for a retirement of my own. I had to get a job, so I started cleaning the library, at night, and it made just enough money to get by. I liked it, too. I could scrub that place clean, and sometimes even get rid of the smell it had, although the smell was always back by the next night. I dusted and vacuumed and sprayed so much air freshener, and when that didn't work I collected the books together and poured bleach over them, and when the smell got in me I poured the bleach over me too, and it ate away all the stories and all the skin and all the smell. I hate that smell. You have it on you too, don't you, er …?"

"Ruth."

"That's right."

The strong wind last night has cast down so many more apples. They lie thick on the ground, and nobody will come for them. Ruth steers the wheelchair around the ones that have fallen on the path, and shoves them back into the wet grass with her foot as she passes them.

Madeleine turns her head, shifting her upper body in the wheelchair, and makes a rare moment of eye contact. She smiles. "That's a pretty dress," she says.

"Thank you," says Ruth, surprised. Perhaps this is it. The breakthrough. The moment when one of her patients begins to find a better way of existing, led by the light Ruth has been providing for so long. She wants to say: *tell me about your childhood*, but she's no psychiatrist. How to continue this conversation?

But Madeleine is still talking. "I had two dresses. One to wear and one to be washed. My mother liked me to be clean. I wasn't allowed to play outside. But inside was terribly boring, too. I had no toys or books. Books had stories in them, and my mother said all stories were lies. That people couldn't go on adventures. They had to stay in Shallow Creek forever. In their houses. Their rooms. And the town would change them into what it needed them to be."

Ruth remembers the patient's file. Never employed, never sent to school. To never go outside. To never be seen, or known about. Empty.

"But you tell so many stories." Terrible stories.

"Who does?"

"You do. You."

"Stories from the library?"

"No," says Ruth, feeling the connection slipping away. How to reach her again? "You. Madeleine Mortimer. You only lived with your mother. You never worked."

"I'm working right now!" says Madeleine. "I'm looking after you."

"No, that's not—"

"You stink of it. The change. You need to get on with it. That's what you're here for. That's what the town wants. I'm here to tell you that. Get on with it. Get on with it."

"I'm not—"

"Get it done," Madeleine says. They reach the pond. She falls into silence and looks out over the water.

What is that smell?

The rot, the rot is not coming from the apples at all. It is wafting from Ruth's armpits, pushing out of her prickling skin and up through the loose material of her new dress. The dress is ruined by the stink, it must be washed clean. It all must be washed clean.

Her father would tell her to wash it clean.

She tips the wheelchair forwards until it overbalances and plunges down into the water.

Then she starts a fast walk back to inside the walls of Arkady. She does not listen, as she walks. She does not look at anything but the path, and she breathes only through her mouth, to avoid that smell.

***

She has washed the dress twice but it cannot be salvaged. It doesn't matter, as the smell cannot be washed from her body, either, and she has tried. She sits on the bed in her underwear, her skin raw from scrubbing, and writes in the back of her bible.

Ruth Usiskin, Age 44:

I was a psychiatric nurse. I was called to it. I believed in the idea of helping people to find their way out of their illness, and I do think my patients were all the better for my care. Then one day a new patient came to my asylum. An old woman who had never done harm to anyone, perhaps because she had never been given the chance. She began to speak to me of her life, except it wasn't her life. It was a smell that had spread through her, and that smell came into me and took me over too. It changed me. It wanted me to be part of a story. So I did as it asked. I drowned that old woman, and then I returned to the asylum and found the morphine and injected the other patients so they could not change, not like me. They held out their arms for me, because they thought they knew me. They called me Ruth, but that is not my name any more.

My name is Shallow Creek. I have become the town and it is in me. This is the story now. There is no need for further alteration.

Ruth finishes writing. She closes the bible, sits on the bed, and waits for the story to end.

TIDE

by Nick Adams

We see sandpipers out on the exposed, fetid-sweating bay sifting through the mud like jaded prospectors. We see the scattered glint of the sea playing hooky two hundred metres out. We see the sunken ribcage of the old lifeboat yawning at the sky, its bones stripped and bleached by the seasons.

An exchange has taken place. She has been given back to us, and he has been taken away. Who are we to say whether we got the better end of that deal or not? There's just a certain symmetry to it.

It starts with the heat.

The heat is everywhere, oppressive and exhausting. The town's a-whirring with a thousand fans variously indolent and geriatric, the shops' fridges and freezers are gouged empty, and the dead are sweating in their graves beneath the crippled spire of St Martin's.

The sandpipers scatter without cause. The vacated mud spends most of the year submerged and lies abandoned now by the retreating tide (even the sea, we say, is eager to escape).

This is how she's found.

Normally it's folk with dogs or metal detectors who do the finding, often lost themselves. Percy Pettigrew is out walking with his terrier and a pair of custom mud-shoes (*used to be perfectly good tennis rackets, we hear*). It's the wedding ring he finds—the wedding ring that leads him to the rest of her, imprisoned down there in all the dank and blind darkness.

In Shallow Creek people are familiar with each other, for better or worse. But truth be told, we never knew Eva Runt all that well. She was a black sheep or a dark horse, or some other manner of outlying creature. She was always over or underdressed—sometimes both at the same time, in flawless make-up and paint-flecked hand-me-downs. She was absurdly early or painfully late, and there were moments when this faraway look came over her and we'd wonder what it was she saw.

This was years ago, mind. We'll admit we haven't given her much thought lately—when someone goes missing there's plenty to say, but as time passes and nothing or no-one appears, talk soon runs dry. We wanted to assume the best too—we didn't like to think of things like this.

Ask other people and they'll say she was well-educated, a smart sort, as far as they could tell. Sure, we say—she *seemed* educated, but didn't she work to make us notice how clever and proper she was? That's what we remember. Constantly scolding her little one—don't do that but this, don't eat with those but these, don't say *ta* but *thank you*. Whose benefit do you suppose that was for?

She was polite though, they'll say.

Up to a point. Not so polite when she had a screaming fit with her chap during Solstice Fair, choosing the zenith of the fireworks to let loose, so what they screamed was drowned out, but we got the gist all right. It was that business with her and the Lighthouse Keeper, as we recall.

Just tittle-tattle, they'll object. Pernicious gossip.

Well. No fire, no smoke. That's all we'll say on the matter.

She was pretty too, they'll tell you, and we'll concede, if that's your taste. The little one's grown up to be her mother's doppelganger, we hear, with her green eyes and curls and lashes.

Mind you. Not so pretty now. Ten years inside the mud and under the water—she's a sorry state when the police disinter her, so it's said. Ted Sylvester claims no—says she looks like she hasn't aged a day, says the mud must've preserved her, says she looks like she's a long-lost marble statue lifted clear of all that muck. But Ted Sylvester also swears wolves the size of horses live in Silverpine Forest. Just to give an idea of where he's at, reliability-wise.

Once it's done, Officer Lopez visits the husband, we know that much.

The *late* husband, they say.

Well, fine. The *late* husband. Though that's jumping forward, isn't it?

In any case, we ask Janet, and she's all discretion and professionalism like always, so she tells us in general terms.

A decade's a long time, she says. Evidence doesn't do well over so many years, doesn't tend to last, especially underwater. Generally speaking.

What about forensics. Isn't there forensics? We ask.

There's a mouth swab, she says. No use now. In general terms, that is.

But the fibres. The skin under her fingernails. The blood spatters?

She says we watch too much television.

We always did prefer Officer Hamilton, before he moved upstairs and lost time for normal folk and everyday troubles.

We're not for public lynchings, far from it. A fair trial's the cornerstone of any civilised society. But they don't come guiltier than Angus Runt if you ask us. He's a big fella who blots out the light but moves like a ghost. He's got silent footsteps, which we agree is an ill omen in such a chunky chap. He wears his guilt the way we might wear an overcoat in winter, and dispenses words like a miser offering change.

You see him on his tug boat—first light or midnight, high tide and low. He strips the wrecks beyond the bay and drags barges laden with rusting containers up the creek. He'd have no difficulty taking his lady out for a twilit cruise, boshing her on the head and slipping her overboard, her alabaster skin sinking beneath inky waves.

Mind you, *were* there a lynching, he'd require three nooses just to hold him off the ground.

Thing is, where no justice is served by man, natural justice soon steps in, and Angus Runt doesn't get away with it for long.

The way we hear it, he wakes up one night after they've dredged her up to find he's soaked through, top to bottom. The summer's an undying thing that's tightening further round our necks each day, so first he thinks it's sweat, but nobody sweats inches deep across the floor.

(We've known some fellas, they say)

Enough of that, we say. This is a serious matter.

The next morning all's fine and the floor's dry like nothing ever happened. He's in the shower gargling under the hissing stream when he notices two peculiar things: first, the water around his ankles is so thick and murky he can't see his feet; second, he can taste salt between his lips.

You might ask, incidentally, how what happens to a person alone in their shower is commonly known. Thing is, this is a small place and we are more than a few. What's taken to be secret usually isn't, and from a pile of overheard fragments and whispered fibres, it is not beyond us to weave a tapestry of near-truths.

Angus turns off the shower and waits for the muddy water to drain away. But it does not drain. He squats and feels around for a blockage in the plughole—a knot of hair or a chunk of soap—and feels the water rapidly chill.

He stands and regards the shower stall with suspicion. Unsure of his jumbled thoughts, he shuts the bathroom door, paces down then up the stairs and turns the handle again. This time the stall is empty but for a nebula of gritty detritus around the plughole.

There is a moment between the noticing of this fact and a second realisation—the carpet beneath his feet is sodden.

In the pits of winter colossal waves howl in off the sea and hurl themselves kamikaze-like against the harbour. Some of us are old enough to remember when the town woke up to fish atop our library steps and seaweed covering the square. But this morning the sea is pancake-flat and the sun has baked everything in the seaport dry.

Everything bar for the puddle under Runt's feet, which spreads and deepens the longer he stands there. The Tugboat Captain stands squinting at the sun outside his cottage, opposite the burnt ruins of the pier. We watch him lift one boot followed by the other, examining the water dripping off. He bends down and stirs the water around with a solitary finger, and it's about now that he begins to attract attention—a grown man squatting in a puddle, behaving like he's never seen one before.

We ask him if he's okay, being community-minded spirits after all.

He says he's grand, just grand, and he stands and moves away, slow and deliberate paces. There's a brief moment of reprieve between each footfall and we think—he thinks, for that matter—that it's nothing, all imagined. Then the water comes again. He swears and wheels in circles, struggling to keep watch on all the water. Beneath his breath he runs through his full repertoire of foul and objectionable language, as if reciting a potty-mouthed mantra.

It bubbles up through cracks between the flagstones, pushing up dust and dirt and slowly submerging each slab around him. The water spreads in creeping fingers, searching for the other pools and subsuming them into a swollen body that ripples unnaturally and trails Angus's every step.

He breaks into an awkward jog, not a man for sudden movement. He succeeds in escaping the water, but as soon as he stops we watch his feet. Shimmering tendrils emerge from beneath his boots and catch the climbing sun overhead. As it begins to spread once more, he turns tail and flees in stomping, heavy footfalls through the trees.

The Sylvester brothers are here too, skulking in the shadows. As we watch Runt run, Barney claims he's seen this before. Alice Mora, twenty years ago. We've never heard of her, we say. Exactly, he says. If either of the Sylvester brothers is a greater fabricator of untruths, then it's a bitterly-disputed title.

If you were to gaze at Shallow Creek from above, it could appear that some vast creature had taken a tremendous bite out of the land. Thing is, in our case, it's all too real. Whatever the beast was that had a chew on our coastline left a poison that's working its way through the veins of the town.

When we were little there were shops all along the seafront. There were people too—people working, playing, talking. We remember the sweet shop selling gum as big and tough as tennis balls and the penny arcade that swallowed everything you gave it. We had a café that sold food in greasy paper bags and a machine that told your fortune.

Time slipped away and so did these places, until there was only Angus Runt, living in the sagging cottage at the end of the harbour.

You'd think he'd have moved away, after what happened. But he stayed, rising defiantly every morning to stare down the sea, knowing she was out there. If you ask us, there's got to be something of a person missing to be able to live with yourself after you've done something like that.

You jump to conclusions, they'll say. They've said it before.

And you think he's innocent, do you? They're naive.

What about Pettigrew, they say.

What about him?

You know he knocked around with Sian Runt?

By *knocked around with*, they mean in bed. They think we're prudes who never did such things.

Angus's kid? And what of it, we say.

They think it suspicious Pettigrew took so sudden an interest in metal-detecting. They find it iffy that in all of twenty minutes he stumbled upon the remains of Sian's mum, a decade after she went missing. It's like the daughter knew something, they say.

We remind them that she was only eleven when Eva vanished. Anyway, doesn't she live in Scotland now?

All manner of ways to keep in touch, they say. Cheap flights too.

Cheap flights to Shallow Creek? Ha, we scoff.

They're just saying, they say. There are plenty possibilities.

The heat and the sun continue to rise, so the water Angus leaves behind dries up in no time flat. If anything, it vanishes faster than you might expect. Maybe it's merely another record-breaking heat, or it could be that the water's interest is solely set on him.

There's a small crowd on Sandhook Lane, whispers faster than people. He's in the square now, they say. He's armed. Violent. Drunk. High on drugs cooked up in his basement, we hear. They haven't seen what we've seen though.

Sandhook Lane connects the seafront to the Town Square, and when we reach the latter, we're met with the sight of Angus stripped of everything but his underpants wading out into the memorial fountain. He stands knee-deep, holding onto the leaping concrete fish like it's a life raft in a storm. The police have arrived and Janet Lopez is fastening tape to a lamp post to secure the no-go zone. Sheriff Hamilton looks on from the shade, sucking on a cigarette that engulfs his head with noxious fumes and discourages folk from talking to him.

Janet walks out into the centre of the square and tries to talk to Angus, but he bats her arm away as she tries to usher him out of the water, drool spilling from his toothless mouth. She looks at Hamilton and shrugs. He shakes his head. We doubt this was covered in their training courses.

The fountain's spilling over already. We suppose he hoped to lose the water in there, trick it maybe, but tiny waves are sloshing over the lip onto the gravel beyond. A dark circle is slowly spreading amongst the stones.

The sun is directly overhead, shrinking our shadows in the pools beneath our feet. Angus's slick skin shines in the midday light. He casts wildly around for help, but we don't want to meet his eye. What could we be expected to do?

As the scorched afternoon rolls on Angus is attended to by Dr. Payel. The doctor is unable to coax him out of the fountain and is forced to clamber in to administer tests. The fountain is turned off so he can check him over and take blood samples.

They say the syringe is so full of water there is no blood to test. We hear Payel slides another needle into Angus's arm, takes extra care to stop the syringe getting wet. It makes no difference, they say. Water, water everywhere.

We wonder if this will be on the news. We wonder what we'll say if they interview us.

He's a quiet sort of fellow, we'll say. And he drowned his wife. Or at least, killed her. She may have been dead before—

Hang on, the young man or woman sent to interview us will tell us—you can't say that.

Can we say he *seemed* like a murderer, we'll ask.

No, they'll object. He might sue.

He won't, we'll say. It's true.

Even so.

We envisage a young woman now. She'll be sweeping her hair behind her ear in an irritating-not-endearing tic and searching for someone less slanderous to interview. That'll be best. We're too honest, see.

Afternoon drifts into evening and the sun slips behind the lighthouse, throwing long blue shadows across the Creek. We've been told to leave by the Police now, but we understand he's still there, the square under a foot of water. There are ducks, there's a heron, there are waterfalls running into the fairground.

They're looking for volunteers, we hear. Not enough folk in the police and fire service, so they need more people to pick up squeegee brushes and drive the flood towards the creek. A few years ago we'd have put our names down, but we'd be no use now. There are plenty younger people. They'll do a fine job.

Come morning, Angus is gone.

The flood's gone too, the waters now subsided leaving only small pools like the residue of a storm, a fine layer of sand and grit across every surface and the lingering smell of rain on a summer's day. Nobody knows where he is, but we suggest the hospital—perhaps Payel enticed him down from the fountain and is fixing him up as we speak. Maybe it's all blown over. He might be in bed at home deep in feverish dreams.

We're not sure we believe it.

It doesn't feel like the kind of story that ends that way.

He is spotted from the harbour.

At first, when we get there, we can't see him. It takes Charlotte Cooper to point him out. She knows him, she says. She used to be friends with Sian. She wonders if she should let her know. What would be the point? What could she do?

We can see him now, his head and shoulders above the waves, silhouetted by the early-morning sun.

Nobody saw him go in, just as nobody saw him leave the square. They ran out of volunteers at three in the morning.

It's fine, they say. Not to worry—the tide's on the way out. Someone will be in to get him. He'll be sunburnt, but he'll be safe.

They're wrong.

Twenty minutes later, it's clear that the tide is not going out. It should be—as it does every day at this time—but it's not. His shoulders are no longer visible, and the waves are breaking over his chin.

People scream and shout, but he's facing out to sea and there's no sign that he has heard their calls. There's talk of a boat, but we realise soon enough that Angus Runt is the only one equipped to help. Could we break into his house, find his keys and launch his boat? Not *us*, obviously—but someone else?

The water is above his mouth now.

The thought occurs to us—is he standing in the spot where she was found? We wouldn't like to say. We're not ones for idle speculation.

Percy Pettigrew and Mike Pollock run into the water and swim out towards him. Their t-shirts are draped on rotting groynes protruding from the mud. It's already too late. The sea has swallowed him.

Pettigrew and Pollock spend an hour searching for him deep in the water before they give up. This is not the Med—the sea is dark and murky, full of sharp-edged rocks and ruins beneath the waves. It's hard to know now where he went under, a struggle to swim, and they can't find him.

In a way we're glad. It's cleaner this way.

The boys come back up the beach, limping over the pebbles. They are told they're brave, they've done a good job, not to blame themselves. It wasn't their fault.

We don't know if we believe this when we look at Pettigrew, long and sinewy and straight-backed with a towel over his shoulders. He's not exactly cut up about it.

We think of the girl, Sian, who has lost both her parents to the sea, the same stretch of water—one given and one taken.

We are not surprised when the tide finally draws back its curtain to reveal that there is no trace of Angus Runt.

There are more birds out on the mud now, but these are different. We think they might be curlews, but we're no experts. The sea appears to come closer to shore every day, burying the stench and bones of the old lifeboat.

Without Angus Runt, the cottage at the end of the harbour is boarded up, and the empty houses along the seafront look like a row of rotten molars that need pulling before the infection spreads.

The daughter is seen around the Creek. She has a drink in Jack's Tavern on Monday, checks out a book of local hiking trails from the library on Tuesday and goes to the cinema with a foreign man on Wednesday.

Or maybe none of those things are true, because she's not there when Eva Runt is finally buried—properly buried—at St. Martin's on Thursday. It's not like she could blend into the crowd, as hardly anyone attends. We go, because nobody deserves to be sent on their way alone, not a second time.

There's talk of the hospital closing, which would mean a thirty-minute drive to see a doctor, but Dr Payel says he'll keep the surgery open till they drag him away. We don't want to tell him that's precisely what happened to his predecessor.

The heat lingers into October, like it forgot to die. Flowers shrivel and the grass turns yellow. There's a fire in the hills and we wake up to a layer of ash on our doorsteps. They say there's rain forecast for next week, that things will get better, but they've been saying that for a long time now.

THE FULMAR'S CRY

by Andrea Hardaker

It was 6am, breakfast time. She'd woken up disorientated. A breath of autumn wind whistled in through the rickety bedroom window. She rubbed her bare arms and rose, wrapped a blanket round her shoulders, and headed downstairs to the kitchen. There, she boiled the kettle, watched a puff of steam billow into the air then vanish, and cast her mind back, back, back, as she did every day to *that* day. The day before.

The telephone screeched from its cradle like a fractious infant.

Martha's heart jolted in her chest. She held her breath and slowly counted, but the ringing continued. She knew the call was important—the phone so seldom rang, but there were voices in her head. One urged her to answer right away. *You're stronger now, let the news sink in, deal with it.* The other yelled at her to ignore it. Which voice to listen to? She hovered in the doorway, tried to quell the tremor inside, and lifted the receiver.

"They've found the bike." The words tumbled out of his mouth like rocks, landing with a thump. She didn't answer. There was a pause, then the line went dead. It was all he had to say. She had no idea how he'd found her, but his words, she understood, were an instruction—*You have to come home.*

Martha replaced the receiver and returned to her trees. Her whole body shook. She chewed over the news like a fish bone, lodged between her teeth. *Thirty years. Thirty years to find a motorbike. How hard could it have been?* James didn't say *where* it was found. In fact, James didn't *say* anything. Acid scorched her throat. *She couldn't go back. She daren't.* She dug a fingernail into the palm of her hand, felt the pince, and allowed her mind to snag once more on the barb of her past.

In the weeks after Charlotte went missing, when it became clear her daughter wasn't coming home, Martha scoured the cliffs near the lighthouse of Shallow Creek, where she was last seen alive. Rumour dictated Charlotte was the latest victim of the waters surrounding Five Finger islands, just a few miles from the mainland. For years locals vanished in the area with no explanation. Most were 'officially' classified suicidal, drawn into the waters by some peculiar preoccupation with death. Yet, there were many in the Creek who hinted at a more sinister force at play.

The fishing community, steeped in superstition, believed the disappearances were linked to an ancient maritime legend, about a beautiful young woman named Sedna. Having turned down many wealthy suitors, Sedna was tricked into marrying a sea-bird by her own father in return for a supply of fish. On the eve of her wedding, she was drugged and secreted away on an island. She awoke confused and heart-broken. Weeks later, her father, wracked with guilt, rowed out to save her. He killed the bird and attempted the journey home but as his boat reached the middle of the ocean a flock of angry fulmars rose up from the sea, causing a huge storm. Panicked, Sedna's father threw his daughter overboard. She reached up, attempting to pull herself to safety but, afraid for his own life, he cut off her hands with his fishing knife.

According to local lore, this was how Five Finger island came to be. Sedna's severed digits bloated and swelled until they grew big enough to act as a permanent reminder to residents of The Creek of what her father had done.

But her anger didn't stop there. The fishing community believed that after she sank to the underworld, Sedna was transformed into a vengeful sea goddess who took control of the waters and all its inhabitants. In her wrath, she promised an endless supply of fresh fish to any bird able to source a pair of human hands to replace the ones she lost. Birds who failed to comply were starved to death.

Martha had heard this story recounted many times over the years and dismissed it as superstitious nonsense. Yet, even she had to admit, something wasn't quite right about the area. The water forever appeared inviting; turquoise, with a sprinkle of silver stars. But Martha, and everyone else in The Creek, knew that swirling tides circled beneath the surface like ravenous sharks ready to gobble up the foolish who tried to navigate its waters. Most people went out of their way to avoid the entire area—Charlotte included.

No one in Shallow Creek knew precisely what life, if any, existed on the islands other than the vast colony of fulmars, —sea birds which obsessively circled the coastline. In the entire history of the Creek only one person reached an island and returned—local campaigner Janet Lopez.

Years after Charlotte disappeared, Janet, whose gay lover Zsofia was another supposedly claimed by the sea, tried to convince the town that the mystery was, indeed, directly linked to the birds.

There could be no doubt of their unsettling presence; diving into the water from great heights to catch their prey, wailing agonising cries as they soared. Janet, perturbed by their menace, organised demonstrations, waved placards, assembled a photographic montage of the missing, and recorded hours of footage of the fulmars rising from the ocean in great swarms.

Occasionally, rows of dead birds were discovered near the lighthouse on Pincer Crag, their bellies slashed open. The stench of death hung in the air and kept hikers at bay for weeks on end. Eager to solve the mystery, Janet donned a gas mask purchased from Colt's Curiosity Corner and documented the birds' movements and subsequent deaths in what swiftly became an obsession. But she needed answers. Martha understood that.

Gradually, a section of townspeople who previously dismissed Janet as crazy, began to pay attention to her claims. The local newspaper carried an article in which she blamed the sheriff's office for failing to investigate. The story was picked up by a national news channel. Documentary makers, scientists and journalists swarmed the Creek, searching for answers. All they found were flocks of sea birds and cagey locals, unwilling to endanger their fate. None of those so-called experts came to The Creek for truth. They came on safari, bolting back to their cosy lives once the answers dried up, taking with them souvenir cuttings of unexplained phenomena.

The official line, fed by authorities, was of a magnetic field surrounding the cliff, drawing folk to their death. It was a common enough theory to be accepted the outside world.

Janet herself vanished not long after the furore died down. She was up on the crag, photographing a flock of birds in the shape of a whirlwind rising from the sea. Her camera was found on a rock, no sign of Janet. Weeks later, she was discovered soaked and delirious by the groundskeeper of St. Mary's, who was still recovering from the tragedy of The Big Dig and now devoted his days to the living, and trying to keep them that way. Onlookers, who stood well back during Jed's heroic rescue, whispered that Janet could not speak when she surfaced from the sea. Dark swathes of seaweed were coiled around her neck and the fingers on her right hand were severed. She was blue in the face, dripping with blood, and covered with cavernous gashes.

Jed rang for the police the minute he got Janet to safety. She was transported to the local hospital on the west side of town, and subsequently delivered to Arkady Asylum. None of her followers were brave enough to probe deeper and the 'investigation' floundered.

Three months later, speculation about the birds heightened when a wealthy entrepreneur descended on the Creek, determined to leave his mark. His arrogance was as sizeable as his estate and after attempting to buy the islands—(nobody really knew who owned them), he vowed to land his private helicopter on the isle most resembling a thumb. With little haste he took off, the entire population of the Creek by the lighthouse to watch. He would have made it, were it not for the rotor on his chopper striking and beheading a bird during his descent. Within seconds the wails of a hundred fulmars crescendoed to a piercing screech. Engine failure beset the chopper as it spiralled like a dying wasp into the sea. His body was never recovered.

And so the rumours continued. Everyone agreed the area off Pincer Crag was the most beautiful spot in town—a picture of innocence. Yet it proved itself, over and over again, a femme fatale.

When the Sheriff's office insisted that Charlotte deliberately rode off the precipice on her motorbike, Martha dismissed them without a second thought. She knew Charlotte well enough to vouch with absolute certainty that her daughter would never be tempted into the waters, no matter how desperate she might have been to end her life. Charlotte almost drowned as a child and was so traumatised by the experience she'd never learned to swim. It was a struggle to bathe her without a fight. If Charlotte was suicidal (and Martha remained adamant she wasn't) she'd have chosen a swifter, less traumatic end. Carbon Monoxide or drugs, Martha thought—nothing prolonged or messy. Besides, Charlotte was far too obstinate to ever contemplate suicide. Her zest for life was often the cause of trouble. Charlotte sought to explore, relished her freedom, refused to commit to relationships. Charlotte was a free spirit, and a damned stubborn one at that.

Still, in the weeks following her disappearance, Martha, stunned by revelations that her daughter was seen riding near the lighthouse, combed the cliffs for clues. She begged the wauling sea birds for answers, listened to the hiss and spittle of the sea, searched for the slightest sign. On day five, after screaming her daughter's name over and over into the haar, she herself was dragged from the waters by Jed. He'd found her wading out towards the islands. A few steps further, he later told the authorities, he would never have reached her. What he didn't tell them was that when he finally grabbed hold of Martha, she too, was embroiled in swathes of seaweed and had no idea where or who she was.

Shaking herself back to the present, Martha threw open the living room window and listened. Sometimes, she imagined the wind whispered to her, calling her out from the house. She would step outside and follow the direction she believed was the source of sound, trying to decipher the message banded in the breeze—it was a hangover from long before, she knew that. On such occasions, of which there were many, she'd often forget to tie her shoes, neglect to dress, and leave her back door wide open. Her neighbours feared for her sanity. They visited to check up on her, armed with casseroles and pie. One of them went so far as to send the local priest, which only made her laugh. If they were worried about her losing it, they were thirty years too late.

But, as was always the case, she was forced to concede that the wind's message was lost to her. She carried her cup of tea up the steep stairs to her bedroom and, despite herself, began to pack.

The journey back to Shallow Creek was long and arduous. The sun blazed overhead, so Martha rolled down the windows, the sea air cooling her skin. She entered the creek from the west side, navigating the narrow road along Devil's Gorge. The Gorge was yet another place locals immortalised in mystery—its name derived from ancient lore about the appearance of the Devil to a local man. Satan offered the man all the wealth in the world to trade places with him. The man, a simple carpenter and uninterested in wealth, declined the offer. Furious at his refusal, the devil invoked raging thunderstorms which split the mountainous land apart, and caused the carpenter to plummet from a freshly forged cliff into the gorge below. Locals claimed that if one journeyed through the Gorge at night, not only did one risk meeting Satan in all his guises, but one could also hear the harrowing screams of the carpenter as he fell.

But to Martha, the Gorge was a place of beauty. The hills rose high around her, standing guard and making her feel cocooned and safe. It was when she approached the sea, she felt vulnerable.

Once at the house she previously shared with James, she remained in the car, trying to get a hold of herself. The second she saw the coast line she almost fled in panic. She cast an eye towards the ocean and all the old sensations returned in crushing waves. The same dank misery which stalked her day and night until she finally left the Creek, descended upon her like a shroud.

Breathe. You know this isn't real.

Shaking, she left the car, gulped back air, and pushed the front door open.

She found him passed out on the settee, surrounded by piles of crumpled newspapers, empty food cartons and a stack of Charlotte's clothes, which she herself had failed to recycle long after their daughter vanished. His way of coping was to drink and smoke into oblivion. How he'd managed to hold down his job at the library was beyond her. Perhaps it was due to the fact few people used the facility any more.

She entered the kitchen and rattled the dirty dishes piled up at the side of the sink. He groaned as if waking from a heavy beating. Martha strode back into the lounge and sat on the seat opposite, staring at him until he finally stirred awake.

"Come in," he said grudgingly, running his fingers through his hair.

Martha made no comment. He obviously hadn't changed the locks and, naturally, she held on to her key. "Where was it?" she asked.

He stretched out, rubbed the back of his neck. "I've just woken up."

"I can see that. I'm not here for you. I'm here because of the bike. Where was it?"

He reached for a cigarette paper and slowly filled it with tobacco. He didn't look at her as he spoke, fully focused on his rolling. "You're not going to go all crazy ass on me again are you? I only phoned because … well, you know … closure."

Martha bristled. *Crazy ass.* This was because of her reaction way back then. For years a gnawing terror chewed at her insides, hour after hour, day and night. It devoured her dreams and mauled her at dawn. James stood by her side, yet she'd never felt so alone. The sensation froze her flesh and bones. She searched everywhere for the slightest of signs from her daughter—something from the other side that would bring her peace; a feather floating through the sky, a trace of some familiar scent. When no signs came forth she convinced herself that Charlotte was still alive, kept captive or trapped.

On the rare occasions she managed to sleep, Martha would wake soaked in sweat, haunted by images of her daughter rising from the ocean, cocooned in seaweed, the fingers on her right hand gone. Worse still was the hatred in Charlotte's eyes as she fixed her stare upon her mother.

The nightmares stopped soon after Martha left the Creek. She relocated to a small town out west, accepted a job in a store, re-built her life. But all that did was trigger a different unexpected issue. Despite everything—*she missed the terror.*

She surveyed the room "Is *this* what closure looks like?" she asked, gesturing. "*This* is your idea of sanity?" The words shot from her mouth like a bullet. James flinched. He waved his lighter beneath the hash and sprinkled it into the open joint.

"I just meant …"

"I know what you meant. I am—and always have been—as sane as the next person."

James carefully sealed the joint and lit up, sucking on the spliff and coughing. "Whatever."

"So?"

He offered the joint, which she flatly refused. "Marsh Lands."

Martha felt something peck at her chest. "Marsh Lands? But that's …"

"Miles from the coast."

"So how …?"

"Environmentalists—a group of 'em. Conducting a survey. Arrived from the east. Drawn to—you know, all the weird shit that goes on around here."

Martha let the information sink in. "Have you seen it?"

"Nope."

"Don't you want to?"

"Nope. Sherriff already confirmed it. The number plates. Too late to do anything now."

Martha bristled. "So why did you call me?"

James took a deep, long drag on his joint and looked at Martha through creased eyes. He's weighing me up, she thought. Trying to assess my stability.

"Lopez girl."

Martha screwed up her face. "Janet?"

"Hanged herself. Found by her old man up at Silverpine. Damned near broke the door to the asylum demanding answers. Sheriff's lot went crazy. Bundled him in a cell, sent her to the incinerator—no autopsy, nothing. Al reckons she had gashes all over her body and her hand was …"

"Why the fuck are you rantin' on about Janet Lopez?" Martha asked.

"Al reckons …"

"What?"

James didn't reply. "He *sounds* like a crazy man. They's threatening to slam him into the loony bed *she* left behind."

Martha sank in her chair. She'd come close to being certified herself after Charlotte disappeared. Like James, she'd hit the bottle, let junkies into her home—school friends of Charlotte's, most of them. She needed the company of Charlotte's friends—those who knew her in a different role from the one she'd always understood. It led to trouble. Inebriated, she was free with accusations as to who—or what—was responsible for her daughter's disappearance. Her mind whirled with possibilities, but possibilities meant hope, and hope ceased to feel like hope, but more like persecution. It was her undying conviction that Charlotte was still alive that finally ended her marriage. Following several run-ins with the Sheriff, she overheard James on the phone talking to Dr Usiskin, at Arkady Asylum. She packed her bags and fled that night, leaving only a short note behind.

In sickness and in health?
Do NOT follow me.

She shuddered, bitter at the memory. Shallow Creek was surely one of the only places left in the US with a working asylum. Countless folk campaigned to shut it down, but it was impenetrable, records and data as securely sealed as 'patients'.

"I wish you'd never brought us to this dump," she said. "Lord knows why you're still here."

He stood, hitched up his trousers. She noticed with a shock, how much weight he'd lost, his torso caving inwards.

"In case you'd forgotten, our daughter's still out there."

Martha studied him. "Thought that was crazy talk?"

"I don't mean she's alive. Christ, Martha, thirty years and you don't think we'd have heard something?' He wandered into to the toilet, not bothering to close the door. She listened to the splash of his pee against the ceramic basin and remembered the forgotten sounds of his morning routines. They were always the same; the tinkle of running water, the flush of the john, the scrape of a toothbrush, the gargle of mouthwash. The sounds he made comforted her. They mingled with cartoon voices rising from the lounge where Charlotte was curled up on the settee, giggling between mouthfuls of dry Weetos. These simple noises were the symphony of a family life long since silenced.

"I gotta go," she said, swallowing the pain in her chest.

As she reached the front door he called over his shoulder. "Damned bike was covered in sea weed, like it had been dragged from the ocean. Go figure."

The lighthouse stood on the highest point of Pincer Crag and looked over The Fingers. It was built in the mid-18th century and beside it sat an ancient canon once used to alert seafarers who drew too close to the islands. Directly behind, loomed the asylum; its elongated shadow stretching out towards the sea.

Jud, the keeper, was painting the side of the lighthouse as Martha approached. She shivered. There was something about Jud that didn't ring true. He spent his entire life in solitude, forever watching the coast from his lighthouse yet claimed to have seen nothing the night Charlotte disappeared. At the very least, he would have heard her bike roaming the cliffs, but when Martha asked him about it he gave her a long, cold stare that turned her blood to ice.

He didn't look round when she spoke.

"Still at it then?"

"Yup."

"Should get a medal. Longest surviving keeper in the Creek."

He turned and squinted at her.

"You here about the bike?"

Martha shrugged. "You know how it is."

Jud's eyes flitted to the asylum. He returned to his painting. "I aint looking for trouble. I aint seen nuthin, aint heard nuthin, don't know nuthin. Know what's good for you, you'll be the same."

"James mentioned sea weed ..."

Jud's back stiffened.

"Please?"

He didn't answer, so Martha gave up. She had no real desire to be around him any longer than she had to. He was always like this—evasive, skulking in shadows with his beat-up walkie talkie, spellbound by static and waiting on veiled words. Nobody knew who he spoke to; they were glad it wasn't with them.

She slept in her car that night. She didn't trust James and couldn't bear the dampness that enveloped her body the second she stepped into the house. She'd find out about the bike in the morning. It would take resolve and courage. Even after all this time, some things remained the same, including the Sheriff and his office. Answering awkward questions was never on their agenda.

She woke in darkness, the handbrake jabbing into her side, groaning at the image in her mind. That day; the day she'd tried so hard to scrub from memory, rose to the surface of her mind like a bloated corpse. They'd been rowing. Charlotte, then 16, had started hanging out with the junkies at Silverpine Forest. Her school work was slipping. She was moody, uncooperative. Then Martha discovered a letter from the hospital regarding a termination she'd known nothing about. She demanded to know who the father was. Charlotte, outraged at the intrusion on her privacy, retorted by shouting and screaming, claiming her mother was stifling her, sucking the life out of her because she had no life of her own. She accused her of being a terrible mom, said the only reason Martha was upset was cos she'd had so many miscarriages herself in the years after Charlotte was born. There was no way *she'd* be used as a breeding machine. Charlotte was high when the argument erupted. She'd been sniffing solvents in her bedroom. But Martha didn't see a junky when she spoke to her daughter. She saw the child she took great pains to raise; the life that twisted out of her cervix during a seventeen-hour labour. She slapped her daughter hard across the face.

The memory haunted her for decades. She tried everything to banish it, singing, whistling, screaming, but she barely made a dent despite her best efforts. Sometimes, she allowed herself to go back, do things differently, say things differently, but it offered no solace. She hadn't said or done those things so what was the point? The thought that Charlotte may have met her fate feeling unloved, that she may have stifled calls for help, unable or unwilling to utter her mother's name, became the largest of all looming phantoms that stalked her every day.

The squawk of a sea bird cut through her thoughts. The red sky was bleeding into morning. She opened the door, stepped out into the street, and headed back towards the lighthouse as if pulled by an invisible force; a mixture of hope and panic rising in her chest in crashing waves. A light sea breeze kissed her face and she heard a familiar whisper, the same babble which led her into the ocean all those years ago when she blindly waded out in search of her daughter.

Ten minutes later she arrived at the crag. She watched a blue-grey haar rising in coils from the shoreline and listened to the buzz of blue bottles, circling the air, several feet in front of her. A foul smell flooded her nostrils, so pungent her eyes stung. Walking towards the flies, she pressed her forearm across her nose to block out the stench.

The beam of the lighthouse swung past, exposing what looked like the dried-up corpse of a woman, left to rot in the sun, arms outstretched as if reaching towards her. Icy fingers slithered up her spine. Her mouth filled with water. *Charlotte.*

She ran towards the rancid shape, yelling her daughter's name, just as she had done all those years before, her voice shrill, even to her own ears. The screech of the Fulmars joined the cacophony. *Charlotte! Charlotte!* They all cried.

The *corpse* was nothing more than a clump of slimy seaweed, twisted in swathes near the edge of the cliff. As Martha inched closer the smell was sickening. She seized a stick and poked at the belly of the putrid clump. Half a dozen birds slithered out, their stomachs slashed open as if gutted by a knife. Pink and grey innards coiled like balls of flabby worms. The birds' heads remained intact, black eyes reflecting no flicker of light, despite the rising sun. Martha jumped back, retched and vomited until her stomach was hollow.

Behind her the tip of the asylum was only just visible through the mist. She was done with all this. She was cured. All those years, all that counselling. She could handle this. Quickening her pace, she searched for a signal on her mobile phone. Nothing. When she looked back in the direction she thought she'd arrived from, she felt disorientated. Her head spun. She could no longer see the lighthouse or the asylum, such was the depth of the surrounding fog, the cry of the Fulmars screeching overhead like an air raid siren. Ice blossomed across the surface of her skin. From the corner of her eye she saw the shape move. *How can it possibly move?* Slowly it slinked towards the edge of the cliff, as if rolling over in its sleep, and dropped beyond the precipice.

The sea hissed and spat below the cliffs. Voices whispered on the wind. Martha scanned her brain. The shape *wasn't* a body. It was seaweed. The innards weren't human, they were birds. A rush of images scrambled her head. Now the bundle *was* a body—*Charlotte's body*. Some bastard had fished it out of the marshlands and abandoned it on the cliff edge, specifically for her to see.

Something light and unfamiliar fluttered inside her chest. Relief? *My only daughter has lain dead in a bog for thirty years and the only emotion I have left is relief? What kind of monster am I?*

She hurried towards the precipice. A few yards along, a ladder spiralled down to the shore, predominantly used by the lighthouse keepers to reach the waters in a hurry. She ran towards the ladder and straggled down its steep decline, her feet slipping on the metal rungs.

When, at last, she reached the sand, it sucked on her toes, dragging her down as she tried to push forward towards the figure which, despite the fall, was crawling in steady movements towards the sea, trailing a long rope of wrack.

Martha fell on to her stomach, yanked her feet free, and reached for the cord. The seaweed burned, slipping through her fingers, but she fought to hold on to the last thread of her daughter's corpse as she was dragged towards the sea. The smell of bird guts engulfed her. Fulmars circled noisily overhead, increasing in number until the sun was entirely blocked from the sky. Darkness cloaked the earth. The sound was unbearable, like the screeches of a thousand souls' agonising death. The beam of the lighthouse swung over the ocean. She saw her daughter's head disappear beneath the water and cried out wildly, tightening her grip on the rope, struggling to pull her back ashore. A searing burn swarmed her right hand and she let go.

When Martha awoke she thought she was staring into the sun. Her thirst was so great it felt as if she'd swallowed an ocean of saltwater. Attempting to sit up, she scanned her surroundings and realised she was nowhere near the ocean, but on a hospital bed.

Her skin was covered in bloody scabs, where the birds had pecked and clawed at her. Her hands were bound with bandages and there was something wrong with her left eye. Everything was hazy and out of focus.

A man in scrubs ambled over, pulled her eyelids apart, examined her mouth. Her heart beat with a memory that flapped like a bird at the edge of her mind. *I saw her*, she croaked. *I saw her*. If the man heard her, he didn't respond.

He reached to raise the pillows behind her neck. As he moved, she noticed an inscription on the white-washed walls behind him. She blinked, straining to read.

He will again have compassion on us; he will tread our iniquities underfoot.
You will cast all our sins into the depths of the sea.
Micah 7:19

The medic returned to his notes. Martha felt a sudden chill, saw the open window, and heard the sea breeze call to her. She sat up, strained to absorb the view, waves of unease rippling through her veins.

She had expected to see the clock which loomed over the town square. The same clock which comforted her following Charlotte's birth—a reminder of the waiting day.

What she saw instead, was the red and white stripe of a lighthouse.

STRANGE BREW

by Eleanor Hickey

James Cooper
17 Chestnut Street
Shallow Creek
Lowridge Co.

Dear Jimmy,

I hope this letter finds you well and that the years have been kind
to you and yours. A peculiar thing happened to me today (and God
knows I am no stranger to peculiar things!) but it brought you to
mind. You see, Jimmy, there are things I need to set straight and my
future is uncertain.

So I was in the store cupboard when I noticed something at the
back of the shelf. Would you believe it was only a box of Krinkles
Crunch! Well, I took it down, turned it over and there we were—
Gerty and Jimmy, Krinkles Kids. *In 20 words, describe why Krinkles
Crunch is the best in the world!* The prize—tickets to a private meet and
greet with Krinkles himself. I remember that photoshoot like it was
yesterday; my hair in bunches, and you in a cowboy hat so big it kept
falling over your eyes, before—well, you know.

Anyway, I've been thinking a lot about the past and about things
that were said or unsaid. Me and you that night on the pier; our
bags packed and our hopes high. If things had been different I like
to think we would still be together; somewhere hot. You'd teach and
I'd grow chillies and mangoes. I want you to know I don't blame
you for keeping your distance after what happened. My father broke
my arm that night, along with three ribs and my nose (no more TV
appearances for me!) and he would have done worse to you. The
police were barely out the door when it began. That first punch threw
me against the window with a wet thud and I remember the Sheriff
turning at the sound. Our eyes met through the blood-smeared
glass, just for a second, but he did nothing and walked on. That's
when I learned to hold my tongue. Seen and not heard, my father
would say. Bad Men will get you in the end, but sometimes, if you
remain hidden, stay *quiet*, they pass you by. Until the next time. Back
then I thought broken bones was the worst he could do but that was
before Gerard.

My father had no time for the human qualities that matter to you
and I, Jimmy. He looked at people and saw only their worth to his

interests. In those terms I guess I was quite valuable—a well-spoken daughter with a careful mouth, pretty enough when my face wasn't bruised. I bet that's how I ended up on the Krinkles show. Making friends, gaining recognition. My marriage was just another deal. You're probably wondering why I didn't just say no—and I almost did—right there at the altar in front of all those people. And then I remembered what happened with the the sheriff. Who would protect me from my father if I embarrassed him in front of the whole town? So I said 'I do' and was handed over from one Bad Man to another. Father died a month later with a bullet in his brain.

I'm sure you heard the rumours about Gerard. Well, every single one was true and no amount of dinner dates with the mayor would change that. Now, I was not permitted to ask questions about the particulars of his job but there were things that couldn't pass unnoticed, such as the packages that were delivered on Sundays and collected by lumpy men with suspicious eyes, or the secret phone calls to the Mayor and muttered talk of mines. Meanwhile, I performed my wifely duties and entertained Gerard's business acquaintances, always with a smile, my lips shut tight. Lucky for me, Gerard's 'work' often took him out of town and it was on one of these occasions I discovered I possessed a very special gift.

The house we lived in was big and spacious—originally built as a holiday retreat for Errol Flynn, they say. Anyway, it meant little to me and offered nothing but more rooms to clean. The best thing about the house was that it backed onto Silverpine Forest—a sparkling diamond in the heart of the monstrous beast that is Shallow Creek. I used to walk through those trees for hours on end when Gerard was away like Little Red Riding Hood, free from the wolf. At first I collected fruit for my jam. Did you know that the damsons in that wood grow and ripen for nine months of the year? Hazelnuts, wild rosemary, mint and raspberries, so full you had to mind they didn't pop between your fingers when you picked them off the bush. I boiled marmalades, pickles, dressings; perhaps you tried them yourself.

Anyway, this one day I woke up with a fierce migraine and left the stuffy house for the cool curtain of the trees. I remember feeling as if some beautiful force was guiding my hands as they sought out garlic, blackberries, chestnuts, and who knew what else. In my stupor, I heard myself muttering out loud; snatches of sentences, words I recognised, and sounds I didn't. At home, I crushed my treasures in water and sipped the liquid. Well, I couldn't explain it, but I never got sick again! Those woods provided me with everything I needed to cure any imaginable ailment and I guess this is where Heather Turner enters the story.

Forgive me, Jimmy, I had to stop for a while and take a nap. Gripping a pen for too long aggravates my ancient bones and there ain't no amount of berries or nuts that can cure old age! It's a funny thing, but I don't know where this particular pen came from. It has 'Bubba's Bazaar' printed on the side. It's like the Krinkles box; sometimes things just appear out of nowhere. Sometimes I think there are other people here, as if from the corner of my eye the shadows change shape and—sorry, I am getting ahead of myself again.

We met around 1986—in your library, to be exact. Heather brought her three children out from the rain and was seeking books to satisfy the literary needs of her eldest two so she could get her baby to sleep. It was damp and muggy in the library and all the tables were taken. She looked around helplessly, inexperienced in library etiquette.

'Would you like to sit down?' I asked, the meek leading the meek.

'Thank you.' She wrestled off her jacket while propping a bottle of milk in her chubby baby's mouth.

I had been studying a pocket book of North American fungi but put it aside to take a closer look at the woman. She removed her scarf and I caught sight of three, of the familiar five, red circles close to her collarbone.

'Good book?' she asked, drawing her blouse up around her neck. I must have been staring. 'Wait, are you the lady that makes the apple and walnut chutney? It's divine!'

'Yes, I'm Gertrude.'

'Heather,' she replied. The baby farted and closed his milk-drunk eyes and we laughed. 'This is George, who is having a rather bad week. He was bitten by a mosquito a couple of days ago and it just won't heal.'

George's arm was swollen to twice its normal size, an angry black dot deep in his flesh and a flaming line snaking out from the centre.

'I think you should take George to the hospital,' I said.

'Oh, he'll be fine in a day or two. Besides, my husband is out of work at the moment and, well, we have no health insurance.' Heather breathed a nervous chuckle.

All I could do was stare at this complex woman—polite and neat on the surface. Perhaps so used to injuries that eventually heal—on the outside anyway—that she failed to realise her own son was terribly sick. I had to intervene.

The problem was, Jimmy, I had a guilty secret at that time. As my skills grew with the treasures of the forest, I began to expand my expertise. Gerard and I had been married a decade and he'd become particularly agitated of late. He'd received death threats, presumably from a rival, and for months we had one of his seedy little friends posted out front for protection while the real danger — for me—was inside! A couple of weeks later Gerard deemed it safe for the night watch to stand down, and on this particular night he was drinking and raving, demanding to know why I hadn't given him a child yet. He'd become unreasonable, said that I was cursed. Then he hit me with a whisky bottle. He hit me so hard that the blood streamed down my face and into my eyes. I could taste it, hear it patter on the ground and my body buckled and fell while he passed out on the couch. I'll admit there was something appealing about staying put, waiting for my heart to slow to a stop, to sink into black oblivion. No more pain and, most importantly, no chance of ever bearing a baby made of Gerard. But this time I could not stop for death.

I thought about the sheriff. Gerard was a powerful man in Shallow Creek and would have no problem covering up a murder, so I dragged my broken body through the French doors, along the garden path, life throbbing out of my shattered skull with every heavy heartbeat. Somehow, I scratched about and found what I needed. Dandelion, moss, almonds, redcurrants. I repeated the name of each ingredient as I chewed them up and fingered the crown of my head, pressing the mixture around the shards of bone sticking out of my skin like cracked walnut shells. I buried my face in the cold ground and screamed, but soon the pain melted away and I forced my breathing to slow. I lay and cried. I cried for Heather and you and for the little girl that wore a checked shirt like Calamity Jane and found her way onto a cereal box. Then I came to a decision, a decision so clear it was like the sun emerging on a dying thunderstorm.

Up until then, I used my skills for good. Well, now my blood was full of red hot rage. My skin was aflame with it. By the time the birds began to sing there was not a single graze on my head. So I turned away from the house and ventured deeper into the woods. I was crazy, my nightdress sodden with blood, my feet bare. I tore rosehips out of the soil by their roots and dug into the earth with broken nails, churning up mysterious bulbs. At the river I got to my knees and tore a strip off my dress, laid it flat on the floor and spread out my treasures. The muttering that usually accompanied these rituals was now replaced by a rasping, dangerous drawl that I had never heard before. I cupped river water in my hands and poured it carefully over the ingredients. Then I found a large rock and smashed them to bits, ground them into a puree, all the while growling those words I didn't understand.

I had more than enough. When I returned home Gerard was exactly where I left him, asleep, so I changed clothes, removed the bloodied rug, and erased all evidence. He couldn't remember a thing. Had no idea why I smiled so widely when I poured his morning coffee.

By the time I met Heather, I'd been feeding that beautiful tonic to my dear husband for almost a year. He had grown bloated and yellow, his liver swollen and cancerous. I'd expected the toxin to take effect far quicker, but I liked this way just fine—listening to him spew his guts up every day, his belly becoming so bloated he looked like he would burst! But always room for a morning coffee.

So, you can understand my trepidation when I realised little George had blood poisoning. I knew I could help him, but it would mean bringing them back to my home. Still, I treated the boy and enjoyed Heather's wonder as she watched the red line retreat and disappear beneath unblemished baby skin. She asked why I couldn't cure my husband. I could have lied. I could have said it was beyond my abilities.

'Because I don't want to,' I said.

'Seems like he's in a lot of pain,' she said.

'Oh, he is.' Then we laughed. We laughed so hard the baby woke up.

That night I gave Gerard a sleeping draught and sat with Heather in the garden, drinking homemade wine and listening to *The Cure* as the kids slept upstairs. Heather had lied to her own Bad Man and said she was visiting her sister. The timid lady who entered the library that morning was gone, replaced by the most radiant spirit I'd ever met.

'Will you tell the police?' I asked.

'Shit no,' she said, lighting a cigarette. 'You're my fucking hero.'

I couldn't help but look over my shoulder, scared I'd see the hulking shape of Gerard as he discovered me and my new friend. Because, Jimmy, that was what Heather was. A friend. My first friend. She removed her jumper, exposing her bruised skin to the summer air. We sat in silence for a few moments until she unbuttoned her shirt to reveal a series of pearly circles spread across her stomach.

'This is what Lenny does when he's angry. This one,' she said, pointing to the biggest burn, 'was when I overcooked his eggs.' She pointed at the remaining circles. 'A forgotten packet of cigarettes, having my hair cut, wearing yellow on a Tuesday.'

She reached for my hand.

'Can you help me?' she said.

'Sure. Scars are easy to hide.'

'No,' she said, looking behind me towards the house. 'Can you help me solve my problem … for good?'

You know, Jimmy, I think I knew she was going to ask and I guess I always knew I would help in the end.

Gerard finally passed on a Friday morning some six months later. During the funeral I looked at all the faces present—men in suits and missing teeth—the Mayor with his cronies. I can tell you I almost squealed when they lowered that big box into the ground. I squeezed Heather's hand so hard I thought I'd break her knuckles. It was just her and the kids. Her own Bad Man was sick, after all.

After the funeral, when it was just the two of us, we drank a toast on the porch.

'Well,' said Heather, chiming her glass with mine, 'you did it.'

'And your time will come,' I told her.

'Oh, I know. Lenny started pissing blood this morning and he's off to the doctor tomorrow. I just can't wait to see what they find. It's like Christmas. And the best thing is, the bastard hasn't touched me for weeks!'

Another chime.

'Actually, Gertie, I been meaning to ask you something,' said Heather. 'This gift you have—can it be taught? It's just that I have this friend.'

She was a tired-looking young lady called Daisy whose father was an abusive, violent man. Then more friends came along; the beaten, the humiliated. So many hurting women! I just wanted to help, to make their lives better, for them and their children. And for the town. Every deadly tonic we brewed made Shallow Creek a little sweeter. They say folk used to lynch witches from the Hanging Tree, innocent women strung up by Bad Men. I was just tipping the scales. For every evil we disposed of, good souls were free of their tormentors, and believe me, Shallow Creek produces many Bad Men!

I won't lie, Jimmy, those years were the best time of my life. With Gerard out of the way, I was free to open my house to these women. Bad Men were dropping like flies and there was even a newspaper article about it. *'Has the Curse of Krinkles returned?'* I guess in a way it had. They called me sister, my girls. Sister Gertie. And as it turned out, some of those skills were transferable. At night we'd go out together—ten or fifteen of us—and reach out with our souls until our arms were bursting with treasures.

And then one day everything changed. Gerard had been dead and buried for a blissful twelve years and I got a call saying that Heather had been arrested. I never knew where the tip off came from but that one phone call was all it took for the police to search her house. In any other town, a few herbs and rose petals wouldn't mean a thing but we all remember what happened with Krinkles and the police, as it turned out, were no fools. Before long a new inquest had been opened into Lenny's death, but it made no difference; Heather pleaded guilty.

Jimmy, it broke my heart to see her incarcerated. I drove to the station as soon as I heard but it was hours before they'd let me see her. I can only guess at what they did to her during that time but when I finally walked into that cold room, she was a shadow of the woman I knew—her eyes shiny and her lips cracked.

'Look after the children.' That was all she said.

The inquest progressed as planned and then began to look at

other Bad Men and the contents of their bellies. I can't tell you the strain I was under over those next few weeks. Not for myself, you understand, but for my sisters, for their kids. In the end Heather pleaded guilty to all of it—28 deaths in total. She saved us for a little while longer but they locked her up in Arkady Asylum and I never saw her again.

The case took a strange turn after that. My sisters and I were forced to stop meeting but I wasn't prepared to stop fighting for Heather. At first, I protested to the police. I told the sheriff what Lenny and the others did to their wives, not caring that I was casting considerable suspicion on myself. But he wouldn't listen, wouldn't allow me to see Heather. So I went to the asylum, feeling so very small outside those enormous walls and miles of barbed wire that stretched right around the building. I was seen by a chirpy nurse with Buddy Holly glasses who informed me that Mrs Turner was making excellent progress but must be left alone to heal. I wanted to tell him that I could make his eyeballs rot in his head or his teeth fall out overnight, but once again I held my tongue, for Heather. Instead, I returned the next day and the next and asked to see my friend. The nurse stopped coming to meet me and eventually security escorted me off the premises, through the iron gates so that I couldn't even walk up the driveway anymore. I changed my tactic and stayed away for a couple of weeks before arriving unannounced, this time successfully reaching the desk. Buddy Holly was talking to the receptionist and I prepared for the the familiar pressure under my arms as the security guards hustled me out, but instead he smiled, as if it was the first time he'd seen me.

'Good morning,' he said.

'I want to see Heather Turner,' I said.

'I'm sorry, Madam, but I don't know that name.'

'Mrs Turner,' I said. 'My friend.'

His smile remained fixed but his eyes slid down to my chest. I had a gift for recognising when people were lying to me and I studied his face, looking for signs of deceit but finding only lecherous optimism.

'Never mind,' I said and went on my way.

Since Heather's arrest I kept my distance from my sisters so as not to attract suspicion. The police had their confession but they didn't believe it for a second. Every day, at the school gates and in the street, Bad Men in black cars cruised past young widows, eyeing them up. But I needed to speak to them, to ask for their help. I called Daisy first.

'Is it safe for us to talk?' she said.

'I had to call. Something strange happened today.' Then I proceeded to tell her about my visit and the staff at Arkady Asylum claiming to have no knowledge of Heather.

'How strange,' she said, although there was something hesitant in her manner.

'Daisy, What's wrong?'

'I'm sorry,' she whispered, 'it's just I'm not myself with this investigation going on. I do hope you find your friend.'

'My friend? Daisy, she introduced us.'

'Oh yes,' A pause. 'It was all so long ago. What did she look like?'

My mouth went dry. My thoughts contorting as I tried to process what was happening. Surely you couldn't just erase a person? I had to do something; after all, I'd got them into this. Daisy was repeating my name, concern in her tone. I took a deep breath and found my voice, made my excuses and hung up. It was reckless of me to ring her and I didn't want to endanger her further. Besides, some dreadful spell had taken hold of the town and I needed to get to the bottom of it.

The events around Heather's disappearance, as I now thought of it, continued. Her children lived with me now and I provided for their every need but even they stopped talking about her and looked vacant when I mentioned her name. Jimmy, I am ashamed to admit that there were times I couldn't remember her face or the sound of her voice. One day *The Cure* came on the radio and I realised I hadn't thought of her in weeks. I ran to the woods, gasping and wretched with guilt, and I chanted her name over and over again until her face came back to me and I promised never to let this twisted trick take hold of me again.

On top of this, other peculiar things started to happen. The phone rang in the dead of night, only to emit a crackling static when I put it to my ear and I began to receive letters in the post with no name on them—just grubby envelopes containing sheets and sheets of blank paper. I started to fear that I'd been found out, not by the police, but by Gerard's men. I hadn't considered it at the time, but his death must have put a lot of them out of work. I would wake often, following breathless nightmares in which tall, weasel-faced shapes pointed guns at me through my windows or from under my bed.

Daisy was the next to be arrested before, one by one, they came for the others. Children were packed off to relatives and houses boarded up and left to rot while my sisters were committed to the asylum. I could have waited for the Sheriff's boot at my door but my memory of my sisters was fading fast. Heather's children were old enough to look after themselves so they stayed in the house, while I grabbed a bottle of the poison I'd created and handed myself in.

As you can imagine, Jimmy, I was quite a different person by then. I had known love and empathy and I had my place in the world. I had faced the devil and knocked him down but I'll freely admit I was scared. When I arrived at Arkady, cuffed and surrounded by Shallow Creek's finest, I was greeted by the nurse with the Buddy Holly glasses. The smile was gone as he looked me up and down, no hint of recognition either. Once again I was handed over, rough fingers pulling me this way and that.

I was marched down a corridor with white walls and fluorescent lights, past a thin-haired woman with coal-black eyes who was slowly wiping the linoleum floor with a filthy mop.

'Where are we going?' I asked. I tried to keep my voice steady but it was as if the nurse couldn't hear me. I knew better than to resist or fight back, so we continued through a maze of corridors that became grimier with every turn. Lights flickered or faded altogether the further we went and I could hear the inmates—talking, screaming, laughing hysterically. Jimmy, I could have sworn I heard Krinkles among them.

Eventually we arrived in a shower room where I was stripped and forced into a plastic seat. I expected a female nurse but it was Buddy Holly who scrubbed me raw with a blackened sponge he found on the floor, a hypnotised concentration on his glowing face. Next I was hosed with freezing water and ordered to wear a thin grey gown. I was used to pain but I couldn't stop thinking about all my sisters who came before me, frightened and alone. For the first time in too many months, I was close to them. I was walking in their footsteps and I felt them nearby. I endured the treatment in the hope that I might see them again.

I was ushered to a tiny room with the same white walls and flickering lights as the rest of the building. Peering in, I saw a bed on fixed wheels, but it was already occupied; a woman was laying on it, strapped down by her chest and legs, her arms sticking out at peculiar angles. Her long dark hair almost reached the floor and I realised it was Daisy! She appeared to notice me and tried to talk but her cracked lips wouldn't budge, a moldy feeding tube hanging from her mouth like a rotting snake.

I was furious and thrusted my elbow at the nurse's face, knocking his glasses to the floor. Then more men arrived. They pushed Daisy's bed out the way and wheeled in another one for me. It wasn't difficult for them to strap me down and stick a needle in my arm. And that was that. I become another resident at Arkady, another voice screeching in the woods.

The drugs came daily, pinpricks bleeding nightmares into my veins that loosened my tongue or held it still, whichever they desired. At first I had a lot of visitors—police, doctors, nurses. I had no way of knowing who or what was real. Sometimes I saw my sisters, sometimes Krinkles, or my father, or Ruth Usiskin standing in the doorway, swinging a locket and chain, smiling. The cleaning lady came frequently with her ragged mop, smearing dirt across the floor before shuffling out the door. Once I could have sworn I saw a tail poking out of her tabard—dark and lumpy like an alligator. Another day Buddy Holly played *Maybe Baby* and crooned in my ear.

And all the time Daisy lay on her bed, her limbs wasting away and her hair dropping falling to the floor strand by strand. Her head was turned away from me, but I knew she was dead. I was the only one who could see her now; everyone else had forgotten her the same way she had forgotten Heather.

That's the way it worked there, Jimmy. Our voices were all we had, and they were taken from us. The more we were silenced, the quicker we were forgotten. Fewer and fewer people came to check on me until eventually they stopped feeding me altogether. I faded away, with only my horrific imaginings for company while my organs slowly failed.

And then one day I walked out. A shadow moving through the grey asylum and returning to the darkness of the forest.

I can't tell you how long it's been as it is always night here. Sometimes I sleep, but when I first arrived there were strange noises outside, and creaking footsteps inside. Sometimes I heard them slowly tread towards me, so close I could reach out and seize a fistful of the unknown. The forest that surrounded me was no longer my Silverpine, or if it was, it had turned against me. Several times I lost my way deep inside the woods, not a single treasure flourishing for me anymore.

Until today. It was after I found that Krinkles box in the cupboard. I left the house and went to the woods and for the first time since I escaped the asylum, the moon was out, full and silver and stunning. Within its wonderful light I saw the caps of countless mushrooms bursting through the soil, cepes and chanterelles and a cluster of enormous puffballs, the biggest I'd ever seen. In the warm embrace of my forest I heard my sisters call my name, and I called back to them, my voice finally returned.

So, Jimmy, I don't suppose you'll ever read this letter. At most you may receive an envelope brimming with blank pages, as I once did, but the forest has granted me another chance and I will not fail it. I will find my sisters and we will reap its treasures once again, and reward it with the blood of every Bad Man that still darkens Shallow Creek.

Your friend always,

Gerty

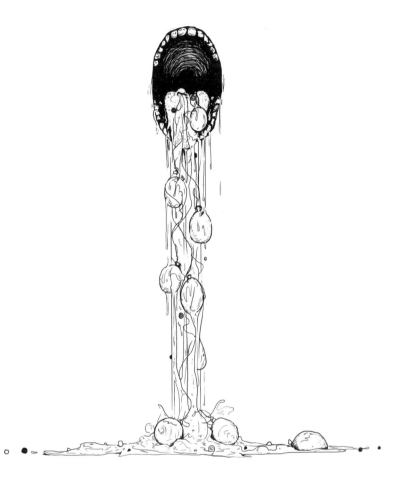

THE CAGED BIRD SINGS IN A DARKNESS OF ITS OWN CREATION

by Richard Thomas

In the most northern reaches of the Silverpine Forest, past the lumbermill, east of the abandoned mine, just this side of Devil's Gorge, there is a hut. It's nothing special, really, scraps of wood and sheet metal, held together with rumor and rusty nails, a roof made out of old billboards, a hint of a cereal ad peeking through, with a splash of red—a faded logo barely visible.

How it is still standing, after all this time? That can be debated.

Perhaps it was built in the shadow of a huge oak tree that shades the structure, protecting it, the occasional acorns raining down on the wood and metal roof, creating a ripple of percussion in the otherwise quiet forest. Maybe it's the animal fat that is slathered over the frame, the sinew wrapped around one board after another, dried now, creating a bond, that might be cemented even further tomorrow, or the next day. Or it might be something else entirely—an illusion, some sort of glimmer of technology rippling under the building, a line of gold running through the tiny house, as if a motherboard had been pressed into the rotting wood, a surge of electricity running over it all, then fading as the sun pushes through the dense foliage. Whatever is happening here, the old man standing in the doorway holds a flickering presence, both daunting in the shadow and void he creates, but vulnerable in his sickly thin appearance, an old flannel shirt barely covering his pale flesh and bony arms, dirty jeans leading down to black boots that are grotesquely oversized, the only bit of joy his shockingly bright hair in a rainbow of colors, as well as a red bulbous nose in the center of his face. He grabs the sphere and rips it off, leaving behind a gap where a fleshy proboscis must have once resided, flinging the spongy crimson ball to the forest floor, where it bounces into a pile of leaves and disappears. He turns and heads back into the residence, the nose back on his face, a bit of magic here, the illusion continuing.

When the acorns fall again, he begins weeping, muttering the name of a long lost love under his breath, his sobs turning into a rasping cough, then to something darker—something wet. Other random noises emanate from the hut—sometimes from him, and sometimes from the dozens of jars that line the walls, shelves full of clear glass, and a curiosity of items. As he rolls about on the cot, transferring white paste and powder to the dirty sheets and blankets, the tension in his stomach builds until he leans over and vomits up a long stream of tangled balloons, in a shocking mix of rubber iridescence. Mixed in with the puddle of primary colors is a smattering of glitter, a few chunks of some glistening meat, sawdust, and a handful of marbles, that go rolling across the floor.

In the jars, there is much more.

A tiny heart floats in a yellowing liquid, somehow still beating. Next to it, a bowl filled with Yoyos, the strings dirty, crusted with brown stains, a meaty smell lifting off of the faded toys. In a large glass mason jar there is nothing but hair—long blonde strands, several puffs of dark, curly tightness, and brown clippings in a number of lengths, all mixed together.

It doesn't stop there.

A little glass music box is filled with glittering metal—rings, and necklaces, in silver and gold, some plastic, some onyx, all inlaid with memory, and trace amounts of DNA. Next to that is a large clear vase filled with toothbrushes in a variety of colors—some brand new, or nearly that, others worn down, the bristles frayed, handles bent and faded, the edges worn away from use. There is a jar filled with flickering fireflies, humming and buzzing in the night. A clay bowl is overflowing with little rubber balls that mix and mingle, vibrating with hate and sorrow. A gilded cage toward the back of the little room is filled to bursting with tiny birds, in a cacophony of pigmentation—chirping red, twittering blue, gasping black into the encroaching night. There is so much pain gathered here, and the sobbing form lying on the floor knows exactly what he's done, the role he has played in all this sadness.

As the darkness settles in around the humble abode, the hut goes quiet, a crinkling of leaves buried under snapping sticks, the tall shadows outside standing in a semi-circle around the building, their long necks, and slender arms extending in ways that are hard to rationalize. Six of these elongated figures hold court in this desolate forest, chittering to each other, a dull glow seeping from their myriad eyes. Their skeletal frames rise nearly to the top of the encroaching trees, their oval heads brushing up against the green leaves, bent over in worship, or perhaps just to get a closer look.

Inside, he stirs, swallows with some effort, a coil of madness unfurling in his gut, the time for his departure at hand. He has played host for so many years now, and a series of black and white photos unfurl in front of his watering eyes—cracking jokes in grade school, sent to the corner of the room, a dunce cap on top of his head; sitting at a bar sipping beer and telling stories, as the women eased in closer, the laughter slipping from their blushed lips, their eyes crinkling with happiness; the television cameras bearing down on his face, as he cavorted for their amusement, the children at his feet filled with wonder, the ache in his gut swirling around and around.

He knows they are here now, returned. But the price he had to pay, it seems exorbitant, out of balance with what he has reaped, what has been sowed. In the beginning there was no length he wouldn't go to in order to get back what he loved. But over time the cost grew, and expanded, one more task, one more item, until there was no turning back.

In for a penny, in for a pound.

And that pound of flesh has been taken. Over and over again.

To what end?

Eventually, it was inverted. Not the death of one for the good of many, but the opposite—the death of many for the good of one. Or the few.

Or so he thought.

As the ripples of his actions scattered across the globe, and beyond, the man with the funny shoes and the sparkling eyes wept into his trembling hands. And the worm in his belly squirmed with a heady anticipation.

They were going home.

***

Somewhere in the dark, millions of miles away, and yet, entirely on top of this event, so very distant, and yet, essentially, filling the same space, a massive pair of hands are busy creating. They are moving quickly, a blur, and yet, upon closer inspection, moving infinitely slow. There is a vast tableau in front of this being, spilling out in every direction, the great presence surrounded by satellites of life, motes of dark energy, electric fields riddled with animation—so many sights, sounds, and smells.

Taking a deep breath in, it exhales into its fists, a flurry of feathers circling like a fixed tornado in blue and white, spinning round and round, forming a murmuration of life and movement. Off to the left several hundred bluebirds scatter into the never-ending darkness.

The hands reach out into the ether and conjure up a handful of dirt, packing it in tightly, then reaching up as if to find a lost memory, pulling twigs, and berries out of nothingness, pushing the wood, and red juice together, tugging here and there, eventually opening its massive hands to spill out a herd of deer, some antlers budding, others fully formed, the creatures standing on tepid legs, then dashing off in excitement, and fear.

Holding one giant hand over the other, its fingertips sprinkle dust and droplets of water over the cupped hand below, and a squirming starts to spool and twist in the palm of the mighty being—dark green, the smell of algae and seaweed swimming up into the air, one tentacle after another pushing out of the mass, growing faster and faster until it overflows the hand that holds it. With a sigh and squinting eye, a handful of sharp teeth are shoved into the wriggling creature, an undulating mass of tiny bulbous eyes crammed into the middle of the rippling mass. When it surges again, it is released into the darkness, a singular monstrosity, destined for a distant planet, an ocean with unlimited depths.

This has been happening for a long time, it is happening now, it will happen for all of eternity.

It bends over and snaps its fingers, lighting a fire at its fingertips, the flames licking at what must be flesh, trying to cajole the flickering light, a difficult task, the smell of meat cooking, an earthy wood burning sweet and smoky, the sinuous form leaping out of the gesticulating hands before it is complete, before it becomes what was planned. But this is life, this is creation—intention, and then chaos.

With a long, steady blow a wind leaves its massive lips, a funnel of cool air whirling about in the space before it, swirling and taking on mass—long, leathery wings extending—the creator narrowing its gaze, shaking its head, trying to manipulate the shape, as a beak elongates and talons scratch at the air, first one winged beast, then two, doubling in number, released with frustration, scales and needles spilling behind them, this experiment another failure.

Only two, it thinks. It could have been worse.

And in its anger it makes a fist, pounding what would have been a table, a surface, if such things existed here, but it finds resistance nonetheless. And in that singular gesture, a spark of atoms spills out of the clenched fingers, a sickly yellow cancer spreading out and over the trembling knot of digits, the tiny flashes of light and oozing sickness taking on a microscopic form, expanding and then contracting, breeding in and of itself, and when its presence is noticed, fully formed, it disappears into the ether, death wandering out to claim its stake—seeking out weakness, and feeding on misery.

It pauses for a moment, this rippling form, taking in a deep breath, its many forms shifting as a wave of emotions washes over it. Calm, collected, legs folded, hand on knees. Then its head tilts back its eyes ablaze, as a deep laughter builds up from inside tinted flesh, feet to hooves, and then nubs bursting from a cracking skull. It inhales and its pale flesh expands, running a hand over its bald head, an expanding belly, a gleam in its eyes, a smile upon its fleshy face. And then its arms double, then triple, a third eye upon its forehead, a glitter of gold sprinkling down like rain from a cloud, a clash of symbols, and then silence.

It was all things, it is all things, it will be all things.

It goes back to work.

It focuses for a moment on mankind—and pulling a sack of what might be seen as marbles out of the darkness—it spills the assortment of spirits upon a false ground. In a flurry of activity, the shapes ping off of each other—a clacking sound, and then a great sigh, a moan of contentment, and then a cry of fear and loss—as it manipulates the dozens of entities with a deft touch and a sharp eye. They shiver into life. A push here, a pinch there, a whisper to this handful, cupped up close to its mouth, and then scattered back on the floor, a sparking of blue and green, and flash of red and orange, a singular white orb spinning and hovering all by itself, while a solitary black sphere sits in one place, vibrating with anger and vengeance.

It scatters the bulk of these new beings out into the universe, some seeking light, others wallowing in the endless darkness. It picks up the only one left, the obsidian globule, bringing it close to its trembling eyes, the hard shell cold in its grip, a shallow pulse of warm light buried within, that sparks white, sparks yellow, flashes a momentary glow that makes its creator smile.

It is given a name now, it is shown how to bring joy to the world, the children, it is told of how other life might exist far beyond its reach, and it warns of how such power and knowledge might corrupt, eventually.

And then it is set free.

It is born unto the Earth.
It will hear laughter in the form of innocent children.
And it will make decisions—both horrible, and inspired.
Such is life.

**

At a very young age Edward Carnby had the first in a series of visions that would transform and define his life. And because he believed what he saw, these moments had great power—to alter his future, and those around him as well.

Some say that the tall shadows were nothing more than a fever, a flu when he was lost in the woods, a sickness that caused the boy to lie in bed for weeks on end, a cancer in his bones that would cause a slight limp in his gait.

Others can confirm what was there in the forest—too many concrete details kept in their fluttering minds, in metal tins at the back of closets, in safe deposit boxes, the keys rusty and lost long ago. There is no real way to explain away the tiny knobs, levers, and bits of heavy black rock that was melted into odd shapes. Found downstream, in the back of caves, and buried deep in an assortment of fields—the materials they were made of cannot be found anywhere on Earth.

But there may be a third explanation here as well.

Three moments, three wishes.

What happened?

At the age of 12 Eddie used to wander the woods in search of arrowheads, empty wasp nests, tree bark curled into sheets of paper, and bright blue robin's eggs—some intact, other cracked open, and empty. He was fascinated by the offerings nature presented to him. He might find a field filled with budding flowers—in yellow and purple, with hints of red. He might see in the ponds, lakes, and creeks a variety of silver-backed fish swimming in schools, some with a wash of shimmer and a stipe of color—perch, trout, bass, and carp. And sometimes he found death—that egg cracked open with a bit of fluff and bone inside, a singular eye gazing up; a skeleton riddled with a sour stench inside a thorny bush, the red of its fur faded and damp; now and then just a splash of blood, and a bit of sinew, nothing left but a stain, with buzzing flies marking the expiration.

It all fascinated him—life, death, and everything in-between.

It was on one of these hikes that he found the shadow child, a thin trail of smoke leading up into the sky, a dent in the earth, and a smattering of flickering metal across a field of puffing dandelions. There was an echo in his head, his ears filled with the sound of cascading water, and at the same time, entirely quiet.

When a baby bird falls from a nest, the story is that it shouldn't be touched, that any kind of interaction with human flesh will taint the creature, the mother bird pecking it to death, sensing only trouble, and danger. This is not true. But that doesn't mean the action goes unnoticed, that the bird is not aware, that the gesture is not recorded—for future action, good or bad.

Of course Eddie bent over and touched the clear gel, the shadow pulsing within it, the strange form lying prostate in the dirt, a hum of some machine winding down, the smell of oil and plastic burning. It was unlike anything he had ever seen.

He thought that there were words slipping from the form, some sort of plea. As he knelt in the field, in the itching grass and moist soil next to the fading silhouette, it was in his nature to touch it, his hand slipping through the glistening form, a gasp from them both, a ringing of bells, a stinging across his flesh, a triggering of some alarm, his body suddenly covered in a sheen of sweat. It was electric, it was liquid, it was a marking in self-defense by the creature lying beneath him.

Pulling his hand back, the shadow dissipated, the remaining gelatinous shape seeping into the earth, Eddie's hand held up high in front of his flickering gaze—glowing red, then absorbing into his flesh, around him the metal and plastic smoking, melting—reduced to ash, the wind scattering the detritus to the far corners of the field.

Standing up, it was all gone. No smoke, no fragments or evidence—just an empty field, the sound of wildlife slipping back into focus. They boy swallowed hard, and turned in a circle. He walked the field, pushing aside long grass, sending dandelion seeds flying, but nothing more. He was unable to see the remnants, his vision distorted forever, altered in some crucial ways. It would be much later when others would find the strange remains.

He looked to the sky, asking for an explanation, wishing for something more. He was eager to learn, to grow, to comprehend.

That would be a mistake.

Later that night he would take a very long time to fall asleep.

The next day the memory would fade, and he would forget it had every happened.

Mostly.

Almost.

But not quite.

It would be twelve years down the road at the ripe old age of twenty-four that he would revisit this moment, in an entirely different way.

Standing in an alleyway outside a local bar, smoking a cigarette, and thinking about a girl that was inside playing pool, Eddie noticed a gathering of shadows down by the trashcans and dumpsters. For a moment he thought it was some local boys he'd had trouble with in the past—simple folk that had no aspirations, often offended by his lengthy conversations, the attention of blonde and brunettes alike stirring up something close to a primal, territorial rage. But it wasn't those kids.

In an instant, Eddie was on his knees, one hand help up, inspected by the shifting shadows, a glow spilling into the night. His mouth open as if to scream, but nothing came out. His vision was watery, *shimmering*, a darkness descending upon him like a ratty blanket, the smell of smoke and burning plastic filling the air, and before he passed out, a sharp pain in his gut. They would hardly leave a mark. The only evidence of this moment was a tiny red dot—something a mosquito, or spider, might make.

When he wakes, there is only one thought in his head.

Wait.

Don't go.

Hold on.

It is fading fast, the memory, but he has glimpsed something extraordinary, and he wants to see more.

And he will. In time.

In the coming weeks he will get sick—a fever of 103; a horrible rash that creeps across his skin in mottled hues; nausea that causes him to vomit into the toilet with a violent upheaval, the blood and mucus dotted with tiny flecks of metal, all triggering some deeper knowledge that he is afraid to truly recognize.

And then it is gone.

The hosting is complete.

His work only beginning.

The third time will cement their relationship, ten years later, as he sits in front of a mirror, putting on his makeup, the lights on the dressing table bright yellow, a smile splitting his face, as he glues on the red nose, pulls the wig on tight, a wriggle of anxiety in his gut.

There is a woman, Gina.

She is everything he has ever wanted in a woman—long blonde hair, sparkling blue eyes, curves hidden behind modest dresses, and an easy smile that fills his gut with mating butterflies.

For Edward, this is the love of his life, a relationship that has bloomed over the last couple of years, through cups of coffee, dancing at local watering holes, seeing her out in the audience at his shows, smiling with glee.

For Gina, these are merely coincidences, a Venti Mocha on the way to work with a nod to the strange pudgy man in the corner booth, a night out with the girls at the only place to dance for miles, a visit to the television station to laugh at the clown, a bit of a local celebrity, kept as a safe distance, after all.

In the shadows of his closet, there is a murmuring, a beckoning, and Edward, soon to be Krinkles (and *only* Krinkles) answers. He stands in the back of the tiny space and nods his head. He listens to what is offered. And it is set in motion.

It will spill out into the future.

Look close, and see what it becomes.

See what you want to see, as Krinkles does.

The truth is a slippery fish.

***

When the tired old man leaves the hut once again, they are waiting. Patient for so long. With all of their technology, their abilities, and their desire, they cannot walk the earth in shadow, for the eyes of the planet are upon them. They have been seen, and they have been hurt.

But their work here is done now.

And in a blink, they vanish.

In a distant laboratory the worm is removed under bright lights and a sterile environment. It is placed into a container where later it will be downloaded, dissected, and documented for the benefit of them all.

In the living room of quaint little cottage, just on the edge of an entirely different set of woods—not far from a rippling stream filled with colorful fish, and a field overflowing with blooming flowers and dancing grass—Edward sits and smiles. He rocks in his chair, sipping a cup of chamomile tea, comfortable in his soft new flannel shirt, his faded jeans, the windows open, birdsong slipping in, the television quietly playing black and white shows from his childhood.

He laughs.

When the woman enters the room, he takes the plate with the ham and cheese sandwich on rye, a bit of Dijon mustard slathered on there, rippled potato chips, and a dill pickle on the side. She kisses his forehead, and he thanks her, saying her name. It's a recognizable name. When she enters the kitchen her skin flickers, the tapestry that is tightly wrapped over her metal frame, plastic shell, and colored wiring dissipating for a moment.

On a wall to the left of Edward is a large mirror. There are days he stares at it, thinking he sees a shimmer. But most of the time he is content. He thinks of his childhood, his career, the woman he loves, and while parts of it feel thin at times, a headache forming if he looks at it too closely, he is grateful.

Behind that mirror there may only be a wall.

Behind that mirror there might be men watching Edward, taking notes, and nodding their heads, smiling in the darkness, their work a success.

Behind that mirror there could be elongated shadows, stretching to the ceiling, hunched over, chirping in the gloom, eyes glowing.

There may not be a mirror at all.

Edward may lay dying in that first forest, his dark deeds finally absorbing the last of his humanity, death a welcome respite.

The jars, the bowls, the DNA—perhaps they were stolen in secret, nobody harmed (especially not the children), saving an alien race from a plethora of sickness and disease.

Or maybe it's something much worse.

In the expanding corners of a never-ending universe, the creator smiles. His work here, is done.

AUTHOR PROFILES

NICK ADAMS
Tide

Nick lives halfway up a mountain in the north of Spain
where he works as a teacher and writes weird fiction.
He can be found on Twitter: @_nickadams

ERIK BERGSTROM
The Soil of Stonier Hearts

Erik Bergstrom lives in Minneapolis, Minnesota. When he's not
writing, he's making friends with the crows in his backyard and
working on his green thumb. He's been published previously with
STORGY in the Exit Earth anthology, and has stories published or
forthcoming in online and print magazines like *Deracine*, *Typehouse*,
and *Coffin Bell*. You can find these and others on his
website at www.erikbergstromwriting.com
Twitter: @erikbbergstrom

SIMON BILLINTON
Blood Moon Bob

Simon Billinton was born and raised in South London, where he still
lives with his one and a half cats. He is a new writer whose debut
publication will be the terrifying short story Blood Moon Bob in the
eerie horror anthology Shallow Creek. He writes across all genres and
is inspired by the fantastical, the profound, and the political.
You can find Simon at www.simonbillinton.com
Twitter: @simonbillinton

DANIEL CARPENTER
Arrowhead
2nd Place Winner of
The Shallow Creek Short Story Competition

Daniel Carpenter's fiction has been published by *Unsung Stories*,
The Irish Literary Review, *Unthology*, and *Year's Best Weird Fiction*.
He lives with his family in London.
Twitter: @DanCarpenter85

MARION COLEMAN
Anchor

Marion Coleman lives in north Cork, Ireland. Most mornings she meets up with fellow writers in Charleville Library where they work alongside each other, help each other with editing and sometimes even talk to each other. She began writing short stories and flash fiction as homework during the writer-in-residence programme in Charleville Library, and found she enjoyed the unique challenges such stories bring. She has read some of her short stories at a number of literary events, one of which was subsequently published in *Ireland's Own*. She has completed one novel and a first draft of a second.
Twitter: @marionbcoleman

J. STUART CROSKELL
Dave Danvers' Final Foray Into All Things Woo Woo
3rd Place Winner of
The Shallow Creek Short Story Competition

As a perspiring writer Stuart Croskell takes full responsibility for several plays, novels and short stories. 'Dave Danvers' is his first piece of fiction to be published 'properly'. He lives in darkest Somerset with Alison and a dog called Paddy (Patrick on Sundays). Stuart teaches Drama to children with special needs and is currently working on a futuristic YA reworking of Frankenstein.

HEATHER CUTHBERTSON
Secret Ingredient

Heather Cuthbertson has an MFA in Creative Writing from Antioch University, Los Angeles. For nearly nine years she has served as the Editor-in-Chief of *Gold Man Review*, a literary journal based out of Salem, Oregon. She teaches writing both at the college level and at writer's groups and conferences

ANDREA HARDAKER
The Fulmar's Cry

Andrea Hardaker is a Scottish writer, based in the north. She has had short stories accepted by various publications and magazines including; *STORGY Magazine* (2018), *The Runcible Spoon* (2018) *Indigo Dreams* (2015/16) *The Federation of Scottish Writers' Soundwaves Anthology*

(2014) and *Firewords Magazine*'s first issue (2014). Andrea has recently
been accepted as a member of the Northern Short Story Academy in
Leeds and is currently working on her first YA novel. She loves dark
fiction.
Twitter: @Bletherinskite

DAVID HARTLEY
Pentameter

David Hartley has written many an eerie and discomforting tale
and some of the choicest cuts have been ravenously consumed by
various literary dinner tables. Previous stories have appeared in *Ambit*,
Structo, *Black Static* and the first volume of *The Shadow Booth*. He is
currently studying for a PhD in Creative Writing at The University
of Manchester, working on a novel about autism and ghosts. Explore
more of his mysterious meanderings at davidhartleywriter.com.
Twitter @DHartleyWriter

TOM HEATON
Janet's Vision of Love

Tom Heaton is a writer and videogame designer.
His stories have been published in *Ambit*, *The Mechanics Institute Review*,
Confingo, *Litro* and elsewhere. He was shortlisted for the *Bridport Prize*
in 2017. He lives in Hampshire.
Twitter: @RealTomHeaton

ELEANOR HICKEY
Strange Brew

Eleanor Hickey has a BA in English Literature and lives in Cambridge,
where she works in education. She writes in a range of genres but is
drawn to the dark side of storytelling, inspired by humour, music and
the grotesque in everyday life. She is also a mother, wife, cat-owner,
musician, reader, trickster, vegetarian, teacher and watcher.
www.beagytales.wordpress.com
Twitter: @EleanorHickey8

ALLYSON KERSEL
Knock, Knock, Knuckle Bone

Allyson Kersel is a writer from Oban, Scotland. Her short fiction and
poetry have appeared in *STORGY*, *Lamplight* and *Moonchild Magazine*,

among others. She is currently working on her first novel; *Harmony of Trouble*, a blend of dark comedy, Gothic horror, and Celtic myth. She is also co-founder, editor and contributing writer at *Dusk & Shiver*, a brand new online magazine showcasing dark fantasy, horror, and speculative fiction. www.duskandshivermag.home.blog. Updates for her novel can be found on www.patreon.com/allykersel.
Twitter: @allykersel

ADAM LOCK
And The World Fades To Black

Adam Lock won the *STORGY* Flash Fiction Competition 2018, the *TSS Publishing* Quarterly Flash Fiction Competition 2018, and was placed 3rd in the *TSS Publishing Cambridge* Short Story Award 2018. He has also been nominated twice for the *Best Small Fictions Anthology* 2019. He has had over fifty flash fiction pieces and short stories published online and in print.
You can find him online at adamlock.net.
Twitter: @dazedcharacter

SARAH LOTZ
The Eyes Have It

Sarah Lotz is a novelist and screenwriter with a fondness for the macabre. Her collaborative and solo novels have been translated into over twenty-five languages. She currently lives in the UK with her family and other animals.

ALICE NOEL
Behind These Eyes

Alice grew up in Norwich, and is now a final year History and English student at the University of York. In 2018 she became a member of the Writing Squad and for the past year Alice has been the Student Liaison Officer for the Society of Young Publishers North, as well as a proofreader for several student publications.
Twitter: @Alice__Noel

IAN STEADMAN
We Live In Dirt

Ian Steadman is a writer from the south of England. His stories have most recently been published in *Black Static, Unsung Stories,*

The Lonely Crowd, STORGY and *Coffin Bell*, as well as in the anthologies
Humanagerie, Night-Light and *The Year's Best Body Horror*.
You can find him at www.iansteadman.com.
Twitter: @steadmanfiction

RICHARD THOMAS
The Caged Bird Sings In A Darkness Of Its Own Creation

Richard Thomas is the award-winning author of seven books—
Disintegration and *Breaker* (Penguin Random House Alibi),
Transubstantiate, Herniated Roots, Staring into the Abyss, Tribulations and
The Soul Standard (Dzanc Books). He has been nominated for the *Bram
Stoker, Shirley Jackson*, and *Thriller* awards. Over 140 of his stories in
print include *The Best Horror of the Year* (Volume Eleven), *Cemetery Dance*
(twice), *PANK, storySouth, Gargoyle, Weird Fiction Review, Midwestern Gothic,
Gutted: Beautiful Horror Stories, Qualia Nous, Chiral Mad* (numbers 2-4), and
Shivers VI. Visit www.whatdoesnotkillme.com for more information.
Twitter: @richardgthomas3

ADRIAN J WALKER
Backwards

Adrian J Walker was born in the bush suburbs of Sydney, Australia
in the mid '70s. After his father found a camper van in a ditch, he
renovated it and moved his family back to the UK, where Adrian was
raised. Ever since he can remember, Adrian has been interested in
three things: words, music and technology, and when he graduated
from the University of Leeds, he found a career in software. His novel
The End of the World Running Club, a post-apocalyptic running fable
about hope, love and endurance, was a Simon Mayo Radio 2 book
club choice. He lives in Aberdeen with his wife and two children.
To find out more visit: http://www.adrianjwalker.com/
Twitter: @adrianwalker

ALIYA WHITELY
The Alteration

Aliya Whiteley was born in Devon in 1974, and currently lives in West
Sussex, UK. She writes novels, short stories and non-fiction and has
been published in places such as *The Guardian, Interzone, McSweeney's
Internet Tendency, Black Static, Strange Horizons*, and anthologies such as

Unsung Stories' 2084 and *Lonely Planet's Better than Fiction I* and *II*. She has been shortlisted for a *Shirley Jackson Award, British Fantasy* and *British Science Fiction* awards, the *John W Campbell Award*, and a *James Tiptree Jr* award. Her latest novel, *The Loosening Skin*, is currently available from Unsung Stories. She also writes a regular column for *Interzone* and occasionally reviews films, books and TV at *Den of Geek*. She blogs at: aliyawhiteley.wordpress.com
Twitter: @AliyaWhiteley

GREGG WILLIARD
The Lurid Trance

Gregg Williard is a writer and visual artist based in Madison, Wisconsin. His work has been published in *The Collagist, Diagram, Wisconsin Academy Journal, Raleigh Review* and *Fiction International*, among others. He teaches ESL to refugees at the non-profit Literacy Network, and does the spoken word radio show, "*Fiction Jones*" on WORT community radio (wortfm.org).

BRIAN WILSON
Distraction
Winner of The Shallow Creek Short Story Competition

Brian Wilson is a writer from Newtownards, Northern Ireland. His writing has been published in numerous places including *Blackbird: New Writing from the Seamus Heaney Centre, The Cabinet of Heed* and *The Bangor Literary Journal*. In 2018 his work was featured as part of the *SMOKE AND MIRRORS* exhibit at the Torrance Art Museum in California. He is currently working on a novel about a fungus. You can find out more about Brian's writing at www.brianwilsonwrites. Twitter: @bwilson4815

SHALLOW CREEK SHORT STORY COMPETITION JUDGE PROFILE
NAOMI BOOTH

Naomi Booth is an award-winning writer and academic, included in the Guardian's Fresh New Voices: 50 Writers You Should Read Now (2018). Her first work of fiction, The Lost Art of Sinking, was selected for New Writing North's Read Regional campaign and won the Saboteur Award for Best Novella 2016. Her debut novel, Sealed (Dead Ink Books, 2017) is a horrifying tale of body mutation and environmental contamination, described by the Guardian as "not for the faint-hearted ... a marvellous first novel". Her uncanny short fiction, "Cluster" was long-listed for the Sunday Times EFG Short Story Award 2018. Naomi is Subject Director of Creative Writing at York St John University.

https://naomibooth.com

COVER DESIGN

CRAP PANTHER

Carrie South is an illustrator and painter from Oklahoma City, who creates delightfully brutal illustrations.

Discover more about Crap Panther on her Instagram page:
https://www.instagram.com/crap_panther/

Visit Crap Panther's shop on *Etsy*:
https://www.etsy.com/shop/warmachineink

ROB PEARCE

Rob Pearce is a Graphic Designer from London who has worked with clients ranging from Nike & The British Film Institute to The Churches Conservation Trust. He designed the cover for the novel The Boy From Aleppo Who Painted The War, which was serialised for BBC Radio 4, and STORGY'S first printed publication; Exit Earth.

SHALLOW CREEK MAP & MALLUM COLT

HARLOTVONCHARLOTTE

HarlotVonCharlotte is an artist living and working in London. She primarily focuses on figurative illustrative artwork of the slightly odd and macabre and has used sculpting, painting, figure drawing and graphic design to create new styles and unique works of art.

Discover more about HarlotVonCharlotte and her artwork via the following links:
https://instagram.com/harvonchar/

Visit HarlotVonCharlotte's shop on Big Cartel:
http://harlotvoncharlotte.bigcartel.com/

ILLUSTRATOR

MICHAEL TO

Michael To is an illustrator based in London with over a decade of experience. While studying animation, he discovered his love for concept art and illustration. He is greatly influenced by films, gaming and art. You can follow him on Instagram @toart0.

ACKNOWLEDGEMENTS

We would like to thank the below without
whom SHALLOW CREEK would not have been possible.

Annaverey, Eleanor Anstruthe, Chris Basler, Erik Bergstrom, Lauren Bergstrom, C. R. Berry, Michael James Bird, Manny Blacksher, Boudica Press, Matt Brandenburg, Phil Breach, Glen Brown, Paul Buck, Gary Budden, M Buley, Kit Caless, Trish Cantillon, George Pursall & Caitlin Catherwood, Bo Chappell, Ian Chung, Philip Circuit, F. E. Clark, Fiona Clark, Lauren 'Prince' Cohen, Marion Coleman, Sebastian Collier, Jim Coniglio, Rachel Connor, Joshua Lee Cooper, Rhett Coxhill, Dan Coxon, Ian Croskell, Jeremy Daugherty, Cathleen Davies, Thomas M. Davy, Jennia D'Lima, Jess Doyle, Cristina Mameli Dzido, Robert Dzido, Tomek Dzido, Laura Elliot, Christopher Hamilton-Emery, Tiffany R Engle, EP Eriksson, Jeanette Everson, Edward Field, Harry Gallon, David Ginsburg w/Tales form the Fandom Podcast, R. D. Girvan, Abi Godsell, Richard Lee-Graham, Michael Graves, Kate Greybanks, S R Griffin, Andrea Hardaker, Lucie McKnight Hardy, Tony Harries, Emily Harrison, Tom Heaton, Eleanor Hickey, Levi Hodge, Kenneth Hooper, Chase Thomas Hopper, Damien Horgan, Catherine Hunt, Stephanie Hutton, Daniel James, Justin James, Lara Jefferies, Paul Jeffery, Ross Jeffery, Susan Jessen, Chris Johnson, B F Jones, Petri Kanerva, Karen, Chris Keegan, Gavin Kendall, Diamond Kennedy, Jan & Bill Kersel, Kyle Lambe, Andrew Leach, Janice Leagra, Kaleigh Linholm, Catherine J. Link, Toby Litt, Adam Lock, Adam Main, Tomas Marcantonio, Benjamin Mark, Simon Marlowe, Alice McCallum, Sean McConville, Erik McManus, Robert McLyslaght, Erina Mettler, Candise Mitton, Neil Moran, Andrew Murray, Alison Neville, Katie Nickas, Beth Noel, Mrs Sandra Noel, Tim Noel, Roisin O'Donnell, Belinda O'Shea, Charlotte Organ, Allan Paltzer, Steve Pattee, Gareth Penn, Henry Peplow, Randalll Perry, Rosie Prince, Susan Purkiss, Rachael Smart, H. J. Ramsay, Rob Reddick, Ashley Rich, Richard Rose, Shannan Ross, Abigail Rutherford, Joseph Sale, Shannon Savvas, Anthony Self, David Self, Priya Sharma, Richard Sheehan, Kenneth Skaldebø, Ronnie Smart, BobbyRoo Smith, Caroline Smith, Ruth Smith, Chris Sorensen, Daniel Soule, Thomas Sparkes, Cynthia Stevenson, Nathan & Eszter Surgenor, Supersplurk, Justine Taylor, Megan Taylor, The Book Spine, The Bristol Methodist Centre, Richard Thomas, Nick Thornton, Maria Pia Tissot, Wayne Turmel, Kit de Waal, Kerri Ward, Stephanie Wasek, Bobby Williams, Drew Rhys Williams, Gemma Williams, Gregg Williard, Brian Wilson, Dawn Wilson, Rebecca Wilson, Elizabeth Withstandley, Christa Wojciechowski, Michael Wood, Lou Yardley.

DEDICATIONS

Well, my little flayed friends, it appears we've reached the end of our expedition in Shallow Creek. Did you have fun? I really hope so. Perhaps next time you venture into an antiquated town located off the beaten track, you'll stop for a while and take a moment's pause to consider all the folk that live there … and the secrets that they hide.

Being able to serve a succulent slice of The Creek to you on my finest china is an honour, dear reader—but rest assured, the making of it was not all unicorn farts, fairy lights and cupcakes. There was blood, sweat and tears involved in creating such a vivid landscape for your devillish digestion … however, the odd visit to Bertha's brothel did help to calm the nerves. I would not have been able to put this torturous tome together without the helping hands of several special people. Firstly I must credit the artists who provided the fabulous illustrations which adorn these pages—creativity is so delicate a flower that praise tends to make it bloom, so I shall lavish our artists like a maniacal gardener. Firstly, the magnificent *Michael To*, who encapsulated each story into a macabre microcosm of The Creek with an effortless and sumptuous style—I thank you sir. May the nib of your pen be forever dipped in the pleasure pools of obsidian reverence. Applause and adulation is also bestowed upon *Charlotte Wosiek*, the evil genius who created the map of Shallow Creek and my gorgeous handsome face! That's right my little oozing pustules, without her iridescent mind and effervescent style, you would find yourself staring at a caricature of an irritated and bewildered stickman. Frida Kahlo once said that she never paints dreams or nightmares, only her own reality. In that case, *Crap Panther* is the mother of monsters, and if her artwork was reality then we'd all be in trouble. Big trouble. And of course, without the digital talents of *Mr. Rob Pearce* the cover would not be the insanely 80's style horror creep show that it is. I thank you all, from the bottom of my black husk of a heart. Kisses.

To all the writers that entered the Shallow Creek Short Story Competition and spent endless hours formulating stories to revolve around my initial concept, I thank you. It was grievously hard to select the stories for this anthology, but I wish you all the best for your future publications. To those writers that made it into the anthology, I can't wait to read more of your words, so write more, my little scurrying scamps.

And finally a special mention to *Kendall Reviews* for their unwavering support and *Richard Thomas* for permitting us to add *Gamut Magazine* to our Kickstarter perks.

Now, my fiendish rabid chihuahua's, there is a special place in Shallow Creek for the following people, who went above and beyond to help finance my little endeavour. They are:

IAN CROSKELL

I wanted to buy you a paid vacation to the Seychelles as a thank you for your generosity, but if I could do that then I would send myself on holiday instead. The only recompense is to imagine that we're both on holiday. Together. Just imagine it Ian, close your eyes and take three deep breaths—can you hear the ocean? Can you feel the Sun on your face? There we are on the whitest of beaches, the shush-shushing of palm trees looming over us. It is an idyllic landscape and we have left our myriad of troubles behind. I look over at you and whisper, 'I think you caught the sun today, Ian.' You laugh. It is a beautiful chuckle, because you are a beautiful person. I offer to apply sunscreen to your chest and you say okay. There is no hesitation. No apprehension. Only love. I apply the lotion with vigour.

ROBERT DZIDO

It's funny that you share the same surname as our editor, Tomek. Coincidence? No, I think not. But that's the kind of person you are, isn't it Robert? You're the salt of the earth type of guy, the one to roll your shirtsleeves up and get stuck in. If you were in World War Two, you'd be the kind of soldier that would jump out of an aeroplane without a parachute, landing by the will of sheer machismo and killing 100 Nazis with your pinkie toe. I imagine Robert, that you have a hero's face, all stoicism and threatened whispers, a phalanx of resplendent manhood that can punch a wolf in the face—and you can walk into any nightclub and leave with forty women. I imagine this. I bet when you wake up in the morning and make a cup of tea (the women having died from exhaustion) you stand, spread your legs and stiffen every bulging muscle in your body. Because that's the best way to make a cup of tea. And by all that is holy, I hope one day to share a cup of tea with you.

BRENDAN HORGAN

Ah, Mr. Horgan—where would Shallow Creek be without your indelible advise to those pugnacious meat heads at STORGY, eh? Yes that's right, my little purring critter—up the proverbial shitter. In fact, I'm so in awe of your magnanimous character and advice over the years that I decided to build a bronze statue of you in our town square. That's right, Brendan—it towers like a monolithic beast looming over the denizens of The Creek, a naked representation of your virtuous character—legs and arms stretched out in a warm and welcoming gesture. Unfortunately, I didn't have enough money to pay for ALL of the statue, so the sculptor had to skimp a little and 'downsize' a particular feature. At first I thought you might take this as a slight towards your masculinity and 'manhood', but many of our residents have begun to refer to this particular part of the statue as a 'lucky knubbin'. They occasionally rub it for good luck, too. Silly fools.

ALISON NEVILLE

I hear the measured lilt of your voice, Alison—the natural way you command a room and I know ... I know you're the one to lead the resistance when the zombie uprising occurs. Perhaps it's the calm intelligence of your voice tinged with a soft aloofness that teeters, but never quite tips into, complete self-satisfaction, which makes me blush like a schoolboy caught with a dirty magazine. Yes, Alison, that's what we need now. Leadership. We've fallen into disarray, and you're the only one to help us escape this rut. When you generously contributed to my Kickstarter, you thought all you would receive is a book and several perks, didn't you? I'm sorry that this burden falls upon your shoulders, but you're the only one we can rally behind—you're the only one who can strap a flame thrower and machine gun together and wail a battle cry the likes of which no human has ever heard, as zombies sprawl over the wall and run towards us like crazed hyenas. But your stiff upper lip only threatens to wobble with tempestuous indignation. Because you're made of sterner stuff, Alison. Now, let's get out there and kick some zombie ass.

H. J. RAMSEY

In a world filled with sub-par people, you're an above-the-crowd-type, aren't you H.J? How do I know this? Because when I look out of my window every morning, I see you—heroically standing in a power stance atop the cliffs, looking wistfully at the sea. Does the sea speak to you, I wonder? Do you hear the crashing waves against the rocks as the Sea Gods whisper your sweet name? What are you doing there at 6am every morning, naked from the waist down? It must be cold, but by Zeus' beard I'm glad you're there. Without your support, I would have been forced to sell some new born pups from my Curiosity shop, and frankly, those things are fugly. I wouldn't have earned a single dime. So thank you, H.J—thank you for saving the puppies from a one way journey to

Shallow Creek's gorge.

ANNA RIVERS

Well, my little courteous jellyfish, it looks like those hawkish eyes of yours have proofed my tome of terror. Did you viddy well, my droogie? I really hope you did—because if we spot any typos the complaints come straight to you! Oh happy days! Remember Anna, to err is human.
To blame someone else is politics. And I'm the Prime Minister in this house.

STEPHANIE WASEK

Have you noticed Stephanie, that the more special something is, the more folk seem to take it for granted? Take your Kickstarter contribution, for example. In a world filled with generic funding campaigns, you chose mine. Do you know how you made me feel, Stephanie? You floored me with your glamour of innate majesty. Not only did you donate, but you donated big. I wonder why you did that Stephanie. In that moment you enslaved me to your will. I realised then, how special you are. People must realise just how special YOU are. That's right, Stephanie—I'm not taking you for granted. The smallest command will bid me to obtain what you desire. Do you have a boss that grinds you up the wrong way, my little lemon sherbet? One word and I'll blast the kneecaps off that ungrateful, officious troglodyte. Friends whining in your ear? Just one luscious whisper from your lips and they'll disappear forever. That's right Stephanie, I'll do anything for you. Anything.

ALSO AVAILABLE FROM STORGY BOOKS

...EXIT EARTH...

EXIT EARTH delves into dystopian worlds and uncovers the most daring and original voices in print today. With twenty-four short stories, accompanying artwork, afterwords, and interviews, EXIT EARTH is a haunting exploration of the sanity of our species... past, present, and future.

Featuring the fourteen finalists from the STORGY EXIT EARTH Short Story Competition, and additional stories by award winning authors M.R. Carey (The Girl with all the Gifts), Toby Litt (Corpsing, DeadKidSongs), Courttia Newland (The Gospel According to Cane, A Book of Blues), James Miller (Sunshine State, Lost Boys), and David James Poissant (The Heaven of Animals). With accompanying artwork by Amie Dearlove, HarlotVonCharlotte, and CrapPanther.

To discover more about EXIT EARTH visit STORGY.COM.

COMING SOON FROM
STORGY BOOKS

HOPEFUL
MONSTERS

STORIES BY
Roger McKnight

AVAILABLE IN SUMMER 2019

S T O R G Y
LONDON

STORGY
MAGAZINE

ONLINE ARTS & ENTERTAINMENT MAGAZINE

BOOKS - FILMS - ART - MUSIC
INTERVIEWS - REVIEWS - SHORT STORIES

For more information about STORGY Magazine visit our
website.

STORGY

@fb.me/morest0rgy @morestorgy morestorgy

www.storgy.com